Ashes
ON THE
Moor

OTHER PROPER ROMANCES

NANCY CAMPBELL ALLEN
My Fair Gentleman
Beauty and the Clockwork Beast
The Secret of the India Orchid

JULIANNE DONALDSON
Edenbrooke
Blackmoore
Heir to Edenbrooke (eBook only)

SARAH M. EDEN
Longing for Home
Longing for Home, vol. 2: Hope Springs
The Sheriffs of Savage Wells

JOSI S. KILPACK
A Heart Revealed
Lord Fenton's Folly
Forever and Forever
A Lady's Favor (eBook only)
The Lady of the Lakes
The Vicar's Daughter
All That Makes Life Bright

BECCA WILHITE
Check Me Out

JULIE WRIGHT
Lies Jane Austen Told Me

ASHES ON THE MOOR

PROPER ROMANCE®

SARAH M. EDEN

SHADOW
MOUNTAIN

Library of Congress Cataloging-in-Publication Data

Names: Eden, Sarah M., author.
Title: Ashes on the moor / Sarah M. Eden.
Description: Salt Lake City, Utah : Shadow Mountain, [2017]
Identifiers: LCCN 2017031124 | ISBN 9781629724027 (paperbound)
Subjects: LCSH: Teachers—Fiction. | Man-woman relationships—Fiction. | Nineteenth
    century, setting. | Yorkshire (England), setting. | LCGFT: Romance fiction. |
    Historical fiction. | Novels.
Classification: LCC PS3605.D45365 A94 2017 | DDC 813/.6—dc23
LC record available at https://lccn.loc.gov/2017031124

Printed in the United States of America
Lake Book Manufacturing, Inc., Melrose Park, IL

10 9 8 7 6 5 4 3 2 1

For William and Ann,
my 4th-great grandparents, who labored in the
19th-century textile mills of West Yorkshire

CHAPTER ONE

Petersmarch, Cambridgeshire, September 1871

hrough a thick fog of grief, Evangeline Blake suffered the blow of each clang of the distant funeral bells. Petersmarch custom dictated that the bell in the church tower toll once for every year of the deceased's life.

Four people were being interred that day. Four lives reckoned one peal at a time. Four irreplaceable bits of herself. Her father and mother and both of her brothers were gone. The bell tolled for them, shattering her heart with its ringing.

Each clang reverberated through her with new pain, new heartache, new loss. The echoes filled the now-empty house where she stood with a comforting arm around the thin shoulders of her twelve-year-old sister, the sole member of her once inseparable family. Lucy's head rested heavily against her.

Unfinished needlework sat on the arm of Mother's chair. Unopened correspondence lay piled upon the side table nearest Father's preferred place by the fire. The miniature George had commissioned of his intended on the occasion of their engagement mere weeks earlier stood on the mantelpiece. James's well-worn schoolbooks occupied their usual shelf near the window.

If not for the bells, she might have believed her beloved family were merely in the corridor, waiting to step inside the parlor, their smiling faces greeting her with amusement and tenderness and love.

"Gone," the bells tolled. "Gone."

Grief washed over her in relentless waves, yet she could not allow it to drown her. She was Lucy's only support and stability.

Evangeline closed her eyes. She needed to hear every last toll marking her family's memory, despite the pain. This was their final tribute, the last impression they would make on a world that would forget them all too quickly. She would hear their memorial in this room where they had once been happy. She would do so with her beloved sister kept close.

"Gone. Gone."

Evangeline waited for the next toll. A long moment stretched out into silence. The bells had stopped. No years remained to be marked. The all-too-short reckoning had been made.

"I do not want to leave here," Lucy whispered. "Could we not convince Aunt Barton to allow us to remain?"

Their mother's sister had descended upon their grief only one day before the fever claimed its first victim. She had allowed no emotion, no tears from Evangeline or Lucy. Her dictates had been unfeeling and unbending, including the one demanding their immediate departure from the only home they had ever known.

"The world does not allow ladies to choose our own futures," Evangeline said. It was a difficult but unarguable truth. "We must go where we are sent; that is the way of things."

"Could we not at least ask her?" Lucy's voice cracked with emotion.

Only with effort did Evangeline keep her own words quiet and serene. "Even if we were to ask her, she could not give us permission to remain. This house now belongs to Father's cousin. We cannot stay." Evangeline hoped being forthright would allow Lucy to reconcile herself to their situation more quickly. "But even in Smeatley, even far from home, we will be together, dearest. We will have each other, just as we always have."

Lucy raised her gaze. Her once clear and naive eyes were clouded with an understanding of how unkind fate could truly be. "Do you promise?" The pleading in her voice was nearly Evangeline's undoing. "We will be together? No matter what happens?"

Evangeline pulled her sister into a tighter embrace. "I swear to you, Lucy. I will not ever leave you. Not ever."

Her sister took a deep breath, a gesture she had employed her whole life when calming herself. This time, however, the movement shuddered through her.

For Lucy's sake, Evangeline clamped down her pain and resolved to be the sure foundation they both needed. "What do you say to pilfering something from this room?"

"Pilfering?"

Evangeline forced a smile. "We each search about for something to take with us when we go, something of our family and our life here."

"But Aunt Barton said we weren't permitted to take anything, that it all belongs to the estate."

Evangeline assumed her most mischievous expression, one she'd often employed when Lucy was younger and they'd undertaken some silly game or another. "We won't tell Aunt Barton, and no one will notice. Nothing in this room is of particular value

3

in the eyes of anyone but us. We will slip whatever we choose into our trunks and never breathe a word of it."

Lucy pulled away enough to look up into Evangeline's eyes. "What if we're caught?"

"We won't be. No one will come in here for a few minutes yet."

For the first time since the true nature of their family's illness had become apparent, Lucy's expression turned hopeful. "And I can keep whatever I choose?"

"You can keep it forever and ever."

Lucy nodded anxiously and stepped away, her wide-eyed gaze scouring the walls. Evangeline turned away, giving her sister a modicum of privacy to make her very personal selection. She hoped her scheme would help in some small way. She knew no other means of easing even the smallest bit of Lucy's suffering. Or her own, for that matter.

Evangeline fixed her gaze upon a framed photograph on the bookshelf. Her father had been fascinated with photography and had, only a few short months earlier, arranged for a family portrait. How they had teased him about what had seemed like a ridiculous novelty.

Yet, there was her family—Father and Mother, George and James, frozen in time alongside Evangeline and Lucy. Captured forever. The sight pained and comforted her all at once, and she knew she had found her item to pilfer.

Evangeline glanced at the empty parlor doorway. She took the photograph from the shelf then moved swiftly to her trunk, opening it with shaky hands. She lifted two folded chemises, slipped the photograph beneath them, then carefully closed the lid.

She remained there, kneeling before her trunk. "Have you found something to claim for your own, dearest?"

"May I take more than one thing?" Desperation touched Lucy's simple question.

Evangeline wished she could allow Lucy to claim everything her heart desired, but Aunt Barton had been quite clear about them taking only their personal effects. She had caught Evangeline attempting to pack away one of Mother's porcelain figurines and had confiscated it.

"So long as whatever you choose can be easily hidden," Evangeline reminded Lucy.

"They are very small," Lucy said. "I can put them all in my wrist bag."

"Will the added weight be obvious? We wouldn't want Aunt Barton to grow suspicious."

"Help me hide them, Evangeline." Lucy begged. "I can't bear to leave anything behind."

Perhaps this had been a bad suggestion. Lucy's fragile heart would be set upon the treasures she'd selected. What if there was no way of secreting them away?

Footsteps sounded.

Evangeline turned quickly to her sister, whose look of panic told her she'd heard their aunt's approach as well. They would have to be swift.

She quickly perused Lucy's stolen goods. Father's pipe would fit in her wrist bag, but would be easily spotted. The book she'd selected from James's stack would also be harder to tuck away.

"Place the book and pipe in my trunk," she said quickly. "Tuck them under the clothes so they won't be easily seen."

What else had her sister selected?

"An antimacassar?" Similar bits of lace could be found over the backs and arms of chairs throughout the kingdom. Why would Lucy choose such a thing?

Lucy clutched it to her heart. "Mother made it for her chair," she whispered. "It still smells like her."

That simple explanation pierced Evangeline's heart. These treasures that Aunt Barton would no doubt begrudge them both were so tender, so personally dear.

"That will fit in your wrist bag. Tuck it in." Evangeline rearranged the items in her trunk, being careful to completely hide the photograph, the pipe, and the book. "Is there anything else?"

"The little shepherd boy Mother said resembled George."

Evangeline held her hand out for the figurine. "That will have to go in here as well."

She hid the final item, snapped the lid shut, and stood. She faced the doorway just as Aunt Barton stepped into view, framed in the light of the corridor. Lucy took tight hold of Evangeline's hand, clutching it for dear life.

"I trust you are ready to depart." Aunt Barton spoke sternly no matter that she must have known their hearts were breaking.

"We are."

Truth be told, they were not the least bit ready. But as she'd told Lucy: ladies, be they young or old, had little control over their comings and goings. They were to be grateful and cooperative. Life was far easier when such realities were accepted upfront.

"The servants will place your trunks in the carriage," Aunt Barton said. "Come along. We mustn't be late; the train waits for no one."

Lucy looked on the verge of falling to pieces.

Evangeline spoke on her behalf. "Might we have a moment to bid farewell to our home and—"

Aunt Barton's mouth pressed tight. "The train waits for no one," she repeated in clipped tones.

"I—"

"Evangeline." Aunt Barton motioned her into silence. "You would do well to set a good example for your sister. Both of your lives have changed, and it would be best if you helped Lucy make her peace with that."

Make her peace? How was the girl expected to ever do that? And how was Evangeline supposed to help her when she hadn't the slightest idea how to reclaim that peace for herself?

She alone remained of Lucy's loved ones. No matter how deeply she loved her sister, no matter how desperately she tried to be strong for the dear girl's sake, she knew she would never be enough to fill that void.

A light rain fell as the train sped north. Rivulets of water covered the windows, obscuring their view of the countryside. To distract Lucy from the gloominess of the ride, Evangeline pulled the ribbon from her hair and tied it in a large loop. It was not the perfect substitute for the string ideally used in a game of cat's cradle, but it proved sufficient.

Lucy didn't grin as broadly as she usually did when attempting the intricate patterns, but her countenance did lighten. Perhaps this was the key to seeing her sister through the difficult weeks and months to come: finding small sources of joy amidst the sorrow. Evangeline could do that.

"Perhaps when we reach Smeatley, we can find a field with daisies." Evangeline carefully moved a length of ribbon from one of Lucy's fingers to another. "We haven't made a daisy chain in ages."

Lucy watched the pattern forming around her fingers. "We could search for honeysuckle, as well."

"Oh, yes. Honeysuckle would be a beautiful addition, and it would smell divine."

Lucy's small smile grew, and some of the pain in her eyes lessened. "Could we sing while we collect flowers?"

Evangeline abandoned her cat's cradle creation to give her sister a hug. "Of course we can, my dear. Flowers. Songs. Games. We will continue to do them all—together."

"You're ruining the pattern." Lucy's complaint contained just enough amusement to make Evangeline smile.

Neither of them were truly happy nor lighthearted, but there was hope. They would be together, and Evangeline would make sure her sister had moments of encouragement each day.

Aunt Barton cleared her throat loudly, drawing their attention to her. She sat with her hands folded primly on her lap. Her lips pursed, and her brows pulled in a straight line. Evangeline had come to recognize that expression over the past week: her aunt was about to lecture. "It is time and past we discussed your future."

Time and past? *Past?* How long was the generally accepted mourning period for the sudden passing of nearly all of one's family? According to her aunt—four hours.

"Your grandfather has made arrangements for you and Lucy," Aunt Barton said.

"Arrangements?" The word boded ill. "I understood we were to live in Smeatley with you and Uncle Barton."

"*You* are to live in Smeatley." Aunt Barton straightened the chains of her chatelaine, separating the various baubles. Did she not intend to offer any further explanation?

"What are Grandfather's arrangements?" Lucy asked.

"He has procured a position for you."

Lucy traded her confused expression for one of concern.

Evangeline leaned closer to her aunt and spoke in quiet tones. "Could we not discuss this at a later time? Lucy has suffered a great deal and certainly does not need—"

"Nothing I am saying should upset her." Aunt Barton's nose scrunched as she spoke. Culling her words on the girl's behalf was apparently distasteful to her. "Besides, the job is for you, not Lucy. She need not be concerned on that score."

"What is this job?" Certainly her grandfather did not mean for her to be employed in his textile mill? Although, considering Uncle Barton managed the factory and Aunt Barton was delivering the news of Evangeline's unexpected employment, the possibility was not so far-fetched as it at first seemed. "In the factory?"

Aunt Barton's look of dry disbelief held ridicule. "You? In a factory? Do you think we are mad? Why, you would not last a single day there."

Evangeline didn't know whether to feel relieved or insulted. Lucy, for her part, still looked worried.

"Do not fret," Evangeline whispered to her. "All will be well."

"And we will be together," Lucy whispered back.

"We have never yet been apart." Indeed, not a day of Lucy's life had passed without Evangeline being there for her. They were as close as two sisters could be despite an eight-year age difference. "That will not change."

"If the two of you are quite finished with your chattering, I would like to return to the topic at hand."

Living in the same home as Aunt Barton grew less appealing with every conversation. Shielding Lucy from her barbs would require all Evangeline's efforts.

"Smeatley is in need of a schoolteacher," Aunt Barton said. "Your grandfather is the most important man in Smeatley, owing to his ownership of the factory—"

"I thought Grandfather lived in Leeds."

"Do not interrupt." Aunt Barton's stern expression did not change. "Your grandfather does not make his home in Smeatley, that is true, but he still wields a great deal of power there. As such, he has been granted the right to choose the town's new teacher."

"And he is asking me?" She was utterly unqualified, not to mention completely disinterested in being a teacher.

"We are not *asking*," Aunt Barton replied.

"We?"

Aunt Barton folded her hands once more. She tilted her chin at a disapproving angle. "Your uncle is the acting head of the school board. He, of course, was included in this decision. I was consulted as well. We are all in agreement. It is essential that you learn not only to work but to work hard. You will not learn that sitting about being idle."

Evangeline shook her head, confused that everyone seemed to have overlooked one simple fact. "I do not know how to teach."

"We are hopeful you will rise to the occasion." She did not sound the least bit hopeful. "You will learn what you must about teaching. Otherwise, you will fail."

Lucy's pallor had grown. Evangeline took her hand and held it comfortingly, though she continued to speak to Aunt Barton.

"I will do my best," she promised. "You will discover that I do, indeed, work quite hard, and I will work hard every day." She set her gaze on Lucy. "And we will gather our flowers and play our songs when I return home each evening."

Aunt Barton cleared her throat again. "You will not be living with us."

"We won't?"

With a sigh of annoyance, Aunt Barton clarified. "The schoolhouse has rooms for the teacher." She thumbed through the small chains hanging from her chatelaine and produced a key. She held it out, its rusty, dingy coloring in stark contrast to her white gloves. "You will need this."

"We are to go directly there? Today?"

Aunt Barton leaned back, settling herself comfortably. "You will begin teaching in only a few days. You'd do well to take the time to prepare for your students and to set your quarters to rights. The building has been empty for some time and will, no doubt, require a great deal of attention." She patted at her perfectly coiffed hair. "You will go directly to the schoolhouse and begin your work. Lucy will remain at Hillside House with your uncle and me."

Shock rendered Evangeline unable to respond.

Lucy's tear-clogged voice broke the silence. "You won't be with me?"

Evangeline focused her thoughts and summoned her determination. "Lucy will come with me. We can make do with whatever we find at the schoolhouse."

Aunt Barton was unmoved. "That is not for you to decide."

"Aunt—"

"Set your new house to rights, Evangeline. That must be your first priority."

"I—"

That pursed-lipped, narrow-eyed gaze of her aunt's returned with full force. "This is why you girls have a guardian. Lucy is too young to be on her own, and you, it would seem, are too selfish."

"How am I selfish for wishing to keep Lucy with me?"

"You desire to have her with you more than her comfort and well-being."

With effort Evangeline kept herself from glaring at her aunt.

Why, in heaven's name, had she required this discussion now, with Lucy present? "You are decided?"

"Your uncle and grandfather are decided. It is not your place to argue against them."

A lady simply did not contradict decisions made by her male relations. Her governess had explained that time and again. A lady did as she was instructed; to do otherwise only invited difficulty, uncertainty, and unnecessary misery. Quiet obedience made life far less complicated. She would do well to calm Lucy's worries and set her own sights on creating a home where Lucy would be permitted to join her eventually.

She clasped Lucy's hand in both of hers and met her distraught gaze. "We will be apart only this one night, dearest. I will work tirelessly to get the schoolhouse ready, then you can come live there with me."

"We'll be together?"

"As always," Evangeline said.

"Just as you promised." The statement was nearly a question, a plea.

"Just as I promised." She took the ribbon, hanging limply in Lucy's hand, and untied the knot. "We will not be living in a place so fine as Blakely Manor, but it will be home to us, just as that beloved house was." She tied the ribbon in a bow at the end of Lucy's long braid. "And you will have family in Smeatley: myself, of course, but also your aunt and uncle. And when Grandfather visits, you will have him as well."

Aunt Barton interrupted her attempt at reassurance. "We have judged it best if you don't bandy about the fact that you're related to your grandfather or your uncle and me. In fact, we insist that you do not."

"But we are family."

"The people of Smeatley did not take kindly to your uncle being placed in charge of the mill; some accused him of being given the position only because he was a relation of the owner." Aunt Barton tugged at her gloves, straightening the wrinkled fabric. "They will never give you a moment's opportunity to prove yourself if they know your connection to your grandfather."

"He feels this way as well?" Evangeline asked.

Aunt Barton's expression turned icy. "He and I have spoken at length about you, and we see eye-to-eye. You would do well to accept that your uncle and I speak for him in these matters."

Evangeline's heart dropped to her toes. As dismal as she had felt about coming to Smeatley, the prospect had only grown more bleak. She was being forced to take a job she'd not looked for nor knew how to properly perform. She and Lucy would be required not to acknowledge the only family they had left and would be disregarded, essentially disowned, in return. She could not imagine how Lucy's presence in the Bartons' home would be explained if she was not to be acknowledged as family.

"How will—" She stopped herself from asking about the requirement to hide their connection. She did not wish to emphasize that within Lucy's hearing. "How long will I be working as a teacher?"

"Until your grandfather is convinced you can be trusted with access to your inheritance."

Evangeline had been told only the smallest bit about the legacy left to her by her parents. Her grandfather controlled it entirely. It seemed, however, that he might be convinced to allow her enough of it to live a life more aligned with the one she and Lucy had known.

She pulled her sister to her side, keeping her arm tucked around her. This one night they would be apart, but Evangeline would spend that night making some semblance of a home for Lucy. She would throw herself into her unexpected responsibilities and prove to her grandfather that she was hardworking and capable. She would gain access to her inheritance, and they could live wherever they chose, perhaps Petersmarch.

They could return home. Together.

CHAPTER TWO

Smeatley, Yorkshire

England was no place for an Irishman. Dermot McCormick knew that well enough. His English neighbors knew it, too. But as they all were quite stuck with each other, Dermot chose to find humor—however dark—in the situation. 'Twas a challenge finding reason to be amused by the unkindness of others.

He'd worked hard and done well for himself. A skilled brick mason was valuable in a town growing as fast as this one. Dermot had helped build the recently opened grand mill. He'd worked the long hours expected of him, never allowing himself to rest on the job.

Mr. Barton, the mill manager, had taken note and placed Dermot at the head of the crew of bricklayers finishing the renovation of his personal home. Though the English work crew had first met Dermot's authority with resentment, they'd soon learned to listen and do their work, else they found themselves off the job.

Thomas Crossley, a local lad new to bricklaying but eager to learn, rushed across the back lawn to where the crew was near to finishing their day's work. At fifteen, he was considered old to be learning the trade, but it seemed to Dermot a far sight better that children be children, and trades and work and professions be delayed a bit. Circumstances didn't always allow for that luxury, as he knew all too well.

"Mistress is back," Thomas called. "She were comin' up t' drive in that fine carriage of hers but a moment ago."

Saints preserve us all. Mrs. Barton's absence the past week was the only reason they'd managed any work at all. The woman was forever changing her wishes, then pitching a very sophisticated fit when inconvenienced by her own fickleness. How any person could be equally stubborn and changeable, he still couldn't say. The woman was an oddity worthy of a traveling circus.

Dermot made quick work of cleaning the trowel he'd been using before setting it in his bucket with his other tools. "I'll face down the she-devil."

Thomas slipped off his cap and held it to his heart, his expression theatrically solemn. "Tha were a good man, Mr. McCormick, and tha'll be sorely missed."

"You think she'll best me as easily as that?"

The look of mourning still firmly on his features, Thomas shook his head. "I never said it'd be easy. But, mark thee, death'll seem right welcome by t' end, as it allus is to those what face down—"

"Enough, lad." Dermot knew from experience that Thomas'd go on for ages if allowed to. "You've my full confidence should the need to eulogize me arise. In the meantime, set your mind to your work or it's your own funeral we'll all be planning."

Thomas smiled as Dermot had known full well he would. The lad gathered the empty water buckets. He was charged with seeing that the crew had water enough for their work throughout the day, and he took his job seriously.

Dermot turned to his other men. "You've a full hour left of working today. You'll not shortchange the master."

They indicated their understanding, some with nods, some with grunts.

He crossed the lawn to the back of the house and stopped at the edge of the terrace where the Bartons always met for their consultations. He crossed himself for good measure and said a preemptive prayer for forgiveness, knowing he'd be thinking uncharitable thoughts in no time. A mere moment passed before Mrs. Barton joined him on the grass.

"How is the work coming along?" she asked.

"All will be in order by Friday week, provided nothing's changed in your expectations."

Mrs. Barton eyed him through narrowed lids. "I still expect what I've always expected, McCormick; work worthy of the generous amount we are paying you."

When he took into account the misery Mrs. Barton had caused him and his crew, that "generous" payment felt far more like a pittance.

"I have a task for you this evening," she said.

"I've a task for my own self," he said. "Working on that wall of yours, in fact. Unless, of course, you're not wanting it to be finished on schedule."

Mrs. Barton ignored him, as she always did. "Mr. Farr has secured the town a teacher."

Mr. Farr, who happened to be Mrs. Barton's father, owned the mill. Though he did not live in Smeatley, the well-to-do man held sway over anything and everything that happened in the tiny town. While Dermot was glad to hear Mr. Farr had found a teacher at last—he'd a boy of his own in need of schooling—he hadn't full confidence in the people Mr. Farr had selected to fill other important positions in the town.

He'd chosen his son-in-law as the mill manager, and Mr. Barton, though not so changeable and frustrating as his wife, was so tightfisted in the running of the mill that corners were often cut and expenses avoided that could be beneficial to them all.

And the vicar he had brought in—though many in town argued that Mrs. Barton had been the one behind the selection—was a toady of a man, who, according to the gossip of Dermot's workers, spent his sermons reminding churchgoers to work hard in the factory and live lives free of complaints.

The teacher might prove just as much of a disappointment.

"As you live near the schoolhouse," Mrs. Barton continued, "you're to accompany her there and see she arrives in the right place, well and sound."

Delivering women to their homes was an odd job for a brick mason, to be sure, and one that'd prevent him from seeing that his crew finished their work for the day. "Could not a servant be tasked with carting the teacher about?"

Mrs. Barton gave him one of her characteristic icy stares. "Perhaps. That would allow me time to discuss with you some of the thoughts I've had about the wall."

"I'll see to the teacher."

Oh, how he loathed that smug look she'd so perfected. The woman thought herself right about anything and everything under the sun.

Dermot turned toward the small copse of trees where his boy, Ronan, spent his days. The lad didn't always respond when his name was called, so placing two fingers in his mouth, Dermot let out a shrill whistle. That never failed to capture the lad's attention. Ronan looked up from his neat rows of rough-carved wooden figures. Dermot waved him over. Obedient as ever, the lad began gathering his toys.

When Dermot returned his attention to Mrs. Barton, she was no longer standing alone.

"This is Miss Blake," Mrs. Barton said, "our new teacher."

The lass beside her wore a black dress, one far finer than any he'd seen in Smeatley, with gloves that didn't appear to have been mended again and again. She stood with perfect, prim posture.

"You have a very peaceful back garden." Miss Blake's wide-brimmed bonnet kept much of her face hidden. "*Très charmant.*"

Unmended gloves. Fashionable dress. And a bit of French tossed in amongst her fine English words. This was no destitute woman looking for whatever work she could find, grateful for any position even if it meant wandering off to a tiny speck on the map like Smeatley.

Mrs. Barton finished the introductions. "Miss Blake, this is Dermot McCormick. He'll be showing you the way to the school-house."

Dermot thrust out his hand to shake Miss Blake's. She didn't take up his offer, but simply eyed his hand.

"You're meant to snatch it up," he told her. "Give it a good shake. 'Tis a way of saying 'It's pleased I am to meet you.'"

"I've never shaken hands with anyone before."

Oh, blessed fields of clover. She was even too high in the instep for hand shaking. "I'll not overtax you, Miss Blake. We'd best trek on. I've supper to put on after we've seen you delivered."

"You speak of me as though I were a parcel." Her muttered words carried a hint of amusement.

He set his hand against Ronan's back and gave him the lightest of nudges, setting him moving forward. Dermot led the way, his lad keeping close to his side. Around the side of the house they went, up the garden path, and through a gate leading to the street out front. Ronan kept pace with Dermot's longer strides. Miss Blake, however, did not.

She dragged a trunk behind her, something he'd not taken notice of at first. She might manage it on the lower streets of Smeatley, but the schoolhouse sat on Greenamble, the steepest of all the lanes and streets and alleyways in town. At the pace things were going, she'd never reach the top.

"Bide here a moment," he told Ronan. "Miss Blake's taken on a load greater than she ought." Heavens, he hoped that was only true in reference to her traveling trunk. Smeatley needed a capable teacher. *Ronan* needed a capable teacher.

Miss Blake had only just reached the iron gate when Dermot reached her. She pulled her trunk with both hands, her progress laborious.

"Were you wanting to be left behind, then?" Dermot asked.

"As a matter of fact, yes." Again a quiet mumble, completely lacking the traditional English irritation.

"Seems you ought to have packed a bit lighter," he said.

She allowed her trunk to drop flat. Her shoulders drooped. "If I'd known I'd be pulling it across town, I would have." She nodded toward the street ahead. "How much farther?"

"Never fear, you've plenty more of this bleak ol' town to see before setting your trunk down for good."

"You don't seem to care for Smeatley." She was likely eyeing him from under her black bonnet. "Is it because you aren't from here?"

"Now why would you be thinking I'm not Smeatley born and raised?" His tone held all the dryness of a vast African desert.

"Certainly I am not the first person to piece together your origins."

"I assure you, Miss Blake, this entire town has sorted that out and decided precisely how they feel about it." He took hold of the handle of her trunk. "Come on, then. You've a bit of a climb ahead of you."

CHAPTER THREE

r. McCormick looked back over his shoulder. His eyes were so dark his pupils were almost undetectable. It was not, however, the color of his eyes but the frustration in them that set Evangeline moving at a faster clip.

This Irishman was not only a touch grumpy but he had also shown himself to be in a tremendous hurry. Perhaps he did not realize that someone new to town would require some time to orient herself and become acquainted with the place. He likely didn't realize that she had, that very day, not only buried the majority of her family but also bid farewell to her one surviving sister and so understandably struggled to find the energy for a quick-paced jaunt across town. She suspected that even if he had realized as much, he still would not have summoned the patience to wait.

She picked up her pace to reach him. Her apologetic smile did not receive so much as a nod in return. He simply resumed their journey, her trunk in his hands. It wasn't overly heavy nor large, but he certainly managed the cumbersome load better than she had during the longer-than-expected trek.

The streets were nearly empty. No dogs barked. No voices were raised in conversation. Not even a birdcall filled the air. The quiet hung unnaturally about her, as though a cacophony would burst forth at any moment. This place felt pushed and pulled and pressed upon, and Evangeline was not at all sure what she thought of it.

"Have you lived here long?" she asked her companion.

"A year and a bit."

That, it seemed, was to be his entire answer. She'd always understood the Irish to be quite talkative people. Perhaps a different question would help, one without such a quick answer. She needed the distraction of a conversation.

"What is it that you do here?" she asked.

"I carry trunks for chatty women."

So that was to be his attitude. She could match him dry retort for dry retort if he wished to tread that conversational path. A series of quick steps brought her to his side.

"Do you charge extra for your cheerful conversation?" she asked.

"Naturally. A man's got to make a living, you know."

Just how far did he mean to take this tongue-in-cheek conversation? "Trunk carrying is a noble profession, I will grant you that. How do you endure the crushing weight of the ceaseless praise you must receive?"

He eyed her sidelong, his mouth an unreadable slash in his otherwise blank expression. Evangeline did not believe that he was truly as emotionless as he appeared. She'd known a tenant of Lord Bentley's in Petersmarch who walked about stone-faced and severe. As a child, she'd found him intimidating, but as she'd grown, she'd sensed something more beneath the facade, and the glare began to feel like a mask he wore.

The reminder of the home she'd not wanted to leave brought to mind the sister who'd watched, with tears streaming down her face, as Evangeline had followed Aunt Barton to the back terrace. Lucy had begged her not to go.

She had disappointed her sister; she knew she had.

Evangeline took in as much air as her tight lungs would allow. She would soon be alone in the schoolhouse that was to be her home. In private, she could allow her emotions to surface, giving way to the tears she'd kept tucked away. By the time she and Lucy were reunited in the morning, their new home would be in order, Evangeline would be the master of her grief, and they could begin this new, if unwanted, chapter in their lives. They would find their happiness again.

"You're to take this lane," Mr. McCormick said. "Greenamble Street."

She stepped around him enough to look up the road. And look *up* she did. This end of town sat directly against the side of a small but steep hill. Who had decided to place the schoolhouse *here*? The children would be exhausted before they even arrived for lessons.

"Is it as steep as it seems?" She hoped the answer was no.

"No."

At last, a bit of good luck.

Then he added, "It's steeper."

Of course it was. There was nothing for it, though, but to make the climb. She squared her shoulders.

"We can go slowly if you're needing to," Mr. McCormick said.

"I love sharply angled streets," she tossed back. "In fact, I believe I love them more than you do and that you will be the one struggling to keep up with me."

24

His mouth didn't so much as twitch. Perhaps he'd not been blessed with a sense of humor. Or, more likely, he had one but was too stubborn and surly to allow it even a moment's free reign.

His son, so quiet at his side, kept his eyes fixed on the toys he held in his hands. Yet there was something in the set of his posture, his shoulders turned slightly toward them, that told Evangeline he was listening more than he appeared to be. Her brother James had often held himself in just that way.

In a single heartbeat, her posturing and frustration with Mr. McCormick dissolved in a rush of grief.

James. Her beloved James. He was gone, just like the others.

Gone. The remembered church bells echoed inside her. *Gone.*

"Were you meaning to stand here all the day long?" Mr. McCormick said dryly. "Or might we jaunt on up?"

"Why are you so sour?" The question flew from her lips before she could stop it.

"Because, unlike you, I don't love steep streets—not when I'm carrying a heavy trunk for a dithering lass who can't make up her mind which way she's going or when."

She raised her chin. "You are not very amiable."

"What I'm not is patient." He twitched his head toward the street.

Evangeline's ongoing feud with fate certainly hadn't abated. Tears clung to her throat. For hours she'd worked for every steady breath, for every dry blink of her eyes, and this man was quickly pushing her to the limit of her emotional strength.

Mr. McCormick set down her trunk and squatted, facing his son. His expression and posture surprised Evangeline. There was concern and tenderness and—despite his insistence that he did not possess this particular virtue—patience.

He said something to the boy, then pointed up the street and gave a quick nod. His son ran ahead, not looking at his father nor at her. Evangeline watched him go, her thoughts and heart in Cambridgeshire. James was— No. James *had been* six years younger than she.

As quickly as that, her grief pierced her. She had spent the past days, even more so the past hours, either feeling everything or nothing. She had little choice but to cling to the latter, at least while she was in Mr. McCormick's company.

He stood up again, her trunk slung over his back.

She made a final attempt at conversation. "Your son seemed in a hurry."

"The lad's anxious to be home." Mr. McCormick's tone hadn't softened. Why was the man so put out with her?

"Home is a comforting place." She walked alongside him as they headed up the street.

"It is that," he said.

Evangeline eyed him. "Did we just agree on something?"

Mr. McCormick glanced up with a look of overdone pondering. "Sky's not falling." He trudged onward.

He was not one for prattling on. It was just as well. Evangeline had lost whatever earlier desire she'd had for lighthearted conversation, however distracting it might have been.

"This'll be you," Mr. McCormick said, jutting his chin at the thick hedge directly to the side of the road. It was too tall to see over.

The hedge? He must be mistaken. She glanced behind them, then up ahead.

"'Tis a bit overgrown." Mr. McCormick motioned to the hedge again. "You'll simply have to press your way through like a water vole squeezing in and out of her den."

"Did you just compare me to a rodent?"

"I'd not dare, miss," he said. "Rodents are far quieter."

If pushing her way through a hedge meant being free of Mr. McCormick's company, she'd gladly do her best impression of a water vole or badger or whatever other animal he meant to compare her to.

Evangeline stepped up beside him and found a small gap in the hedge. She pushed the overhanging branches back, slowly, carefully passing through to the other side.

Tall, wild grasses filled a small front garden. Overgrown trees dotted the area, several with their branches resting atop the roof of an L-shaped building, one hardly bigger than the small tenant cottages of Petersmarch. Even taking into account the upper story, the schoolhouse was tiny indeed.

Narrow windows checkered the building, sitting in uneven intervals. At least one of them appeared to be missing its glass. The house bore all the hallmarks of disuse and neglect.

Evangeline's heart dropped to her toes. Aunt Barton had scolded her for believing her new house had been appropriate for Lucy. That, it turned out, had not been an entirely inaccurate assessment. Perhaps the situation was better inside.

"Have you a key?" Mr. McCormick asked.

Her mind refused to work through the mystery of that simple question. But then she fished through her wrist bag and found the key Aunt Barton had given her during their long train ride. She pulled it from her bag just as they reached the two stone steps in front of the door. The key slid in the hole easily, but turning it required the use of both her arms. How long had this door been locked, unused and unopened?

The hinges squeaked loudly as she pushed open the door. Dust particles hung in the air, dancing in the sunshine spilling in from behind her. Directly in front of her was a staircase and, just to the right of it, another door with another keyhole.

"I was only given one key," she said, thinking out loud.

"Perhaps you're meant to burrow in," Mr. McCormick suggested.

"Like a rodent?" she tossed back dryly.

"Except louder."

She chose to ignore that observation. She hadn't another key; the one that had unlocked the front door did not fit in this interior one. With a tiny, unspoken prayer, she decided to test the knob. Fate chose to be kind in this small thing; the door opened easily.

The room beyond was dim. The air tasted stale and smelled of must.

"Is this the schoolroom?"

"I've not the slightest idea." Mr. McCormick moved past her and set her trunk on the floor.

Fully expecting him to walk away, she turned to thank him for his help. But he simply leaned against the wall and folded his arms across his chest as if waiting for something.

"You needn't stay if you'd rather be on your way," she said.

"I *would* rather be on my way, but you've not the slightest notion yet if your quarters are here or up the stairs."

What did that have to do with him remaining?

Her confusion must have shown because he answered the question she hadn't voiced. "'Tis a bit of a heavy trunk, miss. I'll carry it if you're needing it up there."

He was irritable, there was no denying that, but he was showing himself to be thoughtful. Still, she didn't intend to try his patience.

Evangeline made her way through the dimness toward a sliver

of light peeking through a covered window. Her fingers found the stiff curtains, which she pulled back. More light came in through the dingy glass, illuminating the space enough for her to see a table and a spindle-back chair near a small fireplace and a bench under another covered window.

She spotted another door, this one on an exterior wall. An old iron key, like the one in her hand, sat in the lock, ready and waiting. With effort, she turned it and pulled the door open, filling the space with sunlight. In the corner, barely lit enough to be seen, hung a few pots and cooking implements. She had found her living quarters. Her dingy, dust-covered, sparse, dark living quarters.

"I believe the trunk stays here." Mr. McCormick tapped it with his foot. "We're up the street a few paces—the only house with a yellow door. Should you need anything, give us a knock."

For a moment, she could do nothing but stare in mute shock at his offer. The day had been terrible and sorrowful. He, of all people, had offered a kind word, a moment of compassion. She hardly knew how to respond.

"But we've a limit of one knock per day, so don't go abusing the invitation." There was the Mr. McCormick she'd come to expect.

"I will set a goal of one knock per lifetime," she said.

He nodded firmly. "Then we'll get on just fine, Miss Blake. Just fine, indeed." With that, Mr. McCormick left.

And she was alone.

Evangeline lowered herself onto her traveling trunk, sitting on the edge just as she had that morning in her family's parlor. She had left a warm and inviting home, a place where she'd felt welcome and loved and treasured, to live in a disused and neglected building in a cantankerous and inhospitable town.

How can I possibly bring Lucy here?

Dust sat so thick on the floor she could see her footprints. The window had likely not been cleaned in years. The floor around the fireplace was darkened with soot and ash. She had but one chair and, as near as she could tell, no bed. Or any food. Or a blanket.

A lady quietly performed those tasks expected of her. But what was she to do when those tasks and expectations bordered on the impossible?

CHAPTER FOUR

ermot had reached out to that blasted woman and offered her a kindness, telling her to come by if she found herself needing any help, and she had returned an expression of disgust. When would he learn to simply leave the English be? Still, he stopped in the middle of the road, debating whether or not to turn back. That room had been bare as bones, not a crumb of food in sight or a blanket or lantern. He'd not even spied a bed. Where was the woman to lay her head? What was she to eat?

You're turning soft, you are, fretting over someone you don't even know—one who turned her nose up at you not a moment ago.

Miss Blake hadn't wanted his help, so there was little point offering it again. That reminder set him on his way home.

Ronan was sitting on the step outside their distinctive yellow door. He'd chosen the bright color to aid his lad in finding their house when they'd first arrived in this unfamiliar hamlet but, long after Ronan had learned the way, Dermot had kept the color as a reminder of the colorful doors of his own beloved Dublin. And because it vexed his very staid neighbors.

He unlocked and opened the door, motioning Ronan in ahead of him.

It was the same routine every day. Dermot wasn't certain when it had started, only that it didn't change. Each evening, Ronan rushed inside and carefully placed his carved figurines in a neat line against the wall beneath the front window. The lad then hung up his coat and cap on the nails beside the door. Ronan waited until Dermot was beside him as the boy liked doing that part together.

Then Ronan would join him at the shelves beside the fireplace where the pots and spoons were kept. A chair sat nearby in anticipation of this twice-daily moment when Dermot prepared their meal and Ronan broke his silence.

"Mr. Palmer made the mortar too runny today. Mortar mustn't be runny." With that eager introduction, Ronan dove wholeheartedly into the subject of mortar. 'Twas always that way with him. Whatever he chose to speak about, he spoke of it endlessly, digging down to the smallest of details. Imagine if the boy could learn to read. His mind, already eager to learn, would have endless supplies of knowledge on whatever struck his fancy.

While the boy prattled on, Dermot cut thick slices of bread and cheese. He hadn't the energy to build the fire, so their sandwiches would be cold, as they often were. Ronan never complained so long as the food was familiar.

Ronan stopped talking to begin eating, allowing Dermot a chance to slip in a word or two. "How did you fill up your time today?"

"The windowpanes at Mr. Barton's house needed counting. I got up as high as one hundred, but I didn't know the numbers that came next, so I had to stop."

"At one hundred you're for starting over again at one, but

adding the words 'one hundred' to the front. One hundred one. One hundred two. On like that."

Ronan nodded even as he practiced the new words. "What happens when I've reached the end?"

"Then you begin saying 'two hundred' before all the numbers. 'Tis a terribly convenient thing, that. You needn't remember anything new for ages and ages with counting."

Ronan took another generous bite of his sandwich.

"And did you know," Dermot continued, "if you learn your ciphering, you needn't count each windowpane on its own?"

He had his boy's full attention. "Could I cipher pebbles or bricks or leaves?"

"For sure and certain. Anything at all you're wanting to count can be ciphered."

The sandwich hung limp in Ronan's hands. His wide eyes were fixed on Dermot. "I want to learn that."

"That's what school's for, lad. And we've a school in Smeatley, and now a teacher. You can learn all the fine and useful things Miss Blake means to teach you." He hoped she proved fit for the post. He'd hate to think he was making promises to his boy only to have them broken.

Uncertainty clouded Ronan's expression. "Miss Blake smells like flowers."

Dermot had noticed that, himself, but hadn't dwelled on it overly much. At least not so much as warranted thinking on it again. "You don't care for flowers?" he asked Ronan.

"Only flowers should smell like flowers. People should smell like people." Ronan had always been very particular about things. He could be led to accept new ideas and ways of doing things but only with a great deal of patience and explanation, and sometimes not even then.

"Ladies like to smell of flowers," Dermot said. "I'd imagine because they're fond of them and fond of smelling sweet."

Ronan's brow furrowed more deeply. "People should smell like people."

"Female people smell like flowers sometimes." Dermot tried a slightly different approach. "And sometimes they smell like soap, just as you do after you've washed up."

Ronan scrunched up his face in distaste. No eight-year-old boy cared for a wash. He quickly recovered though, and offered an example of his own. "Sometimes people smell like dirt."

Dermot swallowed a bite of sandwich. "Sometimes they smell like cheese sandwiches."

"Sometimes they smell like mortar."

"Are you telling me I smell?" Dermot bit back a smile.

Ronan shrugged. "Sometimes."

Dermot ruffled the lad's light brown hair. "Finish your sandwich. We'll do a bit of whittling tonight."

'Twas a favorite pastime of theirs, whittling. Dermot had always enjoyed it, and Ronan was showing a knack for it, but neither of them would get far if a lamp wasn't lit. They hadn't nearly as many windows in this house as Mr. Barton had in his. Light was in short supply during the day, let alone in the fast-approaching evening.

The schoolhouse had been quite dim. Heavens knew how Miss Blake was getting along.

As soon as she entered his thoughts, he pushed her aside. He had troubles enough of his own.

He took the glass off the oil lantern and turned up the wick, then he opened the tin box in which he kept both the matches and a small bit of peat he'd brought with him when they'd crossed the Irish Sea.

Dermot stole a glance at Ronan. Finding the lad focused on his sandwich, Dermot returned his attentions to the peat. The texture of it was familiar and comforting, a bit of his childhood he'd lost so young.

Dermot lifted the peat to his nose and took a deep breath. The scent took him home in an instant, first back to his years apprenticed to Mr. Donaughy, then even further, all the way to a white-washed cottage tucked against a hillside overlooking the sea and his own once-tiny footprints in the sand. The smell tied him to a place and time of which nearly nothing remained. Dublin smelled of coal on blustery days, but the country had smelled of peat fires. It had smelled of home.

With a sigh to clear his thoughts of those long-ago years, Dermot slipped the peat back inside its box. It didn't do to go losing himself in memories when he'd work enough in the here and now. With a quick pull of a match, he lit the lantern and placed it on the rough-hewn table near the fireplace.

He pulled down the whittling knives and unfinished work. "Are you still carving a dog?" he asked Ronan.

The boy nodded. "Are you?"

"I am." He bent over his nearly completed Irish wolfhound. He didn't think Ronan had ever seen one in person. They weren't found in Dublin, and he'd not encountered any in England. "Did you see any dogs about today?"

Ronan nodded. "Three, but they hadn't any spots. Dogs should have spots."

"I'd a dog with grand spots when I was younger than you are," Dermot said. "He and I walked along the shore nearly every day."

"Dogs should have spots."

Dermot set his knife to shaping one of the hound's ears.

"Would you like to live along the sea, lad? Feel the spray of the ocean in the air and the wetness of the sand beneath your bare toes?"

"We should live here," Ronan said, his tone both earnest and decided. "This is where we live."

"And you're happy here?" Dermot wondered about that often. 'Twas oddly difficult at times to know if Ronan was happy.

A knock interrupted any answer the lad might have given. Ronan's brow pulled low as he glared at the door. They didn't often have visitors. Almost never, in fact. He'd received a few unhappy droppers-by early in his time in Smeatley, though there'd not been trouble in months.

Dermot set his knife down and rose from the table. "Take care with your work, there. The knife is sharp."

"Knives are supposed to be sharp."

"That they are."

Another knock, faster and louder than the last, sounded before Dermot reached the door. Someone was anxious, it seemed.

He cautiously pulled open the door, ready to cut off any tirade before Ronan heard too much of it. 'Twasn't a mob nor a newly unemployed bricklayer come to wage a complaint, but Miss Blake, her eyes wide, strain pulling at the corners of her mouth. She was terribly pale, though he couldn't say if it was a new development as her bonnet had hidden her face during their earlier walk.

"Miss Blake." His statement of recognition held a bit of a question.

"I need your help." The words came out in a rush, brimming with worry rather than inconvenience.

"What's happened?"

"There's a man in my house." She took a quick, quivery breath. "He won't leave. Please help me."

Dermot needed no more than that; he'd not ignore a woman in distress. "Ronan." The boy had stopped his whittling, clearly aware of the exchange at the door but not joining in. "We've a task, lad. Blow out the lantern and come along."

Dermot reached behind the door and snatched his shillelagh from its spot. He held the door while Ronan stepped out, then snapped it shut behind them all. The lad clung to his side, up-ended by the change in their usual evening pursuits. Dermot gave the boy's shoulder a quick squeeze, having learned early on that a kind touch—if offered by *him*—often soothed Ronan's worries over new things and people and places.

He eyed Miss Blake as they made the quick walk to the schoolhouse. She was pale to the point of being worrisome, with dark circles under her eyes. If he had to guess, he'd say she'd been crying.

"Did this man in your house hurt you, Miss Blake?"

She shook her head.

"You're full certain of that?"

Tension filled every inch of her stiff posture, but exhaustion dominated her expression. "I'm certain."

They passed through the overgrown break in the hedge and into the front gardens of the schoolhouse. Only the smallest bit of light illuminated the windows—a single lantern, he guessed. Perhaps a candle or two.

"Keep to Miss Blake's side," Dermot told Ronan. "I'll step inside first."

Ronan responded by gripping Dermot's coat and shaking his head frantically. He made a noise of distress and frustration. Being left with a stranger in an unfamiliar place would be overwhelming

37

for the boy, but what could Dermot do? Until he knew who was inside, he didn't dare bring Ronan along.

"If Miss Blake stays out here, could you sit on the stairs just inside?" he suggested. "I'll only be on the other side of the next door."

Ronan frowned as he thought. After a moment, he gave a small nod, though he didn't relinquish his hold on Dermot.

"We'll do that then." He only hoped the arrangement truly did work.

The front door wasn't locked. Either Miss Blake hadn't felt the need or she'd left in great haste. Dermot stepped across the entryway and to the stairs.

"Set yourself down just there," he told Ronan. "I'll be through this door." He motioned to the one that led to Miss Blake's rooms. "And I'll leave the door open, so you'll be sure to know when I come back out."

Ronan agreed, though reluctantly. He sat, his posture tense.

"I'll be but a moment," he reassured his boy.

He took a single step inside Miss Blake's living quarters. Only a few candles lit the nearly empty room. Dermot could make out a silhouette. A large, broad silhouette. 'Twas little wonder Miss Blake had been worried.

"Make yourself known," he called.

"McCormick? That you?"

"I'll have your name." Dermot spoke sternly. Until he knew who was in the room, he'd proceed with care.

"Owd Bob," the man answered with a laugh.

Dermot lowered his cudgel. *Saints above.* Miss Blake had sent him over here, fighting stick in hand, on account of Ol' Bob?

"What brings you to the schoolhouse?" he asked.

Ol' Bob stepped near enough to be lit by the candlelight. "I were just deliverin' for the new schoolmistress."

"You can't come stomping in here without warning. You have her jumpy as a mouse in a room full of tabbies." He pointed a finger at Ol' Bob's silhouette. "And if you tell her I compared her to a rodent again, I'll have your neck. She's sore at me over that as it is."

"Is she a friend to thee?"

"I'd not call us friends." Dermot shook his head. "Our acquaintance is only as long as the walk from Hillside House to here. I brought her from there to here, is all. On Mrs. Barton's orders."

Ol' Bob doffed his hat and held it dutifully to his heart. "Ah, her high-and-mighty lordship."

Most of Smeatley called Mrs. Barton that, though never in her presence.

"You'll have to knock if you're coming 'round here, man," Dermot said. "You can't be walking in on a lady unannounced."

"I didn't know she were here." Ol' Bob popped his hat atop his head.

Having sorted the mystery, Dermot returned to the entry-way where Ronan sat anxiously. "Come along, then. 'Tis only Ol' Bob."

Ronan obediently rose and grabbed hold of Dermot's coat, following him onto the outer step. Miss Blake watched Dermot expectantly.

"'Tis only Ol' Bob delivering something," he said.

"Who is he?"

Dermot hadn't intended to play nursemaid, but it seemed that was the job handed to him. "He's a man for hire. Carrying, delivering, moving things about."

"Entering houses without knocking," Miss Blake added.

"A talent of his. I'd suggest you lock your doors if you're not wanting visitors." Dermot couldn't stand about chatting all the night long. He'd a lad to see to and care for and to get to bed on time. And he'd a business proposal to prepare for Mr. Barton, one that meant the difference between a fine, steady future and uprooting the two of them again in search of one.

"Old Bob is not dangerous, is he?" Her tone was quiet, uncertain.

Dermot shook his head. "He's harmless enough."

"Then I am simply to wait until he leaves?"

"*We'll* wait until he leaves."

That brought her worry-filled eyes back to him. "You said he wasn't dangerous."

"So he isn't. Still, you're living here on your own and you've a man you don't know in your house. We'll wait until he's gone."

"And until I've locked the doors."

He nodded. "I'd recommend it."

Miss Blake sat on the top step. "I have a feeling Smeatley will require some getting used to."

"It will at that."

She turned enough to look up at him standing in the doorway. "How long did you live here before you stopped feeling out of place?"

He tapped his chin. "I'd wager another ten years or so. Twenty if all goes as it is now."

She sighed deeply, her shoulders drooping. "That is not very encouraging."

"I'm not tasked with relieving your uncertainties, Miss Blake."

"Apparently what you are tasked with is being offended by every word I say no matter how innocuous." She sounded truly irritated. "I said it earlier and my sentiments have not changed: you are not very friendly."

"We are neighbors, miss. Neighbors needn't be friends." 'Twas the philosophy that'd pulled him through the past year. No one truly wanted him here, and that was fine with him. He didn't need friends. He only needed money enough to see to his and Ronan's care. That was all.

She raised her chin and skewered him with a dagger-sharp glare from her blue eyes. "I am sorry to have bothered you this evening, Mr. McCormick. I assure you I will not knock on your door again this night."

"You've reached your knocking limit as it is," he reminded her.

Her eyes narrowed. "I thought you were jesting about that."

"If you're feeling particularly daring, you can test your theory." Truth be told, he'd not turn her away if she found herself in dire straits, or even in uncomfortable straits if it came to that. He simply preferred peace and quiet and being left alone.

Ol' Bob stepped out and doffed his hat. "I'm bahn ter home." He dipped his head to them. "Good night to thee an' all." He walked down the path and disappeared through the thick hedge.

Bahn ter. Dermot had lived in Smeatley for months before he'd made sense of that turn of phrase. 'Twas the Smeatley way of saying one was going somewhere. The locals had any number of such oddities. "Tha" rather than "thou." They said "nowt" when meaning "nothing" and "owt" when meaning "anything." "Allus" took the place of "always," and "summat" was the Yorkshire way of saying "something." The list had only grown the longer he lived in this particular corner of the world.

Dermot motioned Ronan toward home. Before stepping

away, he paused, intending to remind Miss Blake to lock her door.

The church bell rang out, and Miss Blake jumped, turning with jerking movement toward the sound. She pressed an open hand to her heart. "Why are the bells ringing?"

"It's dusk," Dermot told her.

"They ring at dusk?" Though he'd not have thought it possible, the lass had grown paler.

"And every morning at dawn," he said.

"Oh, merciful heavens." Her voice rasped out. "They ring twice every day?"

"That they do."

She wore a look of absolute horror. "How do I make them stop?"

"Well"—Dermot assumed his most serious expression—"you either marry the vicar and use your wifely influence to convince him to stop ringing them, or you burn the church down. Truth be told, I'm not sure which method I'd consider the more drastic of the two."

"They ring every day." She spoke the four words as a dismayed realization rather than a question. "What kind of purgatory is this?" she whispered.

She spun around and rushed up the steps. The door slammed closed with a loud, reverberating blow.

Purgatory? All on account of pealing church bells? The lass was an odd one, to be sure. And, he feared, a touch too fragile for life in a rough-and-tumble factory town. If she was unequal to the job of teaching here, then Dermot was in a fine pickle, indeed.

CHAPTER FIVE

Evangeline laid atop the straw tick, her coat spread over her for warmth, flinching with every peal of the church bells.

Gone. Gone. Gone.

The pain of grief, which only sleep had allowed her to escape, returned. It spread, reaching the very tips of her fingers, weighing down the very air she breathed, thundering with every beat of her heart.

Gone. Gone.

She rolled over onto her side, focusing on the dim light peeking around the dingy window coverings and illuminating the dancing flecks of dust. She could taste the dirt in the air, could feel the grit in her eyes and on her skin.

Her coat proved an insufficient blanket. The sandwich she'd eaten on the train the afternoon before had long since ceased keeping her hunger at bay. She was cold and famished and so very alone.

Gone. Gone.

She allowed herself to wallow in her suffering only until the last peal sounded.

She had never been apart from Lucy before. When George had gone to school and James had retreated into his books, she and Lucy had spent their days together, growing ever closer, ever fonder. Enough years separated them to add a maternal aspect to her view of their relationship, but she considered Lucy her friend as well as her sister. She simply had to get her sister back.

Evangeline sat upright, pulling on her coat like a knight of old donning his armor. It was time to get to work. The sooner she set her house to rights, the sooner she would have Lucy with her again.

Her assessment of her surroundings the night before had been disheartening. The house held no fuel for warmth, not even a lantern. There was no food. No blankets. No rags for cleaning. The sum total of her belongings were the clothes she'd brought with her, a table and bench, a spindle-backed chair, a straw tick, and three pots. She hadn't a bowl or plate or utensils. She hadn't even a teakettle.

Evangeline sighed and stood, determined to do all that must be done. She crossed to the window and pulled back the heavy cloth hanging over it.

The evening had been dim so she'd not been able to truly see the area surrounding the schoolhouse. She could see it now though. The back bushes were overgrown, just like the hedge at the front of the house. Weeds choked what looked to be a small kitchen garden. Roses grew wild and unchecked in a flowerbed.

Everything about this house felt forgotten. Perhaps that was why Aunt Barton had sent her here: to be forgotten.

She could practically hear George teasing her for that black thought. "Ever the dramatic one, aren't you, Evangeline?" He would have laughed—they all would have—and her spirits would have been lifted.

Evangeline forced a deep breath and pushed away the unwelcome reminder of her loss. She knelt in front of her trunk and lifted the lid. In an instant, she was overwhelmed by the smell of home: Father's shaving soap and the hyacinths Mother grew in her garden. How had those scents followed her here? She'd brought no flowers or soap, but the aroma had come just the same.

I am strong enough to endure this. I have to be.

Her first task was to dress for the day. That bit of normalcy would help tremendously. She pulled her chemise and underclothes from the trunk only to uncover the photograph she'd hidden away the day before. Her heart lodged in her throat. She ran her fingers around the wood frame, then over the cold glass, tracing the outline of her family. Beside the photograph lay Lucy's stolen treasures: Father's pipe, James's book, and "George," the ceramic shepherd.

She would find a place of prominence for these so her family could, in some small way, be with her in this unfamiliar place. She would at least have a tiny hint of home.

Evangeline pulled her corset from the trunk, eyeing it with misgiving. It was not designed for self-dressing, and she no longer had a maid to help her. She struggled, twisting and turning and pulling in whatever way she could. Getting it off the night before had not been easy, but putting it back on was proving nearly impossible.

How can I insist that I be entrusted with Lucy's care if I cannot even dress myself? She knew that the argument was unfair, the trouble being in the design of her corset rather than her own capability, but she felt certain Aunt Barton would wield this point against her if she ever learned of it.

Long, frustrating minutes passed, but at last she had herself corseted, however inexpertly askew. She pulled on her black dress, purposely choosing one that fastened in the front. She shook the dust from her skirts.

The mantelshelf became home to her family's photograph and Lucy's treasures so her sister would be greeted by these familiar, cherished things when she arrived.

The morning passed in long, difficult hours. Evangeline washed walls and windows and dusted every surface. She hadn't a proper broom, but she did her best to sweep the floor with a small hand brush, which proved tedious and ineffective. She didn't want Lucy to be disappointed in their new home, but how could that possibly be avoided? The house was dark, dingy, and cramped, empty of all that would make it comfortable and inviting.

She stood back and examined her work, her spirits dropping even further. Her focus slid to the family photograph, settling on her mother's intent gaze.

"What am I to do?" she asked in a whisper. "How could Lucy be happy in a place like this?"

It wasn't Mother's voice that answered, but Evangeline's own words from the day before: *I swear to you, Lucy. I will not ever leave you.*

Lucy had begged, and Evangeline had promised. Shabby house or not, they would be together. That was what mattered. It would be enough. It would have to be.

She tied her bonnet firmly on her head. She would return to Aunt and Uncle Barton's home, request enough of her inheritance to furnish this house with all it needed, and bring Lucy back with her. Surely they would agree to that.

The overgrown hedge did its utmost to prevent her from leaving, but she pressed through, careful not to snag her dress on the brambles. The tight space knocked her bonnet loose, but she righted it. Trimming the hedge needed to be high on her list of tasks, otherwise her students would arrive in tatters.

How did one go about trimming a hedge? A specific tool must exist for such a task, though she hadn't the first idea what it might be nor how to use it. Good heavens, she was out of her element. Yet even with a small bit of her inheritance, she could set things to rights. With a little more than a small bit, she could pay workers to do the things she didn't know how to accomplish.

With determined steps, Evangeline headed toward Hillside House. There was no risk of getting lost; she need only move downhill. At the bottom of Greenamble Street, she turned in what she was relatively certain was the right direction.

She walked past a dry goods store and thought she spied a person or two inside. The same was true of the small, one-windowed tobacco shop and of the cobbler's. Petersmarch was smaller than Smeatley, but those streets had been busier than this. Why was a town reported to be growing as quickly as this one was so empty?

And where were the children she was meant to be teaching? Other than Ronan McCormick, she hadn't seen a single child. Perhaps she would only have a handful of students. That would not be so unmanageable. Learning how to be a teacher was less daunting when faced with only a half-dozen pupils.

The road curved around a central churchyard, shops lining the side opposite the green. Evangeline slowed her pace, studying her new surroundings, learning the lay of the town. One thing, however, continually pulled her gaze: the massive mill built of a tawny-colored brick, glowering down on the town from its high perch to the west. Little effort had been made at ornamentation. No noticeable details softened its straight lines and imposing solidity. Window after window sat dark against the brick. She wondered how much light actually entered the building.

She knew the mill was not only a symbol of prosperity and innovation, but it also had saved the town of Smeatley from economic ruin, but Evangeline found the sight of it discomfiting. It was so cold and unyielding.

She pulled her gaze away, forcing her thoughts on her final destination and the conversation to come. Aunt Barton was a formidable presence. But Evangeline's need for the basic necessities in her new house, both for her own sake and Lucy's, was a reasonable request. The trouble was, Aunt Barton was not always reasonable.

CHAPTER SIX

Aunt Barton's butler ushered Evangeline inside Hillside House. He silently led her through an ornate vestibule that boasted a colorful mosaic floor and stained-glass windows. Stepping into the entrance hall, Evangeline was met with a grand staircase flanked by gold-leafed statues and the newest in gas-fueled lamps. More stained-glass windows high above the foyer filled the space with a rainbow of color. Every surface shone, free of smudges, free of dust. This was a far sight grander than the schoolhouse. The opulence nearly put even her beloved Blakely Manor to shame, except this luxury felt suffocating, burdensome. There was no sense of comfort and ease.

The butler led her up the wide staircase, his chin held at an angle even a duchess would be hard-pressed to replicate. Aunt Barton had insisted that keeping their relationship secret would require Evangeline to prove herself without the aid of her influential family. Here was evidence that her aunt had been correct. Evangeline was nothing more than a visitor come to beg a moment of the mistress's time.

The butler guided her to an open doorway, gave her a brief nod, and then returned downstairs.

Evangeline paused at the threshold. It was a library, small when compared with her father's but far more ostentatious. Seeing this, no one could doubt that the Bartons were quite wealthy. That, Evangeline suspected, was intentional.

Beneath one of the tall, leaded windows, Ronan McCormick occupied an armchair far too big for him. His gaze rested on a carved figurine in his hand. He didn't look up at her, though Evangeline felt certain he'd seen her. She took the same approach with him that her family had always used with James: greeting him as unobtrusively as possible and allowing him to decide what level of interaction he was comfortable with. She kept her gaze averted from Ronan but allowed the smallest of smiles to curve her lips, just enough of a happy expression that, should he choose to glance her way, he would know she was glad to see him but didn't mean to impose.

It was with that vague expression on her face that she met the eyes of Ronan's father. He sat in an armchair pulled up to a wide, cherrywood desk behind which sat a man Evangeline hadn't seen in years: her uncle Barton.

He was angular, all corners and long lines, with a thick and bushy mustache. The only thing about him that had changed since Evangeline had last seen him was the generous sprinkling of gray in his dark hair and the fine cut and cloth of his suit. Uncle Barton was older, but he was also more prosperous.

"Do continue your business," Aunt Barton said to the men. "I will see to this interruption."

Mr. McCormick didn't wait even the length of a breath. "As I was sayin', Mr. Barton, you'll never be filling your positions to capacity if this town can't hold the workers you're needing."

"And this proposal of yours would provide the hands?" Uncle Barton sounded intrigued.

"All who live near enough to the mill now are working there. All who live too far for coming in and out of town each day won't ever be working there. Their homes are too far afield. I'm proposing you build workers' housing, just as has been done elsewhere." Mr. McCormick pulled out a thick roll of papers. "I've not made this proposal lightly, Mr. Barton. I'll show you how it'll make you money in the end."

Aunt Barton had crossed nearly all the way to the door. In a harsh whisper, she snapped out Evangeline's name, then motioned her to step further into the room.

"What has brought you here? Do you not have a schoolroom and living quarters to set in order?"

Evangeline ignored the scornful tone. "I have come for Lucy."

"Lucy is not here."

"Where is she?" She need only have Aunt Barton point her in the direction of Lucy's room, and they could be on their way.

"She is in Leeds." Aunt Barton spoke those four words as if they were no more exceptional than a comment on the weather or a listing of foods on the menu.

Leeds? Shock rendered Evangeline silent for a long, heart-pounding moment. Lucy—who was only twelve years old, and who had, until yesterday, never been apart from her family—was in Leeds.

"Why is she in Leeds? Who is with her? She is too young to be on her own."

Aunt Barton pressed her lips together even as she arched one of her thin eyebrows. "She is with her guardian. That hardly constitutes being alone."

Grandfather was Lucy's guardian as well as the trustee of both of their inheritances. But Aunt Barton had previously indicated that he didn't wish for them to reside with him. "She is visiting him?"

Aunt Barton nodded. "Only until arrangements are made for her to leave for school."

"Leave for—? He is sending her away to school?"

Aunt Barton stood with her hands folded in front of her, the picture of calm serenity. "He feels it best."

Best? It was not remotely *best*.

"She belongs with me." Evangeline pressed her hand to her heart. "She needs me."

"And what of her education?" Far from empathetic, Aunt Barton's tone was accusatory.

"I live at a schoolhouse, for heaven's sake." Panic and anger mingled at a furious pace. Evangeline forced herself to regain a sense of calm. A lady did not grow forceful. In more serene tones, she spoke again. "I will be working as a teacher. I can see to her education."

"Do you honestly mean to suggest that the education you would provide her would be preferable to what she would receive at a fine school chosen by her trustee? Are you truly so selfish?"

Again that particular accusation was lobbed at her. "It is not a matter of being selfish—"

Aunt Barton's brows dropped in dry disbelief. She turned to Uncle Barton. "Are you hearing this, Robert?"

To Evangeline's dismay, both her uncle and Mr. McCormick looked up.

"It seems," Aunt Barton continued, "that Miss Blake has placed her judgment above that of Mr. Farr."

Uncle Barton made a noise of disapproval, but did not otherwise answer. Mr. McCormick's sharp gaze jumped between

Evangeline and her uncle, impatience filling the lines of his face. No doubt the interruption bothered him. He had come on his own business, and her efforts were interfering with his.

That was hardly her fault. And this matter was too crucial to leave unresolved. Yet his attention made her unaccountably nervous.

"I had no intention of asserting that my judgment was superior," she told her aunt and uncle. "I am simply explaining that Lucy and I have never been apart, and we ought not to be separated at such a difficult time."

"You've not been here twenty-four hours and are already demanding that we bend to your whim?" Aunt Barton tsked. "You will be an utter failure with such an unladylike attitude of entitlement."

Uncle Barton wore such a look of contemplation that there was no doubt in her mind he was evaluating her. This moment, she sensed, would set the tone for their future interactions. Uncle Barton, who had seldom visited her family, had always seemed to be a man who valued logic above sentimentality, but he also possessed an unmistakable air of self-possession. He would not respond any better to an appeal to his tender nature than he would to an attitude of superiority. She must remain thoughtful and calm, and not put herself forward overmuch.

"I did not mean to interrupt." She faced her uncle fully. "Indeed, I would have happily waited until your business was complete. I came because Mrs. Barton instructed me to do so yesterday. I came because I wish for Lucy to be with me again."

The plea did not appear to appease him. If anything, his expression hardened. "I have not completed my business with Mr. McCormick. You may wait near the door until I have time to discuss this." He motioned her toward the threshold, watching her with stern expectation.

Confusion coupled with frustration and worry in her over-burdened mind. Why was she being treated with such disdain? She had explained that she hadn't meant to disrupt, that she had come because she had been told to. She was behaving civilly, appropriately. Yet she was being scolded, reprimanded, and denied the one thing she had asked for.

She made her way back across the room. A chair sat a few paces from the doorway. She lowered herself into it and folded her hands on her lap, prepared to wait with patience and composure and not let any of her frustration and exhaustion show.

Lucy is in Leeds. If Evangeline had access to her accounts, she could join her there or bring her back to Smeatley. Somehow she would keep her promise to her sister.

Emotion burned at the back of her eyes. She could not allow herself to give in to her growing despondency.

She dropped her gaze to her hands and breathed deeply, clearing her thoughts and tucking her grief away. Out of the corner of her eye, she spied Ronan, who sat with a carved horse in his hand and looked nearly at her. How she wished she knew him well enough to move to his side, to ask him about his figurine or his day. He reminded her so much of James. To have been granted even a moment of his company would have been a much-needed salve.

Mr. McCormick resumed speaking to Evangeline's uncle. Her encounters with Mr. McCormick had shown him to be gruff and unpersonable, yet the lilting timbre of his Irish voice proved soothing. "Your factory's not fully staffed because you haven't enough workers nearby to fill the positions. If you're to compete at all, you'll be needing workers, and they'll be needing a place to live."

"You make a compelling argument, McCormick," Uncle Barton conceded. "I can see the value in the houses, but why should I place you in charge of building them? Why not someone else?"

"I saved your mill," Mr. McCormick replied without the least doubt in his voice. "The work was in disarray and so far behind schedule there was doubt it'd ever be finished. I brought the work quality up and cleared your crews of those who ought not to've been employed—something your local foreman wasn't willing to do. Why would you place anyone else in charge of this new project?"

Uncle Barton nodded both his acknowledgment and his approval. *Approval.* Mr. McCormick, despite being difficult and Irish, which was a liability of almost unspeakable proportions in England, had earned her uncle's approval.

She listened closely, attempting to sort out the mystery of how he had done it. If there was a way to impress her family despite a poor beginning, she needed to know what it was.

"Putting local men off the crews didn't earn you any friends," Uncle Barton said.

Mr. McCormick didn't look the least saddened by that fact. "How many people hereabout would've been my friend as it was? I know the history between our people. I know the unlikeliness of that being set aside. As much as I'd enjoy raising a pint in the pub with the local lads, I've too sensible a view of the world to mourn what I'd no right to expect in the first place."

His declaration struck Evangeline with unexpected force. He chose not to mourn what was out of his reach, and that choice, it seemed, gave him a degree of peace. Perhaps there was wisdom in that approach. But how did one determine what was and was not a rational expectation when lost in a situation that was new and unfamiliar?

"I'm not needing an answer immediately," Mr. McCormick continued. "You're too careful a man of business to make such a decision without contemplating it. Keep the drawings and the ciphers. Think it over. If you're not for building the homes, I'll take on the position overseeing the rebuilding of the Lilycroft Mill in Bradford."

"You have been offered that position?" Uncle Barton's full attention rested on Mr. McCormick.

"I have."

Worry filled her uncle's expression. Perhaps he was not so hard-nosed as his wife.

"Grant me a few days to ponder before you make a decision regarding Bradford," Uncle Barton requested.

"I can grant you a week," Mr. McCormick said, "but not much beyond that. I need to be where I have work."

"I understand." Uncle Barton held out his hand to the Irishman, and they shook firmly.

Mr. McCormick turned toward his son. "Come along, then, lad."

Discomfort tiptoed over Evangeline as her neighbor moved nearer. The man made her uncomfortable but not in a fearful way. He simply made her feel even more out of place than she already did. The doubts that had niggled at the back of her mind for the few hours she'd been in Smeatley grew when he was nearby.

She kept her gaze away from him, maintaining the rigid posture her mother and governesses had taught her when she was young.

As the McCormicks passed, Ronan raised his hand not holding the carved horse and gave her a tiny wave. He spoke not a word. He did not actually look at her. But with that gesture, a brief instant of reaching out when she felt so alone, the dear little boy captured her heart.

"Now, Evangeline." Her uncle's sudden words pulled her attention to him. "Let us address your difficulties."

She rose, anxious and uncertain. *A lady does as she is bid. A lady does not draw undue attention. A lady does not make trouble.* What, then, was a lady expected to do in a situation such as hers?

"You are upset that your sister is in Leeds," Uncle Barton said.

"I am upset that she is not here as I was told she would be," Evangeline corrected. Careful not to sound accusatory, she pressed on. "If you had lost nearly all your family, would you not be desperate to keep with you the one remaining member of that family? Lucy needs to be with me. She needs to come home."

But the final word fell flat. Home was in Petersmarch. It always would be.

"Mr. Farr disagrees," Aunt Barton said. She did not need to refer to Evangeline's grandfather in such formal terms now that Mr. McCormick was gone, yet she did. The message was clear: no matter their circumstances, Aunt Barton would always think of her as something less than family.

"Perhaps if I spoke with him—" Evangeline's request was cut short by her aunt's derisive laugh.

"Speak with him? You *do* think your judgment is superior to his. What utter nonsense."

"I do not believe that is what she was implying," Uncle Barton said.

Relief began bubbling inside Evangeline. Despite her earlier dismissal, she had been heard.

Aunt Barton took hold of the conversation. "Dearest," she said to her husband through tight lips, "are you suggesting that she 'speak with' Mr. Farr? You know his stubbornness as well as I do. You know perfectly well how he will respond when told he is wrong. He will not change course without ample evidence that doing so is prudent."

Evangeline saw an unexpected bit of hope in that declaration. "I need to show him that I am fit to be Lucy's caregiver and oversee her education?"

Uncle Barton nodded. Aunt Barton simply glared.

Evangeline's mind spun, attempting to sort it all out. Grandfather would not believe her capable of providing for Lucy's education until he had seen her provide an education for others. She would not begin her work as a teacher for two days yet, and there would be no indication of her abilities until she'd been at her new line of work for weeks.

Weeks. She could not leave Lucy in Leeds for weeks.

"Perhaps he could be convinced to postpone her education until my abilities as a teacher have been determined. Surely he cannot argue against my fitness to look after her in general."

"You have put your house in order?" Aunt Barton spoke with palpable doubt.

Uncle Barton watched too closely for Evangeline to be anything but honest.

"Not entirely. The house needs a few things, and I'm unable to obtain them on my own. As you know, my accounts are under the control of my trustee, and I cannot access my funds to obtain the things I need without your permission."

Grandfather had given Uncle Barton the ability to access her funds should he feel her reason for doing so was warranted.

"You mean to withdraw from your accounts so soon?" Aunt Barton asked. "That is worryingly irresponsible."

Why was her aunt so determined to think and speak ill of her?

"I will not withdraw an exorbitant amount." She hoped her nervousness didn't show. Mr. McCormick had not appeared distressed while making his business proposal. She hadn't a doubt that his confidence had done much to improve Uncle Barton's view of his position.

And, yet, he was a man. Men were permitted shows of confidence and ambition. The same in a woman was viewed as arrogant and brazen. Explaining without being assertive was her best approach. A lady, after all, would not do otherwise.

"I do not intend to purchase furnishings or fine decorations or anything that might be considered frivolous. I need only the most basic of things: linens, blankets, dishes, a bit of fuel for warmth, and enough food to see me until I receive my first pay. I don't even have a broom."

"The school board ought to have provided such things for a new teacher." Uncle Barton no longer addressed Evangeline but spoke directly to his wife. "This was an oversight, one we are duty-bound to address."

Her aunt still seemed set against it. They watched each other with a tension that boded ill. How had a simple question of linens and supplies led to an argument between them?

Aunt Barton's posture grew more rigid. "I would expect you, of all people, to be quite careful with her inheritance, Robert."

Why "him, of all people"? What had Uncle Barton to do with her legacy from her parents?

"I do choose to be prudent, yes," Uncle Barton responded. "But in this instance—"

Aunt Barton's expression hardened. "In this instance *what?*"

His shoulders drooped almost imperceptibly. "I only meant

that this is a matter for the school board, of which I am the acting head. The teacher ought to be provided with the basic necessities."

"Then she shall be provided with them," Aunt Barton declared. "You need only make the vicar aware of her needs, and the church will provide a basket."

"A charity basket?" Evangeline asked in shock.

Aunt Barton turned disapproving eyes on her. "You are living a more humble life now than that to which you were accustomed. Turning your nose up at charity will not serve you well. And it will certainly not secure your grand—Mr. Farr's approval."

"I wasn't turning my nose—"

"We are seeing to the concern you raised." Aunt Barton intertwined her fingers and assumed her lecturing expression. "Complaining about the way in which we accomplish it only gives you an air of unladylike ingratitude."

Evangeline bristled at the accusation. She'd objected because using charitable funds to meet her needs felt wasteful when she had, tucked away in an account, the means of meeting those needs on her own. She suspected her aunt would not believe her if she tried to explain. Indeed, Aunt Barton likely wouldn't allow the explanation in the first place.

"Robert, I do believe this is the best approach." Aunt Barton closed some of the distance between herself and her husband. "We will procure the things she needs, and her account need not be touched."

Uncle Barton did not respond immediately. His brow pulled low as his gaze wandered away, unfocused. He tapped a finger on the desktop.

"Dearest?" Aunt Barton offered the endearment in tones of impatience.

"A basket, yes," Uncle Barton said, "but not through the vicarage. This matter should be seen to by the school board. I will not burden the church with it."

Aunt Barton raised her chin to a painfully dignified angle. "Very well. I assume you will tell me if I am needed at all."

On that declaration, she strode from the room, head held high. She did not so much as glance at Evangeline as she passed.

Her uncle watched his wife leave, a look of frustration on his face. He returned his gaze to the papers on his desk. "I need to see to my work."

"Yes, of course. I will return to the schoolhouse and await the basket of supplies."

He nodded, but didn't look up at her. It was a dismissal, a discourteous one, but likely the sort she needed to grow accustomed to. A young lady born to a family of some means and living in one of the principal homes in a small and tight-knit neighborhood was, by default, treated with some tender kindness. A stranger relegated to the run-down schoolhouse would not be seen in the same light.

"Might I ask one question?"

"If you are quick."

"How am I to show Mr. Farr"—in time she might grow accustomed to referring to her grandfather in such formal terms—"that I can be entrusted with Lucy's care if he is never here to see the evidence for himself?"

"Mrs. Barton will report to him regularly."

That was not reassuring. Aunt Barton had made her opinion of Evangeline quite clear. "Oh, dear."

Her uncle glanced up at her, and for a moment, he appeared almost empathetic. "Mr. Farr visits Smeatley now and then. When he next comes, he will see the evidence for himself."

"How often is he here?"

"Not often, though I expect he will come around in another month or two."

Another month or two. She would be separated from Lucy for another month or two. How could she bear it?

"Send word if you find the schoolroom lacking in supplies." Uncle Barton focused on his papers.

The interview had come to a close. She would be given no further opportunities to plead with him nor make a case for Lucy's swift return. Her only chance of reclaiming her sister lay in convincing her grandfather, a man of legendary stubbornness, to change his mind.

CHAPTER SEVEN

ife had crushed too many of Dermot's dreams for him to live with any degree of hope. He knew he'd presented his idea to Mr. Barton clearly and convincingly, yet he paced the length of his tiny parlor that evening, racked with uncertainty.

"Why should I place you in charge?" Mr. Barton had asked in tones of sincere questioning.

Dermot didn't like to think of himself as suspicious, but he'd interacted with enough Englishmen to know that they viewed the Irish as lazy, undependable, and too simpleminded for anything but the most basic manual labor. Had he not proven himself to the man? If all he'd accomplished was not enough to show he was capable of the work he'd proposed, then what in the name of St. Bridget would ever be testament enough?

"Miss Blake smells like flowers." Ronan spoke so abruptly from his place at the table that Dermot nearly jumped in surprise. "She doesn't smell like people."

Dermot pushed his worries aside and took up the new topic.

"Perhaps she truly is a flower, but the wee folk transformed her into a lady."

"Flowers can't be people." Ronan, for all his innocence, never had been inclined to imagining fantastical things or otherworldly happenings.

"What is it, do you suppose, that makes her smell of flowers if she isn't secretly a flower her own self?" Dermot sat near Ronan.

"She didn't have flowers in her hair," Ronan said. "And she hadn't any in her hands."

What he lacked in imagination he more than made up for in attention to detail.

"I spied not a single flower on her person," Dermot confirmed.

Ronan's face twisted in contemplation. Dermot knew that expression well. The lad would ponder the question for a good long while, sorting the possibilities until he arrived at an answer. He was thorough and thoughtful and bright. Saints knew he'd do well in school if he had a capable and patient teacher. Dermot couldn't say with certainty if Miss Blake could claim either of those qualities.

"What would you think, Ronan, if we were to move to another town?" Dermot hoped their situation wouldn't require it, but if Mr. Barton rejected his proposal, he'd have to hie them to Bradford and the factory being rebuilt there. He'd do well to be prepared.

"We should stay here," Ronan said. He was often soft-spoken, just as often silent, but when he was fully decided upon something, he spoke with determination.

The lad always grew anxious or emotional when the possibility of something different or unexpected was proposed. 'Twas something more than merely enjoying familiarity; he seemed genuinely afraid of what he could not predict. Dermot never knew whether 'twas best to tell him of potential changes far ahead of time or if he'd do better to not mention them at all.

"But if we had to?" Dermot kept his tone as unconcerned as he could, not wishing to cause undue alarm. "We'd manage it, don't you think?"

"We should stay here. Here is where we're supposed to be." Ronan held his carved horse in a white-knuckled grip. His wee mouth pulled in a tense line, his brows jutting down in angry slashes. "We're for staying here."

Clearly, raising the possibility of change had been the wrong approach this time. Dermot pasted a smile on his face and ruffled Ronan's sandy-brown hair. "I think we should as well. 'Tis a fine home we've made for ourselves."

But the damage had been done. The boy would be on a knife's edge for a time. He was not the perpetually lighthearted child so many others seemed to be. Was that the result of some failing on Dermot's part or simply Ronan's natural disposition? He didn't think it a flaw in the boy, but he did worry about Ronan's happiness and lack of friendships and . . . far too many things.

"Miss Blake might keep flowers in her bag." Ronan had returned to their previous topic, though whether out of interest in it or out of a desire to avoid their more recent discussion, Dermot couldn't say. "Or her dress might have pockets with flowers inside."

"Perhaps." Dermot would let the lad weave his way toward soap and scented water on his own. Ronan enjoyed piecing together mysteries. "A few flowers might liven up her black dresses, don't you think?"

Both of Miss Blake's dresses had been unrelenting black. The color didn't suit her in the least, and it gave her an air of cold forbidding that would most likely cause her students a bit of trepidation. Perhaps she would choose less somber colors for school days.

She can wear whatever colors she wants if only she'll teach the lad.

"You can sit up a bit longer and ponder the question of Miss Blake's flowers," Dermot said, "but it's nearing time for bed."

Ronan nodded silently. He set his horse on the tabletop and slowly turned it, eyeing it from all angles. He'd always been content with quiet observation, alone and uninterrupted. In some ways that made things easier for Dermot, but it also made life lonely at times.

A rap sounded at the door. Dermot might've been lonely now and then, but he certainly didn't wish for company, especially not the sort who usually visited him. All too often they came around to wonder aloud when he meant to "return home," as if they weren't talking to him on the doorstep of his own home.

Of all the families he'd interacted with, only the Crossleys, whose oldest son, Thomas, worked for him, had ever seemed truly comfortable with his residence there.

He opened the door, preparing for the worst, only to experience the strongest feeling of reliving a moment. Miss Blake stood on his front step just as she had the night before. He couldn't seem to go anywhere without running into the woman.

"Before you bellow at me," she said, "I remembered your rule about only one knock per day and have waited the required twenty-four hours."

That was quite the "good evening."

"And," she continued, "I would not have come at all except I find myself in a difficult situation, and you are the only person

I know. Further, you did promise that I could ask you for assistance, provided I didn't come more than once each day."

"I give you full credit for your keen memory." He eyed her warily. "I'd give you more points if you'd tell me your purpose."

She made a sound that fell somewhere near a growl. "Why are you always so sour?"

"Why? Because, Miss Blake, I am tired." He was tired of unwelcoming neighbors, of not knowing how to get through to his boy, of facing an uncertain future.

"Then I will be brief." She took a nervous breath. "I—" She stopped, her gaze settling on something behind him. He followed her eye line all the way back to Ronan.

The lad glanced more than once in the direction of the door, but made no move to join them. He'd have to explain to Miss Blake that Ronan wasn't likely to even acknowledge that she was there. Those neighbors who had taken enough notice of the lad to realize his odd quirks had seemed more than a little put off by them.

She would have to know eventually. If she were to have any success schooling Ronan, she'd need to understand him.

Dermot squared his shoulders, determined to broach the subject without eliciting either pity or revulsion toward the lad. But his words died in his throat when Ronan raised the fingers of one hand and bent them once in an almost unnoticeable wave.

He'd waved. He'd acknowledged another person, one only slightly known to him. That never happened. Even the men on his crew hadn't been granted his notice until after weeks and weeks of daily encounters. He'd seen them at work. He'd listened to their conversations and repeated them at night over supper. But Ronan hadn't looked at them or spoken to them. He certainly hadn't waved.

Dermot turned toward Miss Blake. Had she noticed the gesture? Did she have any concept of how exceptional it was?

She stood just where she'd been, not a hair in a different place. But the corners of her mouth had pulled upward and something like excitement shone deep in her eyes. She raised her right hand mere inches and bent her fingers just as Ronan had.

Nothing more passed between his lad and this frustrating new neighbor, but the moment rendered Dermot too shocked for words, almost for thoughts. Ronan had reached out to someone, and that someone had reached back.

"I will come to my point quickly." Miss Blake didn't dwell on the astonishing exchange. "I've come to ask if I might borrow a blanket."

This grew odder by the moment. "A blanket?"

She nodded. "I will bring it back tomorrow. I won't even knock; I will simply leave it on the doorstep."

"Why are you needing a blanket?"

"There is not one at the schoolhouse." Her air of confidence was undermined by the way she held her hands tightly together. "Mr. Barton declared that was an oversight on the part of the school board, but the basket of items he said would be sent has not yet arrived. I only wish to borrow a blanket. I am certain the basket will arrive tomorrow."

"He's sending you a basket of items? How many things are you in need of?"

She hesitated. "A number."

"Anything else you're needing to borrow?"

"One does not 'borrow' food, does one?" A fleeting smile accompanied the comment, as if she'd been attempting a jest that she knew would fall short of the mark.

"You haven't any food?"

Her gaze dropped. "I am certain they will send the basket tomorrow."

If she had no food at her house, then she likely hadn't eaten since before her arrival the evening before.

"Ah, begor," he muttered. She was full starving, he'd wager. How in the name of all that was fair in the world had he been appointed her keeper? He'd worries enough of his own. "Step inside. I'll fetch you a blanket."

She didn't move. "Do you have a one-per-day limit on entering your house?"

"The check on ya, woman," he grumbled. "I've told you before that I'm not patient, but I'm no ogre either. Come in and get your blanket."

She took a single step inside and stopped, folding her arms in a posture of defiance. Stubborn colleen.

"Have a seat, then." He motioned to the spindle-back chair near the low-burning fire. "And don't you go jutting your chin out at me over the invitation. The night's a chilly one, and the warmth'll do you good."

For a moment she looked as though she meant to object, but her gaze slid to the glowing embers and the bravado left her stance. In a voice quieter and far more subdued than he'd yet heard from her, she said "Thank you" and crossed to the fireplace.

I'm playing nursemaid to a fine lady—one who resents the effort. How did fate and I come to have such a falling-out?

He pulled a bowl from its shelf, snatching up a spoon at the same time. The ladle was yet in the pot hanging over the fire. Without a word, he filled the bowl with stew and held it out to her.

She eyed it and him with obvious misgivings. "I don't understand."

"It's food. You eat it."

Her eyes were snapping. He suspected she had little enough experience with life to have encountered difficulties of this nature. The fine and fancy were treated quite differently than those living hand-to-mouth. He shouldn't delight in watching her grapple with her change in situation, but the way her frustration lit her eyes was oddly fascinating, as was the fierceness she used to keep that dissatisfaction in check.

"I came only for a blanket." She began to stand up, still not having accepted the stew. "I know better than to depend too heavily on your benevolence."

"Starving yourself to make a point will do no one any good, least of all yourself." He set the bowl in her hands. "Take the food, and stop being stubborn."

"*You* stop being overbearing."

He groaned as he stepped away. "Serves me right for opening the blasted door."

Truth be told, he was grateful she'd come by. Though they weren't friends, he'd no wish for her to be cold and hungry with no one to turn to.

He pulled a heavy woolen blanket from the chest in the corner and set it, still folded, on the floor beside her. "Once you're done with your supper."

"I won't inconvenience—"

"I swear to you, Miss Blake, if you can't find a means of graciously accepting what I'm generously offering you, I'll dump that bowl of stew right over your head. And what's more, I will enjoy it."

Instead of returning his quip with one of her own, Miss Blake pressed her lips together. The slightest of quivers shook her chin. Her gaze dropped to her untouched bowl.

Sweet mercy. "Don't cry, now. Not over something a quarrel-some ol' dog like me said to you."

"I *do* appreciate your generosity." Her words were thick, a clear indication she was indeed close to tears. "I'm simply over-whelmed, and tired, and hungry, and . . . I have had a terrible few days."

Those terrible days, no doubt, had something to do with the Lucy she'd mentioned at the Bartons' home, the one who was in Leeds. Dermot hadn't sorted that mystery entirely, but 'twas plain as the nose on his face that this Lucy meant a great deal to Miss Blake and that her absence was a point of great concern.

"I'm not bothered by you being here," he assured her, "and Ronan won't be either." He'd have thought otherwise if not for the boy's unexpected wave. "I know what it is to have terrible days, Miss Blake. I'm sorry you've had a few of your own lately."

She turned her haunting blue eyes on him. "How did you get through your terrible days?"

"I ate a great deal of stew." He nudged the folded blanket closer to her. "And I got a good night's sleep."

She raised an eyebrow. "You aren't one for conversations, are you?"

"Not with the English." He walked back to the table where Ronan sat, working at his whittling.

Miss Blake was not done discussing the matter at hand. "That decision must have rendered your life rather quiet."

"'That decision,' Miss Blake, was not mine."

She turned in her chair to look at him. "Your neighbors don't talk to you?"

"Not a soul—except for *one*," he said dryly.

He swore he saw amusement flash in her eyes. "Perhaps that's because you're a quarrelsome old dog."

"I would say that's exactly why." He took up his knife and a block of uncut wood. "Ronan, I'll wager you a tuppence that Miss Blake'll not finish her stew but rather will spend the evening flapping her gums like she's been doing."

"Quarrelsome dog."

Miss Blake had a sense of humor after all, it would seem.

"Eat your stew, woman."

A fleeting smile crossed her features as she faced the fireplace and tucked into her stew. She'd jested with him. Had tossed him a smile. The woman was being friendly.

Dermot wasn't at all accustomed to that.

CHAPTER EIGHT

Evangeline's basket of supplies arrived sometime the next day. She couldn't be certain when, as the items were simply left on her doorstep without so much as a knock. Perhaps that was for the best. She would have asked whichever of the Bartons' servants had been tasked with the delivery if they had been present when Lucy had departed the day before and if she had seemed afraid or lonely. The answer, no matter what it had been, would not have offered any reassurance. Indeed, the only comfort she'd felt of late had come from Mr. McCormick last evening. It was a sad state of affairs when one's own family could not muster as much kindness as the town curmudgeon.

She told herself that Lucy knew full well that Evangeline would not rest until they were together again. She imagined that Lucy's new school was a warm and inviting place, staffed by teachers who were kind and gentle and filled with students who would become her dear friends. Lucy would be well. She would be. Evangeline would believe that no matter her doubts.

Her gnawing hunger alleviated a bit by an apple she found in the basket, Evangeline made the trek upstairs to the schoolroom for the first time since her arrival. Her concerns for Lucy had occupied her every thought, but Lucy was gone, and Evangeline could delay no longer. Her students would begin arriving the next morning.

Evangeline needed to put her time to good use. She needed to prove herself capable enough for even her grandfather's exacting standards.

The schoolroom door was unlocked. Indeed, it hadn't even a keyhole. She wondered if the omission was a good sign or not. The hinges protested as she pushed the door open.

She stepped inside the dimly lit room. Dust sat upon every surface. This space was no better than her neglected quarters downstairs. The town was required by law to educate its children, but the evidence pointed at a clear reluctance to do so.

Evangeline had done her best to address the state of things below, but without a broom and only a few rags, she had been hard-pressed to make any progress. Sweeping an entire building with a brush would take a tremendously long time and, once the children began coming, would need to be done every day. It was far from the only job she needed to do. The windows required washing. The room needed arranging for school. She had yet to locate any schoolbooks or slates. Of course, somewhere in the midst of everything else, she needed to determine what in the world she would do come morning. She hadn't the first idea how to be a teacher.

Dust stirred as Evangeline crossed to the far end of the room. Though she had always preferred soft colors and pale laces, she was grateful in that moment to be dressed in black. The color would hide any smudges and smears of dirt from her cleaning efforts.

Her arms and shoulders ached from the hours she'd already spent cleaning her own space. They protested the prospect of more time spent in the same pursuit. But what option did she have? She could not welcome her students to such a neglected space.

The first order of business was arranging the long benches in a way that made sense for a schoolroom. What that arrangement might be, she couldn't say. Her schoolroom had been the nursery in her home, with only herself and her siblings learning under the watchful eye of their governess. They'd sat at a single table, surrounded by books and maps, paper and slates. They'd had all they needed and an educational guide who knew what she was about. The children of Smeatley would have neither.

I will simply have to do my best.

She decided on a U-shape for the benches, as that would allow her to see all of the children and all of them to see her. Of course, she was assuming the number of students matched the number of spaces on the benches. What if the numbers were far larger? Heavens, that did seem likely. From all she had heard, the town had grown during the past few months and seemed likely to continue doing so.

The benches proved heavier than she'd expected. Inch by inch, she pulled and pushed them into position. The scraping sound grated on her ears, as if declaring that she was thoroughly unfit for the task she'd been assigned. She could not even set up the schoolroom in a proper and efficient fashion; how could she ever hope to oversee the room when it was filled with children?

She tried to clear her mind of doubts as she worked well into the afternoon. Her empty stomach loudly protested the physical exertion. She might have simply hurried downstairs for a quick bite if not for the fact that she hadn't the first idea how to prepare any of the items she'd been sent. The basket consisted mainly of vegetables, few of which could be eaten raw. The carrots might have made a quick lunch eaten as they were, but she could not bring herself to face yet another glaring example of her deficiencies.

Mr. McCormick knew how to prepare such things. The stew she'd eaten at his house had included potatoes and turnips and carrots. If he would help her learn how to cook, then she would be ready for Lucy when she returned.

But a lady ought not cause difficulties or inconvenience people. Heaven knew she'd done enough of that already where her neighbor was concerned. Yet, what choice did she have? She would utterly fail without help, and failure meant losing Lucy.

She would simply have to ask for help in a way that did not make her too much of a burden.

She headed downstairs and crossed directly to the photograph on the mantelshelf. "What do I do, Mother? I don't wish to disappoint you, but I do not know how to navigate these waters."

She watched that still, silent face, desperate for one moment of reassurance, one single word of guidance.

"I will do my best," she whispered. "I only hope it will be enough."

Evangeline returned to the rough-hewn table. She dropped a potato, turnip, and carrot into her upturned apron, then pulled the apron's hem to her waist. She smoothed her finger over the glass covering her beloved family photograph and offered silent words of love and longing. She straightened Father's pipe, brushed a bit of dust from the edge of James's book, and touched the tiny crook held by George's shepherd figurine. Then, her vegetables held fast in her apron, she hurried out.

She barely managed to pull the heavy door closed with a thud.

The key fought her, but she forced it to turn. Mr. McCormick had advised her to lock up; she hadn't neglected to do so since. He knew this town and its inhabitants better than she did. He also had far more experience of the world than she could claim.

Reaching the McCormick home would be easier and faster if not for the steepness of the street. She felt like she was navigating stairs rather than taking a quick jaunt.

Her knocks generally went unanswered for a moment or two. Whether the hesitation was common for him—he did not, after all, seem the type for eagerly welcoming visitors—or he took his time answering her knocks in particular, she could not say. Her father had often praised her for her patience, so she stood on the McCormicks' front step, her apron clutched tight, and waited.

When Mr. McCormick opened the door, his brows pulled low in the middle while remaining still at the ends, forming the opposite of his frown. The effect was likely meant to be intimidating, emphasizing his grumpy demeanor, but for reasons Evangeline couldn't explain, it inspired an inarguable desire to smile, not with amusement, but something far closer to relief.

"Ah, is it yourself, Miss Blake?" His usual tone of irritable exhaustion had changed to dry acceptance. "What is it brings you 'round claiming your daily knock?"

She knew she was pushing the bounds of polite hospitality, but she did not know anyone else; at least, no one who would help her.

She revealed the three pathetic bits of vegetable tucked inside her apron. "Do you know how to cook these?"

He eyed her collection, then looked up at her, his pulled-brow frown still in place. "You've come begging cooking lessons?"

"A few words of instruction would suffice." That should allow her to learn a necessary skill without proving truly burdensome.

It was as good a balance as she was likely to strike. "The stew you so kindly shared with me last evening contained all three of these, so I know you know what to do with them. A bit of guidance, however small, would be most welcome."

"Have you never cooked a vegetable or made a soup?"

Not a week past, that lack hadn't been the point of derision it apparently was now. Evangeline kept her expression of friendly determination firmly in place. "I have not."

He tipped his head slightly to the side, eyeing her sidelong. His eyelids narrowed to slits. "And what of being a schoolteacher? Have you ever done that before?"

"I have not." Uttering those three words damaged her pride more than she could have predicted. She had never professed to be a teacher, nor had she chosen to be one.

He muttered something that did not sound at all like English. Irish, if she had to guess, and, she would further wager it was not an age-old expression of confidence. Mr. McCormick turned away from the door. No doubt he meant to leave her in her ignorance and uncertainty.

"Please, sir," she said, softly. "I have been forced into a situation for which I neither asked nor wished, but I am doing the best I can."

He stopped but did not look back at her.

"I know my best is not good enough," she continued. "Not yet. I need a little help while I am finding my footing. Surely you can feel some degree of compassion for someone in such a situation. I am in dire enough straits to accept pity if need be. I am hungry, sir. I am hungry, and I cannot cook these things without some help. And worse still, I am without my family, and proving myself capable and competent is my sole means of being reunited with the only kin I have left in this world. Please, help me."

Mr. McCormick looked at her at last. His mouth still formed a sharp frown. His brows had not returned to a position of ease or pleasure. Yet his countenance seemed softer.

He stepped aside and waved at her to come inside.

He meant to help her? As easy as that? She'd had to work hard to convince her aunt and uncle to aid her situation, yet a simple appeal seemed enough for her gruff neighbor.

"Either you're not hungry or you're not in a great hurry," he said.

She pulled her wandering thoughts back in order. "Forgive me. I am unaccustomed to receiving help when I need it. I've known so little of that these past days."

"Odd. I seem to recall you receiving ample help here the last few nights. Every night, in fact. At about this hour."

Despite his gruff tone, she found herself nearly smiling at him. She ought to have felt unwelcome or at least unsure of herself, but somehow his grumbling eased her uncertainties.

"You did give me permission for one knock each day," she reminded him.

"Ought to have made it one each fortnight." He waved her inside again. "How is it you're wanting to prepare your vegetables?"

"Any way at all, really. I haven't the first idea how to go about any of it."

"Easiest is roasting them. You poke 'em a time or two with a fork, then set them amongst the coals. That'll take a bit of time, though."

She nodded, committing the simple instructions to memory. "What if I don't have a great deal of time?"

"Meaning, what if you put off your meal preparation until supper time and have nothing to eat though you're hungry enough to have a go at the vegetables raw?"

She shrugged a single shoulder. "I suppose that is one possible scenario."

"Then there's but one thing to do."

She was intrigued. "What is that?"

He motioned with his chin toward the chair near his fire. "Same thing you did last night."

"I can't take more food off your table, Mr. McCormick."

"Fair enough." He held out his hand. "You can trade me your potato for a bowl of soup."

It still felt as though she was taking advantage of his reluctant generosity. A single potato would hardly replace a bowl's worth of soup.

"I can see you intend to argue with me," he said. "I'd advise against it."

"Because you fear I will best you in a battle of wills?"

He shrugged a single shoulder in a rather impressive imitation of her own earlier gesture. "I suppose that is one possible scenario." He even managed to recreate her Cambridgeshire accent. Quick as lightning, he resumed his usual tone and demeanor. "Mostly I'm too weary for arguing civilly, and I've no desire to curse at a woman."

"I thank you for that. And, in deference to your forbearance, I will skip over my planned arguments and simply take my place near the fire."

"Thank you." Those two words were filled with conflicting emotions: annoyance, relief, amusement, weariness. For a man who put forth nothing but grumpy standoffishness, he certainly could pour a lot into only a few syllables.

She set her single potato in his hand. The carrot and turnip she kept in her apron pocket. She sat in her seat.

Mr. McCormick dished her a bowl of soup and left her at the

fireplace. Ronan kept to the same seat he'd occupied the evening before. He didn't speak to her nor look directly at her, but neither did he seem truly bothered by her presence. He offered his tiny wave, which she returned in kind.

This evening, however, Mr. McCormick did not keep to the other side of the room, busying himself with tasks. Instead, he returned to the fireplace and leaned against the mantel.

"Aside from roasting amongst the coals, you can cut up your vegetables to put in a soup or stew, like you have there." He tossed her potato in the air no higher than his eye level, catching it in his hand again. "Simply cut it to the sizes you want, drop in a pot of simmering water, toss in a bit of spices—whatever suits you—and let it cook 'til all is tender."

"Spices?" Oh, dear. This was more complicated than she'd anticipated. "Which spices? And how much? And where would I find them? I don't suppose they might grow in a kitchen garden?" She shook her head at the thought. "Except there is no kitchen garden at the schoolhouse, only weeds choking out roses that have gone to wood."

"You know flowers but not herbs, then?"

She sighed. "My parents envisioned a very different life for me than the one I now have. They prepared me for that other future, not this one."

"Sounds as though you'll go hungry if I don't help you."

How she hated being the constant recipient of such displeased charity. And, yet, she couldn't blame Mr. McCormick for begrudging her the frequent aid she required. He hadn't brought her here so ill-prepared, neither had he asked to be given so useless a neighbor. Her position as teacher had not been his idea. He was not the reason her grandfather and Aunt and Uncle Barton had pushed her away, nor why Lucy had been taken from her.

And he was not to blame for the loss of her family. There was no one to blame for her circumstances other than cruel fate.

"I can roast the vegetables for the time being," she assured him. "Someday, when my welcome is not worn quite so thin, I'll ask for instructions on another method. Better still"—she quickly changed directions—"I will endeavor to make the acquaintance of someone in town who can teach me. The mother of one of my students, perhaps. Or the vicar's wife."

"I complain and mutter a great deal," Mr. McCormick said, "but I'll not begrudge you the knowledge you need to keep your belly full. No one should ever go hungry, and there's a far sight too many in this ol' world who do. You come here in the evenings, and we'll see to it you learn what you're needing."

"Would that not inconvenience you a great deal?"

"Of course it will," he said. And yet his surliness was not off-putting.

"Why would you help me if it is such a bother?"

An actual smile tipped the corners of his mouth. It was small and subtle but utterly unmistakable. She found herself unexpectedly reciprocating the gesture.

"I know perfectly well I'm a curmudgeon," he said, "but I can be a decent person now and then."

"Never you fear," she said. "I'll not share your secret with the neighbors."

"I'd appreciate that." Quick as could be, his expression turned serious. "I'd further appreciate you helping Ronan with his studies should he need it. He's not had any schooling before, and I can't say how he'll take to it."

The straight-forward declaration held more than a hint of uncertainty. Evangeline knew little of Ronan, yet she understood Mr. McCormick's concerns. The boy was quiet and withdrawn.

He didn't speak, didn't interact other than the occasional wave. There was every possibility that an attempt at schooling would prove futile or overly frustrating. But there was also the possibility that he would flourish, however quietly, however inwardly, and prove a fine student.

"I will help him in whatever way I can."

"Be as good as your word on that," Mr. McCormick said, "and you can come knocking on this door as often as you wish."

She meant to keep her promise, and not merely because she wanted to do right by the students she'd meet tomorrow. She also wanted to forestall causing Mr. McCormick additional inconvenience. But most of all, she wished to help Ronan because she held out hope that he would prove to be like her brother James in more ways than she'd yet seen. James had behaved in much the same way Ronan did, the same quietness, the same insistence on a barrier between himself and others. He had also been a dab hand at a number of school subjects.

More than that, though, he had been, quite possibly, the best soul she'd ever known.

CHAPTER NINE

Evangeline woke to the sound of tiny voices, dozens of them, right outside her windows. For a moment she feared she'd overslept. But the church bells had not yet announced the arrival of dawn. She never slept through the church bells. Heavens, she hardly *breathed* through them.

She was not late. Her students were early.

With no time to struggle with her corset, she pulled on her coat, grateful it was long enough to hide nearly all of her night-gown. She quickly smoothed and braided her hair, tying it in a loop with a length of ribbon. Feeling rather like a vagabond, Evangeline hurried out of her rooms and across the entryway to the front door.

The early morning light illuminated the faces of a handful of children. They sat on rocks, in the dirt. Some leaned against the schoolhouse. A few of the younger children rested with their heads in the laps of the older ones. No one seemed to think it odd that they had arrived before the sun.

Had Evangeline misunderstood? Surely school didn't begin

so early. Why, most of these children had likely not even eaten breakfast yet.

She caught the eye of a young girl, one approaching eleven or twelve years of age, the same age as Lucy. The reminder of her sister struck deep at her heart, but she rallied. Her first day of teaching was no time to fall to pieces.

"Are you all here for school?" Evangeline asked.

The girl answered with what sounded like a haphazard collection of noises, though Evangeline firmly suspected they were words.

"I beg your pardon?"

The girl repeated herself, though Evangeline still couldn't make sense of the answer.

"One more time, please," Evangeline requested. "But slowly. I do not hale from this area of the kingdom, and my ears are not yet accustomed to your manner of speaking."

The girl's ginger brows pulled low in consternation. When she spoke again, her words were slow and overly pronounced, as if Evangeline didn't understand English. "We're come for skoo-il."

Skoo-il. *School.* They had, indeed, arrived for school. The day was proving more difficult than she'd imagined; and she hadn't even started teaching yet.

"Why are you here so early?" she pressed.

"It i'n't so early as that."

She sorted that sentence in her head and hoped she understood it correctly.

"Does school always begin before sunrise?" Evangeline asked.

"Tha are t' teacher. Tha'll know better'n I."

Good heavens. Did the people of Smeatley speak a different language? *Tha are t' teacher.* That likely translated to "You are the teacher," though how, precisely, she couldn't say.

"Will you be coming this early every day?" Perhaps she would fare better with a simple yes or no answer.

The girl nodded. At last, something Evangeline could understand without effort. The words that followed, though, were still a struggle.

Evangeline recognized the word she felt certain meant "school," as well as "parents" and "factory." If she was filling in the remainder correctly, the girl was saying that the children came with their parents, who were headed to work at the factory, and were left here to await the start of school. How she hoped she'd guessed right.

"I'll be but a moment," she said. "Please tell the other children."

Another indiscernible answer followed. Perhaps, given time, Evangeline would grow accustomed to this West Yorkshire style of speaking, but for the moment, she was lost. How in heaven's name was she supposed to teach these children if she could not even understand them?

She posed the question aloud once she had returned inside. The empty room did not answer. Her family, ensconced behind glass, did not either. She, herself, hadn't any solutions.

Her corset fought her as much as ever. Surely women who hadn't the means of retaining a lady's maid still wore corsets. How did they manage? Were they more limber than she or simply more practiced? Perhaps they wore more cooperative corsets.

Her hair neatly, if simply, pinned up, her button-front dress donned, and her boots on and tied, Evangeline stepped from her rooms. While she'd been uncertain ever since learning she was to be a teacher, she found herself even more nervous than she'd expected to be.

I can do this. I must *do this.* Her future as well as Lucy's depended upon her success.

As if mocking her, the church bells chose that moment to peal out their greeting to the sun. Evangeline's heart stopped as that now-hated sound filled the otherwise quiet morning. Each clang reverberated inside her, a full-fisted punch delivered directly to her most tender of emotions.

Gone. Gone.

Its unyielding declaration refused to allow her a single day's escape from her loss.

Gone. Gone.

The intrusion would stop soon enough if only she waited.

Gone. Gone. Gone.

The onslaught ended, though her heart continued to pound. She could breathe. She could think. She could go on. That was how she would survive: one breath, one thought, one moment at a time.

With one more fortifying lungful of air, she resumed her most proper posture. If she could appear confident, her students would never guess she was utterly overwhelmed.

She stopped in the open doorway, overlooking the front garden. The children were more awake than they'd been when last she'd seen them. A few had taken to chasing each other about the unkempt grass. The same girl Evangeline had spoken to earlier sat patiently near the door.

Evangeline resisted the urge to ask her further questions. She likely had already made herself appear incompetent. She didn't know how students were called in to school, never having attended one herself. Her governess used to simply call out their names.

"Children." Her first attempt emerged far too quiet and uncertain. She steeled her resolve and, in a more commanding voice, called out, "Children."

That captured the attention of most of them in the yard. She gave a quick clap, hoping to gain the notice of the rest. "Come inside," she instructed. "We'll begin."

The responses varied considerably. Some were eager, skipping over and inside. Others appeared resigned or nervous or still half asleep. A few could not possibly have given a less enthusiastic performance as they dragged themselves through the tall grass and inside the schoolhouse.

Evangeline offered each of them a "Good morning" as they passed, regardless of their level of enthusiasm, and motioned them toward the schoolroom. When the last student had entered, she climbed the narrow stairs. She left the exterior door ajar for those students who hadn't arrived in the wee hours.

The chaos of the front garden had recreated itself in the schoolroom. Children sitting, chatting, running about, testing their balance by walking the length of the benches. How had her governess retained control all those years ago? Evangeline hadn't the slightest idea.

She assumed her authoritative voice and called out, "Children. Please have a seat on any of the benches where you can find space." She would organize them later either by families or age or academic level. That last approach might not work, though. The chances were good that none of her pupils, regardless of age, had any previous education. They would all be on the same academic level.

Good heavens, I am in deep water.

She clasped her hands in front of her and surveyed her group of ragamuffins. In many ways they all looked alike: clothes faded, well-worn, and made of sturdy and simple fabrics, hair combed but generally in need of washing, feet bare and thick with the dust of the road. Some of the children were thin—too thin—with sunken eyes. Others at least appeared to be sufficiently fed, though without the rosy glow so common with more well-to-do families.

That observation brought another thought: was she meant to feed them? The school day would last several hours. The children would, no doubt, grow hungry. She hadn't food enough, nor any idea how to prepare it.

Focus, Evangeline. You'll do yourself no good by borrowing trouble when you've trouble enough.

"First things first," she said to her students as much as to herself, "I would like to get to know you a little bit. Would the oldest here from each family take turns introducing yourself and your siblings? If you are the only member of your family here, then you need simply tell me about yourself."

Had that sounded as pathetic as she feared? How could she ever instill in her students any degree of confidence in her teaching skills if she continually displayed to them her lack of ability?

She brought her thoughts back around and addressed the group. "Who is willing to go first?"

The one girl Evangeline had spoken with rose from her seat, apparently volunteering to begin.

Evangeline spoke quickly. "I am newly arrived from Cambridgeshire, and no doubt you have noticed my odd style of speaking." Their giggles and nods confirmed what she'd suspected: she sounded as strange to them as they did to her. Their response also told her, however, that they understood her far better than she did them. At least communication was working in one direction. "Until I grow more accustomed to your Yorkshire speech, I will ask that you say your words as clearly as you can and even a touch slower than you might otherwise. Can you do that for me?"

No one objected. She hoped that counted as agreement. Eager for information, she uncorked the inkwell, grateful that necessity had been included in the charity basket along with a bit of paper. She dipped her pen in the ink and held it at the ready.

She turned her gaze to the only child standing. "If you will, please tell me your family name and you and your siblings' Christian names, as well as a little something about your family. I would like to know you all better."

Honestly, she would settle for knowing them at all. The room was full of tiny strangers. How could she know the best way to teach them if she knew nothing about them?

The girl's long ginger braids draped over her shoulder. "We family name is Crossley. We've one sister more who'll be comin' t' school, but she's a' we 'ouse as she were feeling poorly."

She jotted down the family name. *One sister more . . . feeling poorly.* Evangeline felt she'd sorted through the gist of it. *She's a' we 'ouse,* though. That part was indiscernible. The last word was likely "house."

"I'm Susannah," the girl continued, poking her chest with her thumb. "This is Billy and John." She motioned to the two ginger children sitting beside her, each with brighter hair than the last. At least the Crossley family would be easy to spot.

Evangeline added their Christian names to the accounting. "Do you live far from here?"

Susannah shrugged. "Two mile."

A long walk for so early in the morning. "And do your parents bring you here on their way to the factory?"

"Us aren't a factory family," Susannah said. "We live on t' moor, but we've come to town with us brother what works for Mr. McCormick."

She realized a clue to their manner of speaking, one she

hoped would help her understand them more easily. They cut out every sound in the word "the" except for the *t*. Even more surprising than the fact that Evangeline had sorted out a bit of their language was hearing the sound of her neighbor's name. "Mr. McCormick?"

"That's m'self." Indeed, Mr. McCormick stood in the doorway, looking perplexed. "Is there a reason you're tossing my name about?"

"One of the Crossley children works for you."

"That he does." Mr. McCormick eyed Susannah. "Have you been gossipin' about me?"

"We's lot are for it now," she said, tossing her hands upward in defeat. "I'll be threaped for this, mark tha, though I'd nowt to do with it."

Merciful heavens. No matter how closely she listened, Susannah's words were impossible to understand.

Mr. McCormick seemed able to decipher them. "Hush your worries, lass. I've no intention of scolding you."

Scolding. Something Susannah said had indicated an anticipated scolding. Perhaps the "threaped."

Mr. McCormick nudged Ronan inside the room. The little boy clutched his carved horse as though his life depended upon it. At first glance Evangeline feared he was angry, but his tightly pulled lips quivered and his brows jutted at sharp angles above eyes that bore the telltale shimmer of unshed tears. The poor child was afraid.

"Have you any place in particular where the lad is meant to sit?" Mr. McCormick asked.

Evangeline shook her head. "Everyone is sitting wherever he or she would like for today."

Mr. McCormick said something to Ronan, then motioned

toward the benches. Ronan didn't budge. His grip on the wooden horse turned white-knuckle, and his expression grew mutinous, even as his legs began to tremble.

The other children were watching him. Ronan stood firm, clearly determined not to take a seat. Mr. McCormick seemed unsurprised. He sat on the bench nearest his son, leaving enough room on the end for Ronan to join him but without forcing his compliance.

"Go on with your lessons, then," Mr. McCormick said to Evangeline. "I'll wait a spell with m' lad."

He meant to stay and watch? Though she doubted his decision had anything to do with her, Evangeline found the prospect unnerving. She was doing little more than stumbling her way through her first day. The last thing she wanted or needed was a parent in the audience. Children were more forgiving. At least she hoped they were.

She set her gaze on the child nearest the Crossley siblings. "Would you introduce yourself and your family, please?"

Several times she had to ask the children to repeat themselves. Sometimes that was enough to solve the mystery of their words and odd pronunciations. But more often than not, she simply offered a nod of acknowledgment, having resigned herself to never fully understanding them.

How had she found herself facing such a difficulty? She was a teacher in a county in England. These were not students from far-off lands who'd recently arrived on British soil. They were speaking English, and she could hardly understand them.

In the end, she was able to add five new families to her list of pupils.

The Shaws had two sons and one daughter in attendance. Also attending were the Palmers, who appeared worse off than the others, both in the state of their clothing and the thinness of their bodies. The Sutcliffes were both thin but in better condition than the Palmers. Lastly, little Cecilia Haigh, who'd proven too timid to share anything beyond her name.

She had expected that all of her students had parents who worked at the factory, but that was not the case. The Crossleys raised sheep, in addition to the eldest son being on Mr. McCormick's bricklaying crew. Mr. Palmer also worked for Mr. McCormick, with Mrs. Palmer taking in sewing. The Sutcliffes were the only factory family, though the Haighs remained a mystery. Perhaps more students were yet to come who would tip the balance in the other direction.

"Ronan," she said, keeping her tone gentle. "Would you care to introduce yourself to the other children?"

He made no indication of having heard her, though she suspected he had. James had been that way. So much about him had been baffling, but so much had been beautifully endearing. Ronan was still standing, stiff and unmoving. How easily she could picture James doing precisely the same in an uncomfortable situation.

"Allow me to introduce you to the other children," she said to Ronan, hoping that would be a satisfactory alternative. His father began to stand, no doubt meaning to object, so Evangeline pressed on before he had the chance. "Ronan's family name is McCormick. He lives not far from here. His father is a brick mason, and Ronan has accompanied him on many of his jobs and, no doubt, has a vast knowledge of bricks and bricklaying. Ronan also whittles. I have seen a dog he is carving, and I did not need him to tell me that it was a dog because he is doing such a fine job with his whittling that I could tell for myself."

Mr. McCormick lowered himself back down, clearly relieved.

Ronan's expression and posture hadn't changed in the least. Evangeline hoped that in time he might grow more comfortable.

She addressed the group as a whole. "I look forward to knowing all of you better," she said. "And I hope there will be more children joining us." Her hope was not born of eagerness but concern. Why were so few students present if education was required? Were they staying away out of fear of her incompetence? Was there another school of which she was unaware?

"We don't know owt about thee," Susannah said.

Owt—Evangeline hadn't sorted that word yet, though it sounded like the girl wished to know a little about Evangeline. That was a fair request.

She carefully set down her pen. "I was born in a small town called Petersmarch in the county of Cambridgeshire, and I lived there all my life until a few days ago."

"Does tha have any family?" Susannah's question was easy to understand despite her heavy accent.

Another piece of the linguistic puzzle clicked into place. What sounded like "tha" was actual the word "thou." It was not a pronoun she'd generally heard used outside of holy writ or sermons. Knowing the pronunciation of it and its usage, she could make more sense of what was being said. *Tha.* She repeated the word in her head a few times, hoping to make it more familiar. *Tha. Thou.*

The look of confusion on every face, including Mr. McCormick's, told her that she'd allowed her thoughts to wander again.

"I had a mother and father, a brother older than I, and a brother younger." Speaking of them in the past tense would never grow easy. "I also have a younger sister who currently resides in Leeds." The simple explanation proved more difficult to make than she'd expected. Evangeline swallowed the sudden thick lump in her throat and forced a smile. "This is my first time in Yorkshire, and I fear I know very little about it. So, for today, I will be the pupil and you will be the teachers. I wish for you to teach me about Smeatley and Yorkshire and your lives here."

She hoped, by doing so, to find her own place in this all too foreign land.

CHAPTER TEN

Dermot had expected some resistance from Ronan on the matter of school. He'd taken pains to prepare the lad for the change in his routine, but it hadn't been enough. He'd hoped to spend his morning working with his men on the wall. Finishing it quickly would go far toward convincing Mr. Barton to approve the proposed houses he wanted to build for the workers. Instead, he'd sat in the schoolroom, watching Ronan stand defiant and unwavering. After an hour, he'd offered their excuses to Miss Blake, and he and Ronan had made their way to the job site.

The instant they'd stepped from the schoolhouse, Ronan's shoulders dropped from the tautly held position by his ears. His tense frown eased. He'd pushed out a breath so deep and long that Dermot wondered if the lad had breathed at all during the long hour in the schoolroom.

What was he to do if Ronan never warmed to the idea of school? The question hung heavy on his mind as the workday moved forward.

"Straighten that row before the mortar hardens," he barked out.

Gaz Palmer was a fine bricklayer, when he was watched closely enough. Left to his own governance, he tended to cut corners and rush his work. Dermot hadn't decided if he meant to keep the man on should Mr. Barton approve the house-building plans. More hands'd be needed than he'd required for this smaller project, but hands that produced poor results would hardly be an asset.

Dermot surveyed the rest of the crew, checking their work, their mortar, the state of their tools.

"Your brick there is near to touching the line," he told Thomas. "Straighten it out. I'll not have this wall leaning or bowing."

The young man still made a number of mistakes common to those new to the trade, but he was learning quickly and he'd come along; Dermot had no doubt of it.

"I knew it weren't right, but cursed if I could make out the trouble." Thomas quickly followed Dermot's instructions. "My little brothers and sister were right feather-legged this morning. Never seen 'em so tired."

"I saw them at school." Dermot watched Thomas work as they spoke.

"Were they bawlin' or making a fuss?"

"They were well-behaved and seemed happy enough. That sister of yours hasn't a bashful bone in her body, I'd wager."

Thomas grinned. "She's a right 'un, our Susannah. Holds her head high and don't abide trouble off anyone."

Dermot approved. The poor, women and girls especially, needed to be resilient in this cruel world. A touch of stubbornness and confidence would serve her well.

"And Ronan, there. Did he enjoy school?" These Yorkshire

folks had their own way of saying "school," with an extra sound tossed into the middle, one Dermot couldn't precisely explain but knew when he heard it.

"Ronan's unsure of schooling. He'd rather come here as he's used to doing."

"He'll come around, I know it. Once he sees t' other children laikin', he'll want to join in t' fun."

To *laik* was to play. 'Twas one of the words Dermot had learned early on.

Thomas talked more than the rest of the crew combined. But so long as he did all the work required of him, and did it well, Dermot didn't mind. He'd known a few masons who required near-silence from their crews. 'Twas a miserable way to spend one's day. He'd not be so hard-nosed.

"See that you don't spend your afternoon laikin'. I'll not have you whiling away the day when you're meant to be working."

Thomas grinned again. "Aye, Mr. McCormick."

Dermot continued his perusal of the crew's work. Despite the many setbacks and myriad interruptions, he meant to finish the job on schedule.

"McCormick."

He turned at the sound of Mr. Barton's voice. "That's m'self."

Mr. Barton's brows drew down in bewilderment as they always did when Dermot answered his name with that particular response. 'Twas a bit confusing to the English. Truth be told, Dermot would have used it less if not for the amusement it offered him.

"A minute of your time," Mr. Barton said, though it was not truly a request.

"I could spare a minute or so," Dermot said, "but not much

more than that. We're near to finishing this wall, and I mean to do so in the time I promised."

Mr. Barton nodded. "I will not keep you long." The man had employed a very different tone when Dermot had first come to work for him, always demanding things and dismissing any argument to the contrary. But Dermot had stood firm, maintained a respectful tone, and allowed the quality of his craftsmanship to do the rest. He was not viewed as an equal by any means, but he was no longer treated like an underling.

Dermot turned to Thomas. "Keep an eye on this lot for me."

Before the lad could answer, Gaz did. "Tha'd set a boy in charge of a crew of men?"

"I wouldn't, but I'd set him in charge of you."

The rest of the crew chuckled and tossed good-natured jests Gaz's way.

"He'll not be in charge in the full sense of the word," Dermot clarified for all their sakes. "Merely be a watchful eye to let me know if anything's needing my attention."

"A snitch, then?" Gaz sneered.

"If you're not giving him reason to snitch then you've no reason to worry, do you?" Dermot tossed back. "And straighten that row while you can. If the mortar hardens on you, you'll be knocking those bricks out and fixin' them on your own time."

Gaz muttered something which Dermot didn't try overly hard to hear. As he stepped aside with Mr. Barton, Dermot glanced at Ronan. The boy was under his tree again, lining up his figurines as always. This was not how Dermot had imagined the boy living out his life.

At least he's not slaving away for some unfeeling taskmaster, learning a trade before he's old enough to even know what that means. Most children from poor families had no other choice. He'd not had one himself.

"I've given some thought to your proposal," Mr. Barton said.

Though his and Ronan's future would be determined almost entirely by Mr. Barton's next words, Dermot didn't allow his anxiety to show. He simply maintained an air of calm expectancy.

"I can see the reasoning behind your idea." Mr. Barton's hesitancy hadn't diminished.

"Sounds to me as though you can't see *enough* reasoning behind it."

Mr. Barton's bony fingers smoothed his thick mustache even as his forehead creased deeper. "It simply seems a great deal of money to spend on workers."

A grand house stood directly behind Mr. Barton. With its ornate stonework and many smoking chimneys, manicured shrubs and grass, and dozens of servants, *that* seemed a great deal of money to spend on only two people.

"Do as you see fit." Dermot covered his disappointment with an unconcerned tone. "I'll be passing through Leeds on m' way to that job in Bradford, after all, it seems. I'll be certain to drop in on Mr. Farr and let him know that if he's expecting all the positions in his fine new factory to be filled, he'd do well to set his hopes elsewhere, seeing as how there's nowhere in all of Smeatley for any new workers to be living, and therefore no reason for potential workers to not move on to a town with accommodations."

Dermot straightened his cuffs and made to turn back to the wall and his crew, but not before tossing back one last observation. "I'm certain he'll believe it so grand that you saved a bit of blunt that he'll not care in the least that he has a factory that's bleeding profits for want of the very workers you're not wanting to invest in."

"Now, see here, McCormick." Mr. Barton could be difficult when his pride was pricked. "I may have placed you at the head of this crew, but that does not give you leave to address me in such a surly manner."

"'Tweren't anything surly about it." Dermot slipped his hands into the pockets of his trousers and spared a glance for Mr. Barton and his chastiscment. "I'm plainspoken, and that can send some people into high dudgeon. But it is what it is."

"You would truly speak with Mr. Farr?" Mr. Barton's tone was both defiant and uncertain.

"I would. He's spoken with me on a number of occasions when he's been here in town. He respects my opinions said so his ownself. And he further said that he values m' willingness to be honest with him." Dermot didn't look back but allowed his words to sink deep into Mr. Barton's thoughts.

A long moment passed. Dermot watched Ronan sitting in the shade. What if Mr. Barton didn't yield? Dermot could take the job in Bradford, but that'd mean uprooting Ronan again, something the lad didn't endure well. He'd need time to adjust to a new place, new people, new surroundings. There'd be no chance of getting him to school for a long while after that. For both their sakes, Dermot didn't want to leave Smeatley.

"I'll strike a bargain with you, McCormick."

Dermot turned enough to see his employer out of the corner of his eye.

"I will approve building one set of these back-to-back houses, as a trial. Should they be completed in a timely and economical manner, then we will discuss building more."

"You'll not learn the whole truth if this first set isn't built the way you mean to build the others. I'd be needing a full crew, access to quality materials, fair pay, and full control over the project."

"Full control?" Mr. Barton scoffed.

Dermot nodded. "You'd approve the plans, and I'd build to them. But neither you nor your missus could come 'round insisting on changes."

'Twas a testament to Mr. Barton's understanding of his wife's nature that he didn't immediately deny that she'd do precisely that. Instead, he gave a regal but firm nod of his own. "Agreed."

Dermot tucked his relief and excitement away. "This wall will be done by week's end, you've my word on that. I'll have a full set of detailed plans for the houses to you by then for your approval. We'll begin as soon as that's finalized."

He held out his hand. Though Mr. Barton had objected to Dermot's addressing him in a manner that didn't befit an employee nor a person of the lower class, they shook hands as equal partners. Dermot knew he wasn't truly viewed that way, but he found in that moment a reason to believe he might be someday. Perhaps, beyond Ronan's education and his own job security, Dermot might have something of a future in this odd and all-too-often unwelcoming town.

Once he'd enough for the undertaking, he'd build them a fine new home—one without neighbors to either side, complaining of every noise, every Irish dish he prepared, the color of the door, and anything else they could think of. They'd have a measure of peace and a degree of comfort.

"McCormick." It seemed Mr. Barton didn't mean for Dermot to have that peace today.

Dermot met his gaze.

"Your son is not in school," Mr. Barton said. "Why is that?"

"The lad went this morning," Dermot said. "He'll be needing

a bit more time to feel enough at ease there to remain for the entire day."

"Ah." Mr. Barton nodded. "I was afraid something had gone wrong or that Miss Blake had not begun teaching today as expected."

"Nothing was wrong, but the lass didn't begin teaching, not truly."

"What do you mean by that?"

Dermot hadn't intended to talk about Miss Blake, but it seemed he couldn't avoid the discussion. "She spent the morning asking questions of the wee ones: what were their names, where'd they live, what sort of work did their parents undertake, those sort of things. 'Twasn't really teaching is all I meant to say."

Mr. Barton made a noise of contemplation, and not of the "surprisingly impressed" variety.

"The children were well-behaved, and Miss Blake kept charge of the schoolroom," Dermot added. "The floor had been swept and the windows washed. While 'tis true no one was learning reading or writing, I'd not see that as a sign that anything was amiss."

Mr. Barton sighed again. Something about the situation apparently weighed heavier on him than Dermot would've guessed. The man was acting as head of the school board. That likely accounted for his deep interest.

"If you're not needing to discuss anything further, I've a crew to oversee and a wall to complete," Dermot reminded him.

"Yes. Of course." And with that, Mr. Barton left, his steps carrying him back to his grand house with its rows and rows of windows.

Ronan never seemed to tire of counting the panes of glass. When Dermot built their home, he fully intended to include windows enough for the boy to number. And a garden large enough for Ronan to run and play—something he seldom did in their poky space. And he meant to plant a tree for the lad to sit under. They would be happy, the two of them, and all the toil and heartache of the past years would finally be worth it.

CHAPTER ELEVEN

ermot hummed as he prepared supper that evening. He'd passed a fine day despite the uncertain beginning. For once, the future was looking promising. He'd been given a chance to prove himself and to step onto a path that might lead to prosperity at the end. A bit of the music of home seemed a fitting celebration.

Ronan picked up the tune, singing the chorus when Dermot reached it. *"Trasna na dtonnta, dul siar, dul siar, Slán leis an uaigneas 'is slán leis an gcian."*

'Twas good to hear the lad wrapping his tongue around the unique sounds of the Irish language. Too many Irishmen had lost that; Dermot meant to see to it that Ronan knew at least a few songs. He didn't know enough to truly speak Irish, merely a few words sprinkled here and there, but, having been apprenticed to a man who had passed the time singing as he'd worked, he knew a great number of songs in that ancient language.

Dermot also had vague recollections of his parents having spoken Irish, something more common in the country than in

Dublin. Had he remained at home, he'd've had the language, and he mourned that loss. But, had he remained at home, he wouldn't have Ronan, and that didn't bear thinking on.

"*An Maidrín Rua!*" Ronan loudly requested. He was a quiet and placid child, but when he grew excited about something, he could hardly contain himself.

"We've not finished this song yet." Dermot wasn't certain how to teach his lad patience without damping his enthusiasm.

"I'm wanting to sing about the fox." Ronan looked up from his whittling, abandoning what was his usual evening activity. "And the dogs. I like dogs with spots."

"The song doesn't say the dogs have spots," Dermot pointed out.

"But they should. Dogs should have spots."

Dogs should have spots, and people shouldn't smell like flowers. Never let it be said that Ronan didn't have very particular ideas.

"Did you enjoy school today?" he asked.

Quick as that, Ronan's eyes were on his carving again, and his talkativeness disappeared.

"You'll be going back in the morning," Dermot warned him. "'Tis a fine thing to have some learning. Not every lad gets that. I didn't, though I wish I had."

Ronan didn't look up at him. Early on, Dermot had assumed his long moments of silence or his lack of acknowledging him when he spoke were signs of obstinacy. He'd learned differently over time. He truly believed that Ronan grew overwhelmed, whether with fear or uncertainty or some other difficult emotion, and found himself unable to respond. He didn't know how to reassure the boy enough to stop it from happening. So much about Ronan confused him.

A moment later, the knock that Dermot had been listening for ever since returning home sounded at the door. Miss Blake was meant to join them for their evening meal and a bit of learning herself in return for offering Ronan some extra tutoring.

"That'll be Miss Blake." He hoped Ronan heard the warning. Unexpected arrivals upset him sometimes.

"School is in the mornings," Ronan said. "School isn't at night."

School is in the mornings. If ever five words brought a man relief, those did. Ronan might not've been entirely accepting of going to school, but he had it in his mind that school had a place in the day. That was a step in the right direction.

"She's come for supper," Dermot explained.

Ronan nodded, eyes on his work. "Supper is at night. Not school."

"Right you are, lad."

Dermot reached for the door, finding himself unexpectedly pleased. The day had been a good one, and he was in a fine mood.

He pulled open the door. "Good evening to you, Miss—"

Her glare, which could easily have felled a weaker man, stopped his words. He couldn't be entirely certain it hadn't temporarily stopped his heart. 'Twas a good thing the woman wasn't armed.

"I've come from Hillside House." That, it seemed, was both a greeting and an explanation.

"Have you, now?" What had he done to earn her ire? They'd not talked since that morning. "And had you a fine visit with the Bartons?"

"It was illuminating." Her terse tone and glare told its own story.

Yes, she most definitely was put out with *him.* "Would you

care to tell me the how and why of your ire, or am I to begin guessing?"

Her lips and jaw tensed with her next breath, and he sensed an outpouring of complaints was about to follow. While he was interested in her grievances, he'd rather not have them listed on his front step for all the neighbors to hear.

"Come inside, then." He stepped aside to clear the threshold. "I'll set myself at a mark so you can fire at will."

"Do not tempt me," she muttered as she stormed past him.

The devil mend it, she truly was vexed.

She took a few steps, then spun about to face him, her hands set on her hips.

Dermot kept himself at a distance—far enough to be safe, but near enough to show he wasn't cowed by her flare of temper. "State your grievances, lass. I've courage enough."

"State *my* grievances? I believe lodging complaints is more your strength than mine."

What complaint he had made? What had that to do with her visit to the Bartons? "I'll be needing more specifics, there."

"I called on Mr. Barton this afternoon, as instructed, to make my report of my first day as teacher. Imagine my surprise when he already knew all he felt he needed to." Her eyes narrowed, her gaze skewering him like an arrow. "Someone—the only someone over the age of twelve to have been present for any portion of my lessons today—had informed him that I was a failure, not teaching anything and wasting my students' time with questions."

"That someone would be myself, would it?"

"Did you notice any other grown men in my schoolhouse?" she asked dryly.

"I didn't tattle on you, woman. I—" But then he remembered. "Mr. Barton did ask me about school."

"And you told him I was miserable at it."

He might have taken exception to her accusations had there not been a hint of truth to them and had there not been more than a touch of pain beneath her unusually fiery demeanor. She'd had a difficult day, he'd wager.

"I said nothing about you being miserable at teaching. I only told him that you didn't teach a lesson while I was there. And before you go tearing my head off for that, 'twas nothing less than the truth."

"It was nothing *more* than the truth."

"You'd have preferred I lied in your favor, then?"

"I'd have preferred—" She pressed her lips closed and shook her head.

He motioned for her to finish her thought. He wasn't afraid of what she meant to say.

"I would have preferred you not talk to him about my morning in the first place." She'd a bit less wind in her sails, though clearly the storm had not entirely blown by. "He had already formed his opinion before I had a chance to present my position. It was unfair."

"I hate to put too fine a point on it, lass, but you charging in here accusing me of speaking ill of you without giving me the chance to present my position is a bit unfair as well."

She held his gaze. The defiance slowly melted from her posture and with it much of the fire in her eyes. Quick as anything, she resumed the expression and posture of a lady of refinement, that impersonal air they all seemed to have perfected.

'Twas a shame, really. While he didn't care to be on the receiving end of unfounded complaints, he'd seen more life in her these past minutes than in all their previous encounters.

"We're for making soup tonight," he told her, crossing to the table and the basket of vegetables waiting there. "'Tis a simple enough thing. You'll have it mastered in no time."

She nodded silently, following slowly in his wake. She was regal Miss Blake, thoroughly and completely. A shame.

"Come along, then. I'll not bite no matter that you came here with your own teeth bared."

She stood still and impassive, her expression nearly empty. "I appreciate your forbearance." Good heavens. She'd turned as bland as boiled cabbage.

"Are you feeling unwell, Miss Blake?"

"I am perfectly well, thank you. Please, proceed."

He preferred his own personal concerns remain personal, so he'd not press himself into hers. "Take up a knife. You'll be chopping the carrots."

"Is there any particular trick to it?"

"Only one." He pushed the pile of carrots closer to her. "Aim for the vegetables, not your fingers."

The cooking lesson was uneventful. Miss Blake listened closely, followed his instructions, and spoke little. A heaviness hung about her, not unlike what he'd been plagued with his first few weeks in this unwelcoming place. He was far from the only new arrival this past year, yet none of the others seemed as unwanted as he.

The Bartons hadn't been kind to her during the brief encounter he'd overheard not three days ago. Mrs. Barton, in particular, had been scathing.

"Did you speak with Mrs. Barton today as well?" he asked as he hung the pot over the fire and stirred the soup.

"I did." She seemed surprised that he'd guessed that bit.

"She's a difficult one to endure," he said. "I thought that might be why your spirits seem so low."

Miss Blake lowered herself into her usual chair. "I have had a difficult few days."

"Aye, you've said that once before."

She rubbed at her forehead with her fingers. "My days have not grown easier. I fear I haven't the strength to endure much more without some kind of hope."

How well he knew that feeling. "'Tis the hunger talking. Life always looks bleak when the belly's empty."

"I am hungry," she confessed.

"And likely tired as well."

"Exhausted." How she managed to fill that single word with such desperation, he couldn't say, but it told quite a story.

"Sleep and food. That's just the thing, you'll see."

She sighed and looked up at him. "I will tell myself that. Perhaps it will help."

"I'd wager it will."

When the soup was ready, she ate, but not with the sunny disposition of one whose optimism had been restored. She thanked him dutifully for the meal and the cooking instructions, then she turned her attention to Ronan.

She sat near him at the table but not so close that the lad would be uncomfortable. "I am quite certain you had more than your fill of schooling this morning. I know you will need time to grow accustomed to this change, so I will not press you tonight with lessons."

Dermot kept an eye on Ronan, unsure how he would react. 'Twas difficult to predict at the best of times.

"I have brought you something." Miss Blake pulled a folded paper from a well-hidden pocket in her dress. She laid it flat and slid it toward the boy. "These shapes are letters, and these letters spell your name. You needn't learn them or memorize them.

I simply thought you would enjoy seeing what your name looks like."

Ronan's gaze took a rare departure from his carved horse and settled firmly on Miss Blake's paper.

"Tomorrow when I come, I would very much like for you to tell me what other word or name you'd like to see written out. I will write it for you. Then, when you are ready to stay at school longer during the day and we begin practicing the letters, they will be familiar to you."

Familiarity. Ronan desperately clung to what he knew and what he understood. Miss Blake had offered the lad a chance to be familiar with something as unknown as school.

True to her word, she didn't press Ronan for anything else. She simply told him that she hoped to see him in school the next day, then rose from her seat, and left, pausing briefly to thank Dermot again for his hospitality.

For his part, Dermot was too shocked for much beyond a nod. Miss Blake was not the least suited for a life of poverty spent teaching the children of this hardened and difficult area of the kingdom. Yet, for that brief moment at the table, she had been very nearly perfect for Ronan.

CHAPTER TWELVE

ould you please repeat that again?" Evangeline was at her wit's end. They'd nearly completed their school day, but had accomplished little, mostly because she struggled to simply understand what her students said to her.

Hugo Palmer growled out his own frustration. But when he spoke again, he did so more slowly. "Why do we have to know t' letters' names if their names have nowt to do with their sounds and t' sounds are how we use them?"

She'd heard the word "nowt" enough to decided it meant "nothing," and she was nearly accustomed to their odd way of saying "the" with nothing more than a *t*.

"Why are the letters' names important? That is your question?"

"Aye." That word she knew perfectly well, having heard it from Scotsmen occasionally over the years and even from Mr. McCormick.

"When you are told how to spell something, you will be told

using the names of the letters. Knowing their names will be important."

He rushed out a response but stopped partway and began again, more slowly. "But their names aren't their sounds."

"That is true."

"Seems a lot o' bother to me." During the course of the day, Hugo had proven himself to be "a lot of bother." She had never met a more obstinate child. At ten years of age, he was more of a handful than those smaller than he.

"You have been given the task of learning to read and write and do arithmetic." She addressed all of her students. "This is no small feat. You will have to work hard. If you do not work hard, you cannot possibly hope to succeed."

"Us father doesn't read. He doesn't need to, and neither do I."

Though the frequent but inconsistent changeability of "we" and "us" and "our" still settled oddly on Evangeline's ears, she'd grown accustomed to it, not having to switch the words back in her mind.

"Hush, Hugo." May, the littlest of the Palmers, glared her brother down. She had thick, dark hair and a fiery tenacity that belied her tiny frame. "Father'd not be sending the lot o' us to school if he didn't want us to learn."

May had spoken slowly without needing to be reminded. That, Evangeline felt, was a sign of progress.

"Even that Irish lad comes, and no one expects him to learn owt."

She mentally translated "owt" as "anything."

"'That Irish lad' is Ronan," Evangeline corrected. "And I fully expect he will learn plenty."

John Crossley, a thin boy and near in age to Hugo, entered

the fray. "He's a bit swaimish, aye, but being quiet is not t' same as being gaumless."

Swaimish? Gaumless? Every time she thought she could understand the people of Smeatley, she encountered new, indecipherable words.

"And being loud is not t' same as being smart," May tossed back, pulling laughter from the other students and a glower from her brother.

If "swaimish" meant quiet, then "gaumless" might mean simple or unintelligent. Her heart sank for the absent Ronan. She had every confidence that he was a bright boy, but his oddities and his reserve would leave him open to the ridicule and teasing of his classmates. What could she do to prevent that, to protect him? It was little wonder that Mr. McCormick did not leave Ronan at school for long. He must have anticipated this difficulty.

Had James been likewise needled when he'd been away from home? She hoped not. The thought of him unhappy only added to her grief.

"Let us review the letter names again," she said.

As she held up the papers on which she'd written in large, block lettering the first portion of the alphabet, the children dutifully repeated the letter names. She tried to determine which children had learned them and which were simply copying the others. She felt certain they would not all learn at the same pace. The older students would likely learn faster, provided they were willing to try. She did not wish to discourage anyone by moving too quickly or too slowly, but not one of the children knew the entire alphabet nor how to write or recognize numbers. The entire class was starting at the very beginning.

They'd spent the day focusing on only ten letters. By the third time through, Susannah Crossley had the letters memorized.

She would need something more challenging, but how could Evangeline do that while trying to help all of the others? She needed to think of something.

"Susannah, will you come up here, please?"

Far from cowed by the summons, Susannah made the short walk with confidence. What must that be like? Evangeline had always struggled to feel anything but anxious when faced with uncertainty. She had learned to put on a brave face, but beneath it all she quaked like an aspen leaf.

Summoning her acting skills, Evangeline addressed her oldest pupil. "I noticed you have mastered these first letters rather quickly."

"Aye, miss."

That morning, Evangeline had inscribed the entire alphabet on a sheet of paper, unsure how far her students would progress in one day. She had, as it turned out, been overly optimistic. She handed the paper to Susannah.

"I need to help the other students learn the letters we are working on, but I thought you might appreciate learning the remainder of them. When I have the chance, I will tell you their names, but for now you can practice writing them."

"Aye, miss." Susannah took the paper and returned to her seat with little enthusiasm.

Was that to be the way of it? Drudgery and acceptance in her best students, rebellion and complaints in her most challenging?

"I'm finished," Hugo said.

She needed to find a means of ridding him of his tendency to simply shout whatever he wished to say whenever he meant to say it. Though this particular instance was not a true interruption, many of his other outbursts had been.

"Let me see your work," she said.

He rose with all the languid annoyance of one asked to perform a task decidedly beneath him. Upon reaching her lectern, Hugo held his slate out with minimal effort, its face tipped downward. Evangeline took hold of it and examined his efforts.

"Your *B* needs two distinct bumps." Heavens, that sounded ridiculous. Was there a proper term for the shape of these letters? "And your *I* and *J* must be written precisely so as not to look so much alike."

"I'n'it good enough?"

"I'n'it" was "isn't it" pushed together into a single quick mouthful.

"Without clearly drawn letters, no one will be able to read what you have written," she said. "And until you learn the precise shapes of those letters, you will not be able to read what others have written."

His grumbled answer was too low, too clumped together, and too fast for her to understand.

"Again, Hugo." She held the slate out to him.

His mouth turned down in a mulish frown. "Neya."

She didn't need to translate Hugo's refusal to follow her instructions.

"You will never learn the remainder of your letters if you don't—"

"I'll not."

"Quit complaining, Hugo." His sister was clearly put out with him.

"Quit jabbering," he tossed back.

"Don't talk to her angry," another voice insisted loudly.

"Children," Evangeline started, but none of them seemed to hear her.

A shouting match ensued, one covering everything from learning letters to who had traveled furthest onto the moor.

"Children! Enough!" No matter how Evangeline tried, she could not regain their attention.

They were nearly all up out of their seats, except Susannah, who appeared annoyed by every last one of them, and little Cecilia Haigh, who was on the verge of tears.

Into the shouting and pointing and chaos stepped Aunt Barton.

Evangeline didn't know who saw her first, but an immediate, tense silence fell over the room.

Aunt Barton stopped not two feet inside the room. "Well," she said, eyeing them all with stinging disapproval.

"Mrs. Barton, you have caught us at a difficult moment." Evangeline attempted to strike a tone both conciliatory and competent, but feared she sounded more pathetic than anything else.

"And on your second day of school," Aunt Barton observed. "That is not encouraging."

Evangeline sent a desperate look to her students. They appeared as overwhelmed by her aunt as she was. She would do well to take advantage of the temporary cessation of hostilities.

"Back to your benches, children," she instructed firmly. "You will continue copying your letters."

The children obeyed without a word or a glance or a moment's hesitation. All was quiet and still and decidedly uncomfortable.

Evangeline stole a glance in her aunt's direction. The look she received in return was one of delighted disappointment.

If only she had come a moment earlier. The room had been controlled, and the children had been learning.

"Miss Blake," Aunt Barton said. "A word, if I may."

She would much rather have refused, but civility did not permit her to. Though she was obliged to work for her keep and earn the right to her own family connections, Evangeline would behave as a lady ought.

She carefully corked the inkwell. "Keep to your letters," she told the children, her voice commendably steady.

She crossed the small room more swiftly than she would have liked.

Aunt Barton watched her every step, her gaze not wandering in the least. "I had come today to construct my initial report to Mr. Farr. Imagine my astonishment."

Evangeline suspected her aunt was not the least surprised by what she had seen. "You happened to arrive at a moment when the children's hunger overcame their manners. They are here for hours, you realize, and I have not been provided with anything to feed them."

"I expect decorum, Miss Blake, not excuses."

"I am simply stating the situation."

"The situation"—Aunt Barton climbed immediately onto her high horse—"is that the school board is not obligated to feed them. Their families should provide food for them at midday if they are hungry."

"I suspect many of them cannot afford to do so." The Palmer children, in particular, were worryingly ragged and thin.

"Then they likely would not have been eating at home, either." Aunt Barton looked over the children studiously bent over their slates. "Do you think them capable of learning?"

The slight against her students, whom she'd known only two days, emboldened her. "Of course I do. Being born poor does not make one"—what was the word John Crossley had used?—"gaumless. And being wealthy does not automatically make one clever."

Her aunt's attention returned on the instant. "'Gaumless'?"

"It is a Yorkshire word."

"I am well aware of that." And, it would seem, she did not approve. "You are here to improve their minds, not adopt their ignorance."

"I do not see how a different word choice equates to ignorance."

Aunt Barton straightened the chains of her chatelaine purse. "I believe I have seen what I came here to see."

"You have seen almost nothing."

She pierced Evangeline with her harsh, pointed gaze. "Precisely."

CHAPTER THIRTEEN

Evangeline's first week of school blurred together. Each day was just like the last. She taught the students letters, telling them the letters' names and asking them to copy them out. Susannah looked utterly bored. Cecilia spoke now and then, but never loudly and never without encouragement. Hugo blustered and complained and, at least once each day, provoked the other boys—and occasionally a few of the girls—into a shouting match. Thankfully, no fisticuffs erupted, though Evangeline suspected it was merely a matter of time.

She was not failing, but neither was she truly succeeding. Haphazard, accidental progress would not impress her aunt. And if her aunt was not impressed, her grandfather would likely never hear a good word about Evangeline's accomplishments, such as they were. And without her grandfather's approval, she would never have Lucy back.

"Miss Blake." Mr. McCormick's indifferent tone was the same each morning. He was more personable in the evenings, but not by much.

Evangeline nodded to him and offered Ronan one of their customary small waves. "We have only just begun learning the sounds associated with the first few letters of the alphabet," she told Ronan before returning to her lesson. She could only assume that, beneath his defiant demeanor, he was listening and, she hoped, learning something. He had not responded verbally or otherwise to her attempts to speak of school in the evenings.

Her eyes settled on Mr. McCormick, occupying his usual seat on the bench beside where Ronan stood. He always remained for an hour, then gave Ronan the choice of staying or leaving. His departure each day brought her a sharp sense of relief. Struggling with her students was difficult enough without anyone witnessing it.

"Why does t' letter *A* have so many sounds?" Hugo's questions always sounded like complaints.

"Because it is a vowel," she said, "and vowels all make many sounds."

"Why?" If Hugo spoke any word more often than that one, Evangeline didn't know what it was.

Why did vowels make multiple sounds? Was there an answer to that question? Every pair of eyes was on her, watching her with clear expectation.

"The vowels make many sounds because . . . they are very talkative."

Something like a smile touched Mr. McCormick's somber expression.

"Very talkative," she repeated, her tone lighter. "They chat and gossip and never stop."

"Which other letters are vowels?" Susannah asked.

She had their attention. Taking advantage of the rare moment, Evangeline pushed on, answering the question and talking at greater length about letters and sounds and hoping the children understood what she said.

By day's end, she suspected a handful of her students had a firm grasp on some of the letter sounds and another handful were beginning to understand. But at least half seemed lost. A true teacher would have known for certain. A true teacher would have known how to help them—all of them.

She stood at the outer door of the schoolhouse, bidding farewell to her students and feeling the weight of her own inadequacy. The Crossley and Palmer children were met most afternoons by their mothers. The other children waited for their parents to finish their day at the factory.

Evangeline waved to Mrs. Crossley. Rather than nodding back and leaving with her children in tow as she usually did, she made her way to the door. They'd never truly spoken, and Evangeline wasn't sure what to expect.

"Good afternoon," she greeted.

"Ey up," Mrs. Crossley returned.

Evangeline had heard that a few times over the past week. As near as she could tell, it was a greeting.

"Our Johanna's right sad not to be at school," Mrs. Crossley said. "She were bawlin' all night. But she's not well enough to be here yet."

"I hope it is nothing too serious."

"She has allus been sickly, but she'll rally." Mrs. Crossley cast a quick glance at her children before continuing. "How are us bairns gettin' on?"

Evangeline took a moment to sort through all of that. "Allus" was "always." She was almost sure "bairns" was "children." And, of course, there was the use of "us" instead of "our." Only after all that effort did Evangeline realize Mrs. Crossley was asking after her children.

"They are doing very well. Susannah is bright and learns quickly. John and Billy both work exceptionally hard and are learning as well."

Mrs. Crossley nodded. "I'm pleased to hear it. We weren't certain school were a wise choice, seeing as it takes brass out of t' family coffers."

"You are charged for their schooling?" Evangeline hadn't heard a word about that.

"Aye. Though them as can show enough financial hardship, t' school board will pay for. And them what work at t' factory"— Mrs. Crossley waved vaguely in the direction of the mill—"Mr. Farr pays for their little ones."

That made little sense. She had only three factory families. If their schooling was paid for, why weren't more children of factory families attending? Evangeline wanted to ask, but she didn't know Mrs. Crossley very well. Neither did she wish to look incompetent in front of her pupils' parents.

"Listen to me, going on about fees when I've a matter to speak of." Mrs. Crossley smiled lightheartedly. "I've come to ask tha if we might borrow a slate. Susannah means to show her sister t' letters she's learned, but we've nowt for her to write on."

"Of course you may take home a slate."

Mrs. Crossley's smile grew.

Evangeline waved Susannah over and instructed her to return upstairs and fetch a slate. Her remaining students were running about, keeping themselves occupied with their play. The respite from her duties was a welcome one. Did all teachers feel that way at the end of the day?

"Our Johnny tells me that you've that swaimish little Ronan McCormick coming to school each day."

Evangeline remembered "swaimish" from the children's use of it several days earlier. "He is quiet, yes. He is also quite welcome at school."

Mrs. Crossley's eyes widened. "I'd not meant to imply that he weren't. I were right happy to hear it when t' children told me. The schools would not have bothered with his sort before t' law said they had to."

"And what sort is that?" Evangeline felt more than a little affronted on Ronan's behalf and, truth be told, on behalf of her dear, departed brother.

"I've talked myself into trouble again, haven't I?" Mrs. Crossley's smile only grew. "My husband tells me I speak my mind a bit too freely. I make my words misunderstood." She looked genuinely apologetic. "I only meant that he's quiet and doesn't seem to know quite what to do around other folk. That doesn't mean he shouldn't have learning like t' others, only that, before this law, he'd likely have been turned away."

"I would not have turned him away."

"I believe thee. I've a sense about people. Tha's a right good one, I'm certain of it." Mrs. Crossley gave her the first look of approval she'd had in Smeatley. Oh, how she needed it!

Evangeline tucked her sudden rush of embarrassment behind a jesting comment. "Would you mind telling Mrs. Barton that? She is convinced I'm a rather sorry sort."

"Ah, her high-and-mighty lordship."

A laugh pulled loose. "What is this?"

"Mrs. Barton doesn't approve of any of us. T' whole town knows it." Mrs. Crossley's smile was reassuring. "Our opinion of thee will not be tainted by her."

"That is more of a relief than you know." If only Grandfather was as immune.

Mrs. Crossley glanced past Evangeline. "On with thee, Susannah. Nip on home. Johanna'll be fair itching to see thee."

Susannah hurried past, calling to her brothers to follow. Mrs. Crossley smiled at Evangeline. "Thank thee again for t' slate."

"You're welcome."

"And for teaching t' children—mine and t' others. I know t' Palmer lad is a difficult one, but they're a good family who've fallen on difficulties just now. Their children getting a touch of schooling has given them all a bit of needed hope. And Mr. McCormick gave up his homeland for his boy's chance at learning. What tha does here is important to a lot of people." Mrs. Crossley nodded and followed in her children's path.

Though Evangeline was filled with questions, she had no opportunity to ask a single one. She watched the Shaw and Sutcliffe children playing happily in the school yard. Cecilia Haigh seemed perfectly content by herself, making a woven chain from long stems of grass. The children would be fine if she stepped inside for a rare moment to herself.

Evangeline walked back into her rooms, her mind whirling. She wasn't certain she could think of Hugo's attempts at learning as anything other than frustrating. Yet, Mrs. Crossley had spoken of it as a source of hope. What did that mean? If education was so important to the Palmer family, why did the boy continually make the task so difficult? Her most troublesome student had unexpectedly become . . . complicated.

She lowered herself into the spindle-backed rocking chair beside the empty fireplace. This was the moment each afternoon when she closed her eyes and breathed out the tension that had built over the day. She couldn't manage it just then.

Her students' families were paying for their schooling, families who appeared ill-equipped to do so. And Mr. McCormick had left Ireland specifically to secure Ronan an education. Was she providing her students with anything worthy of those sacrifices?

She finally pushed out a long, slow breath. It didn't help. Her eyes settled on the photograph of her family.

I am in sore need of one of your hugs, Mother. And a few words of advice from you, Father.

Lucy's treasures sat on the mantel beside the frame, reminding her dozens of times every single day that not only had she broken her promise to her sister but that she was powerless to rectify it.

She took James's book from the fireside bench. She knew Lucy had chosen it as one of her treasures because it had been a favorite of the entire family. James had insisted that someone read from it every evening. They all had its passages nearly memorized.

With tremendous care she opened the book, turning page after page. The process brought fresh pain and grief, yet she did not stop. There was something in her suffering that was healing and comforting, as if allowing herself to ache instead of ignoring it served as a much needed acknowledgment that her pain was real.

In that moment, alone with nothing but the inanimate reminders of all she held dear, Evangeline gave herself permission to feel the weight on her heart. Even if no one else saw her grief, she would feel it, and in time she would heal.

CHAPTER FOURTEEN

An idle soul shall suffer hunger.'" The vicar's pronouncement echoed through the nave. He pressed his finger against the open page of his Bible as his gaze fell over the gathered worshipers. "What do you hunger for?"

Evangeline had not yet attended services in Smeatley, having been too grief-stricken on her first Sunday in Yorkshire to bring herself to traverse the churchyard. She had come today in search of some solace. Mr. Trewe, however, was anything but comforting. His tone rang with accusation, and his glare seemed to pierce every person in turn.

"Do you hunger for friends, for material comforts, for direction in your life?" His bushy brows shot upward, as if the intensity of his question had pulled his eyes as wide as possible. "Are you without the things you need? Are you hungering?"

Across the way sat the Palmer family; Evangeline recognized their children. Mr. and Mrs. Palmer listened raptly to the sermon, their expressions both concerned and earnest. Mrs. Crossley had said that this family was facing hardships. Of the children attending school, they were, by far, the most obviously "hunger-ing" for a great many things.

"You have your answer here." Mr. Trewe thumped his Bible. "The idle hunger, and they hunger because they are idle. Take up your work with determination and gratitude before wallowing in complaints."

Did he truly mean that *only* the idle hungered, only the sloth-ful found themselves in need of things they did not have? Surely not, for that did not ring true.

"You have within your grasp ample opportunities for better-ing your situation through hard work." The words might have been encouraging, but Mr. Trewe's thunderous tones and hard stare rendered the sermon almost threatening. "Do not resign yourself to misery by choosing to be indolent, but rather remem-ber, 'An idle soul shall suffer hunger.'"

He closed his Bible with a quick, reverberating snap. That was, it seemed, the entirety of his message. Even as the rites moved along in their predictable pattern, Evangeline could not entirely move her thoughts beyond the brief, pointed, and, frankly, disconcerting sermon. Most people in attendance bore all the markings of poverty and want. Was there truly an epidemic of laziness as Mr. Trewe's words seemed to indicate?

She, herself, was in need of many things, not all of which were material belongings or comforts. She longed for the love of family, the reassurance that she would find her path in life, the presence of her sister. Were these hopes, these wishes, these hun-gers truly the result of slothfulness on her part?

I have worked hard this past week or more. I most certainly have.

Mr. Trewe's words of castigation struck her deeply, feeding the doubts she'd been unable to shake. Uncle Barton had warned her that her only hope of being reunited with Lucy lay in proving herself through diligent labor. Perhaps she truly was at fault.

With a heavy heart, she left the church once Mass had ended, stepping out into the churchyard and the blinding sunlight. Solace, it seemed, was not to be found.

"Ey up, Miss Blake."

A smile pulled at her mouth at the sound of John Crossley's voice. "A good day to you, John."

His mother stepped up alongside him. "Ey up, Miss Blake. How did tha enjoy t' sermon?"

Was that a laugh Evangeline detected beneath the question?

"The vicar's words were . . . thought provoking." That seemed the safest way to describe her response.

"And familiar," Mrs. Crossley added.

They walked beside one another down the churchyard path.

"He has offered this sermon before?"

Mrs. Crossley glanced back to the vicar standing by the church door. She lowered her voice. "His words are t' same week after week: work hard or suffer."

"That is always his sermon?"

Mrs. Crossley nodded, amusement in her weary eyes. "He were chosen by her high-and-mighty lordship."

"Mrs. Barton?"

Another nod. "Everyone hereabouts suspects Mr. Farr left the choosing to Mrs. Barton. We shouldn't be surprised that she chose a vicar who preaches t' virtues of labor. It keeps t' factory hands workin' after all."

The words that had felt so directed at her had been nothing more than Mr. Trewe's usual call to labor? And a message insisted upon by her aunt? That ought to have brought her comfort but didn't. It was not her place to speak ill of the vicar, and yet she could not approve of what she had just learned.

A man Evangeline did not know joined them on the path. He set an arm around Mrs. Crossley's waist. *Mr.* Crossley, it seemed. "We had best be on our way, love. T' children are feeling right famished."

"Well, if they weren't so idle they wouldn't be hungry, would they?"

The couple laughed wholeheartedly. Evangeline held back her own amusement, though it bubbled near the surface.

Their steps took them to where the Palmer family stood. Mr. Palmer, a craggy and worn man, held his hat in his hand, and nodded a greeting.

"Mornin'," he said, not to the Crossleys, but to Evangeline. "I'm Gaz Palmer. Tha's us children's teacher."

For a moment, Evangeline was overcome with surprise at having fully understood his heavily inflected words—an introduction of himself and the observation that she was his children's teacher—without requiring they be repeated.

"Greet thy teacher, Hugo," Mr. Palmer said as he pressed his son to the front of their small group.

Hugo muttered something. He likely didn't appreciate being in the company of his teacher on a day he was not obligated to attend school.

To his parents, she said, "Hugo has made progress with his letters. In time, he'll learn to string them together and form words, to read and to write."

An unfamiliar voice entered the conversation. "A right waste o' time."

Evangeline turned to see a man dressed in the rough, plain

clothes of the working class, hair neatly combed, and face free of any smudge or stubble.

"Tha'll give t' young ones learning, but what good'll it do any of them?" His question held no argument or anger. He was perfectly calm but firm.

"Keep thy little ones in ignorance if tha thinks it best, Husthwayt," Mr. Crossley said. "My children will learn and grow their minds."

"To what end?" Mr. Husthwayt asked. "None of this'll keep them from t' factory."

"We're not a factory family."

"Not yet," Mr. Husthwayt said.

"Not *ever*," Mr. Crossley insisted.

Mr. Husthwayt gave a quick dip of his head. "A good day to thee an' all."

The families dispersed without further discussion, but with more than a few somber glances in one another's direction. In a matter of moments, Evangeline alone remained. She had wondered why more children didn't attend school. Perhaps Mr. Husthwayt's objections were shared by others in town. Perhaps they all thought the education Evangeline offered their children was worthless.

Her heart dropped and, with it, her gaze. Seeing the rows of grave markers in the churchyard sunk her spirits further. Would anyone bring flowers to her family's final resting place? Would anyone ever take note of those four names, so beloved to her?

Aunt and Uncle Barton stood near the door of the church, speaking with the vicar. Any moment, they would bid farewell to him and walk down the path leading directly to where she stood. They were nearly the last people with whom she cared to have a conversation. They would scold, perhaps even gloat a little. Her grief was too raw for their company.

She headed toward the schoolhouse. The town, for once, was not empty. The pulsing, pushing crowds, their voices raised in a cacophony of conversations, moved in and out of the shops. This was the busy town she had envisioned when Aunt Barton had spoken of Smeatley as a fast-growing factory town. But why did it only fit that description on Sunday?

She caught a few glances as she wove through the crowd but felt generally overlooked. Other than her handful of students and their families, no one knew her or cared that she was among them. At the break in the overgrown hedge, she stopped. Her room at the schoolhouse would be quiet and peaceful, but it would also be terribly lonely. She didn't think her heart could endure it.

Evangeline looked up the street to the bright yellow door. The McCormicks would not be expecting her. She and Mr. McCormick had agreed that she'd learned enough about soups and stews to feed herself on the days she didn't have school. Would Mr. McCormick mind if she used her once-daily knock in search of simple company? She would be happy with a wave from Ronan.

She felt certain she could manage a visit without being too much of a burden.

Silently repeating those words of resolve, she crossed the street. Her knock, as usual, was not answered immediately, and, when it was, Mr. McCormick looked more than a touch annoyed that she was there. Also, as usual, she didn't fully believe his show of frustration. Indeed, his dark eyes betrayed a hint of amusement.

"We'd not been expecting you, Miss Blake," he said. "What brings you 'round?"

"I only wished to bid you a good day—you and Ronan."

He motioned her inside. That simple gesture warmed her heart. Perhaps she wasn't entirely alone in the town, in the world, after all.

"I didn't see you at church this morning." That seemed as easy a way as any to begin a conversation.

"I've had this argument with plenty enough in town without you takin' it up, lass."

She hadn't intended to offend him. "I was making no accusations. I simply . . . missed you both." Heavens, that sounded pathetic.

"Truly?" He could not have looked more incredulous.

She hid her embarrassment behind a flippant remark. "Mostly Ronan."

Mr. McCormick chuckled. "That is far easier to believe."

Ronan sat at the table, but he was not whittling nor playing with his carved figurines. A dinner plate sat on the tabletop filled with what looked like flour. Ronan drew shapes in the powder. Evangeline took a step closer, not wishing to make him uncomfortable. It was enough to give her a clear view of his undertaking.

"Is he drawing letters?" she whispered to Mr. McCormick.

"He is. The lad's taken to the letters like a cat to cream."

"But he is only at school for an hour, and he doesn't participate."

Mr. McCormick watched his son with unmistakable fondness. "He listens, though. And he remembers." He shook his head in amazement. "He remembers *everything*."

Evangeline pressed her hand to her heart. She felt a touch

breathless. "He is learning. I have actually taught someone something."

"Miracles never cease." Too much laughter hung in his words for the observation to be an insult.

She pushed down her answering grin. "Tease all you'd like, Mr. McCormick, but I *have* wondered."

Ronan smoothed the flour, his hand covered in white, and began drawing new letters. She watched them form: R-O-N-A-N.

"He is writing his name."

Mr. McCormick nodded. "He studied that slip of paper you gave him for days and days. He's committed it to memory."

Evangeline pressed her palms together and touched her fingertips to her lips, amazed. Ronan was eager to learn, and she hadn't failed him. Given time, he could learn to read and would likely find the same joy in it that James had.

"A right waste o' time." She took a deep breath, hoping to shake loose Mr. Husthwayt's declaration, but it had lodged too firmly in her memory. How was it her doubts seemed to multiply in the face of any accomplishment?

"Why so pensive?" Mr. McCormick asked.

"Are you happy that he's learning?"

He eyed her sidelong. "'Tis something of an odd question."

"I was told today that educating children—educating *working* children—was a waste of time, that it wouldn't do them any good."

"Ah." Mr. McCormick nodded.

"Do you suppose that is why I have so few students?"

He shrugged. "I'd wager 'tis among the reasons."

"There are multiple reasons?" She brushed a strand of hair away from her eyes. "I don't understand. How could any parent not want their child to learn to read and write?"

"Did these complainers give you any reasons?" He pulled a chair back from the table, offering it to her.

She sat, thankful for a quiet moment and a place to think. "The argument was that their children are bound for the factories one way or the other, that there was no point educating them when it wouldn't change anything about their futures."

"That's likely true. Most families hereabout work at the mill, or will before long." Mr. McCormick sat in the chair beside hers. "Life is hard in these parts, and the mill offers stability and wages a poor family can depend on."

"But those who spoke of it today didn't sound happy about the prospect of working there. The Crossleys insisted they never would."

He leaned back in his chair. "I've heard people speak of their days at the factory. 'Tis something of a misery from all I hear."

"Could not an education save them from that fate?"

He shook his head. "Likely not. Poverty is too tenacious to be dislodged so easily. Her grip is reinforced by disdain and indifference and by the devastatingly vital role she plays in the current balance of things. Too many who are wealthy are only wealthy because so many others are poor. Such a deeply rooted truth cannot be dug up merely by offering a meager bit of learning to a handful of children."

That was not the answer she'd hoped for. "Then I truly am wasting everyone's time."

"I never said 'twas a waste."

She felt certain he had, or at least something near it. "You told me it would not make a difference."

"I didn't say that either." He sat straighter with an air of earnestness about him. "'Tis a frustrating thing not being able to read the day's events in a newspaper, to not know what's happening in the world. A man in search of employment who can't read advertisements nor write out inquiries will likely never find work beyond what he can see directly before him. Most of your students will go to the mill and live out their lives here in Smeatley. Reading and writing and such may not change the path they walk, but it might give them more joy than they'd otherwise have."

"The majority of children in town aren't coming to school as it is." She sighed. "Any difference I make will be miniscule."

"Seems to me you're needing to decide if a small difference is a difference worth making, if changing just one life for the better or changing a mere dozen would be a waste of your time."

She had thought of her role as a teacher only in terms of proving herself to her aunt and grandfather. Lucy's future depended on her success. But, she realized with a sudden weight, so did the futures of her students.

Ronan had written his name in his plate of flour, showing himself capable of learning if permitted to do so at his own pace and in his own way. James had found solace in reading. Through words, he had explored a world that, due to his unique challenges, would not otherwise have been open to him.

Susannah Crossley was teaching her sister the alphabet and would likely in time teach her to read. Someday she could teach her own children, and they theirs. Perhaps Susannah would one day be a teacher herself.

Even Hugo, who could be quite contrary, was learning. His family had greeted her warmly and had seemed relieved to hear that he was progressing. Education meant a great deal to his family, whose circumstances were even more strained than she had suspected.

How many of her students stood on the brink of changing

their lives? They might work in the factory when all was said and done, but if her efforts brought them something of value, how could she do less than her best for all of them? Were they not worth her time and efforts?

With a surge of resolve bolstering her confidence, she met Mr. McCormick's eye. "If Ronan would like to borrow a slate to practice his writing, he is welcome to. The Crossleys borrow one every night."

"We'll gladly accept your offer, Miss Blake. The flour gets a bit messy."

Evangeline turned to Ronan. "When you come to school in the morning, I will have a slate ready for you at the small table just to the side of the benches. You can sit there and write for as long as you'd like."

Ronan, to her surprise, nodded his understanding.

"Begor, Miss Blake," Mr. McCormick whispered, his eyes wide with amazement. "It's not a *small* difference you're making at all."

His praise warmed her heart and reaffirmed her resolve. "Well, as someone once said, 'Miracles never cease.'"

CHAPTER FIFTEEN

iss Blake was as good as her word. When Dermot brought Ronan to school the next morning, he'd a small table all to himself a bit away from the other students. She claimed not to know a thing about teaching, yet she understood exactly what his boy needed to be at ease and to learn. The woman was a mystery in so many ways.

Ronan stood in his usual spot, but only long enough to offer one of his finger-curling waves to Miss Blake and receive one in return. Then the lad set himself down and took up his bit of chalk.

"Why does he get his own table?" the Palmer boy demanded.

"Because he has learned his letters without complaining." Miss Blake turned to address the rest of the class, but was interrupted by the same demanding boy.

"He's learned his letters? He doesn't even talk."

Miss Blake kept her composure; Dermot was struggling with his.

"Here you have proof, Hugo, that a student need not constantly be speaking in order to do well in school," she said.

"Simply because a person does not speak to you does not mean that person does not speak at all. And just because he doesn't speak doesn't mean he is simple. We mustn't judge people based on our limited experience with them."

That was not at all a sentiment Dermot had expected to hear from a lady born to ease and comfort. Judgment seemed near about the only thing the lower classes received from the upper, yet she'd cautioned against it.

A mystery, and no denying.

Dermot kept to his usual place on the bench while Miss Blake taught her students. He kept one eye on the papers on which she'd written the letters from her lesson and kept the other eye on Ronan. He didn't know how much his lad was hearing, and he wanted to be able to remind him later on. He, himself, didn't read. Like most poor Irish, he'd had no opportunity to learn. And since the recently passed law requiring towns to offer an education to any student no matter how poor or unlikely to learn did not extend to the children in the Emerald Isle, that ignorance wasn't likely to be relieved any time soon.

He did his best to commit the instructions to memory, though he was glad to know Miss Blake could provide extra help during her tutoring session with Ronan. 'Twas their agreement.

The customary hour passed. Dermot rose and crossed to Ronan's small table. The lad was no longer drawing an endless stream of letters, but sat quietly, not looking at anyone or anything, not showing that he was listening, though Dermot suspected he was.

"Are you wanting to stay a bit longer?" Dermot asked quietly.

"Mornings are for school," Ronan answered, his tone just as hushed but filled with earnest insistence.

How tempting it was to snatch at the change in Ronan's

opinions, but he knew better than to allow the lad to push himself beyond what he could endure. "An hour more," he said. "I'll fetch you then, and you can come to the new work site."

Ronan thought on it a moment. He held his carved horse in one hand and his bit of chalk in the other, a fitting show of the debate no doubt waging inside. Traveling to the site was familiar to him, but he'd set his mind to spending the morning in school. Yet, remaining at school meant being left there. It was a great deal to ask of the boy.

At last he nodded. Dermot nodded in return, both surprised and relieved.

"An hour more, and I'll return." He turned toward Miss Blake. She met his eye, a question in her gaze.

"I'll return in an hour," he said. "I believe the lad'll be grand until then."

"He will be perfectly grand." She spoke in finer tones than nearly anyone he'd ever known, yet there was nothing truly superior in her air or manner.

Dermot tugged his hat on his head once more and stepped from the schoolroom. Only with great effort did he drag himself down the stairs and out the front door. He'd not been away from Ronan for more than a moment or two in all the years they'd been together. He'd watched over and protected his lad. 'Twas a difficult thing to leave that watching and protecting to another, especially one he struggled so mightily to understand.

Yet, she's better with the lad than anyone else. She knows him surprisingly well. He reminded himself of that as he made his way down Greenamble and onto Market Cross and then to the newly named Farr Street. Mrs. Barton had suggested the name for the lane on which the first row of back-to-back houses would be built. Dermot hadn't argued. Mr. Farr owned the factory, after all, and it was the factory's profits that were financing the project. If that bit of acknowledgment would sway the owner even a small bit, Dermot'd go along with it.

He reached the dig site and frustration bubbled immediately. His crew was standing about, shovels in hand.

"Why've you stopped digging? We'll not get the footing laid if the ground's left where it is."

"Tha weren't here yet," Gaz tossed back, leaning on the handle of his shovel.

Dermot looked at them in disbelief. "You've not done any work all morning? I left you ample instructions on what you were to be doing. You haven't any excuse to be standing about."

He set his gaze on Thomas. The boy would give an honest tale of the trouble.

"We were digging," Thomas said, "but t' work halted on account of an argument."

Dermot could guess as to who'd started the trouble though he addressed his next words of warning to all of them. "You've each of you a job to do. I was quite clear the work expected of you today. You haven't any excuse to not have done it."

Bertie Gardner looked as though he meant to interrupt. Dermot didn't let him.

"I've brought the lot of you over from our last project in the hope that you'd prove yourself useful on this one. I'll be sending to Keighley soon, where most of the bricklayers who worked on the mill went in search of jobs. There are others there as well, eager for work. Show yourself worthy of the trust, and I'll place you in charge of a crew. Interrupt your workday with foolish arguing, and you'll find yourself looking elsewhere for your day's pay."

He held Gaz Palmer's gaze a touch longer than the others.

It seemed every bit of trouble he encountered on the job started with the man.

"Back to work," he barked out. "All of you. I want to hear the ol' blade slicing into the dirt."

The crew set to work immediately, though Gaz paused long enough to send Dermot a hard look. He returned it in full measure. A great deal depended on the success of this endeavor. He'd not allow an ill-tempered grumbler to risk it all.

With Gaz back to work, Dermot set his attention on Thomas. "A word, lad."

He received a wary look in response.

Dermot slapped a hand on the young man's shoulder. "You're not in deep mud, don't you fret. Neither do I mean to ask you to tell tales on your fellow crewmen." He offered up the last bit loudly enough for the others to overhear. "I only meant to ask after your family. Your youngest sister wasn't at school. Is she still ailing?"

"She's not well." Thomas straightened his cap. "Our Johanna's allas been poorly. She's frail, she is."

'Twas testament to the lass's condition that her usually jesting brother spoke so plainly and soberly.

"And this is no place for the fragile." Dermot knew that well enough. 'Twas the reason he worried over Ronan so much.

Thomas's face lit up all of a sudden. "I mean to ask thee, where's little Ronan?"

"He wished to stay at school for a bit."

Thomas whistled long and high. "Now i'n't that a wonder?"

The wonder repeated itself the next day, and the next. By week's end, Ronan no longer needed Dermot sitting in during the first hour of the day, nor did he wish to be fetched after another hour. Midway through the next week, Ronan chose to stay for the entire school day.

Dermot only hoped fate was generous enough to grant him another bit of good fortune. He'd need to organize his newly hired bricklayers and set them to work before the project slid off schedule.

He'd hired back a number of workers from Keighley along with a few new men, dividing the lot into smaller crews. He'd spent hours going over the building plans in great detail then assigning specific tasks for the day.

The heads of each crew were doing their best, but not all were suited to the job. He'd have to rethink his assignments if they didn't ease into their new roles.

"You can't scrimp on the footings, men," he called out. "The width on either side has to be at least one-half the thickness of the wall, and the depth at least two-thirds. Shoddy work'll see you off the crew, don't you doubt it."

Dermot climbed into the trenches dug for the footings and counted bricks for his own self. He'd not build his future, figurative or otherwise, on a shabby foundation.

"Mortar's too runny," he called out. "This'll have to be remixed."

"I've made it this runny before," Gaz said. "Tha never made me remix it."

Dermot scooped up a handful of the mortar, roughly the consistency of undercooked porridge. He might've known Gaz was the culprit. "On dry, hot days, you're able to make your mortar wetter and not have it fall apart. We've had rain for three days and are likely due for more tonight and tomorrow." A fellow didn't learn bricklaying in Ireland and not pick up a thing or two about working in wet weather. "Remix it and rebuild."

"That'll take hours."

"It will."

The others on the same crew as Gaz, the one Bertie Gardner oversaw, watched with looks of frustration and the first hints of anger. 'Twouldn't do to have a revolt on his hands so early.

"I'll work alongside you," he told them. "We'll have this fixed quickly enough."

He kept close watch on Gaz mixing the mortar, making certain he did it right. The sidelong glares he received from the man told him that the scrutiny was not appreciated. The rest of the crew, though, set to work without much complaint. Those men he'd not worked with before even commented on the rarity of the overseer laboring alongside his workers. They'd find he did things his own way.

He knew the new arrivals all by name by the time the footing was relaid, and they looked to him with a bit less suspicion. He'd need time to build trust with them, he being both unknown and Irish.

"I want you here at first light," he told them as they finished cleaning their tools. "The sooner we start each day, the sooner we're done."

That earned him a few approving nods. Those who'd worked with him before trusted him. He'd gain the loyalty of the new men in the end, he felt certain of it. He'd managed it before; he'd do so again. He did not, however, know if Ronan would forgive him for being late.

He lugged his bucketful of tools up Greenamble. If all went well in Smeatley, he meant to build a new house for himself and Ronan. He would choose a site on a street with a more gradual slope, that much was certain.

The hedge outside the schoolhouse still hadn't been cut back.

The children might pass through the narrow opening with little trouble, but a man grown and carrying a heavy bucket didn't navigate so easily. If Miss Blake was particularly miffed by his tardiness, perhaps he could offer to trim the hedge as penance.

A little girl with dark curls sat on an enormous rock not far from the schoolhouse. She turned brown eyes on him as he stepped forward. He knew her from his mornings spent in the schoolroom: Cecilia Haigh. Hers was a factory family, though they'd only recently become one.

"A fine good evening to you, lass," he said, eyeing her for signs of distress. "Why're you standing about the schoolhouse? Have you forgotten your way home?"

She shook her head.

"Were you afraid to walk alone?"

Another head shake.

He set his bucket down and crouched in front of her. "What's kept you here so late, then?"

She turned red but didn't answer. Hers was a different kind of quiet than Ronan's, one born of pure timidity and shyness.

Dermot folded his hands in front of him, assuming his most unthreatening posture. "Are you waiting for someone? Your folks, perhaps?"

She nodded. Her gaze slid in the direction of the factory.

"They've not come to fetch you?"

A head shake.

"Does Miss Blake know you're still here, sweetheart?"

Her eyes dropped to her wringing hands. That, he guessed, meant "No."

Dermot held a hand out to her. "'Tis more than a touch chilly tonight. I think we'd best go inside and wait for your da and ma where you'll be warm."

She set her hand in his, but still looked uncertain.

He offered a reassuring smile. "Only as far as the school-house," he promised.

They walked up the front steps and through the unlocked door. The door to Miss Blake's living quarters was open. Either she'd made her peace with Ol' Bob or she'd left it open in antici-pation of Dermot's arrival.

He stepped across the threshold, the girl's small, trembling hand still in his. Miss Blake sat at her table and looked up as he approached.

"I found a wee angel sitting outside," he said.

"Cecilia." Miss Blake leaped to her feet. "Have you been out-side all this time?"

The little girl sniffled, but didn't release her hold on his hand. Dermot slipped free of her grasp and nudged her forward.

Miss Blake knelt in front of Cecilia and took her hands. "Sweetie, why did you not come inside? The weather is cold to-day."

"My parents wouldn't know where to find me," Cecilia whis-pered.

"They would have, I assure you." Miss Blake rose and led her charge toward the low-burning fire. "Sit here on this stool. You'll be warm in no time."

'Twas then Dermot spotted Ronan, curled up in a rocking chair near the fire, asleep. For the lad to be so at ease in Miss Blake's company to have been lulled to sleep boded well for his future at the school. Dermot needed the building project to be a success; he'd be hard-pressed to find another school Ronan would take to so quickly.

"What could be keeping her parents, do you suppose?" Miss

Blake had stepped closer to where Dermot stood. "Their schedule is usually so predictable."

"They're a factory family."

She nodded. "One of three in the school."

"Do the other factory family children usually wait for their parents?" 'Twas odd this girl was the only one remaining.

"Usually," Miss Blake said. "Though they are older than she, and not the only children in their family. They have ventured home on their own before."

"Factory time must be running slow today," he said.

"Is factory time not the same as everyone else's time?"

She clearly had spent little time in a factory town. "The machines in the mill run the clocks in the mill. If the machines run slow, the clocks run slow, and the clocks rule all."

"Were the bricklaying clocks running slow today as well?"

He crossed to Ronan, checking on the boy. "We had to relay a bit of the footing. The task couldn't be left for mornin'." Ronan didn't feel overly warm or cold. He was sleeping deeply, that was for certain. "How'd m' lad do today?"

"He was as good as gold," she said. "I hope he will stay throughout the day from now on."

"So do I."

Little Cecilia was watching him. Dermot tossed her a bit of a smile. She didn't smile back, but did look less apprehensive. What was it about him that had her so unsure? His manner of speaking, perhaps. Many in Smeatley disliked that he was a foreigner. Even the children weren't immune to that preference.

Dermot scooped up Ronan and turned to Miss Blake. "I'll endeavor not to be late tomorrow. I'm not meaning to make more work for you."

Her gaze, soft and tender, fell on Ronan's sleeping form. "He can stay as long as he needs to, whenever he needs to. He will always be welcome here."

That was surprising. "I've not met anyone so comfortable with him and his oddities."

She met Dermot's eyes. Sadness crept into her expression. "He is very much like my brother. Having him near is like having my James with me again."

"You're away from your family?"

She took a quick breath before answering. "Yes. All of them."

"I'd not have believed it when we first met, but it seems we've a vast deal in common, you and I."

A little smile appeared. "Enough that I can knock on your door more than once a day?"

"You'd best not count on it."

Her brow drew down and a flash of hurt passed through her eyes.

"Eventually, lass, you'll learn when I'm teasing you."

Her expression turned to frustration. "Do you realize how nearly impossible it is to tell when you're jesting?"

He adjusted his hold on Ronan. "I know it."

She shook her head and motioned him toward the door. "I'll see you both in the morning."

Dermot stopped in the doorway and tossed back over his shoulder, "Keep your chin up, Miss Cecilia. Your folks'll be by directly. You'll see."

Miss Blake smiled at him. "Thank you," she said.

He nodded. Only when he'd reached home and had laid Ronan in his bed did he realize how remarkable his visit had been. He'd received trust from a child of the town and kindness from a lady of refinement, he'd broken an established routine without

Ronan falling clear to pieces, and he was overseeing a project of his own design.

For a man who'd begun life near starving with little hope of better times to come, the future was looking surprisingly bright. Like any true Irishman, though, he couldn't help wondering how it would inevitably fall apart. History taught all his countrymen that good fortune always ran out. Always.

CHAPTER SIXTEEN

wo additional families sent their children to school the next week. While Evangeline felt this was a success, she also found herself faced with a predicament. These new students had yet to learn their letters, while the rest of the class had passed that portion of their education and were, at varying speeds, learning their letter sounds. How could she teach her new students when her existing students still needed so much guidance?

After struggling with the dilemma for a few days, she was struck with an idea she hoped would prove the right solution.

One morning, she approached Susannah Crossley before school began. "May I speak with you?"

The girl nodded and stepped inside the entryway with Evangeline. She watched, wary and curious.

"We have several new students," Evangeline began. "They are behind all of the other children and need help learning what you have already been taught. Knowing that you have been helping your sister learn what she has missed at school, I wondered if perhaps you would be willing to take part of your day at school to help teach the new students so that I can continue working with those who need my help."

Susannah, who generally maintained a calm and serene exterior, grew eager and excited. "Tha aren't hoodwinking me, are thee?"

"I am entirely in earnest."

A cloud of uncertainty touched Susannah's expression. "I don't know how to be a teacher."

Oh, how tempted Evangeline was to admit that she didn't either, but she dared not risk her students' confidence in her.

"I would not have asked you if I did not think you fully capable," she assured Susannah. "Now, do not worry that this will interfere with your own learning. I have seen how quickly you grasp new concepts and how readily your mind opens to new information. I believe you can learn all you need to even with a bit less time devoted to your own schooling. Should this arrangement cause you difficulties, though, we will revisit it and make whatever changes are necessary."

A smile as full of relief as it was of excitement appeared on her usually weary face. "I think I'd like to be a teacher."

"Here is your opportunity to discover whether or not you will truly enjoy it, whether or not you have an aptitude for it." This experiment would also prove whether or not Evangeline had stumbled upon the solution to her problem or simply added more difficulty to what she was attempting to accomplish.

"May I ask a favor of thee?" Susannah asked, nervous.

"Of course."

"Would tha tell us mother an' father? They'll never believe it if I tell them missen, but they'll be right chuffed to have t' teacher come braggin' of it."

Evangeline had grown accustomed to a number of the

Yorkshire peculiarities in speech. Mr. McCormick had explained the utterly perplexing "missen" and "thissen" as the local version of "myself" and "thyself." Evangeline had not yet heard the word "chuffed" and hadn't the first idea what it meant. However, if Susannah, who had so eagerly agreed to help her, wished for her parents to be chuffed and if that chuffing required that the teacher deliver the news, then she would gladly do precisely that.

"I will tell your mother when she comes to pick you up this afternoon."

Susanna shook her head before Evangeline even finished the offer. "Mother isn't coming to fetch we today. Johanna is still sickly, and she doesn't wish to leave her, but Father's out tending t' flock on account of there being illness among t' sheep."

"Who will be walking you and your brothers home?" As far as Evangeline knew, the Crossley children had never made that walk on their own.

"I've been given t' task. Thomas dare not leave his job early."

While Susannah was capable of guiding her siblings home, Evangeline felt a twinge of nervousness on the girl's behalf. She had been given additional responsibilities by her family and her teacher on the same day. It was a lot to ask all at once of someone so young.

"I will walk home with you and your brothers," Evangeline said. "Then I can meet Johanna *and* tell your parents of your news. I will need to bring Ronan McCormick with me, as he always remains at school until supper time."

Susannah shrugged. "Us parents know Ronan. They'll not be bothered by him."

The morning went relatively smoothly. Susannah copied Evangeline's methods of teaching letters to the newest arrivals.

Whether or not that was the best approach, she could not say, but it was all any of them had known.

Hugo, though still difficult at times, was possibly her brightest student after Susannah. He had reached the point where he was ready to begin piecing together words. While the other students quizzed one another on the various letters and letter combinations and the sounds they made, Evangeline attempted to help him.

"Nee-vur." He had made multiple attempts to sound out the word and was getting steadily closer.

"What other sound does the letter *E* make?" she offered by way of a hint.

He thought a moment, then tried the word again. "Neh-vur."

"Precisely. The word is 'never.'"

"It can't be," he insisted. "'T' letter *E* don't make that sound."

"I don't understand."

"Can't be the word 'nivver.' I remember all t' sounds for letter *E*, and that i'n't one of 'em."

Oh, heavens. She hadn't thought of that. The sounds she was teaching them to associate with each letter and letter combination did not necessarily match the way they spoke. All the Yorkshiremen she'd met, be they men, women, or children, pronounced the word "never" as "nivver." It was hardly the only word they pronounced differently than how it was spelled.

Beyond that, there were some words that would simply be wrong for them. What happened when she attempted to teach them the word "you"? They all used "thee" and "thou," though they pronounced the latter as "tha," which would only add to the confusion. She couldn't simply teach them the Yorkshire equivalent because they spoke it in such a different way from how it was written that the proper spelling would make no sense.

She attempted an explanation. "The word is spelled to match the way it is pronounced elsewhere. Indeed, you will find that to be generally true. The written language more precisely matches the language as it is spoken elsewhere."

Hugo eyed her with disgusted disbelief. "Then this reading is more for them what lives elsewhere. It weren't meant for us in t' north."

"It most certainly *is* meant for you."

His gaze narrowed in an unmistakable challenge. "How does t' language spell 'tha'?"

Sometimes the boy was too clever for his own good—certainly for *her* own good. "It is pronounced 'thou' elsewhere, and it is spelled *T-H-O-U*. However, outside of Yorkshire, the word used is 'you,' and when doing your reading, that is the word you will see most often."

He shook his head. "Seems those what live elsewhere think themselves above us, making t' words match their speaking and giving nowt of us words."

Nowt of us words. How on earth was she to teach these children to read when they nearly spoke a different language? She took a moment to decipher his meaning, frustrated that she still had to translate in her mind so often.

Nowt of us words. Nowt was "nothing." *Us* was likely being used as "our." "Giving nothing of our words" was the exact phrase, but probably not precisely what he meant. He was saying those outside Yorkshire who didn't write the way Yorkshiremen spoke either didn't include any of their words or didn't care about their manner of speaking. Regardless of the precise translation, she understood the gist. Further, she understood the implications for her as a teacher. She was, in many respects, attempting to teach these children to read a foreign language.

She refused to give up on her students, but she feared they would give up on themselves.

"There is some truth in your criticism, Hugo. But this is worth learning to do." She spoke firmly but quickly, not wishing to give him the opportunity to declare himself finished with the endeavor. "If you will be patient and keep working, I promise you I will try to find a way for what you read to match the way you speak."

He didn't look convinced, but he did look curious. A quick perusal of the room told her that nearly all of her students were listening as well. The others would encounter Hugo's same difficulty as they progressed in their studies. This was her opportunity to give them reason to keep trying.

"Can tha find books written t' way we speak?" Susannah asked. She likely had already begun to realize the discrepancy in what she was seeing and hearing.

"I do not know." Evangeline felt honesty was her best approach. "But I will try."

The look on her students' faces told her this was no small promise. She smiled at each of them in turn, then repeated in tones of confidence and sincerity, "I pledge my word: I will try."

CHAPTER SEVENTEEN

he children worked well the rest of the day, though frustration was rampant. They were attempting to learn a difficult skill, made harder by the mismatch of language. The topic of Yorkshire-specific reading materials did not resurface during school hours but was the first subject Susannah broached during their walk toward the moors that afternoon.

"Does tha truly think tha'll find books written for us?"

"I do not know."

Susannah's mouth dipped on the ends, her brows furrowed in thought. "Why would there not be any?"

Evangeline wished she had a definitive answer, or at least some words of encouragement. Truth be told, it was most likely that the Yorkshire manner of speaking was not considered "proper," and books meant for schooling were unfailingly proper.

"It's because they think of us as nowt but clapt heads."

"What is a clapt head?" Evangeline asked.

"Someone what's not very clever or smart. Someone what can't learn."

"Who has been speaking so unkindly of you?" She couldn't imagine Susannah had ever left Smeatley, but who in town would say such things to a child?

"Many local girls work as maids for Mrs. Barton. She scolds them for being ignorant and not speaking proper."

Embarrassment heated Evangeline's cheeks not only at the realization that her aunt would be so cruel but also that Susannah's revelation was not the least surprising. "Mrs. Barton ought not to treat them poorly."

Susannah shrugged. "She's south folk."

"I am also from the south." Evangeline hazarded a glance at the girl and immediately regretted it; there was no hint of reassurance in Susannah's expression. "Do you believe I look on you with disdain?"

There was no response, which was answer enough. The silence stung Evangeline's heart.

John and Billy walked a few paces ahead of their sister. The two, while always respectful during class, seldom spoke to Evangeline directly. Most of her students were the same way. While she had assumed that it was the inevitable result of concentration on their studies, a different explanation now arose in her mind. They were not comfortable with her. They felt and responded to a distance they believed existed between her and them.

She had come to care about her students, but they viewed her with suspicion. How could she overcome that? How could she prove her worth to them?

She was so distracted she'd hardly noted the distance they had traveled. Upon looking around, *truly* looking around, she was struck by the change in her surroundings. They had alighted over the hill to the east of Smeatley and stepped out onto the vast expanse of the moor.

She had heard tales of moorland, of its barren and desolate character. The sight that met her eyes, however, did not match the picture she had formed in her mind. True, there were few trees or bushes, but the endless sea of hills was covered in tall grasses waving in the wind, and dotting the landscape were patches of deepest purple. It was an untamed beauty unlike anything she had seen before. She could not look away.

Susannah moved ahead, joining her brothers. Evangeline adjusted her pace until she came even with Ronan, who had been walking between the two groups.

"Have you been on the moor before?" she asked him. "I have not, but it is beautiful."

"Moors do not have many trees," he said. "They've a few, but not many. They have grass, but the grass is not always green. They've shrubs sometimes. Sometimes trees. But always grass, and always hills."

Evangeline had known Ronan for weeks, but this was the first time he had ever spoken to her. She had not been entirely certain he could speak. He continued delineating the nature of the moors and their particular assortment of flora. He did not once veer from the subject matter, neither did he pause for her to join the conversation.

As he waxed long, memories of James flooded her heart, and a lump formed in her throat. The two boys shared the same quietness, the same earnest concentration, and, now, the same infatuation with facts and information.

She managed to interject only one word in the midst of Ronan's litany: sheep.

That sent the boy on another soliloquy. Sheep, he told her, grazed on the moor, and sheep farmers raised and looked after them. The sheep gave wool and meat and lambed in the spring.

His was clearly a curious mind. If he could be taught to read, he could learn anything his heart desired. Books had been James's haven and his greatest joy.

"This is us house, Miss Blake," Susannah called back, drawing Evangeline's attention to a humble stone home tucked into the small dip created by the gentle slope of two adjacent hills.

Small outbuildings dotted the land, and stone walls cordoned off fields. The sheep she had seen as they'd approached likely belonged to the Crossleys. The fields must have been for grazing, as nothing appeared to be growing in the vast stretch surrounding the home. Could crops be grown on the moor? Had the family any source of income beyond their flock and Thomas's bricklaying money?

Mrs. Crossley stepped out of the front doorway as they approached. Her gaze slid over her children before resting, wide and worried, on Evangeline. "Miss Blake. We weren't expecting thee."

"I have come with good news," she reassured her. "I wished to tell you in person."

That relieved the worry in Mrs. Crossley's expression though none of the discomfort. "Come inside."

Evangeline followed the children, but Ronan stopped short at the doorway. She recognized the anxiety in his face. This was an unfamiliar place and situation. Few things had upended James more quickly or more thoroughly than the unknown.

"You know the Crossleys," she reminded him. "There is nothing to fear here."

But he only shook his head and kept his feet firmly planted. This was a complication she should have foreseen. Mother had always been able to soothe James, though Evangeline suspected it was as much a matter of her familiar presence as it was the influence of something she had said. Ronan was not familiar enough with Evangeline for her to have offered that same comfort.

"He doesn't have to come in." John stepped back out, joining Ronan on the pathway. "We'll have a look at t' sheep. He allus likes watching 'em."

It seemed Ronan had visited the Crossleys before. Something must have been different this time for him to refuse to enter the house. A different person present or someone missing who was always there. In an instant, the obvious answer occurred to her. His father was not here. That would be plenty enough to disconcert him.

John urged Ronan to follow him. After a moment, he complied. The two boys walked toward the nearest stone wall, neither of them speaking yet seeming comfortable with the silence.

Evangeline watched a moment. Whether it was a lingering sense of the protectiveness she'd always felt for James or her growing fondness for Ronan, she could not say, but she found herself fighting the urge to call him back. John had shown himself a dependable child and in possession of a good heart. He would look after Ronan.

"It's right parky out," Mrs. Crossley said. "Come in and warm up."

"Parky" must have meant "cold" or "bad weather." Heavens, she hoped the language would eventually become easier to understand.

The interior of the Crossley home reminded her of the many tenant cottages dotting Petersmarch. It also reminded her strongly of her own residence in Smeatley. A few short weeks earlier she might have found such a place cramped or dreary, being accustomed to the bright and open spaces of her childhood. This new life, however, had taught her a different view of things.

What she had once thought of as mere accommodations had begun to feel like a home to her. Her small space was cozy and warm even on a "parky" day like this one. Having set the space to rights herself and invested her own toil and effort in keeping it clean and well-maintained, she felt a sense of ownership she'd never had before. Her small corner of the schoolhouse was not large or impressive, but it was hers.

She saw that same pride in Mrs. Crossley's face as she offered Evangeline a seat at their rough-hewn table.

"Might I meet Johanna first?" she asked. "I have long wished to make her acquaintance."

"Aye." Mrs. Crossley turned to Billy and said something that sounded distinctly like "Put wood in the oil." Billy immediately crossed to the front door and closed it.

How did "put wood in the oil" indicate closing the door? She could think of absolutely no explanation.

"T' little one is just in here." Mrs. Crossley led Evangeline past the table and the wood box, toward an interior doorway set in the same wall as the fireplace. "It's a warmer room."

The small bedchamber held nothing beyond a bed pressed against the opposite wall, a small chest at the foot of the bed, and a rocking chair on which sat a small girl—tiny, truth be told—wrapped in a faded quilt. The fireplace opened into the room, adding much needed warmth.

Brown eyes looked up at her from within a pale and weary face.

"You must be Johanna." Evangeline kept her tone as light as she could despite her growing concern for the little girl's health. "I am Miss Blake, and I am so pleased to be meeting you at last."

Johanna sat up a little straighter. "I've been practicing us letters." Her voice held more air than it did strength. "On t' slate."

"I know. Your sister has told me how well you are doing."

A smile, strained with effort, made a brief but sincere appearance. "Susannah means to read to us once she learns how. Stories and such."

"Do you like stories?"

Johanna nodded, though the gesture required greater effort than it ought.

"I will see if I can find some stories for her to learn to read." Even as she made the promise, Evangeline's mind worried over the difficulty of teaching the children to read using books written in English as it was spoken in the south counties. Could these Yorkshire children learn to decipher it? Or would they simply be frustrated at the unfamiliar words and turns of phrase?

Mrs. Crossley slipped past Evangeline and moved to the chair. "Best lay down for a time, babbie. Tha looks terribly pulled."

There was no objection. Mrs. Crossley slid a trundle from beneath the bed, and Johanna settled on it, her blanket tucked around her.

Silently, and with a smile of apology, Mrs. Crossley indicated that they ought to step out.

"Poor girl. She's allus jiggered and needs rest."

Jiggered. Yet another word she had no experience with. "Tired" or "worn" was her best guess.

"Tell me t' news tha've come with," Mrs. Crossley said as they returned to the main room of the house.

Susannah stood nearby, watching Evangeline with anticipation.

Evangeline assumed a bright and cheerful expression. "I asked Susannah today if she would consider assisting me in teaching the children at the school."

Mrs. Crossley looked to her daughter and received a broad smile in response.

Evangeline pressed on, encouraged. "Knowing that Susannah

has been teaching her sister and, seeing how quickly she, herself, is learning, I feel confident that she will be a tremendous help to those students who are struggling."

"Ah, dear girl." Mrs. Crossley pulled her daughter into an embrace. Though Susannah was likely not twelve years old yet, she was nearly of a height with her mother. "We must tell thy father. He'll be right chuffed, he will."

As if brought by fate itself, Mr. Crossley stepped inside. He tossed his weather-beaten hat onto an obliging nail and worked at the buttons of his mud-stained coat. "Right parky out today, i'n'it?"

"Don't bother those boys none. They're bahn to t' west field," Mrs. Crossley replied.

"They're meaning to spot t' black sheep. Full fascinated, they are. We've t' makings of two shepherds in them, we do." Mr. Crossley kissed his wife, not the quick greeting Evangeline was accustomed to seeing among her parents' friends, but an unmistakably affectionate kiss directly on the mouth accompanied by a full-armed and lingering embrace. "Have tha missed me, then?"

Mrs. Crossley smiled up at him. "I've not missed t' mud tha brings in with thee."

Mr. Crossley chuckled and kissed her again, quickly this time. "Palmer's come for a chat. Said to ask thee first if tha minds."

Concern filled Mrs. Crossley's face. "At this time of day? Why's he not workin'?"

Mr. Crossley lowered his voice, though Evangeline could still hear him. "I'd wager that's what he means to talk about."

Why *was* Mr. Palmer not at the building site like Thomas Crossley? They both worked for Mr. McCormick, but Susannah had said that the workday was too long and too rigid for her brother to slip away long enough to walk his siblings home.

"I'll set Mr. Palmer's mind at ease," Mrs. Crossley said. "Hear what news Miss Blake has come with."

Mr. Crossley dipped his head in her direction. "Ey up, Miss Blake."

"Good day to you, as well. I came to tell you that Susannah has been appointed an assistant teacher at the school."

He turned to Susannah. "My girl! Assistant teacher. That's a fine thing, i'n'it?"

Susannah nodded. "I'll be learning to teach, just as we'd hoped."

Just as they'd hoped? Had the family discussed it before?

Mr. Crossley's next question was addressed to Evangeline. "Does tha think, with t' practice she'd get, she might one day be a teacher hersen?"

Hersen. Herself. "I do not see why not. Having experience could only help her chances."

"A teacher." Mr. Crossley gently took his daughter's face in his hands. "Tha'd not have to go to t' factory."

"I know it."

"You'd live your life baht that misery," he added.

"Baht" is "without." When the word continued to sit odd on her ears, she repeated the translation. *"Baht" is "without."*

"Oh, girl." Mr. Crossley pulled Susannah into an embrace.

Hoping she would not give offense, Evangeline asked the question weighing heavy on her mind. "Why is it you dislike the factory so much?"

It was Mr. Palmer, who had only just stepped inside, who answered. "It's a place of misery and death," he said. "Those what get through t' day baht injuries only grow more unhappy, their souls dying by inches."

CHAPTER EIGHTEEN

W hy wasn't Mr. Palmer working this afternoon?"

Dermot eyed Miss Blake, attempting to sort out her unexpected substitute for a greeting.

"I know he works for you, as does Thomas Crossley. Thomas was not able to leave the work site to walk his brothers and sister home from school, yet Mr. Palmer was at the Crossleys' house."

Ah. "Why did you not ask Palmer your own self why he was not working?"

"He did not seem to wish to talk about it," she answered. "At least not to me."

The Crossleys, no doubt, had received an earful. "Palmer was let go today." And that was all Dermot intended to say on the matter. He held his hand out to Ronan. "Come along, lad."

Miss Blake, however, was not satisfied. "You fired him?"

"I did, and not without cause."

Far from placated, she appeared more concerned. "Then he does not have a job. His family has no income."

"It couldn't be helped."

Miss Blake's forehead creased deeply with worry. "What will they do?"

"I'm telling you, lass, it couldn't be helped."

She was unimpressed. "He has children to feed."

"Perhaps that fact ought to have entered his mind each day when he chose to laze about instead of doing his work."

"His work was lacking?"

Why did that surprise her so much? Did she know Palmer at all?

"His skills were fine enough, but he far preferred to stand about chatting rather than doing the job I was paying him to be doing. The crew is small, barely sufficient for the work we're undertaking in the time we've been given. I could not justify taking any ot m' men from their duties to spend the day hounding Palmer to do his part. I gave him ample warnings and opportunities for changing and doing better, but he heeded not a single one. And why"—exasperation filled his words—"do I feel the need to defend this to you? I did what needed doing, and that ought not to earn your censure."

"And I am concerned for my students, which ought not to earn yours."

"Your students?" He folded his arms across his chest. "The Crossleys' oldest works for me, and his income is crucial to them. The Bennetts, too, depend upon the work Mr. Bennett does for me; their children are new to the school, I believe. The houses we're building would allow the Haighs to live near enough to the factory to save their wee lass the long and difficult walk to and from town every day, allowing her to sleep a bit more and have a more reliable roof over her head. If this project is a failure, what happens to *those* students?"

She watched him, silent.

"I'm not heartless. I do worry about the Palmer children. 'Tis the reason I gave their father one chance after another, one warning after another. But too many lives depend on these houses being completed correctly and on schedule. I could not risk all of that any longer."

"Could you not have found something else for him to do? A different task than the one he had been undertaking?"

He tempered his response, knowing that she meant well, that she spoke not out of condemnation but concern. "He is not a reliable worker. I was as merciful as I could be."

"But he'll have to go to the factory." Her voice hardly raised above a whisper. "I have heard him speak of it as a place of death for the soul."

Dermot couldn't fault the man for that view. 'Twas one of the reasons he'd waited so long before finally sending him on his way. "The mill values efficiency above all else. The work is monotonous and miserable at times. And they've not enough workers for the load, meaning they're all doing too much to make up the difference.

"Though I've not been inside the building myself since it was completed, I've heard others speak of the thickness in the air and the overly warm, overly crowded rooms. They say the machines are deafeningly loud, and that the smell of wool and oil is so strong it lingers on the workers long after they've left for the day. A man raised on the moors, as Palmer was, likely sees those confined spaces and lack of fresh air and freedom to be something of a death to the soul."

"Yet, you would resign him to that?"

Saints, the woman knew how to twist the knife of guilt. "He resigned himself to it."

"That is rather cold."

ASHES ON THE MOOR

He shook his head. "It is the truth, unvarnished. I did all I could."

She squared her shoulders, a posture of proud defiance. "And is that enough to appease your conscience, Mr. McCormick?"

"If all my crew lost their positions and incomes, and the factory workers lost their opportunity for better housing, all on account of me ignoring Mr. Palmer's poor work, would that appease *your* conscience?"

She held her chin at a dignified angle. "Clearly we are not going to see eye to eye."

"That would be difficult, seeing as you're not terribly tall."

Her eyebrow shot upward at a sharp angle. "You are turning this into a jest?"

He shook his head. "Only wishing to put an end to an argument." He took up Ronan's hand. "Have yourself a fine evening, Miss Blake."

Ronan offered his teacher his customary wave, which she returned as always. Though the lass had shown his boy kindness and patience, she did not always extend that forbearance to Dermot. Perhaps 'twas just as well, being disposed as she was to assume the worst in his intentions.

Why, then, did her words weigh so heavily on him as he went through the routine of supper and seeing Ronan to bed? He knew he'd been as merciful as he could be with Gaz Palmer. He'd kept the man on through the entire wall building project despite the continued problems he'd caused. He'd even brought him along when the back-to-backs began, hoping for the best.

That afternoon had forced the decision. The crew had been working themselves to exhaustion trying to get caught up after fixing an error made that morning. Every man had been pulling his weight, except Palmer. He'd wandered away and set himself to sitting with his back against the tree, just watching the sky.

Dermot had waited to say anything, hoping to see the man rethink his decision and return to work. But a half hour passed with no change. Then another. He could see the frustration in the faces of the other workers as they'd glared at Palmer. A few even muttered to each other about him being paid to laze about when they had to slave away.

Palmer not doing his work was bad enough, but creating resentment in the other workers would bring the entire project to a halt if left unchecked.

He'd had no choice.

Feeling guilty was a particularly Irish talent, having been perfected over centuries, and Dermot was well-acquainted with the experience. This time, though, it felt different.

He could not have done anything but what he'd done—not with so many depending on the success of the project. Yet he knew the Palmer family would suffer for it. In that, Miss Blake had been correct.

There I go, feeling the ol' guilt.

He pushed back the niggling thought, but it resurfaced again and again. His childhood had been spent learning a trade, far from his family and far from the only home he'd known. He'd suffered the loneliness and the separation because having one less mouth to feed and one less body to clothe had kept his family afloat in the vast ocean of poverty. He'd suffered for the good of others. His life had been turned inside out to save the lives of those around him.

He had been the lamb at the slaughter, and he had just resigned Gaz Palmer to the same role.

The chief difference being that Palmer had been given chance after chance to avoid his fate. Dermot hadn't even been warned. He'd simply been handed off and told to be a good lad, and he'd never seen nor heard from his family again.

Life was far too often cruel.

CHAPTER NINETEEN

Evangeline's day had not been going well. That morning, Mr. McCormick had informed her, in chilled tones, that Ronan would be walking home with the Crossley children rather than remaining with her after school, no doubt the result of her disapproval of his firing of Mr. Palmer. The children were increasingly frustrated with their attempts at piecing together words, something which likely would have been alleviated had they the advantage of a teacher who actually knew how to teach. Her newest students were progressing, but slowly and with obvious concern that they were falling behind their friends who had been attending school longer. To top all of it off, Hugo Palmer was worse than usual.

He questioned everything, spoke sharply and at times unkindly to his fellow students, and refused to do many of the things she asked of him. Knowing the strain that existed in his home, Evangeline tried to be patient and understanding, but his behavior was both discouraging and disruptive.

"If you stop trying," she told him for perhaps the hundredth time, "then you will never learn."

"What's the point of learning owt? We'll all end in t' factory no matter what we do."

It was exactly the argument she had attempted to counter in the churchyard, that education was pointless when set against the inevitability of the mill. "Wouldn't you like to learn to read?"

His shoulders slumped. "What would I read?"

She attempted to maintain an encouraging tone despite having nearly expended the last of her patience. "Books and stories."

Hugo harrumphed. "They're all written for south folk."

"I am looking for books written for Yorkshiremen," she told him. "I simply do not know yet where to find them or whom to ask."

Hugo folded his arms across his chest and glared at her. "I'll read those stories if tha finds them."

"You will refuse until I find something I don't even know for certain exists?"

"Aye." His expression and posture spoke of such stubbornness that she could not doubt he was fully in earnest.

She pushed out a long, deep breath. Remaining calm was as much the mark of a proper upbringing as was serenity of countenance and precision of posture. "Oh, Hugo. What am I to do with you?"

Footsteps sounded in the entryway, pulling all eyes in that direction. They never had visitors. Evangeline watched with as much confusion as curiosity. Perhaps one of the children was being called home early. Perhaps another student would be joining them.

The footsteps reached the top of the stairs.

The new arrival wasn't a student or a parent. Aunt Barton had arrived without warning or welcome.

Worry and discouragement filled the children's faces. For Evangeline, the arrival brought a feeling of dread.

She gave a quick signal to her students, having practiced the appropriate action for this scenario. They all rose quickly to their feet—all except Hugo, who maintained his contrary air.

"Class," she cued them.

"Good afternoon, Mrs. Barton," they all said, nearly in unison.

In what amounted to something akin to a miracle, Aunt Barton actually looked impressed. Perhaps this visit would not end with the same disappointment as the others had. Evangeline had not been privy to the reports her aunt had sent to her grandfather, but she had no difficulty imagining what they had said.

"Continue with your work," Aunt Barton instructed the class.

Evangeline gave a smile and nod of encouragement to her students. "You may be seated."

With a fervor that she hoped her aunt would interpret as an eagerness to learn rather than the fear Evangeline knew it to be, the children bent over their slates.

"They are very studious," Aunt Barton acknowledged, eyeing the children the way one would an unwanted annoyance or a difficulty that is beneath one's dignity to address.

"They wish very much to learn. It is an admirable trait." Somehow she kept the response serene.

Aunt Barton merely nodded.

Pushing back her nervousness, Evangeline gestured to the left side of the schoolroom. "These are our students who are learning fastest. Many are beginning to read basic words. Beside them"— she indicated the middle benches—"are our students who are making progress toward the goal of reading. And this group here"—she motioned to the cluster of students gathered around Susannah—"are children who have only joined us in the past few days and are, therefore, beginning their studies."

Aunt Barton indicated Susannah. "This girl was here last time. She is not new."

"No. Susannah Crossley is our most advanced student and quite bright. She is assisting the newer students."

"Assisting students is your job, Miss Blake." Aunt Barton turned a piercingly disapproving gaze on Evangeline. "Are you so incapable of it?"

"Providing more direct instruction will allow them to progress more quickly and catch up to the other children. It is not a matter of being capable or not."

"Odd that." Aunt Barton lifted her chin a fraction. "I understand the school in Greenborough has far more students and only one teacher, and there are no reports of any difficulty keeping the students progressing."

Evangeline clasped her hands together, maintaining a calm demeanor. "I am doing what is best for my students. Surely that is what a teacher ought to do."

Aunt Barton's disapproval did not ease. "My purpose in visiting is to determine whether or not you are, in fact, doing what is best for the children of Smeatley. Your defensiveness gives me reason to doubt it."

Defensiveness? Evangeline had been reasonable, offering answers to Aunt Barton's questions without accusation or undue emotion. She had acted precisely as she ought, yet she was being criticized. Had she stepped out of line? She didn't think so. Maybe Aunt Barton simply needed to see for herself that all was well in the classroom.

"Perhaps you would care to see what the children have learned, to measure their progress by witnessing a demonstration of it."

The corners of Aunt Barton's mouth tipped ever-so-slightly upward, but her expression was far from warm or kind. "I believe your attitude tells me all I need to know—and all Mr. Farr requires."

With that, she turned and swept from the room with a regal posture and without a single glance in the direction of the children in whose interest she claimed to be acting. That was to be it? On one brief visit, not one moment of which was spent actually observing anything, Aunt Barton meant to denounce her efforts to her grandfather?

It was unfair. Surely Aunt Barton could be made to see that.

Evangeline followed in her wake, tossing instructions to her students to continue with their studies and the assurance that she would return quickly.

"Mrs. Barton." She caught up with her at the bottom of the stairs.

"It is no use begging," Aunt Barton said. "I have seen all—"

"What is your grievance with me?"

"I beg your pardon?" She truly sounded surprised by Evangeline's question.

"Every interaction we have had these past weeks has begun with your already established disapproval, and I am at a loss to understand why."

Anger flashed in her aunt's eyes. "Your behavior is hardly ladylike."

The accusation stung. She had tried so hard to behave as she ought despite her unfamiliar and difficult circumstances.

Aunt Barton stepped closer to her, skewering her with contempt. "So sure of yourself. So very top-lofty. I knew you would

be. Elizabeth could not have raised a daughter who was anything
but her equal in pretentiousness."

Elizabeth was Evangeline's mother, and Aunt Barton's sister.
How could she speak so ill of a woman who had possessed such
a gentle heart?

"I told Father that you would be this way," Aunt Barton continued, "but he simply would not listen. He never saw the truth
about her, either." Aunt Barton took hold of the door handle,
but spared Evangeline one last look of condemnation. "Give a
thought to your future, Miss Blake, as it seems you think too
highly of your capabilities."

Evangeline sat at her table that evening, her head down and
her heart heavy. She was too overwhelmed to even think of preparing herself a meal and too exhausted to drag herself to her bed.

Her aunt's condemnation sat uneasily on her mind. Though
she did not think she had truly pushed the boundaries of decorum in their discussion, she could not say the same for all of her
interactions of late.

She had grown agitated with the local seamstress when she
had, without explanation, raised the price for a front-fastening
corset.

She had spoken sharply when Old Bob stepped inside to drop
off school supplies without knocking. He hadn't had any nefari-
ous intentions, he'd simply forgotten.

She'd had more than one conversation with Mr. McCormick
that would not have passed the scrutiny of her governess or her
mother. She had scolded, accused, contradicted. Ladies were
meant to influence with quiet gentility.

She had acted out of character in those instances. Yet, had she been so wrong? Was she truly deserving of her aunt's censure or of the castigation she was heaping on herself?

Life had grown so discouraging, and she felt helpless to do anything about it. Arguing with those who were contributing to her frustrations had, in the moment, offered some relief. Now, however, she felt dissatisfied. She knew who she was raised to be, and she was failing.

Someone knocked at her door. She was not particularly in the mood for visitors, but she had breached enough rules of etiquette already. Summoning her best manners, Evangeline rose, crossed the small room, and answered the door.

She hid her surprise at seeing Mr. McCormick, of all people, standing there. "Good evening."

"You were meant to come for a cooking lesson this evening," he said.

He had still been expecting her? "I thought, after our discussion yesterday and Ronan not staying after school . . ." Her explanation trailed off at the hurt look in his eyes.

"You think me as petty as all that, Miss Blake?" Heavens, he *sounded* offended as well.

"I suppose I don't know what to think."

He nodded. "Fair enough. From this point forward, you can think of me as a man who keeps his word. Now, come along. Tonight I mean to teach you to make colcannon."

The invitation brought relief and warmth. Perhaps it was simply the joy of receiving a kindness on a difficult day. Perhaps it was the reassurance that yesterday's poor manners were not to be held against her.

She fetched her key and sent a silent word of affection to her family, watching her from within the frame on the mantel. She often greeted them or bid them farewell and even spoke to them during the long, lonely evenings. Outside of school hours, those shadows of her loved ones tucked behind the unyielding glass were her only companions. They alone listened to her worries and hopes and struggles. They alone sat with her during the quietest, coldest hours.

Who was looking after Lucy during her hours of need?

As they walked the dirt path leading away from the school-house, Mr. McCormick pulled a folded parchment from his jacket pocket. "Mr. Barton asked me to deliver this to you."

She accepted it with a small degree of nervousness. Had her aunt made a scathing report to her husband? Was she to be scolded or dismissed? No, the paper was a letter, folded and sealed.

"It is from Lucy," she said in surprise.

"A friend of yours?"

"My sister," she explained. "We are separated just now. I have longed to hear from her, and had nearly given up hope."

"Read it, then." Mr. McCormick tucked his hands in his jacket pockets as they walked, his posture easy and calm. "I'll not begrudge you learning how your sister fares."

"I will be terrible company," she warned him.

"'Twill make you easier to recognize." He immediately caught her eye. "That was a moment of teasing. I know you don't always recognize it as such."

She almost smiled at him. "We need to work on your approach to teasing, render it a little less biting."

"Very well. You learn to make colcannon, and I'll set m' mind to some more tender jests."

That was an unexpected concession. "Are you in earnest?"

"I am." He spoke with conviction. "I know I am woefully out of practice at kindly conversation. I've had little enough opportunity for it this past year. Mark you, though, I'm willing to try m' hand at it, and I'm hoping you'll do as you have been and point out to me when I'm being more peevish than I ought to be."

Would the surprises of this man never end? "You wish for me to tell you when you're being grumpy? That is not generally encouraged or welcome."

"I've backbone enough to endure criticism, Miss Blake. And I've human nature enough to need it now and then." He opened his yellow door. "I'll quit my blatherin'," he said. "You've a letter to read."

Once inside, she exchanged waves with Ronan, then set herself at the table. Nervousness tiptoed over her. Lucy had written at last, but what had she said? What if she'd written to say she didn't miss Evangeline and didn't wish to live with her? How could she bear that?

With shaking hands, she broke the seal and unfolded the parchment.

Dear Evangeline,
  Please do not leave me here.

With those six words, her sister broke her heart.

  My room is cold, and the other girls do not like me. The teachers never smile, and they are unkind when I answer a question wrong. I am so very lonely. Please come and fetch me. Please.

That was all she wrote. Even her name was hastily scrawled without the customary valediction. The hurried nature of Lucy's pleas only added to her urgency.

"Miss Blake?" Mr. McCormick sat at the table by her. "You appear to have received bad news. Are you needing to talk about it? I'm a dab hand at listening."

She shook her head, her spirits sinking. "You don't wish to hear my troubles."

"On the contrary. It'll help pass the time while we chop and mix our supper." He pushed a bowl of boiled potatoes and a large spoon toward her.

She hesitated. Had she not just spent a long hour berating herself over the proper way to behave? Speaking so personally was not terribly appropriate, but, heaven help her, she needed someone to talk with. She needed to lift some of the weight on her heart.

"What do I do with the potatoes?" she asked.

"Crush 'em up as best you can. When you're done, we'll add a touch of cream."

She nodded her understanding and set to work.

Mr. McCormick crossed to the pot hanging over the fire and stirred something inside. The steam smelled heavily of cabbage, as it often did. When he didn't press her further to share her worries, her faith in him rose. He was inviting the confidence; it would not be wrong of her to accept.

"My sister is all the family I have left," she heard herself say as she crushed and stirred the potatoes. "We are separated, though, and we are neither of us happy about it."

"Why are you apart?" he asked, scooping heaps of dark, limp cabbage from the pot.

"Our grandfather was given full control over our residence and my occupation after our parents died. He has determined that my sister should be in Leeds." Evangeline chose not to explain that he had also insisted she come to Smeatley and be the teacher. Admitting that she had not had any choice in the matter felt oddly like giving up on it, on herself, even on her students. She had not sought the position, but it had become important to her. "Grandfather is not convinced that I am capable of caring for her and won't allow her to live here with me until I can prove otherwise."

Mr. McCormick returned to the table with a bowl of boiled cabbage strips. "What is it your sister's written that's added so much to your misery?"

"She tells me she is unhappy." Her shoulders drooped at the reminder. "She is pleading with me to help her, but I cannot."

He dropped his cabbage into her bowl of potatoes. "Stir it all together."

She obeyed with vigor, finding satisfaction in being able to accomplish *something*.

"You know the pain of being separated from those you love," he said, fetching a cream pitcher. "Now, seeing that same pain in your wee sister, you're finding yourself desperate to save her from it."

"You speak as one who understands."

His eyes turned sad and distant. "I've not seen m' family since I was as young as Ronan, there. I've missed them ever since."

"I am sorry to hear that."

He poured a bit of cream in the bowl and indicated she should stir it again. "'Tis a difficult thing not having those we love with us."

"You have Ronan with you," she pointed out. He was not entirely alone.

"I do, at that." He looked on the boy with unmistakable love. "I have him because I couldn't bear to see him endure what I had, being alone in the world and aching for someone to care about him."

That answer did not make a great deal of sense. Why would a father be worried about his son being alone in the world if they were together? "Was there a risk of you being separated?"

He set bowls out for them and began scooping the potatoes and cabbage mixture into them. "I'll tell you something I've not told anyone hereabout. I'm not ashamed, mind you, I simply prefer to keep private matters to m'self, especially where Ronan is concerned."

She glanced at the boy, who had not looked up from his wooden figurines, then returned her gaze to Mr. McCormick.

He sat and pulled a bowl over to himself. "Ronan's not m' son."

Shock silenced her. Of all the things he might have said, she would never have guessed that.

"At an age just younger than I was when my family apprenticed me to a brick mason, Ronan found himself in the same situation, except the man charged with his training was a brute." Mr. McCormick took up his spoon, though he didn't eat. "I knew the sort of life Ronan would have, the misery awaiting him. I couldn't stand by and let that happen."

"What did you do?"

"I convinced the man to apprentice Ronan to me instead. Took a fair bit of doing, but he eventually allowed it."

"But Ronan is not a bricklayer."

Mr. McCormick shook his head. "He's a child, as he ought to be. As I ought to have been. As your sister, no doubt, deserves to be. You worry for your sister, just as I worried for the lad while trying to secure his release from the misery life had placed him in."

Evangeline scooted her chair closer to his. "How did you manage it?"

"How? By being as dogged as I knew how. I never stopped pushing or trying. In time, I found the thing that motivated the man who kept him from me. Once I knew that, 'twas finally possible to convince him."

"What was it?" Perhaps it was something she could use to bring Lucy home.

"Money." He took a bite of his supper. "Not in the direct sense, though. I offered the man a project of mine that was sure to make him a fine sum. I knew he had no care for the lad and was certain he'd make the trade. He did."

Evangeline tried to imagine Ronan with such a person, someone who could toss him aside so easily for the sake of financial gain. The thought brought a thickness to her throat and a burning sensation to the back of her eyes. "What a terrible man."

"That he was."

"My ability to do well at my job will serve as proof of my ability to care for my sister," she said. "But my grandfather's knowledge of my success is limited to Mrs. Barton's reports on my progress." Heavens, she was tiptoeing close to revealing secrets she had sworn not to disclose. "Mrs. Barton, however, has as much as admitted that she does not intend to make a flattering accounting of my abilities, regardless of what I may or may not accomplish."

He did not seem as puzzled as she'd thought he would be. "Why not tell your grandfather yourself? Send your own report."

"He'd likely not believe me." Her heart dropped. "And he would not approve of me being so bold. A lady is not meant to be assertive."

"Aye, but you'd be acting as a sister, not a fine lady. Sisters are family, and family is meant to fiercely protect one another."

She had never, in all her twenty years, imagined a situation where the rules of conduct could change entirely. Yet, she was eating a meal she'd helped prepare, fretting over her employment, and pondering the possibility of contradicting the witness of her aunt and of arguing her point directly to her grandfather. For one taught from the cradle to be unfailingly prim, it was a daunting prospect, and a confusing one. She doubted her own ability to choose the correct course of action.

"I do not know if I have the boldness to contradict Mrs. Barton." She shook her head.

"You give yourself far too little credit," he said. "I think you have fire enough for this."

His words touched her. So few people had shown confidence in her of late, including herself. "Thank you, Mr. McCormick."

"Dermot," he said. "I think we've shared enough confidences to be on less formal footing."

Before coming to Smeatley, she would have rejected the idea out of hand. Such familiarity was unheard of between a woman and a man to whom she was not related. Yet, she felt nothing but reassurance in that moment.

"Dermot," she acknowledged. "And I am Evangeline."

He shook his head and sighed in unmistakably feigned annoyance. "That is a mouthful, that is."

She grinned back at him. "I think you have fire enough to manage it."

CHAPTER TWENTY

After debating long into the night, Evangeline decided not to write to her grandfather. His few visits to Petersmarch while she was growing up had always included praise for her mother's poise and dignity. Showing herself to be in possession of those same qualities would help her cause. She was certain of it.

Then, when he eventually made a visit of his own, he would see for himself that she was everything her mother had been, as well as a good teacher. The contradiction of her aunt's words would be evident, and Evangeline would not need to make the argument herself. She would focus, instead, on seeing that her children began to truly read.

Without money or a sympathetic school board, she felt certain she would not be able to search out Yorkshire texts as she'd hoped to. Her uncle had, however, provided a quantity of paper, which had mostly gone unused as her students used slates for nearly everything. That pile of parchment sparked an idea. Once her students had left for the day, excepting Ronan, who was again remaining with her after school, she planned to trek out onto the moor and speak to Mrs. Crossley.

Mr. Palmer arrived at the same late hour as the Haighs to collect his children. He had taken work at the factory, and the change in him was striking. Though he'd shown signs of strain and worry during the brief moments she'd spoken with him at the Crossleys' home, his appearance had grown haggard and careworn. He was no longer simply concerned; he was falling to pieces.

"A good evening to you, Mr. Palmer." Her greeting was met with a silent nod. "The children did well today. Hugo is making great progress, as are the others." In truth, the Palmer children were more withdrawn during class, and Hugo was more defiant.

"Fine, fine." He shooed his children along. Unhappiness sat heavy on the entire family. Their financial difficulties would have been lightened by his employment with the factory, but that seemed little comfort to them.

She understood Dermot's arguments for dismissing him, yet her heart broke for their misery. If only Mr. Palmer had been permitted to keep his position, to remain out of the factory, and on a job that did not tear away at his soul.

She stepped beside Ronan sitting on the front step of the schoolhouse, writing his name again and again on the slate. "I need to visit the Crossleys. Would you like to visit with John and look at his sheep?"

Though Ronan did not answer, verbally or otherwise, he did set aside his slate and stand.

She began walking and he joined her. How grateful she was that he had learned to be comfortable with her. James had struggled to warm to strangers, at times refusing to try altogether.

She knew that Ronan's acceptance of her was a gift, and she did not mean to take it lightly.

"How do you like school?" she asked him as they made their way down the narrow road that led west of town. "Do you like it as much as being on the building site?"

"We build with bricks," Ronan said. "Bricks are for building, but the mortar must be right, else the bricks don't stay. It cannot be too wet or too dry. It needs to be right. When 'tis raining and misty out, the mortar's needing to be made more dry because the rain'll wetten it. But if the day's a hot one, the mortar'll be made more wet on account of the heat'll dry it out. It has to be right. 'Tis the rule. It has to be right."

"That sounds like a good rule." Evangeline tucked a comment into the conversation as soon as Ronan paused long enough to allow it. "What other rules do you know?"

"Dogs should have spots," he said. "They don't all, but I like the ones what have spots."

Every now and then, the little Irish boy said something that rang with the Yorkshire manner of speaking. He did not interact with the other children much, and he almost never spoke to any of them, but it seemed he was listening and absorbing what he heard.

"People don't have spots. And people smell like different things than people. That's a new rule. People can smell like dirt or flowers or like the factory. 'Tisn't wrong for them to. That's a rule."

Having engaged in similar conversations with her brother, she could easily imagine Dermot having to explain the "rule" about odors that clung to people. It had likely baffled Ronan until then.

"What about sheep?" she pressed.

"Sheep smell like sheep. They sound like sheep. There are

black sheep, not just white ones, but there're not as many. That's a rule as well."

"Did John tell you that rule?"

Ronan shook his head. "I sorted it on my own. I've seen the sheep. There're always more white sheep than black."

The boy was clever, there was no denying that.

By the time they reached the Crossleys' home, the topic had moved to music and the songs he sang most often at home. Though Ronan had been silent during the first weeks of their acquaintance, when they were alone of late he did not stop talking. Her heart never failed to be warmed by it.

Evangeline knocked at the door.

"Miss Blake," Mrs. Crossley said. "What brings thee 'round?"

"I have come to ask a favor, actually." Hearing the words aloud drove home how presumptuous they truly were. "I will, of course, understand if what I ask is inconvenient or unappealing to you."

Mrs. Crossley nodded and watched her closely. Ronan's attention had wandered to the sheep grazing in a distant field, no doubt searching for the rare black dot among the white.

"The children at school are struggling with their reading, in part because the materials I have for them to read are not written in the language with which they are most familiar."

Mrs. Crossley's attention hadn't wavered.

"I would like for them to have stories to read that are written in Yorkshire English, but I do not know how or where to find such a thing. That is what I am hoping you can help me with."

"I've not owned a book in all us life," she said. "I'd not have t' first idea where to find one."

She had not been as clear she'd thought. "I meant that I had hoped you knew of some stories or tales that the children would find familiar that you would be willing to tell me, in your own words. I would write those stories down exactly as you told them to me with the same words and phrases. The children could then practice reading what I had written out. The language would be *their* language, and their frustration at the unfamiliar words and sounds they have been attempting to read would be lessened."

"They'd be reading t' words I say?"

Evangeline nodded. "They would eventually have to learn to read words as they are spoken and written in other parts of the country, but building their confidence by giving them something familiar will help, I think. I hope, at least."

Mrs. Crossley's expression turned thoughtful. "Tha're an odd sort of southerner, miss. They usually turn their noses up at us way of speaking. Allus have done."

"I wish to help the children more than anything," Evangeline said. "And this, I firmly believe, will help."

Mrs. Crossley nodded. "I'll help thee, though I can't this day."

"Of course. Whenever you are able, simply tell me when or where, and we can begin."

She nodded. "It's a grand thing tha're doing. Any other southern teacher wouldn't've cared owt for t' children's comfort."

The idea of a teacher neglecting her dear children hurt her heart. "I would hope that any teacher would care deeply for her students."

Mrs. Crossley offered an empathetic smile. "Tha has a good heart, so tha can't imagine being so cold. We need only look to her high-and-mighty lordship to know how most southern folk feel."

"Mrs. Barton is not always as kind as she ought to be," Evangeline acknowledged. "I am pleased to know that I have shown myself to be preferable to her."

An immediate sense of disloyalty grabbed her. Despite her own difficulties with her aunt, they were family. Yet, having been subjected to Aunt Barton's unkindness, she could feel nothing but relief at knowing she was not guilty of the same transgression.

"Tha and Ronan had best hurry back to town. There's a storm brewing overhead."

The sky had, indeed, turned an ominous shade of gray, and a cold breeze had begun to blow.

"Thank you, Mrs. Crossley. I appreciate your willingness to help."

She urged Ronan onward, and they moved quickly back to the schoolhouse, not slowing to look at anything nor to have a leisurely discussion on whatever struck his fancy.

She had the fire burning low and Ronan deposited in front of it by the time the first flash of lightning lit the dark sky. The day had not grown overly late, but almost no light penetrated the thick clouds. It felt as if night had come far too early.

A low rumble of thunder shook the windows. Wind whistled through unseen gaps in the walls.

Ronan pulled himself tightly into a ball, cringing with each crash of thunder.

Evangeline knelt before the rocking chair where he sat. "You do not care for the storm, do you?"

He sat in tense, shaking silence.

"What is it you do at home during a storm?" she asked.

"Sing," he whispered.

"We can sing now if you'd like."

He nodded, quickly, anxiously.

"What song would you like to sing?"

He hesitated, then, in quiet tones, began to sing. It was not a song she knew nor had ever before heard. In fact, the song was not even in English. After a moment, he stopped, looking at her in confusion, no doubt having expected her to join in.

"I do not know that song," she confessed.

He tried another, also in what she suspected was Irish, and it ended in the same look of disappointment.

"What if I taught you a song that I used to sing when I was your age?" she suggested. "It was a favorite of my brother's. His name was James, and you remind me a great deal of him. I think you would like this song as well."

He looked curious enough to convince her to move ahead with her plan.

"This song involves a great many numbers," she told him. "I suspect you are fond of numbers and counting."

His curiosity increased on the instant.

"I will sing the verses, and you can join on the chorus. It is numbers, but listed in reverse order and skipping over some. It can grow tricky, which only makes it more fun to sing. When I sang it with my brother, tripping over the numbers would make us laugh and laugh until we had to start again." She smiled both at the memory and at Ronan's unwavering interest. "Would you like to try?"

Lightning lit the room, followed closely by thunder. Ronan's gaze flew to the ceiling, and he tensed.

James had often grown clingy when he was afraid, though at other times he refused any contact. Predicting which he would prefer had proven difficult. Ronan was likely equally indiscernible. Evangeline took a guess.

"What if I were to sit in the rocking chair and we were to wrap you up in a warm blanket? You could sit close to me and need not worry over the storm or the cold." Pulling a blanket tight around himself had often been a source of calm for James.

Ronan's ready agreement told her he too was comforted by it. In a moment's time they were settled, and she began teaching him "As I Walked through London City." As she had hoped, the complexity of counting backward using only every other number kept his mind occupied enough to lessen the impact of the storm. Each time they stumbled over a number, they would laugh too much to continue, and he would eagerly ask to begin again.

She did not know precisely how long they worked at the amusing song, but slowly his tension ebbed away and he grew more comfortable. Evangeline found her gaze returning again and again to James's image on the mantel. He and Ronan would likely have appreciated one another, though she knew James had not been particularly adept at making friends. She was not well-acquainted enough with Ronan to know if he had difficulties in that area. He had never made the attempt at school, and, though he did not object when John Crossley invited him to look at the sheep, he was never the one to suggest it nor did he seek out John's company.

Dermot stepped inside before they managed to master the song. He was soaked to his skin, yet stood rooted to the spot the moment his gaze fell on them. Shock filled every line of his face.

"The lad's sitting on your lap."

Evangeline nodded. "We have been learning a song."

"'Tis about numbers," Ronan added.

Dermot's eyes pulled wide. "He's talking to you now?"

"We have become good friends." Though she knew that would not appear true to most observers, Ronan's willingness to talk and sit with her and trust her was, for him, an act of real friendship.

Dermot said something in Irish, though with a tone of

amazement. "Go on with your song, then," he instructed. "I'll put supper on."

"You'll catch your death if you don't return home and change out of your sodden clothes," she warned.

"I'll hang the wettest of it up near the fire. The rest'll dry out as I work."

"You're certain?"

"You've worked a bit of a miracle here, Evangeline. I'll not interfere with that for all the dry clothes in the world."

A different kind of warmth filled her. She had devised a plan for bringing Yorkshire words to her students, had seen Ronan through a storm, and had built a bond with him in the process. Perhaps she was not such a failure after all.

CHAPTER TWENTY-ONE

Nothing could have prepared Dermot for the sight of Ronan curled up on Evangeline's lap. The position had seemed so natural, yet Ronan never let anyone but Dermot so close to him.

More confusing still was how his heart clenched when his thoughts turned to her. He'd grown undeniably fond of the confusing and at times frustrating colleen. She was thoughtful and kind, witty and determined—and from an entirely different world than he was.

Though she spoke little of her past, 'twas not difficult to discern her history. Her posture and demeanor and manner of speaking all testified of a higher birth than he could claim. Theirs was an unexpected friendship and would never be anything but. Some things could simply not be overlooked or overcome.

He reminded himself of that any time his traitorous heart thudded out its affection for her. His had been a humble upbringing, and he'd no education to speak of, but he was not so thick as to think he could change the ways of the world. Life had challenges enough without seeking out more.

His crew had made great progress on the row of back-to-back houses. Despite the fierce storm a week earlier, the foundation had held fast. The portion of the walls they had erected had taken a beating from the wind and pelting rain, yet had remained perfectly square.

He surveyed the men's work, impressed with what he saw. Even young Thomas Crossley, inexperienced as he was, had laid a tidy, straight row.

"You've done grand work here, lad." He leaned a touch closer, eyeing the newly laid bricks. "Well done."

"Thank thee." The response lacked the boy's typical enthusiasm.

"Have you something on your mind?"

Thomas's jaw worked against the tension in his face and posture. "Father fears t' sheep are growing ill. Looks to be scrapie."

"I don't know a thing about that, I'm afraid."

"Scrapie is a disease, terrible and swift." Thomas slid his trowel into the pocket of his heavy work apron. "It can't be treated or cured. It spreads through flocks, killin' most all t' sheep."

The Crossleys' livelihood depended on their flock. "What'll your family do?"

"We'll try to save enough sheep to get by." He sounded not the least bit confident in that possibility. "More likely, we'll not."

"Your family'll be ruined."

Thomas took up his jointer. "We nearly are now, as it is."

The bright and laughing lad had disappeared entirely, replaced by a careworn and burdened young man. Dermot had seen similar transformations far too often over the years. He was helpless to do anything about it. Even if this project led to the larger one he'd proposed to Mr. Barton, he'd never be a wealthy man able to lift a family out of ruin.

"'Tis right sorry I am." He meant it.

Dermot had few friends in Smeatley, but he counted George Crossley as one. They'd spoken on a number of occasions, and he was always sociable and welcoming. They were a good family who did not deserve the string of bad fortune they'd endured.

The vicar happened past a moment later. Dermot nodded his acknowledgment, assuming the vicar would continue on his path. Instead, Mr. Trewe veered toward the work site.

"Best not come much closer," Dermot warned, his voice raised to be heard over the sound of men and bricks and movement behind him. "'Tisn't safe if you're not familiar with the dangers and what to watch for."

Mr. Trewe stopped, then watched him expectantly.

Dermot closed the distance between them. Apparently, there was to be a conversation. "What is it I might be doing for you?"

"I have yet to see you for services on Sundays."

Ah, this ol' back-and-forth. "We still make the trek to Greenborough."

Mr. Trewe laughed as though Dermot had spoken in jest. "Why would you go all the way to Greenborough? Do you not care to worship with your neighbors?"

"I'd not mind it, but what you do in your church each week is not my idea of worship."

Mr. Trewe looked confused. "Are you Catholic? I know a great many in Ireland are."

"I am not."

The confusion on his face only grew. "Then what is your objection?"

"My preference is for a sermon meant to help, written with the needs of the congregation in mind, not one dictated by her high-and-mighty lordship with her own profit in mind."

"Neither of the Bartons *dictate* my sermons," the vicar insisted.

"And yet those sermons don't veer much from the chosen topic, now, do they?" He had heard his workers speak of the Sunday sermons many times. The entire town had noticed the pattern, the adherence to the subject of work and obedience. They all knew perfectly well where the requirement to focus on the godliness of labor had originated from, and it wasn't from on high.

"You do not think I care about the people I am here to serve?" Mr. Trewe's posture straightened to a dignified height. "Rather than only hearing their complaints about my sermons, you would do well to ask the Haighs or the Gardeners or the Palmers—or any number of other families in Smeatley—whether or not *they* think I care about them."

Dermot could not doubt Mr. Trewe's sincerity.

"I know I have little latitude regarding the subject of my weekly discourses. I know I am ridiculed for the grip the Bartons have on my words. If I veer from the topic, as you say, I will lose my position. My acquiescence seems a small price to pay for the ability to quietly assist those in need. My works are not seen by many, excepting those whom I am serving directly. That, to me, is the essence of who a vicar ought to be, one who serves out of love and not for praise."

"Do you never worry that the impression you give of being more loyal to the Bartons than you are to your congregation will prevent the people from turning to you in times of need or trusting you when you offer your help?"

Mr. Trewe's expression turned rueful. "In the words of the immortal William Shakespeare, 'Ay, there's the rub.'"

Much to Dermot's surprise, he felt a kinship for the man. "Life's never simple, is it?"

"Not ever." Mr. Trewe recollected himself and resumed his posture of confidence and his expression of benevolence. "If you ever decide that Greenborough is too far a distance, know that there's always a place for you here."

Dermot nodded, then watched as the vicar made his way up the street. Even for the seemingly unapproachable Mr. Trewe, life was a messy and difficult business. It seemed it was for everyone, particularly here.

That somber reflection remained with him throughout the day and was still weighing heavily on his mind as he climbed Greenamble Street toward the schoolhouse.

"McCormick," a voice called out from behind him.

He spun around to see Gaz Palmer hurrying up the hill toward him. He had been walking alongside a few other factory workers, no doubt on their way to fetch their children. The school had gained several new students of late, most of whom had a parent or two working at the mill.

"Palmer," Dermot said once the man had caught up to him. "Is factory time running slow today?"

"Aye." He took a moment to catch his breath, giving Dermot a chance to study him.

The man was gaunt, his features drawn and pulled, the lines in his face deeper than they'd been. His eyes were wide, not in anxiousness or surprise, but in clear worry. He did not look well at all.

"I know I likely ought not ask, but would tha consider hiring me back to t' crew? I'd be willing to fetch or haul. Tha need only name t' task."

Just as he opened his mouth to remind Palmer of the struggle he'd had with him on the crew before, Evangeline's words of reproach filled his mind. The man was suffering. His family was suffering. But could Dermot risk the success of the project when other families would suffer if it failed?

"I don't know that I could do that," Dermot said. "You caused me no end of trouble before."

"I know it. And I've no right to ask thee. But I can't abide t' factory any longer. I can't." Desperation filled the plea.

Dermot knew perfectly well that he ought not hire back a man who'd shown himself a poor worker, yet he found himself saying, "I'll think on it."

The first inkling of hope entered Palmer's eyes, small and weak but unmistakable. "Tha are a good man."

"I made no promises," he reminded him.

A quick, almost frantic nod. "I know it. I'm grateful that tha're thinking on it."

Dermot stayed back as Palmer continued up the street. The other factory parents passed him, similar looks of weariness on their faces. They were, perhaps, not so desperate as Palmer, but they were careworn. The mill meant reliable work and an income they could depend upon, but it came at a price.

Life in this part of the world always exacted its toll.

The last of Evangeline's students, except for Ronan, had been collected. The mill, it seemed, was running slow today. More students had begun coming to school, which made her happy, but it also made her days longer and more exhausting.

She stepped into her living quarters and offered a quick

apology to Mrs. Crossley. "We had no end of interruptions this afternoon."

Ronan was engrossed in his wooden figurine, content as a bee in honey.

Evangeline sat at the table and took up her pen. "We left off with Mary stumbling upon the fairies' feast."

"I feel right bold," Mrs. Crossley said, "puttin' my words on paper like they was important."

"They are important," Evangeline insisted. "The children will appreciate them, and the story is a good one. I haven't heard it before, and I am eager to discover what happens next."

Mrs. Crossley laughed. "Any of t' students can tell thee how t' story ends."

"And now they will be able to *read* how the story ends."

Mrs. Crossley's eyes danced. "It's exciting, i'n'it? We're making a book."

This had been their second afternoon spent on the endeavor, and Evangeline grew evermore convinced of the wisdom of this approach. Not only was she compiling materials that would assist the children in their studies, she was also making a friend. Mrs. Crossley was many years her senior and their lives had been drastically different, yet they had found the beginnings of a kinship between them.

"Once we've finished this book, we should find other things to do together," Mrs. Crossley said. "I've enjoyed this."

"You might teach me to sew a dress," Evangeline said with a laugh. "This one is worn nearly to threads." She had only the one dress that could be donned without help, so she wore it every day, taking time at night now and then to scrub it clean and hang it to dry.

"That'd be grand." Indeed, she seemed almost eager. Perhaps

she truly was enjoying their interactions as much as Evangeline was.

"Between you and Mr. McCormick, I might manage to survive here."

"Mr. McCormick?"

"He is teaching me to cook, though I have found he is fond of cabbage."

They both laughed, something they did often when together. It was a blessing having a friend to cheer her.

"I should nip on home," Mrs. Crossley said. "Us family'll be right clemmed."

Clemmed means hungry. Evangeline had learned that word quickly from her students.

"Of course. Whenever you have the time again, please come back, and not simply on account of the book. I enjoy your company."

"An' I enjoy thine."

She pulled open the door only to find Dermot standing on the front step, apparently lost in thought.

"Good evening." Evangeline's greeting caught his attention.

He doffed his hat. "I've come for Ronan."

"I assumed as much."

Mrs. Crossley slipped past them both, but did not get far before Dermot stopped her with a question.

"How is the flock faring?" he asked.

She took a heavy breath. "Poorly. We're choosing to be hopeful."

"Send word with Thomas if there's anything I can do," he said.

She nodded and slipped into the darkening evening.

"Is something the matter with their sheep?" Evangeline had not heard a word about it from Mrs. Crossley.

Dermot nodded as he stepped inside. "Thomas says 'tis a disease of some kind, fatal for the sheep and catching."

"Oh, heavens."

"Are you ready, then, lad?"

Dermot was clearly not in a talkative mood. Had something happened, or was he simply tired? A closer look revealed worry in the lines of his face and dark smudges beneath his eyes.

"You look as though you've had a difficult day."

"I've much on m' mind, is all. Far too much."

"You aren't the only one who is a 'dab hand at listening,'" she said.

He eyed her, hesitant. She set a hand on his arm, the light touch sending a wave of warmth through her. She hadn't been expecting that. A friendly connection, perhaps. Even a moment's empathy. But this was something different, something more.

"You'd truly listen to me complaining?" he asked.

"I truly would."

A hint of a smile touched his eyes, and the warmth inside her burned ever brighter.

"I'll hold you to that, Evangeline, someday when I'm not too exhausted for conversation."

Though she felt a twinge of disappointment, it was tempered by the realization that he felt enough of a kinship with her to welcome future confidences. It seemed Mrs. Crossley was not her only friend in Smeatley.

Dermot set his hand atop hers, giving it a quick squeeze. Her heart thudded against her ribs. Heat rushed to her face.

He stepped past her, granting her time to cool her cheeks

and settle her thoughts. Had she not just silently declared them friends? This was no way for her to react to a friend.

Dermot wandered to the mantel. "Is this your family?"

"It is, yes." She crossed to the picture and took it from its spot. "This is my mother and father. My brother George. This is my brother James." She glanced at Ronan, then back at Dermot. "James was so much like Ronan. And this dear girl, here, is my sister, Lucy."

"The one in Leeds."

He hadn't forgotten. She appreciated that. It meant someone in this vast and lonely world was listening to her.

She carefully returned the photograph to the mantel. As she always did when near enough, she brushed her fingers along Father's pipe, George's statuette, and James's book.

"I thought about what you said about being bold enough to tell my grandfather directly about my work here." She faced him. "I have not written to him, but I am increasingly tempted to do so."

"Are you beginning to see how wise I am after all?"

She recognized his dry humor. A few weeks earlier, she would have mistaken it for arrogance.

"I could tell him the good I'm doing and the progress I am seeing. I could tell him not only about the school and the children but also of the other skills I am learning. I can cook, mostly potatoes and cabbage, but I *can* cook."

Dermot's mouth twitched at one corner, causing a small flip in her heart. "Potatoes and cabbage are the most heavenly of foods, lass. Don't dismiss 'em."

"I've become quite good at cleaning and mending and laundering. I've been prudent with the money I earn from my teaching. There is no reason for him not to allow me to be reunited with my sister." She took a fortifying breath. The action she had decided to take went against the behavior she had been taught to embrace all her life. But choosing decorous responses to her current situation had accomplished little, especially where her sister was concerned. "I plan to write to my grandfather and ask him to allow Lucy to come here and live with me."

Far from the look of approval and words of encouragement she had expected, Dermot seemed taken aback. "You wish to bring her here?"

"Yes." Even in the face of his surprise, her determination to follow through with her plan grew. "I wish her to be with me."

"In Smeatley?"

Why was the idea so shocking? "Yes, in Smeatley."

He shook his head, repeatedly, firmly, emphatically. "I'd advise against that, Evangeline. As miserable as you say she is at that school of hers, she'll be more so coming here."

Confusion rendered her mute. He had said only a few days earlier that she ought to fight to keep her family together, that she needed to be bold and confront her grandfather about his refusal to let her be with her sister.

"You have Ronan with you," she reminded him.

"'Tisn't at all the same, lass."

"It is the same. She is my family, and she is alone. I won't resign her to that fate."

He took up Ronan's hand. "You'll resign her to this one, then."

"What do you mean by that?"

He turned toward the door. "I'm only saying, before you drag her here, make fully certain she wouldn't be better off where she's at."

On that confusing and frustrating declaration, he simply left. No words of farewell, no smile of friendship.

Make fully certain she wouldn't be better off where she is. It was precisely the argument her aunt had made, and her grandfather in a roundabout way. They all thought Lucy was better cared for by indifferent and unkind teachers at a school far away from the person who loved her more than anyone else in the world.

When everyone else had doubted her, herself included, Dermot hadn't dismissed her out of hand. He'd helped her when she'd needed it. He'd listened to her concerns and had expressed confidence in her abilities and encouraged her to champion her own cause. He had been a source of reassurance.

Now even he doubted her.

CHAPTER TWENTY-TWO

Though the schoolroom was nearly full on Friday, Evangeline noted that not one of the Crossley children was in attendance. She worried for them even as she attempted to guide her ever-growing class through myriad different levels of learning.

Greenborough school has more students and only one teacher. You can manage this. You must manage this.

Hugo sat on the end of a bench, ignoring her most of the day. She hadn't the time nor the energy to argue with him. Ronan, thank the heavens, had kept to his table and found means of occupying himself. Yet, she'd felt guilty leaving him to himself for so long. She usually made certain to slip over to his corner and give him new things to do or comment on his progress, but she could not find the time that day.

Perhaps she really was as incapable as her aunt reported her to be. Perhaps she truly was as unready for Lucy's arrival as Dermot had implied she was. The possibility of dictating her own future was a new one. She simply did not know what to think or what to hope for.

On Saturday morning, she pulled on her thick outer coat and made the now-familiar journey toward the moor. Her mind would not be at ease until she knew the Crossleys were well.

Cresting the first hill at the edge of town, she could see a plume of smoke in the direction of the Crossleys' home. She sped up her pace, concern gripping her. The night had been a wet one, and the dirt beneath her feet had turned to mud, yet she moved as quickly as she could manage. The air held a pungent smell, a rancid smokiness that only grew thicker the closer she came.

Heavens, what if their home was on fire? What if they were hurt or worse?

In the next moment, however, she spotted a large bonfire in the fields, smoke rising from it.

Her headlong rush slowed. It was not the family's home. She let herself breathe again, hoping her heart rate would slow. She looked away from the fire and over the surrounding land. Sheep dotted the field, but not in the way she expected. The entire flock was lying on their sides, unmoving. She looked over the expanse, trying to make sense of what she was seeing.

At one end of the field, two men lifted a sheep from the grass and tossed it onto the back of a cart where several other sheep lay.

She lifted her skirts and made her way swiftly down the side of the hill, out toward the field. "Hello, there," she called out.

Thomas Crossley looked up at her as she approached. Next to him stood Dermot, which she had not been expecting at all.

She reached the stone wall and spoke to them over it. "What's happened?"

Thomas set his hands on his hips and looked out over the field. "Scrapie."

Evangeline didn't know what that meant. She looked to Dermot.

"They'd an illness, you'll remember. It spread through the flock like a flood."

"Are they all lost?" She dreaded the answer.

"Everything's lost," Thomas said. He nudged a nearby sheep with the toe of his boot. "Everything."

Dermot moved to Thomas's side and set a supportive arm around his shoulders. He spoke to him as they surveyed the gruesome scene. Evangeline couldn't make out what they said, but hoped he offered the distraught young man more reassurance than he'd offered her only a few days earlier.

Voices floated on the breeze, pulling Evangeline's gaze toward the hill behind her. Up the road a bit stood John Crossley and Ronan. She climbed upward, joining them at the top of the slope. John—cheerful, buoyant John—was in tears.

Evangeline held her arms out to him, and he stepped into her embrace. The poor boy wept against her, his shoulders shaking with emotion. He and Ronan loved the sheep, spending long hours watching them graze. How heartbreaking they must have found the sight of the flock so tragically still.

Ronan watched, not the fields, but the fires—for there was more than one—in the distance. She followed his gaze.

Mr. Crossley stood by the flames, his back to the hill. After a moment, Thomas and Dermot arrived with their cart of carcasses. The three men hefted one after another onto the fire. The putridness of the smoke, uncomfortable until that moment, turned instantly nauseating. It was not merely the smell of fire, but of death.

She stood there for long moments, keeping John close and watching Ronan for any sign of distress. After a time, they sat, not caring that the wild grass was wet and the day cold. Not a word passed among them, yet she knew the boys did not wish to return to the Crossley home nor walk over the moors away from the sight of such loss.

"Please sit close, Ronan," she whispered. "You need the warmth."

He didn't object, though he did not come near enough to touch. Again and again the scene played out: the arrival of the cart, the thud of one casualty after another, the rush of flames, and a scattering of ash. Between arrivals, Mr. Crossley built a new fire while the others consumed their burdens. How many would be smoldering by sundown?

John rested his head against her shoulder. The position set his cap askew, hiding most of his face. She didn't know if he watched the horrors below.

After a time, Ronan slid up beside her and leaned against her other side. She laid her arm over his, hoping to give a little warmth. The cold seeped up from the ground through every layer she was wearing. The boys, who had been outdoors longer than she, must have been positively frozen.

"Perhaps we should go down to the house," she suggested. "You will be far warmer, and far drier."

She felt John shake his head, though he didn't speak beyond a sniffle. Ronan kept still and quiet.

"Then, let us sing a song. That will keep our spirits up on this dismal day." She rubbed John's arm. "Do you have any songs you like to sing? Ronan knows many, though they are unfamiliar to me. I know quite a few, but you two might not recognize them."

Neither answered for a long, drawn-out moment. On the hill below, the burning continued, the smell of the fire and the trail of ash growing, even as the number of white dots dwindled.

"I will sing one that Ronan enjoys. The chorus is all numbers, sung backward and skipping every other one. It can grow rather silly as the brain and the tongue trip over each other." She did not wait for either boy to voice their approval or disapproval of her song choice. This was distraction, not democracy.

By the time she sang the chorus for the third time, Ronan was mouthing the words along with her, and John had sat more upright, though he had not joined in. When she tripped over the numbers, both boys silently laughed. That small response did her heart a world of good.

After a time, Mr. Crossley came climbing up the hill toward them, his clothes covered in mud and soot, his expression as grim as she'd ever seen it. He dipped his head to her but offered not a word nor a smile.

"Come along, John. We're bahn to home for awhile. Tha'll be right starved out here."

John stood obediently. Though his father's expression remained bleak, he held out a hand in a gesture of unmistakable kindness. "I thank thee, Miss Blake, for sitting with t' lad. This has been a difficult day."

She nodded, struggling for something wise to say in reply. All she could manage was, "I wish there was more I could do."

Her heart broke as she watched them return to the path below, join Thomas, and slowly drag themselves toward home. This family, who had shown her kindness and welcome, who had supported her efforts at educating the children, who had ever been optimistic and cheerful, gave every appearance of being broken.

The sheep were their livelihood. If they had lost all their flock, or even nearly all, what in heaven's name were they to do? Was their fate to be the same as poor Mr. Palmer, whose soul was being crushed inside the confines of the mill?

From beside her, Ronan's small voice began to sing. The

words were not familiar and they were not English, yet they were oddly comforting.

"Trasna na dtonnta, dul siar, dul siar,

Slán leis an uaigneas 'is slán leis an gcian;"

Dermot joined in, coming up the hill toward them and pulling off his mud-encrusted work gloves.

"Geal é mo chroí, agus geal í an ghrian,

Geal bheith ag filleadh go hÉirinn!"

Evangeline fully expected Dermot to follow Mr. Crossley's lead and simply tell Ronan they were leaving. At the very least, she thought he might sit down beside the boy. Instead, he sat on the grass beside *her.*

He was warm, a buffer against the brutal wind off the moor. She silently willed him to move a touch closer, yet part of her hoped he didn't. His presence proved unexpectedly unnerving. Every inch of her felt tense and on edge, an unidentifiable wish mixed with equal parts uncertainty.

The two McCormicks continued their song, both looking out over the expanse, neither seeming the least bothered by the cold or the wet or her presence between them. Her gaze fixed on Dermot. There was worry in his eyes, yet he was calm and unshaken.

She took a deep breath only to be assaulted by the taste of rancid smoke and the reminder of all that had been lost. John's shaking frame. Mr. Crossley's deeply lined face and slumped shoulders. A humble home not far distant where a family was in crisis. Her own family home, so far away, so empty. Her sister, alone and miserable.

It proved too much. She had kept her chin up and her eyes dry for weeks, but she couldn't manage it any longer. She needed a moment of the strength she sensed in Dermot.

Just as John had leaned against her, and just as Ronan rested on her arm, Evangeline set her head on Dermot's shoulder. She closed her eyes, shutting out the sight of the flock, the blackened ash on the grass, and pushed back the tears threatening to fall.

Dermot shifted, his arm slipping behind her, supporting her as she grieved. She kept her arm around Ronan, offering him the same comfort.

Their song had ended, and they didn't take up another.

"'Tis a horrid sight, is it not?" Dermot said.

It was, indeed. "What will the Crossleys do now?"

"I've not the first idea, but I've a few suspicions." He moved a bit, rendering her position instantly more comfortable. "Losing their flock to scrapie is the reason the Haighs are working at the factory now."

Pain pulsed through her. "They cannot go there. They would be so miserable."

She felt him sigh deeply. "I don't know that they've a choice, lass. The moor giveth, and the moor taketh away."

She looked up at him. "But it is not fair."

"Life seldom is, especially here." He adjusted his position again, this time so he was looking at her and she at him, though it meant his arm fell away from her shoulders. "I know you were vexed with me for not supporting your idea of bringing your wee sister here to live with you, but this"—he motioned to the scene before them—"is the reason I . . ." The sentence dangled unfinished, his face pulling in thought. "I've spent this morning burning what remains of a family's dreams. This, Evangeline, is far too often what becomes of the fragile and delicate souls who come to this harsh and unforgiving land. Their hopes are dashed, reduced to ashes on the moor."

Her lungs ached with her next breath and not from the

smoke in the air. His words drove deep, ringing with a painful, undeniable truth. Yet what could she do? "Lucy is so unhappy where she is."

"I'm not suggesting she isn't," he said. "I'm simply hoping you'll consider that perhaps the harsh realities she'd find here are not such an improvement over the unhappiness she's experiencing where she is."

Evangeline did not care for either possibility. "I will not resign her to misery without attempting to alleviate her suffering."

Dermot slipped his hands around hers. "'Twas a fine thing you did today, Evangeline, comforting the lads as you did. I thank you for that."

Though being outside without her gloves would not only be cold but also horrifyingly improper, Evangeline found herself wishing she had left hers off. To have felt the warmth of his touch directly . . .

No sooner had she indulged the thought then Dermot released her hand. His expression turned stern, almost too stern, as if he assumed the air because he felt it proper and not because he truly felt it. He stood rather abruptly.

"Come along, then, Ronan," he said. "We're for home."

She watched them go, confused, relieved, exhausted, overwhelmed. He had held her hand. He'd spoken gently. On this horrible day of loss and sorrow, he'd offered her kindness and comfort and had acknowledged her efforts to help.

The irascible, unapproachable neighbor whom she'd first met upon arriving in this strange and difficult town had shown a side of himself that was, in a word, wondrous.

CHAPTER TWENTY-THREE

Dear Grandfather,

I thought you might appreciate hearing of my work here in Smeatley. When my students first began their schooling a few short weeks ago, not one of them could read or write, and they had no knowledge of mathematics. I am pleased to say they are making remarkable progress. Many are beginning to read. Nearly all know their alphabet and basic mathematics. My newest students are keeping pace as well.

Though the teacher's quarters were in abysmal condition when first I arrived, the space is now well-maintained, clean, and inviting. I have learned to keep house, work well within a budget, and have diligently expanded my repertoire of dishes I am able to cook.

Lucy will be quite content here, I am certain of it. I look forward to hearing from you regarding her expected arrival in Smeatley.

With all my love,
I am yours, etc.
Evangeline Blake

She had carefully worded the letter so as not to sound overly forward or give the impression that she thought her grandfather's judgment lacking, while still encouraging him to reevaluate his decision. Striking that balance had proven exhausting.

Evangeline posted the letter on Saturday. She doubted her judgment throughout the day on Sunday, but by that evening, as the church bells tolled, she had reconciled herself to accept the outcome, whatever it proved to be. Though, in her heart, she held on to the unshakable belief that if Lucy was to be unhappy regardless of her location, she would do better to be unhappy in Smeatley than in Leeds.

In the meantime, she had students depending on her; she would not fail them. She rose earlier than usual on Monday morning, determined to greet her students ready and eager and hopeful.

She had spent a portion of her first pay on a simple shirtwaist that buttoned in the front. With some effort, she had altered one of her dresses—one that fastened exclusively in the back—to a skirt. Combining her new blouse and her refashioned skirt, she at last had another suit of clothing to wear. Better still, her new clothing allowed for swift and easy dressing each morning. Fewer days began in a state of struggle and panic. That was a step forward.

The sun rose later than it had when she'd first arrived in Smeatley. Even those students who arrived later in the morning now did so in darkness. She would need to ask her uncle for a larger allowance of coal to warm the schoolroom as well as lanterns to light it.

She greeted each child by name, reviewing silently his or her particular challenges and progress. When Susannah Crossley reached the door, though, Evangeline could not prevent herself from saying, "You've returned."

"I've missed being at school," she answered. "I hope tha was not too upset that I were gone."

"I was not upset at all." She set her hand on the girl's arm, rubbing it gently. "I have been worried for you and your family. I am so grateful to have you and your brothers back—" Only Billy was with her. Evangeline tried to remain calm. "Where is John?"

Susannah's gaze dropped to her shoes, strain evident in her posture. "We've had troubles." The short, quiet reply held a world of hurt and worry.

"Is he ill or injured?"

A subtle head shake served as her answer.

"Is he helping at home?"

Another shake of the head. Susannah seemed upset by whatever she was not telling Evangeline. That only made her worry more. She turned to Billy.

"Where is your brother?"

Billy's brow strained. When he spoke at last, he did so quietly. "He's bahn to t' mill."

The mill. Evangeline's heart turned to lead. "Why—" She swallowed against the sudden dryness in her throat. "Why is John going to the mill?" How she hoped he was simply delivering something or running an errand.

Susannah squared her shoulders, her show of determination undermined by the heartbreak in her eyes. "We lost nearly all t' flock. Come spring, we'll not have enough ewes lambing. We'll not have enough for t' sheering or t' slaughter." Susannah's gaze turned pleading. "Thomas has his work. I'm learning to be a teacher. Billy is too little. John had to be t' one."

John was too little as well. Far, far too little. "How long will he have to work at the mill?"

"All day," Billy said.

That wasn't what she'd meant, but she let it go. "When will he be able to attend school again?"

The defeat returned to Susannah's posture. John, it seemed, would not be coming back.

Worry weighed heavy on Evangeline's heart.

She motioned the two Crossley children inside but remained in the doorway a minute longer herself. John had been making such progress. He was enthusiastic and a joy to have in the class each day. He cared about the other children. He worked so hard.

"None of this will keep them from the factory." Mr. Husthwayt's words, which she'd dismissed as unnecessarily cynical, were proving prophetic.

She moved to the front of the room, attempting to focus her thoughts. Looking over her students' faces, though, she could not bring herself to even speak. Were they all truly destined for a life in the factory? Even if they learned to read and write, even if they were taught mathematics and geography and any number of other things she longed to teach them, would it matter?

She had already lost John to the mill. How many others would follow?

"Good morning." Her customary greeting felt like a lie.

Her gaze traveled to the place on the front bench where John always sat. She breathed slowly through her nose, reminding herself that the class was watching and waiting. They would take their cues from her.

"We'll spend the first part of the morning as we always do before the remaining students arrive."

Susannah rose from her spot and crossed to where the new

students gathered for help and direction. The children went through the motions, moving with automatic steps to their groupings. A somber air hung over the room. Susannah's charges bent over their slates, practicing letters and writing. The other children huddled around the two primers Evangeline had received from the school board.

Billy sat with his group, but his eyes remained on the window. His eyelids sat heavy. His shoulders drooped. Susannah did not appear to be in any better state than her brother. Their family had lost so much.

Was John as tired, as beaten down? Had he been given a hazardous job at the factory? Was he safe? Scared?

None of this will save them. No matter what she did, they would all end up in the mill.

Dermot stepped inside on the heels of that thought, Ronan in tow. Evangeline's heart ached with relief at the sight of him, as if she'd been struggling for breath and air had arrived at last.

She crossed to the doorway, intent on telling him of her worries, wanting his thoughts and his views. A growing part of her also hoped he would take her hand again. That moment had repeated in her mind again and again, bringing new comfort and an undeniable delight.

Dermot motioned Ronan to his usual table, then turned his attention to her. "You seem troubled."

"John has gone to work at the mill." The words brought a fresh wave of pain.

Dermot's jaw dropped a fraction, and his eyes widened. "John Crossley?"

She nodded. "Susannah told me this morning."

"Their situation must be worse than I'd imagined." The observation was as much directed at himself as to her.

Worry clutched at her chest. "What if John is in danger or afraid? He ought to be here. He ought to be where he is cared about."

Dermot took her hand in his. "I know you're worried for him, but just now, your students need you. The Crossleys' situation is known to all the children, I'm certain of it. And they're worried. Life is terribly uncertain for the lot of them."

"Like ashes on the moor." She quietly repeated the comparison he'd used on Saturday. She'd thought of it often since then.

His concerned expression eased her burden. The kindness in his dark eyes and the gentleness of his touch captured her thoughts for a long, tender moment.

"Look after your children," he said. "I'll talk with Thomas and see what I can learn."

His hand dropped away slowly, though his gaze lingered.

Her heart pounded loudly in her ears. She managed to utter a "Thank you" though the two words emerged quiet and uncertain.

A smile tugged at his lips. "Was that a question?"

Heavens knew she had a great many questions. More every time she saw him, in fact.

"I will see you this evening," she said.

He nodded. "Chin up, lass. 'Twill all be well in the end."

She told herself as much many times as the morning went on. She was not truly certain he was right, but she was willing to hope.

After the children enjoyed a small, quick tea—she did her best to have slices of bread and butter for them, since very few brought food from home—they all sat on their benches. She made a habit of reading to them each afternoon from James's book of folktales, which she brought up to the schoolroom every morning. Today, however, she had something else in mind. The children needed a bit of cheer after the blow of John's departure.

"I have a special treat for you today," she said.

The few smiles she saw looked no more genuine than hers felt. It had been a difficult day all around.

"Mrs. Crossley has been helping me write out a story for you, one told in the language of Yorkshire." That gained her a bit more interest. "I hope you will be able to read it yourselves in time, but today I would like to read it to you, as much of it as I have written out thus far."

She and Mrs. Crossley had not finished their efforts. With all that had happened, it might be some time before they were able to continue working on the Yorkshire-language stories. But a single page or two was better than nothing at all.

"Of an August nooin—"

The children snickered at her attempts to pronounce "noon" in a Yorkshire manner. She smiled back at them and pressed on.

"—Mary were sittin' in t' garden, in t' front on her were t' orchard. T' leaves were spent ower—"

More laughter. More smiles.

"—wi' flahs."

Though they grinned more broadly, Evangeline could also see that they were confused. Her pronunciation, even with the words spelled the way she had heard them from Mrs. Crossley, was clearly not great.

"I am attempting to say 'flowers,'" she told them. She tried again. "Flahs."

Laughter filled the room, Evangeline's included. Even Hugo smiled, something he almost never did anymore and certainly not that day.

"The sooner all of you learn to read this, the better," she said. "My Yorkshire speaking is terrible."

"Don't us know it," Billy Crossley tossed back.

The room erupted in laughter again. Into this happy moment came the one person capable of dispelling it: Aunt Barton. She hadn't come alone. Uncle Barton stood beside her, and, next to him, was a man Evangeline did not recognize. The stranger wore somber colors and a look of pointed concern.

Evangeline nodded to the class and motioned for them to stand as she'd taught them to do when Aunt Barton visited. The show of respect had seemed to soften her view of them.

"Miss Blake." Aunt Barton always managed to make her name sound vaguely insulting.

Evangeline offered the obligatory curtsey, encompassing all three of the visitors in the gesture. "Welcome."

Uncle Barton spoke for them. "Miss Blake, this is Mr. Garvey, the school inspector."

CHAPTER TWENTY-FOUR

Evangeline had never heard of a school inspector, and she didn't like the sound of it. She allowed not the slightest hint of uncertainty or worry to touch her expression. "A pleasure to meet you, Mr. Garvey." She executed a curtsey worthy of her governess's approval.

He gave a brief dip of his head before passing her and stepping further into the classroom. He looked over the students, though whether his impression was favorable or not, Evangeline could not say.

"Students," she said. "This is Mr. Garvey."

"Good afternoon, Mr. Garvey," they said in near unison.

He made a sound of ponderous surprise. "Good afternoon, pupils." With those three words, Mr. Garvey showed himself to not be a Yorkshire man. That would make the children more wary.

Mr. Garvey turned to Uncle Barton. "I am ready to begin my evaluation. Are there particular areas of concern?"

Aunt Barton answered. "I have observed the school many

times, Mr. Garvey. Though progress has been made, the children are struggling with their reading. And I have not yet observed any attempts at mathematics."

Concern and embarrassment crossed the children's faces. Only with effort did Evangeline maintain her aura of calm lady-like civility. How dare these three come in and belittle her students?

"Please be seated, children," she said, giving them her most reassuring smile.

"First," Mr. Garvey said, "I will examine your school log."

Evangeline hadn't the first idea what that was. "You will forgive me, but I was not told anything about a school log."

"Have you not kept a daily record?" He sounded both shocked and annoyed.

"I did not know I was supposed to."

Mr. Garvey shook his head and muttered, "I warned them about untrained teachers."

"I will begin keeping a record if that is required."

"It is decidedly required." His chest puffed out and his tiny chin jutted. "A log of attendance, visitors, and subjects taught each day."

"Yes, sir."

"I would like to hear someone read," Mr. Garvey said. "Choose one of your students, Miss Blake."

He would be impressed by what he heard; she felt certain he would be.

"Susannah. Would you be willing to read for Mr. Garvey?"

She held Susannah's gaze for a long moment, hoping to convey that she had faith in her but also that she would not be disappointed if the girl's efforts were less than perfect.

Susannah rose, her chin high and her posture firm. "What'd tha like us to read, Miss Blake?"

Evangeline pulled a well-worn sheet of paper from her pile on the lectern and handed it to Susannah. She knew the sentences were familiar to her; they had spent much of the previous week studying the words. She stepped back, giving Mr. Garvey ample space to hear and be impressed.

"No," Aunt Barton said. "Something new."

Susannah paled. Evangeline likely did as well. The students weren't as comfortable with their reading as she would have liked. Unfamiliar text would present a challenge.

"If you truly wish to measure their progress, would it not be best to hear what they have learned to read?" Evangeline pressed.

"The ability to read is more than merely repeating memorized words," Aunt Barton countered. She took up James's book from where it rested near the window. "The child can read something from this."

"Mrs. Barton, that is unrealistic. These children have only been learning for a few weeks—"

"Two months," her aunt interjected.

"Six weeks." Evangeline couldn't help the correction, though she knew she would likely be scolded for it. "These children cannot possibly be expected to read a book as advanced as this one."

The look she received ought to have left her quaking. A few short months earlier, it would have done precisely that. But she would not permit her students to be trampled on simply because her aunt held an inexplicable grudge against her.

"Miss Blake is correct." Uncle Barton came to her defense. "We will learn nothing of the children's progress if we ask the impossible of them."

Aunt Barton set the book down with a thud. "Of course you would defend *her*," she muttered.

The cryptic declaration remained unexplained, but it filled her uncle's face with weariness. The couple neither looked at nor spoke to one another.

"The girl may read the paper you have chosen," Mr. Garvey said to Evangeline.

She nodded for Susannah to proceed.

With only the slightest wobble in her voice, Susannah read aloud, "'T' cat is fat. It has a hat. T' cat sat on t' mat."

Mr. Garvey spoke before Susannah could read the next set of sentences. "The paper, please." He held out his hand.

Susannah glanced at Evangeline, who nodded.

Mr. Garvey looked over the sheet, his thick brows knit.

"The sentences are very simple," Evangeline acknowledged. "We have been working on the letter *a*, and the most basic words seemed best."

"I have no objection to the words," Mr. Garvey said. He gave the paper back to Susannah. "This girl simply was not saying what was written."

Evangeline had heard enough students practicing those exact words to know quite well that Susannah had, in fact, read each one perfectly. "On the contrary, sir."

Mr. Garvey turned to face her fully. "You are charged with more than teaching them to piece together letters, Miss Blake. You are required to improve their minds."

"I believe I am doing precisely that." She refused to look at her aunt, knowing the disapproval that would be there. Contradicting a man with authority over her actions was seen as undesirable behavior. "When they first began attending, not one of these students could identify a letter, let alone knew what sound it made. They can do that now. Many of them can even read, though perhaps not at the advanced level Mrs. Barton hoped for. They also can do basic mathematics, though we have focused mostly on reading, as I feel that will be the most difficult for them to master."

Mr. Garvey offered only the slightest acknowledgment. "While I am pleased to hear that, my concern lies with more than the acquisition of a list of skills. This girl may well have read every word on that paper, but I could hardly understand her."

Was that all? She smiled. "The people of Yorkshire, you must remember, have their own unique way of speaking. Your ears will grow accustomed to it in time."

"One of the express purposes of this nation's educational system is to teach children to speak properly," Mr. Garvey said. "You are charged with that every bit as much as with teaching them academic skills."

"You wish me to change the way they speak?" Her shock rendered the question a bit broken.

"There's nowt wrong with t' way we speak," Hugo loudly declared.

Evangeline looked over her shoulder at him. "Please, Hugo. Not now."

"But there i'n't." He was on his feet, every inch of him exuding defiance. It was the first bit of life she'd seen in him all day. "Happen we speak different from thee in t' south. Don't mean we talk wrong."

"I agree," she said. "There is something lovely in the Yorkshire voice. I did not appreciate it when I first arrived, but the sound has become beautiful to me."

"Miss Blake," Mr. Garvey said. "Language usage is a directive for *all* schools in the kingdom. This one is no exception."

"I will not take away their language," she said.

Mr. Garvey looked anything but pleased. "I wish to speak with you. Alone." He walked to the door. If the school inspector insisted on speaking to her, she was required to listen.

He stopped at the bottom of the stairs but did not step outside. She descended at a dignified pace, not the least encouraged by his tense posture and firmly set jaw. His fingers tapped against his leg with ever-increasing speed.

Upon reaching the landing below, Evangeline summoned her calmest voice. "What is it you wished to discuss, sir?"

"You seem to be under the impression that yours is a position of some privilege."

"Not at all, sir."

He either didn't hear her words or chose to ignore them. "I have been appointed Her Majesty's Inspector for all the schools in this area. You are not here to put forth your own ideas of education and schooling. You are not here to bandy about your opinions on what these children ought to be taught. You are here to do as you are told." His words snapped and echoed off the narrow walls of the entryway, reverberating against her with growing force. "I have been trained in the intricacies of education. I have authority from the Committee of Council on Education. You, Miss Blake, are simply one of hundreds of replaceable cogs in this machine."

Though she attempted to hide the pain his words inflicted, she suspected her effort was not wholly successful. His description stabbed and twisted inside her, adding an edge of agony to her uncertainties.

"Fortunately for you, this visit was not a formal inspection. I will return at a later time to undertake that assessment, and I will expect to hear your students reading, doing their mathematics, and speaking properly." He emphasized the last two words. "If I discover otherwise, you will find yourself unemployed." His unforgiving eyes bored into her. "Am I understood?"

In a voice quieter than she would have liked but as loud as she could manage, she answered, "You are asking me to trade their language, their identity, and their dignity for my economic peace of mind."

"I would advise you to choose wisely." He left on that declaration.

Aunt Barton made her way downstairs, her air one of triumph. She slowed as she approached Evangeline. In a pitying voice, one hardly above a whisper, she said, "You are not the beloved daughter of a fine house any longer. It is time to stop acting as though you are."

She swept past as regally as a queen. The effect was fitting; Evangeline felt rather like a peasant.

Uncle Barton reached her side. Evangeline hazarded a glance, not daring to hope that she would see even a hint of the same approval she thought she had spied earlier. He looked at her with confusion and concern, though without any earnestness.

"I—" Whatever else he meant to say was cut off by Aunt Barton calling to him.

He looked at Evangeline for one brief moment, then set his hat atop his head and slipped out.

She remained alone, the words spinning in her mind. *"Do as you are told. You are not the beloved daughter of a fine house any longer."*

For weeks she had managed to push aside her loneliness and the ever-present feeling of being adrift. All her doubts, all her uncertainties rose to the surface. She had no formal training as a teacher. She had never even been to a school herself.

But I know these children. I know the lives they live. Surely that gave her some degree of expertise. Surely.

A small cough from above pulled her attention upward. At the top of the stairs, several of the students stood, watching, their faces pulled with worry. The sight proved both encouraging and heartbreaking. In the few short weeks she had been their teacher, these little ones had found a permanent place in her heart. What if she truly was providing them with a second-rate education, one marred by her own inexperience? What if she was forced to leave?

"Is he gone?" Cecilia Haigh spoke before anyone else. Quiet, bashful little Cecilia. And her words, so rare and precious, were filled with distress.

"Yes. He is gone." She moved swiftly up the stairs, offering quick embraces and reassuring words.

The children retook their seats, but their eyes retained the wariness that had entered them when Mr. Garvey and the Bartons had arrived.

"I am sorry for the interruption," she said. "We were having such a lovely afternoon. And I am sorry that our visitors did not recognize how well you all are doing and how much you are learning. I could not possibly be more proud of each of you."

She heard the break of emotion in her voice and quickly pulled herself together. Her students needed steadiness. She was determined to give them that in full measure.

Mr. Garvey had been quite clear on what he expected of her. She knew her directive to do as she was told, and she further knew that not doing so would likely cost her this job and her time with these children.

She eventually had to make a choice.

Her income or their language. Her job or their identity.

Her future or theirs.

CHAPTER TWENTY-FIVE

Dermot reached the overgrown hedge of the schoolhouse chilled to the bone. Rain had fallen off and on all day, leaving the air painfully frigid. 'Twas miserable weather to be working in.

His discussion with Thomas Crossley had been sobering. The family'd been on the verge of disaster for some time. The factory was not paying as much for wool as it once had, preferring the lower cost of buying from larger providers than from local farmers. This area of the country had been chosen specifically for woolen mills on account of the abundance of sheep. Yet, the mills were driving to ruin those who'd raised the sheep for generations and forcing them into the factories. The seeming inevitability of it was heart-wrenching.

The path leading across the school yard was riddled with puddles, some too large for hopping across.

None of the factory children sat on the interior stairs as they often did when waiting for their parents on rainy days. Dermot was later than he'd realized.

He hung his hat and coat on the hooks near Evangeline's door. He gave a quick knock, then pushed the door open. That had become their agreed-upon entrance. How he'd come to be on such familiar footing with her, he couldn't rightly say.

Evangeline stood near the fireplace, her gaze on the flames, her back turned almost entirely to him. Ronan sat in the rocking chair nearby.

"Good evening to you both." Dermot summoned something of a sunny tone, not wishing to burden them with his own heavy thoughts.

He received a small, indiscernible reply from Evangeline, one not accompanied by even a brief glance in his direction. What had happened?

He moved to Ronan's chair and patted him on the head, a gesture usually permitted without objection, but also without comment. This time, however, Ronan spoke.

"A man came and shouted at Miss Blake."

What was this? "Someone shouted at you?" he asked her.

She made a small gesture of dismissal, still not looking at him.

"Who was it?"

"It doesn't matter." She turned away, clearly intent on moving further from him.

"She's been crying," Ronan said.

"Evangeline." Dermot followed her to the window. "If someone's made you cry, it most certainly does matter."

She brushed back a strand of her hair, her eyes fixed on the darkness outside. "Did you know there are school inspectors whose job it is to go about deciding if teachers are worthy of their posts?"

"And this inspector was here today?"

She nodded.

"And he shouted at you?"

What began as a shrug, turned into a waving of her hands as if batting away the experience. Then she clutched her hands together and pressed them to her lips. Her next breath trembled with emotion.

The unnamed man had indeed made her cry. "You tell me who the inspector is, lass, and I'll introduce him to the Irish way of expressing disapproval."

His bluster died when a sob escaped her.

"You know how I hate when you cry." He ran his hand along her arm, unsure how to offer comfort.

She brushed a tear away. "*I* hate when I cry. I've managed not to for weeks and weeks, then one discouraging conversation, and I'm falling to bits."

Dermot slid his hand around hers and held it gently. "What did this inspector say to you?"

"Nothing that wasn't true," she said quietly. "That I don't know how to be a teacher. That I have no chance of keeping my position if he disapproves of me. That I am merely stumbling about doing a poor job."

"And he shouted all of this?"

She shook her head. "He didn't shout, but he spoke forcefully."

"Within hearing of your students?"

She turned away, though she did not pull her hand free of his. "I told myself I would not take his criticisms so much to heart, but what if I lose my position?"

"Did he give you any indication of what it is he expected you to be doing differently?"

She nodded solemnly.

"And is it something you're able to do?"

"I could do it, yes, but I'm not—" Whatever she meant to say died unspoken.

He lowered his head to look her fully in the face. Worry and exhaustion filled the lines around her eyes and mouth. She had nearly reached the end of her endurance for the day.

"Troubles only multiply when one is worn to a thread," he said gently. "Come sit by the fire. I'll fix us something to eat."

He made to guide her back to the warmth of the hearth, but she held her ground. Hers wasn't a posture of defiance or protest, but rather one of determination.

"What did you learn from Thomas Crossley?" she asked.

Saints knew the last thing she needed was further bad news. "That can wait 'til after you've eaten, don't you think?"

She shook her head. "I've worried for John all day. Knowing would be far better than continuing to wonder."

He could appreciate that. "I'll tell you all I've learned *while* you warm yourself. Can we strike that deal, then?"

The smallest hint of a smile touched her lips. "You have quite a knack for negotiation, Dermot McCormick."

He raised her hand to his lips and pressed a light kiss there, something he instantly discovered he enjoyed doing far more than he likely ought. This woman, who hailed from a place far above his station, who at first had seemed such a sour sort of person, who likely looked down on him and his situation in life, had somehow found for herself a tender and welcome place in his affections.

He motioned her toward the bench near the fireplace. She went without protest or hesitation. Either she was more chilled than she'd admitted or she did not feel the same urge to remain near him as he felt toward her.

He distracted himself from that unwelcome thought by

kneeling in front of Ronan. "Other than the shouting man, did you have a grand day?"

"John was gone." With that, Ronan's attention returned fully to his slate.

Dermot knew him well enough to realize there'd be no further conversation. He returned instead to his discussion with Evangeline.

"Thomas told me that the family is in a bad way, more so than any of us suspected." He dug through her produce basket as he spoke. "Come spring, they need enough money to replace some of the flock, but 'twill be a difficult thing to manage, being poor as they are."

Evangeline unfolded a light shawl hung over the back of the bench and wrapped it around her shoulders. "Which is why John has gone to the mill."

"It is." He dropped a handful of potatoes and an onion on the table. "'Tis also the reason Mrs. Crossley's gone to work there herself."

"Mrs. Crossley?" She spun to face him.

"Aye. Mr. Crossley's finding what work he can, odd jobs here and there. Susannah's been permitted to keep at her schooling on account of their hope that she'll one day find herself a teaching position."

Slowly, painstakingly, Evangeline lowered herself onto the bench. Her eyes had pulled wide and her mouth hung the tiniest bit open. She clutched her shawl closed with one hand, the other hiding somewhere within its folds.

Dermot whistled to capture Ronan's attention. The boy looked up at him. "Come tear up some herbs, lad," he instructed. He glanced at Evangeline.

"I know you've heard awful things about the mill, and I'll not argue that it's a joyous place for a person to work, but Mr. Farr required it to be built to the latest standards of safety and with a great many windows for allowing in sunlight. The equipment is new and well-maintained." He took up a knife and began cutting the vegetables. "I'd not wish to work there m'self, nor would I want Ronan to while away his days within its walls. Yet, I don't believe John is in truly dire straits, especially with his mother there. She'll look out for him."

"He was doing so well in school." She tucked herself into the corner of the bench, leaning against its low back. "And he loved being out on the pastures. I can't bear to think of him working at a job I know he will hate and missing the opportunity to learn."

"The Crossleys have a plan for being free of the factory by spring. I've known them from almost the moment I moved to Smeatley, and they're a family that accomplishes what they put their mind to."

She seemed comforted by the thought. "And until John returns, Susannah can teach him, just as she's done with—Oh, heavens. Johanna." Quick as anything, her fear returned. "What'll become of the little one? She's too ill to be left alone all day, but her mother is at the mill."

"I've not an answer for that, I'm afraid. But I've full confidence the Crossleys have sorted it out."

He dropped the cut-up vegetables in the pot hanging by the fire, then poured in water from the pitcher. Ronan dropped in the herbs he'd been meticulously tearing. The lad had become more of a help with meals in the time they'd spent teaching Evangeline how to prepare them. The arrangement had not been comfortable at first, but they'd all benefited from it in the end. And Dermot had come to value their evenings together. He'd not truly understood before just how lonely he'd been.

"What I do not fully understand is why, of all the children in Smeatley, so few actually come to school and those who do come can stop when they choose to. Does not the new law require children to be educated?"

Dermot had learned all he could about the Education Act, wanting to make certain Ronan couldn't be turned away. "The towns are required to provide education to all of the children. The children and their families, however, aren't required to accept it."

"But it would do them good," she countered.

"You can't force good things on people," he said. "You can only hope they'll see the good and want it for themselves."

"I suspect you are trying to gently tell me that I am worrying too much."

He sat on the bench beside her. "I'm only saying that you love your students and that you've come to care about the people of Smeatley. Neither is a bad thing."

She sat up straighter, facing him. "When I first arrived you hardly had a good word for the people of this town."

"I know it. They'd given me precious little reason to think well of them."

"Is that not one of the greatest tests of a person's character?" She spoke as if asking herself the question. "Caring about the welfare of people who do not seem to deserve it."

"I suppose it is." He let his shoulders droop from the exhaustion he'd been fighting all day. "Life'd be far easier if we weren't required to be decent."

She laughed as he'd hoped she would. "I, for one, am grateful that you are a vast deal more than decent."

He leaned back and folded his hands on his belly. "You didn't know me before you came here. I was gruff and unfriendly and meaner than a bull with his tail on fire."

"Oh, no, you were like that when I arrived."

He looked at her, then burst out laughing at the mischievous amusement lighting her features. "I'm glad you've come to Smeatley. You're a joy, you know that?"

"Those are kind words coming from a man who is meaner than a smoldering bull."

His first urge was to laugh again, but the truth of her words struck him with unexpected force. The sentiment *was* odd for him. He didn't consider himself an unkind person, simply an aloof one. He'd never been inclined toward sentimentality or any real closeness with other people. He'd been apprenticed at such a young age and that loneliness, coupled with the gruff personality of his master, had taught him to keep a distance from people. 'Twas simply easier that way. Evangeline had been a thorn in his side early on—an annoyance. How, then, was she pulling this tenderness from him?

"Dermot?" Her voice recaptured his attention. "I didn't mean to offend you. I was only teasing."

He recovered to a degree. "I know you were." He rose abruptly and crossed to the pot, giving it a stir and keeping her out of his line of sight. Quite suddenly, he was upended and uncertain.

A man didn't discover he'd changed so wholly without being tossed about by the realization.

"I do seem to have offended you," she said. "I am sorry."

He shook his head without looking back. "I'm not offended, only hungry."

She didn't speak, and he didn't look at her, but the sudden tension in the room was unmistakable. His discomfort was apparent, and she didn't know what to make of it. He wasn't entirely sure himself.

"I have a bit of bread left from the children's tea," she said. "I'll fetch it. We can have some with our supper."

He stirred the pot again. "A good idea."

He heard the rustle of her skirts as she moved swiftly from the room. He kept his gaze on the flames even as he yearned to follow her from the room, to catch her before she climbed the stairs to the schoolroom and keep her with him. The longing was strong and unshakable.

Ronan sat in his chair, making his wooden horse run along the arms of the rocker.

"Do you like Miss Blake?" Dermot asked the lad.

"I do." Ronan didn't look up from his figurine, but his answer was sincere.

"And do you like having her with us?"

"I do."

Dermot's tension lessened. "I like her too, and I like having her with us." He liked it quite a lot.

"We should keep her." With that declaration, Ronan turned in his seat and focused fully on whatever game he was playing.

Dermot turned his back to the fire and paced away. Evangeline had extended her friendship to him—to *them*. That was a far cry from what he was feeling for her. Somewhere between his gruffness upon first meeting her and this very moment, he'd grown incredibly fond of her, more than fond if he were being honest, though he was not yet ready to put a word to it.

Did she share any of those same tender feelings? Did she think of him as anything other than a neighbor and a help and a friend?

He passed the doorway just as she stepped across the threshold. His pacing stopped. His eyes refused to leave her.

She stepped further inside, pulling her shawl more tightly

around her shoulders. "I did not find the bread. Sometimes one of the children takes it. I cannot begrudge them the bite to eat. So many of them are terribly hungry." She moved directly to Ronan and tucked the quilt more snug around his lap, managing the thing without disrupting his play. She brushed her hand lightly over his hair before moving to the fire and giving the soup a quick stir.

Dermot took a single step closer to her, then another. Uncertainty added an edge of strain to his movements, to his breaths, to the very beatings of his heart. He'd not any idea of her feelings for him, but he no longer had any doubts about his attachment to her.

She straightened the book on the mantelpiece, then ran her fingers the length of the pipe beside it. She patted the head of the little shepherd statue. Her attention lingered longest on the photograph of her family. Dermot had studied it before, seeing in the unmoving faces a story of love and loss and a glimpse into Evangeline's past. She had come from ease and privilege to this place of want and sorrow. What remained unknown was who and where she would be in the years to come.

We should keep her. If only it were so easy as that.

She turned. Their eyes met. Did she see the questions he grappled with? Did she know how unsure he was of so many things? He had always been one for decisiveness and moving toward a goal without hesitation. Why, then, was he suddenly overcome with doubt?

"Dermot?" She stepped closer. "Are you unwell?"

He shook his head.

"Are you certain? You've been out all day in horrible weather." She stepped even closer and lightly pressed her hand to his forehead. "I would not be the least surprised if your entire crew has pneumonia." Her fingers skimmed his cheek. "You do not feel overly warm."

He slipped his hand along hers, threading their fingers. She bent her fingers around his, holding onto him just as he did to her. He kept their entwined hands at his cheek, simply breathing.

He kissed her fingers one after the other. He lingered longer with each touch of his lips. It was foolish of him, inviting the heartache he felt certain would come of this, but there was no helping it. His heart spoke far louder than his mind.

A knock sounded at the door. They pulled away on the instant, both watching the other, wide-eyed and silent. Surprise registered in every inch of her face, though whether 'twas a pleasant surprise he couldn't rightly say.

Another knock shattered the tension in the room.

"I—I should answer that." She spoke breathlessly, her voice heavy with uncertainty.

He nodded. "That you should."

She stepped away from him and to the door.

Dermot moved immediately to the window, taking advantage of the draft as well as the privacy to settle his own thoughts. He'd not intended to share such an intimate moment with her. He didn't regret it; he simply didn't know what to make of it. She'd not objected when he'd kissed her hand and held it so tenderly, yet the shock on her face afterward cast that into question.

Keep your head, man. All's not lost.

Ronan, thank heavens, appeared to be oblivious to it all. They'd simply go about things as before until he knew with greater certainty what Evangeline was feeling.

She returned shortly, a look of distraction on her face.

"Who was at the door?" he asked, proud of his steady voice and unaffected demeanor.

"One of the Bartons' servants. Mr. Barton wished to inform me that Mr. Farr will be coming at week's end to make an inspection of his mill, your building project, and my school." She sounded worried, a sentiment he could appreciate. Mr. Farr was the most powerful man in Smeatley. He controlled nearly everything in this town, including both of their livelihoods. "What if he is as unimpressed with my efforts as Mr. Garvey was?"

"He will not catch you unawares," Dermot reminded her. "Be ready for him when he comes. Have your students prepared to show him all they've learned."

She nodded vaguely, making a small circuit of the room. "I can do that. I can prepare the proof he is looking for. I can. I *must*. This is my one chance to show him all I have accomplished. If I can convince him, he might speak to Mr. Garvey, which would help secure my position. Otherwise, I'll have no hope of being with my sister again."

And if Mr. Farr was not overly impressed with the housing project, Dermot had no chance of being permitted to continue with it. He would be forced to move at the very time when remaining in Smeatley was of paramount importance to him. Ronan was thriving and learning. He, himself, had opportunities for precisely the kind of work he wished to do. And Evangeline was here, their future unknown but showing promise.

"You do all you can to be ready to prove your worth to him," he said. He knew all too well how difficult it was for someone of the working class to impress those of Mr. Farr's social status. "I'll do the same. We'll both succeed, I'm certain of it."

She squared her shoulders, a posture he'd often seen her assume. Though she too often hid her fire, Evangeline Blake was a woman of determination, and he loved her all the more for it.

CHAPTER TWENTY-SIX

he next few days passed in a blur. Evangeline spent the school hours practicing with her students as they read aloud and solved mathematical questions. She wanted them to feel confident when they were asked to display their knowledge for her grandfather. She had heard them and their parents speak of Mr. Farr in hushed whispers, filled with both awe and apprehension.

What would they think if they knew she was his granddaughter? She hoped it would not change their view of her, but she feared it would. She had rankled at first when Aunt Barton had demanded that she keep her connection to them a secret, but seeing the change in her students at the idea of Mr. Farr's arrival made clear the wisdom of that condition.

Her evenings were spent cleaning her living quarters, the schoolroom, the entryway. She scrubbed every surface until her back ached and her fingers refused to straighten. The gardener at Hillside House allowed her the use of a large pair of sharp trimmers. Though her work was inexpert, she managed to cut back the overgrown hedge, ensuring that passage in and out of the schoolyard would not involve an altercation with the shrubbery.

She dropped into her bed the night before her grandfather's visit utterly exhausted yet found that sleep eluded her. She had not seen her grandfather in several years; he'd not even come for the funerals. What would she say to him? Was she permitted to acknowledge their relationship in private, or was she to maintain the formalities at all times? And suppose he was entirely unimpressed with her progress and her work?

What if he agreed with Mr. Garvey's assessment regarding the children's language and demanded her compliance? Grandfather had the ability to prevent her from being with Lucy. The thought pierced her with such pain that she feared the ache it left behind would never leave her.

Her sister did not write to her often, and the letters she did send were brief and unhappy. Life was difficult in Smeatley; Evangeline would not deny that. But life was difficult everywhere. No one ought to be required to face it alone.

Grandfather was cruel to keep them apart. If only she knew the right words to make him see that. He was not a man of sentiment. Rational arguments would go much further. Unfortunately, effective debating was not a topic generally covered in the education the upper classes deemed appropriate for girls. She was intelligent, and her position was sound. She was simply unsure of her ability to present that position in a way that would ring true in the mind of a man of business.

She had heard Dermot make just such an argument when proposing his building project to Uncle Barton. He knew the proper means of doing so. Surely he would help her.

Of course, that help required that he visit her, something he'd not done since the very personal, very tender moment they'd shared. Her pulse picked up pace at the thought of how he'd held her hand so gently and kissed her fingers. It was seared in her memory, hovering in a close corner of her mind, sliding into her consciousness during periods of quiet reflection and momentary distraction. Dermot, who had seemed so unapproachable all those weeks ago, who had pushed her so firmly aside and treated her to such a cold welcome when she'd first arrived, had kept her near him and had looked at her with such warmth.

Was that how love generally happened: by surprise? She didn't know when her feelings for him had turned so tender, only that they had, and she could not imagine ever being indifferent to him again. His pointed absence these past days had riddled those new and sensitive feelings with doubt. He was not the sort of person to treat a woman's affections with insincerity; she knew that much of him. She simply could not say whether or not those sincere feelings ran as deeply as hers did.

Time would tell, but the waiting was difficult. The weight of it remained as the morning dawned, as her children arrived, and as they waited on tenterhooks for the arrival of judgment. Dermot came earlier than usual, Ronan, clearly bathed and dressed in his best clothes, sleepily following along beside him.

With the children extra alert, little could pass between them. They stood at an inarguably proper distance. He smiled a touch awkwardly. She felt certain she blushed.

"Will you be coming by at the usual time this evening to take Ronan home?"

"I will be, and I'll wish to hear how Mr. Farr's visit went." He hadn't forgotten. Of course he hadn't. Dermot McCormick, for all his bluster and standoffishness, was thoughtful in a way few others were.

"I know he will be visiting your building site today," she said. "I hope you will tell me how that goes."

"I will." He dipped his head and made as if to leave, but turned back. Stepping a bit closer and lowering his voice, he said, "Keep your chin up, my dear. You've every right to be proud of what you've accomplished here."

Those words remained with her throughout the morning as the children continued their practicing. She listened with new ears to their reading and their mathematics and heard confidence in their voices. They had learned and grown and blossomed. Though much of that credit belonged to the children for the hard work they had put in, she felt a measure of satisfaction at the role she had played in their accomplishments.

Grandfather would see that. She knew he would. She hoped he would.

Fate exercised its typical cruelty. Grandfather arrived, her aunt with him, just as the children were to adjourn for their daily tea. Hunger combined with weariness and anxiety would not make the coming task any easier.

Still, she held herself with dignity and grace. "Welcome, Mr. Farr," she greeted, offering a curtsey.

He made a noise of acknowledgment and plodded into the room. The children rose respectfully and waited, still and quiet, for further instruction.

"Children," she said, "please greet Mr. Farr, the head of the school board."

"Good afternoon, Mr. Farr."

Grandfather gave them the same indiscernible response he'd given her. She hoped he would be more articulate moving forward. How was she to know if he approved of her work if he never said anything?

"Be seated, children."

They obeyed, but sat in near terror, watching the new arrival. Mr. Garvey had been greeted with wary uncertainty. Mr. Farr was feared.

Looking at her grandfather, she could well remember responding that same way to him when she was as young as her students and he would come to visit. His thick brows, now snowy white, jutted at angry angles over his piercing eyes. His mouth was forever pulled in stern lines. Age had not stooped him in the least. His was a broad and intimidating bearing. Had she not, on occasion, seen moments of kindness between him and her mother, she might have still been afraid of him. He was not overly friendly, nor did she deceive herself into believing his was a soft heart. She simply knew he was not the cold man he too often appeared to be.

"The students are eager to show you what they have learned," Evangeline said. "They wish to read for you and answer some mathematical questions."

Her aunt crossed to Grandfather's side and, in a conspiratorial voice loud enough for all to hear, explained, "Mr. Garvey objected to this performance style of reporting. He, of course, preferred that the students demonstrate abilities rather than memorization."

Aunt Barton would not ruin this for them all. Too much depended upon it.

"Mrs. Barton," Evangeline said. "Today's visit is for the benefit of the head of the school board, not for you. Kindly step aside and allow me to do my job and Mr. Farr to do his."

"Did you hear that?" Aunt Barton asked her father in feigned tones of shock.

"I did, and it happens I agree with her."

Her aunt's pretended shock turned genuine. "Well."

Grandfather took little notice. "I want to hear what the students have learned."

This was the moment. Nervousness tiptoed over her.

"Who would like to go first?" she asked the children, praying someone would volunteer.

Hugo stood. "I will."

Hugo. Defiant, difficult Hugo. He looked directly at the man all the children were afraid of and didn't flinch. Bless the dear boy.

"This is Hugo Palmer. He is one of our older students and has been attending for nearly seven weeks."

Grandfather nodded. "I want to hear him read."

Evangeline gave Hugo the paper the more advanced students had been studying. Hugo took it and, without hesitation or the slightest show of nervousness, read the simple but pleasant poem. She watched her grandfather out of the corner of her eye. His expression didn't change in the least.

Hugo finished and waited, holding himself with palpable pride.

"Can you write?" Grandfather asked.

"Aye. Us spelling is not grand, but Miss Blake is teaching we to write better."

Aunt Barton scoffed from the corner. "Miss Blake certainly hasn't taught you to *speak* better."

Evangeline pushed down the hurt of that declaration and focused, instead, on Hugo, intent on intervening should he grow combative at the insult. But the boy held himself with dignity.

"I'm not interested in how he speaks," Grandfather said. "I want to know what he's learned."

Relief replaced some of Evangeline's worries. Her grandfather was brusque, but he was showing himself to be fair as well. There was no guarantee he would not eventually require her to teach them to speak differently, but for now he was focused on what they had learned.

"Can you do any deciphering?" he asked Hugo.

"Aye."

Grandfather stepped closer to the boy. "If I were to order ten pounds of wool and needed to divide them evenly between two mills, how much wool would each mill receive?"

That was a more complicated question than she'd prepared the students to answer. "We have not delved into division yet," she told her grandfather.

"I doubt Mr. Fair has come to hear your excuses," Aunt Barton interjected.

"Enough, Berta," Grandfather said. "Have you an answer, boy?"

"Five pound to each mill, sir."

Evangeline clasped her hands together and let her smile blossom.

"Well done, Hugo Palmer." Grandfather looked at Evangeline. "I'd like to hear more."

"This is Susannah Crossley. She wishes to one day be a teacher herself."

Grandfather nodded his approval. "This world needs young people with ambition." To Evangeline, he said, "Has the girl done any teaching?"

"Yes. She helps instruct the younger students."

Aunt Barton sneered again. "What, then, are *you* being paid to do?"

"Berta." Grandfather's tone had only turned more stern.

Susannah kept her composure, though she showed some signs of strain. Evangeline moved to stand beside the girl, hoping her presence would offer some strength. "Perhaps Mr. Farr would like to see you work with the little ones."

"I would." Grandfather stood in front of the class and watched, still showing no signs of pleasure.

Susannah made a wonderful showing, guiding the youngest children through their letters and numbers. He asked questions of several other students. He listened as they read, looked over the words they wrote on their slates. No matter Grandfather's impression—though she felt nearly certain it was positive—Evangeline was inordinately proud of them all.

The school hours ended, and Grandfather was still there. The children rushed off, even those awaiting the return of their parents from the mill. She could hear them outside, running and laughing and letting out the energy they'd built up during a day of being stuck indoors.

Evangeline straightened the classroom, gathering slates and papers, sliding the benches back into place. Grandfather stood at the windows overlooking the back garden, not the front where the children played. He had not told her what he thought of her teaching or the children's progress. Aunt Barton had not offered her thoughts either, though the flash in her eyes told its own story.

"You are welcome to stay up here as long as you'd like," Evangeline told them both. "I need to go downstairs and prepare my evening meal."

Grandfather kept his gaze on the window. "You mentioned in your letter that you've learned to cook."

"I have. And clean and sew. I wash my own clothes. I trim the hedges. I look after thirty children every day. I go to market for my food. I manage my finances." Deciding she had pushed her luck enough, she finished by saying, "I will be downstairs."

Only when she reached the landing below did she begin to

breathe again. She pressed her open palm to her racing heart. The students had done well. She had kept her composure, more or less. All she could do now was wait.

Cecilia Haigh slipped in through the front door, watching her uncertainly.

"Is something the matter, sweetie?"

Her voice as quiet as ever, she asked, "Will Mr. Farr let thee still be t' teacher?"

Evangeline hunched down in front of her. She took the girl's hands in hers. "I believe he will. You all did so wonderfully today."

Cecilia's gaze dropped. "I were too scared to read for 'im. I'm sorry."

Evangeline hugged her. "Do not be sorry, Cecilia. I know how well you read, and I am so pleased with you."

Oh, how Evangeline hoped her words weren't overly confident, that Grandfather truly would allow her to continue being their teacher.

Cecilia pulled back and, with a quick smile, ran outside. She was still quiet, but she'd made friends with the other children.

Evangeline stood as Grandfather began his decent from the schoolroom.

"The children seem to like you," he said.

"The feeling is mutual."

He studied her. No doubt he was attempting to decide what he thought of her and her work. She had grown quite weary of being constantly evaluated, but if continued judgment meant she could have Lucy in Smeatley with her and continue teaching her students, she would endure it for the remainder of her grandfather's visit.

"I do need to begin my meal preparations," she reminded him. "And one of my students remains here until suppertime, so I need to look after him. His father, actually, is overseeing the building of the mill workers' housing."

"McCormick?" Grandfather rocked back and forth on his heels. "He's doing good work. Manages his crews with a firm hand. They all respect him despite his origins."

Despite his origins. How often did people hold that against him? Being Irish was a liability in England. As was being a woman at the mercy of her relatives' decisions about her future.

"Once McCormick claims his child, come by your aunt and uncle's home for supper this evening," he said.

"Are you certain they will permit it?"

Grandfather pulled his coat from the hook on the wall near the exterior door. "I am your grandfather. If I wish for you to join us for a meal, no one will deny me that request."

At the top of the stairs, Aunt Barton watched her. Though she had been the recipient of many of her aunt's cold scowls, the one she received in that moment was utterly frigid. Her presence at dinner that evening might not be denied, but she felt certain she would not be the least bit welcome.

CHAPTER TWENTY-SEVEN

ermot couldn't say just when the change had occurred, but lately when he arrived at the schoolhouse, the sight filled him with the oddest sense of relief. He'd a feeling of coming home, despite not living there, despite having no family residing within its walls. He'd have assumed the response came from knowing Ronan waited inside, but he'd been fetching the lad from the schoolhouse for weeks and weeks and yet this feeling was a new one.

Love did odd things to a man. He'd at last admitted to himself the true state of his heart.

He hung his hat and coat on the hook near Evangeline's door just as he always did. This evening, though, he paused to smooth out his hair and make himself as presentable as a fellow could wearing work clothes covered with the results of a day spent laboring. Had Evangeline ever seen him look anything but raggedy? He was always in his working clothes or, like last week out on the moor, in clothes just as worse for the wear.

Still, she seemed fond of him. That was encouraging.

He gave a quick rap on the door then pushed it open.

"Dermot, you're here." She crossed directly to him.

"I am," he answered, watching her for signs of happiness or disappointment. What he saw was something far closer to panic. "What has you so on edge, my dear?"

She held up a small oval pendant on a dainty chain. "I want to wear this necklace. My father gave it to me, but I can't manage the latch. I don't usually struggle with it, but I'm nervous and that's making me clumsy and—" She stopped abruptly, folding her fingers around her necklace. "I just need you to tell me that everything will be fine. Even if you don't fully believe, I just need to hear you say it."

The poor woman truly was in a panic.

He took her face gently in his hands. "Everything'll be grand, Evangeline. Grand altogether."

She met his gaze. "And if it all falls to pieces?"

"We'll put it back together again."

She took what sounded like a fortifying breath. "Grand altogether," she repeated. "I believe I shall adopt that as my rallying cry."

He dropped his hands to her shoulders, then slid them down her arms, watching her for signs of further distress. Though she appeared overwhelmed and concerned, there was a calmness in her demeanor that was reassuring.

He took her hands in his. She offered a tremulous but determined smile. He leaned forward and pressed a light kiss to her forehead. His lungs seized on the instant, and his pulse began racing.

How fond he had grown of the scent of flowers, and how quickly he was growing enamored of the warmth of her when she was near.

"I wish I could have been here during your inspection today," he said. "I suspect you could have used a friendly face."

She sighed. "I was terribly nervous, though I'm embarrassed to admit it."

"But you faced it. That's reason to feel proud."

She stepped back. 'Twas tempting to reach for her again, but she'd moved all the way to the window. She pulled the jewelry around her neck, fumbling with the clasp in the back.

"Are you needing help with that?" he offered.

She shook her head. "I'll manage it."

Ronan sat in his usual seat, content with his wooden horse and dog. He hadn't even looked up when Dermot had arrived. 'Twas a wonderfully odd thing for his lad to be so at ease in another person's home.

"How did the school inspection go?" Dermot asked.

She was still working at her necklace clasp. "I cannot say with certainty, but I do believe Mr. Farr was not displeased. Mrs. Barton clearly was, but her opinion is not nearly of as much importance."

"You're not intimidated by her, then?"

"Certainly not."

Dermot couldn't help but grin at the thought of how many of his men were thoroughly daunted by "her high-and-mighty lordship," yet Evangeline, whose well-being depended so heavily on the largesse of the Bartons, was no longer cowed by them. "There's the fiery Evangeline I've come to know."

Evangeline shook her head as if she thought he was teasing. She secured her necklace. She straightened the pendant, then turned to face him. "I understand you had something of an inspection today as well."

"I did at that, though I can't say what Mr. Farr's impression was of the work."

She smiled at him. He rather adored that smile. "I can tell you what he thought."

"Can you, now?"

A teasing glint entered her eyes. "Would you like to know what he said?"

He'd not have guessed when they'd first met that she'd be one for playful banter. Truth be told, he'd not known that about himself before Evangeline had arrived in his life. "I'd not object to it, though it'd depend on how much you're meaning to charge me for that bit of information."

"Are you saying that I could make my fortune on this?"

"Well, I'd have to pay you in coddle."

Her eyes pulled wide. "Cuddle?"

He laughed long and hard. "Good heavens, woman." His attempt at controlling his mirth only led to a deeper fit of laughter. "Coddle. Not cuddle. It's a stew from Dublin."

She pressed her hands over her mouth, color splotching her cheeks. He likely should've stopped laughing then, but saints above, the particular nature of the misunderstanding coupled with her look of shock was simply too much.

"Stop it." Her eyes danced, a sure sign she was not truly humiliated by the error. "It was an honest mistake."

"What was that you said? A *hopeful* mistake?"

She nudged him with her shoulder as she passed. "Hopeful on whose part, Dermot?"

Oh, on his part, to be sure. He'd have enjoyed a bit of cuddling with Evangeline, but that was getting a far sight ahead of things. He knew his feelings but not hers. Slow and steady was the safer course.

"Is it for a special reason you've put on your father's necklace?" He'd not known her to wear jewelry in all the months she'd been in Smeatley. In fact, a closer look showed she'd also done something different with her hair.

"I've been asked to have dinner at Hillside House." She made the statement as if being invited to dine with the wealthiest and most influential people in town was nothing out of the ordinary.

"Dinner with the Bartons? Mr. Farr will be there, I'm assuming."

She nodded. "He extended the invitation."

"You're not quaking in your boots at the prospect, I see. Most would be."

"It seems I missed my calling." Evangeline flourished her hands. "I should have been an actress." Then she dropped her smile and her posture slumped. "I am not looking forward to this evening. Mrs. Barton will most certainly spend the evening speaking ill of me in every way she can manage. Mr. Barton will do nothing to contradict her. And Mr. Farr will hear every word. I will spend the evening either allowing the disparagement of my character, because contradicting them would be unladylike, or defending myself in an impolite show of defiance. So much hangs in the balance: my continued presence here, the possibility of having Lucy with me again, the children's education. What if I choose the wrong approach? What if I only make things worse?"

He took her hand once more, something he was quite fond of doing but which also seemed to give her some comfort. "'Tis a difficult thing being in the position we are, is it not? So much depending on others, having so little power over our own lives."

"It is difficult, yes."

He kissed her hand. "We're rather alike, you and I, struggling to make our way in a world where we don't belong, where we have no one."

A degree of sadness entered her expression. "Do you really feel so terribly alone?"

There was something pleading, something deeper in what she was asking. The question beneath her words was not lost on him. "I've not felt as alone these past weeks."

"Neither have I," she said softly.

They stood a moment, neither one looking away, neither one stepping away. He'd spoken the truth of the situation. He'd been on his own for a long time, depending only on himself, answering to no one but also receiving support from no one. He'd buoyed and cared for Ronan and believed he was cared about in return, but that was not the sort of companionship he'd been unknowingly searching for. Evangeline had come to Smeatley, with her vulnerabilities and determination and loneliness, and by a miracle, he, a poor Irishman in an isolated corner of England, had found a kindred soul.

"I do need to be going." She seemed to genuinely regret the idea of parting. "Mrs. Barton will be even more unpleasant if I am late."

There was wisdom in that, though he wished she could remain. "I'm wishing you a fine and happy meal with the Bartons and Mr. Farr. I truly hope they're pleasant to you and that Mr. Farr is as impressed as you deserve for him to be."

"I hope so too." Her gaze moved to Ronan. "You had best hop up. It's time to be on your way home."

Ronan slid from the chair, a figurine in each hand. He crossed to the door, not even slowing as he passed them.

"The lad's liable to leave without me," Dermot chuckled.

Evangeline set her hand in his. "Then we had better walk quickly."

An easy affection existed between them. She knew the difficult details of his life; he knew hers. They shared and they trusted.

He waited while she locked her door. Ronan sat on the front step. Only a few short weeks ago he'd have rushed straight home, not wanting to stop or change their routine in the least. Evangeline's home and the time she spent with him had become part of his life—of *their* life.

They walked toward the recently trimmed hedge. Ronan's coat hung open, but at least he had it on. Evangeline secured the buttons on her own, fumbling over the task.

"All will be grand, you'll see," he assured her.

She nodded. "Grand altogether."

"You do realize that is an incredibly Irish turn of phrase."

She tucked her hands into the pockets of her coat. "I believe I am English enough to endure an Irish expression or two."

"'Endure'? I believe you mean 'enjoy.'"

Evangeline laughed lightly. "Perhaps I should use a few Irish phrases tonight and see if that endears me to the Bartons."

"I wouldn't recommend it. Most in this country, especially those in a position of power and wealth, are a bit *too* English to endure the reminder of the existence of the Irish with our odd take on the language and our poverty and our unwillingness to be content with the hand they have dealt us."

She didn't say anything further, but simply walked quietly at his side as they crossed the street. He didn't regret speaking aloud the frustrations he'd long held with her countrymen. She wasn't like so many others. The two of them were more the same than different.

Upon reaching the other side of the street where their paths diverged, they paused.

"Have a good evening, Ronan." She offered him a small wave before looking up at Dermot. "Thank you for the encouragement. If the fates are at all kind, this evening will go well, and I'll be reunited with my sister again soon."

Throwing caution to the wind, he kissed her cheek. She blushed but offered no objection. Then she was walking away, leaving him standing there, watching her go. How had he grown so fond of her so quickly, he who'd always guarded himself against personal connections?

He waited until she turned off Greenamble and disappeared around the corner. If only he'd been invited to the meal as well, at least she'd have someone standing beside her. The Bartons and their ilk never did speak well of anyone not from their walk of life. Despite her origins, Evangeline's current circumstances placed her decidedly beneath the Bartons' rung on the social ladder. Mr. Farr seemed less concerned with those boundaries, but he could be a harsh man.

Ronan made a noise of impatience.

"My apologies, lad. I'm dragging m' feet tonight, aren't I?" He followed his boy up the steep hill. "You're to be especially good for Miss Blake next time you see her as she's likely to have a difficult evening tonight. The Bartons, as we know full well, aren't always welcoming."

"Mr. Farr told her they would be," Ronan said.

"Mr. Farr said the Bartons would be civil to her?"

Ronan nodded. "Because he's her grandfather."

Every muscle, every thought, every movement stopped in the wake of those four words. "Where did you hear that?"

"Mr. Farr said it to Miss Blake." Ronan wore the anxious

expression he always did when his expected routine was being disrupted.

"He said that?" Mr. Farr wouldn't lie about such a thing.

Ronan rocked in place, his eyes darting continuously toward the yellow door only a few feet away.

Dermot motioned the lad on ahead, following mindlessly. *He is her grandfather.* Evangeline was family to the most powerful man in all of Smeatley. That made her family to the Bartons as well, who wielded almost as much influence as Mr. Farr. How alike he'd thought they were. What an utter fool he was. She did not merely come from a place of relative ease; she hailed from greater privilege than he could even imagine.

In all her talk of regaining her sister's company, of her grandfather who made that decision, never once had she told him who her grandfather was. He'd told her of how Ronan had come to be in his life, something he'd not told another soul. He'd shared his thoughts and worries. He'd reached out to her in genuine, open affection. And she'd not told him even the most basic truths of her own life. There'd been more than ample opportunity to do so.

Why hadn't she? And what else was she not telling him?

CHAPTER TWENTY-EIGHT

Evangeline wished her family could have known Dermot. She felt certain they would have liked him and, she hoped, approved of her growing attachment to him. He was good-hearted the way Father had been. He was kind to those around him in the way Mother had been. And, as she'd discovered recently, he had a dry sense of humor not unlike George's. They would have adored him.

If only the few remaining members of her family adored *her*. She stood in the entrance hall at her aunt and uncle's home, alone, waiting for the butler to return. He had left her there saying he needed to ask the mistress of the house where she intended to "place" her. Never mind that she had come specifically for the family dinner to which she had been invited. Aunt Barton clearly meant to make certain Evangeline knew how unwelcome she was.

"Mrs. Barton has instructed that you be shown to the drawing room." The butler spoke from the bottom of the stairs, not having returned to her side as would be customary for a guest with any claim of importance. No matter. She had not come to impress the butler.

Evangeline crossed to him, her dignity tucked firmly around her. The butler motioned for her to step through the second set of doors. She did so with chin held high. She might have been about to put herself forward in a most unladylike fashion, but that did not mean she was not a lady at heart.

The drawing room was opulent. A chandelier, so heavy with crystals Evangeline half expected the ceiling to sag under its weight, hung over a lush carpet woven around the repeating motif of the letter *B*. An ornate screen sat before the tall window draped on either side with heavy burgundy velvet. An oil portrait of Aunt Barton, so large it appeared nearly life-size, hung in a place of prominence. Treasures of every imaginable shape, size, and color filled the nooks and crannies of the room.

She had seen some of the extravagance of her aunt and uncle's home during her brief visit many weeks earlier but found it even more overwhelming now. Perhaps her time spent in her own humble surroundings and among her students and their families had adjusted her view of what constituted plenty and what fell firmly into the realm of excess.

While she would not have objected to a closer claim on "plenty" within her small living quarters, she found that she did not truly feel the same sense of deprivation she had upon first arriving there. She had the necessities and a bit to spare, which was more than many families hereabout could claim.

"Ah. There you are." Aunt Barton's words took her by surprise. "We had nearly despaired of you arriving."

Evangeline had been so distracted by the room she had not taken note of who was standing in it.

The ormolu clock on the intricately carved mantel indicated she was nearly ten minutes ahead of the appointed time.

"I am not—" But she stopped. Her aunt would enjoy nothing more than to see Evangeline turn defensive and uncertain. Instead, she took a breath, regained her calm, and stood as an island in a storm.

"I seem to remember that you do not care for asparagus," Aunt Barton said.

"I did not when I was a small girl."

For the briefest moment, her aunt's eyes narrowed. Her lips pressed together. She recovered quickly. "I hope you are not so particular about your meals now."

"My culinary tastes have actually expanded since my arrival in Smeatley." Evangeline summoned a conversational tone, pretending that her aunt had spoken out of sincere concern rather than an attempt to speak ill of her. "I have developed a distinct fondness for cabbage and potatoes and a number of other vegetables. I can prepare them in dozens of ways."

Her grandfather spoke from somewhere behind her. "Cabbage?"

She turned to face him. "I have. A neighbor of mine has a son in school. I have helped the young boy with his schooling in exchange for cooking instructions. That neighbor cooks with a great deal of cabbage."

Grandfather eyed her with what she reasonably believed was approval. "Very resourceful of you to trade lessons."

"We do not want to delay our meal," Aunt Barton said, gesturing toward the door.

"We've a few minutes yet," Grandfather said. He looked toward the far corner. "What have been your impressions of the school?" he asked Uncle Barton.

Until that moment, Evangeline had not noticed her uncle sitting in the corner.

He glanced at her before addressing Grandfather. "I have not visited the school often. What I saw a few days ago, however, was reassuring."

"Reassuring?" Aunt Barton scoffed. "The school inspector left utterly vexed."

That brought Grandfather's pointed and expectant gaze back to Evangeline.

She pushed down a lump of apprehension in her throat. The school inspector had far more clout than she did, even with her own family. "The inspector was upset that I had not undertaken aspects of teaching that I had not been informed were required of me. He was further disappointed that I was not eager to undertake all of them."

Aunt Barton spoke an overly loud aside to Grandfather. "She has far too much of her father in her."

Her aunt usually insisted that *Mother's* influence on Evangeline was the most detrimental. However, Grandfather had not cared for her father and had not been shy about saying as much. There were few evaluations her aunt could make that would turn Grandfather's opinion more quickly.

"On the contrary," Uncle Barton said, "I believe her fiery determination is a trait inherited from her mother."

Evangeline could hardly have been more shocked. She had not, since arriving in Smeatley, heard a kind word of her family. She'd had almost no words at all from her uncle. But these words, these unlooked-for words, had been offered with a degree of fondness.

"Dinner," Aunt Barton snapped, crossing through the open

doorway without a backward glance or a moment's hesitation. A single step beyond the threshold, she added, "Now."

If Uncle Barton could see something of her mother in her and approved, Evangeline would most certainly call upon that resemblance. With a serene countenance, she addressed her grandfather. "Perhaps we had best follow her. There is little to be gained from provoking our hostess."

"True." Grandfather all but grunted the word. "She's a misery when she's on her dignity like this." He glance over at Uncle Barton. "You're likely to have a difficult night."

Uncle smiled with weary acceptance. "It will not be my first."

"I did warn you," Grandfather said.

"I know."

The odd conversation was not further explained. Grandfather offered Evangeline his arm and walked with her to the dining room, Uncle Barton following behind. The aura of unwelcome Evangeline had felt during her previous visit to the Bartons' home had increased. The tension, however, felt more complicated than her aunt's apparent dislike of her. It had expanded to include both her and her aunt and uncle and, in a smaller but just as real way, her grandfather.

They were seated and the meal began. Aunt Barton directed the servants with nothing more than a raised eyebrow or the tiniest movement of her head. Evangeline knew perfectly well what the servants thought of their mistress. Most of the staff came from local families. All of Smeatley knew of Aunt Barton's disapproval of their Yorkshire mannerisms and way of speaking.

When a servant Evangeline knew to be a cousin of Hugo's set a dish before her, she offered a genuine smile of gratitude. He did not return it—his training was clearly too extensive for that—but she felt certain he held himself with more confidence and fewer worried glances in Aunt Barton's direction.

The moment the servants left the dining room, excepting the butler who remained on hand should anything be required of the staff, Aunt Barton broke her frigid silence. "Your time among the people of this town seems to have undermined your memory of how a lady is to behave."

That was unfair. Evangeline had behaved with complete decorum.

"One does not grow overly familiar with the servants," her aunt censured.

"My education in proper behavior included a great deal about how a lady should treat everyone with respect, no matter their station. Acknowledging a servant who has performed his duties well is, in fact, a mark of gentility."

Aunt Barton buttered a roll with greater force than was necessary. "The look you gave him seemed more than mere acknowledgment of a job well done."

Evangeline did not bat an eye. "He is cousin to a student of mine, a student whose father works at the factory, actually." She looked to her uncle. "Mr. Palmer."

Uncle Barton wiped a bit of food from the edge of his mustache with his napkin. "I do not know all of the workers. The mill overseer interacts with them more than I do."

"He has only been working there for a few weeks. He had been part of Mr. McCormick's crew that worked on your home and wall."

"I might recognize him if I saw him," Uncle Barton said, "but I cannot recall him just now."

"McCormick's crew?" Grandfather's brow pulled low in

contemplation. "A good man, McCormick. Good head on his shoulders."

"And, apparently, a very friendly neighbor," Aunt Barton said a touch too innocently. "All the town knows he spends an inordinate amount of time with the schoolteacher."

That brought the gentlemen's eyes to Evangeline.

She maintained her ladylike bearing and folded her hands in her lap. Without a hint of shame or uncertainty, she said, "Mr. McCormick is the neighbor I spoke of earlier who has a son in the school. His son remains after the other children have left and I help him with his studies. When Mr. McCormick is finished with his work of the day, he fetches his son home. One evening a week, he remains long enough to teach me to prepare a meal. There is nothing untoward about our neighborly interactions."

Aunt Barton's features twisted in smug victory. "An unmarried young lady spending the evening alone with an unmarried man? And one of the working class? One who has, as far as anyone knows, never been married yet has a son?"

Heat rushed over Evangeline's face, not in embarrassment but anger. She would not reveal the personal information Dermot had shared with her about his and Ronan's connection, but neither would she allow these aspersions to go unanswered. "Mr. McCormick may not hail from exalted circles, but he has shown himself to be a man of impeccable propriety. I think I need not remind anyone in this family that one's birth does not determine one's worth."

Grandfather was a self-made man. His voice no longer held more than a hint of his lower-class origins. He had worked hard over the years to refine his speech and manners, finding that many with whom he did business were more receptive if he sounded more polished, yet he maintained his adherence to work as the mark of a man.

Before her aunt could say anything further, Evangeline turned the topic of conversation. A lady not acting in the role of hostess was not meant to force topics upon dinner guests. She did not care; she had come to make strides toward reclaiming her sister, and she would do just that.

Her governess would not have approved. Mother might not have either. But they had not prepared her for the situation in which she now found herself. Months of demure, serene obedience had accomplished nothing. She had to be firm; she could no longer simply do as she was told while her life and Lucy's were torn to pieces.

"I have not had a letter from Lucy in over a week," she said to her grandfather. "As her previous missives have been filled with expressions of unhappiness, I am concerned. How is she faring?"

"She is receiving a first-rate education." Grandfather popped a piece of boiled potato into his mouth.

"One thing I have learned these past months," Evangeline said, "is that a child who is experiencing misery in her life is unlikely to learn anything, no matter how expertly taught."

"What experience could you possibly have had these past months with 'expert' teaching?" Aunt Barton's tone of derision could not be mistaken.

Evangeline chose to ignore her. "When will I be able to see my sister? We have been apart ever since our family's funeral, though I have met every requirement given me to be permitted her company."

Grandfather's expression remained impassive. "I have not yet decided what to do about the matter of you and your sister."

"I can feed and clothe her, give her a clean and safe home,

and I can provide her with an education." Evangeline did not flinch though she could feel her aunt's glare. "I hope you will bear that in mind while weighing the possibilities."

Her aunt jumped into the discussion unbidden. "And also bear in mind that you would be sending Lucy to a home where an unmarried man spends a questionable amount of time."

Evangeline maintained her calm, though tension tightened her jaw. "I have already explained that situation, and its propriety has been established. Only a mind with a tendency to see the tawdry where there is none could possibly find reason to condemn me for it."

"The 'tawdry'?" The question might as well have had an exclamation point at the end. Fire filled her aunt's glare. "How dare you sit at my table and question the cleanliness of my thoughts."

Evangeline did not quiver nor cower from the anger thrown at her. "And how dare you invite me to be a guest in your home and then question my virtue. You have been nothing but unkind and dismissive from the moment you arrived in Petersmarch. While watching my family die, I was subjected to your cruelty again and again, as was Lucy. And now, here, in this place where I am making my new home, you continue to toss your unfounded judgments at my head and then blame me for them." She slid her napkin from her lap and set it on the table as she stood. "You are my mother's sister, and for her sake, I will not say all that is in my mind at the moment, but will rather offer my excuses and depart."

Evangeline turned to her uncle, who, along with Grandfather, had stood when she did as decorum dictated. "You have never been unkind since my arrival, and I thank you for that. I hope that the school board will make its own inspections moving forward rather than leave the undertaking to the tainted view of

Mrs. Barton, and that their evaluation will be done with fairness." She faced her grandfather. "I hope that you will come to visit me before you leave. My living quarters may not be as fine and richly furnished as this house, but you will find a civil welcome there and a hostess who will not mistreat you."

She stepped away from the table. Head held high, she walked out of the dining room with deliberate step, not adding any haste to her departure lest her leaving be seen as cowardice. She felt certain she gave every indication of being calm and in control; inside, however, she was anything but.

She had arrived at Hillside House prepared to defend her work and progress if need be. The unexpected need to defend her morals had left her drained, mentally and emotionally. By the time she climbed up Greenamble, her exhaustion had become physical as well.

Her feet took her not to her own home but directly to Dermot's familiar yellow door. She needed his reassurance and his unfailingly logical insights, his tender kindness. She needed . . . him.

Ronan might be asleep, so she knocked lightly, not wishing to wake him. There was no answer. Perhaps Dermot hadn't heard. She knocked again, a little louder. The moments dragged by. He didn't answer.

Evangeline set her open palm against the door, resting her forehead beside it. "Please, Dermot," she whispered. "I need you."

Standing there alone, facing his closed door, the tears she had been holding back began to fall. Her aunt's insults, her uncle's silence, her grandfather's utterly unfair behavior had hurt, but Dermot's unexpected absence fractured her composure.

All her life she'd clung to the safe familiarity of behaving as a lady, of doing as she was told. She no longer had that firm foundation to stand upon.

"You've fire enough for this," Dermot had told her. He saw strength in her when she struggled to see it in herself.

He had become an integral part of her life. She felt stronger with him nearby—braver, happier.

"I love him," she whispered in amazement to the closed door. "I love him."

CHAPTER TWENTY-NINE

Throughout the next day, Dermot struggled to wrap his mind around Evangeline's previously unknown station in life. Mr. Farr was her grandfather. Though he was a man of business and not truly of the most exalted station in English society, he was wealthy as Midas and far above Dermot's touch.

And she is his granddaughter. The time he'd spent thinking on how alike they were, how much they understood one another's struggles and circumstances, seemed rather ridiculous now. They were no more alike than the sun and moon. She was English upper crust, while he was the Irish crumbs.

What bothered him the most, though, was that she hadn't told him. After all the things they'd shared, she hadn't told him, though there'd been ample opportunity. As they'd spoken of the dinner party, she might have mentioned it. As he'd held her near, she could have told him. She might have even said something in passing as she'd walked down Greenamble on her way to the evening's engagement.

But she hadn't.

Did she not trust him? Did she not feel the same closeness he did?

When a visitor knocked at the door, he hesitated. It might well be her, though he wasn't at all certain he was ready to see her, not when he had so many questions. Still, he was no coward.

'Twasn't Evangeline who stood on the other side of the door, but Mr. Trewe, the vicar.

"Good afternoon to you," Dermot greeted. "Have you come to complain about m' church attendance?" He let the jest show in his words and received a light laugh in reply.

"Not at all," Mr. Trewe said. "I've come with a young boy who wishes to ask a favor but finds himself a bit nervous."

That was certainly unexpected. "What lad? And what favor?"

Mr. Trewe tugged Hugo Palmer into the doorway.

"This is Hugo," Mr. Trewe said. "His family has fallen on difficult times, and he is supposed to begin at the factory tomorrow. He—"

"Hold that thought a moment," Dermot said. He turned to Hugo. "I suspect I know what it is you're wanting to ask, lad, but I'll need to hear it from you."

"McCormick," Mr. Trewe objected immediately.

Dermot was unmoved. If young Hugo had indeed come to ask for a job, the boy had best demonstrate a bit of backbone. "I'm not trying to be unkind, I'm simply needing to know that he can speak for himself and stand firm on his own behalf. That's crucial if he's to survive on any kind of work crew."

Mr. Trewe nudged the boy forward. Hugo looked up at Dermot. Though there was nervousness in his eyes, he'd also a fair bit of fire as well.

"Us family is in need of brass," the lad said. "Father can't keep working at t' mill, so I'm to go instead.

"Your father's stopped working at the mill?" Dermot hadn't heard that bit of news.

"It's too great a misery for him," Hugo said.

"'Tis too great a misery for your da, so you're to go in his place?" Dermot frowned.

"I need to work so us family'll have money." Hugo had clearly accepted the necessity despite the unfairness of it. Poverty taught children cruel lessons. "I'd rather be outside, making things. I'd like to learn to lay bricks."

"You're young yet," Dermot said. "You ought to be in school."

Hugo scuffed the toe of his left shoe against the flagstone step. "Us can't bide it. Money's too short."

An all too common problem. "Tell me truthfully, now. Are you wanting to learn the bricklaying trade because you're fair dying to follow that path, or are you simply wanting a way out of the factory?"

The boy held himself proudly, a reassuring sign. "It'd not be my first choice. But my father were a bricklayer."

"I know it," Dermot said. "He worked for me."

"I know it," Hugo said.

"Why'd your da not come asking after work, then?"

The smallest touch of embarrassed color spread over Hugo's face, though he didn't flinch or slump or hang his head. "He did, sir. But tha've not taken him back. He says tha can't be blamed, as he weren't a good worker."

"Are you a good worker, Hugo?"

Mr. Trewe stepped into the conversation. "Let us not punish the children for the sins of their fathers."

"Are you preachin' at me, now?" Dermot found he could almost smile at the idea. "You've given up getting me to attend your sermons, so you mean to bring them to m' door instead?"

"I'll have my message heard one way or another." Mr. Trewe chuckled.

Dermot would not have thought it possible, truth be told. The vicar had always seemed a rather sour man.

Dermot returned his gaze to Hugo. The lad had come, brave and uncertain, asking to be apprenticed, which Dermot generally objected to for boys of such a young age, especially in a town where Hugo had every opportunity for an education. Yet, if his family needed him working, the boy's only other option seemed to be the mill, which took a toll. Were that not enough of a quandary, the lad was Gaz Palmer's, and Palmer had been something of a disastrous worker.

Evangeline would know more of the boy, having had him in class all these months, and would have some idea how likely he was to cause difficulty.

"Let's gab a piece with Miss Blake, then. She can tell me a bit more about you."

Hugo swallowed audibly, his brow creasing, but he offered no objection. Dermot leaned back inside and called to Ronan to fetch both their coats. When he received a look of rebellion in response, he explained, "We're for Miss Blake's house. You'll get to visit with her," which put an end to any objections.

How quickly she'd become an easy and welcome part of their lives, yet how little they seemed to know of her.

The four of them crossed the street and made their way to the hedge-covered archway that led to the schoolyard. Mr. Trewe, however, did not follow them through it. "I believe Hugo is equal to the remainder of this task, so I will leave him to sort it out. Do, however, let me know what is decided. I'd like to know the family's situation."

Dermot had misjudged the vicar, having accused him not

many weeks earlier of caring little for his congregants. The man might not have been what Dermot hoped for in a preacher, but he was a good man.

Hugo dragged his feet, though he didn't slow their progress toward the school. What report was he expecting? Perhaps he wasn't confident that his teacher would say good things of him. That didn't bode well.

The outer door was unlocked, and when they stepped into the entryway, they were greeted immediately by the aroma of potato and leek soup. How was it this very English home could smell so much like Ireland?

A man's coat and hat hung beside the closed door to Evangeline's living quarters. In that moment, Dermot knew a surge of pure jealousy, one he clamped down immediately. She had found a place in his heart, that much he couldn't deny, but he'd not lose his mind over her.

Ronan reached for the handle, but Dermot stopped him. "You remember the rule, lad?"

He let his arm fall to his side. "If it's not m'door, I have to knock."

"Do it, then."

Ronan rapped firmly against the wood.

Dermot felt Hugo's eyes on him and looked down at him. "Have you a question?"

Hugo shook his head. "He sounds like thee."

"You mean Irish?"

"Aye."

Dermot watched him more closely. "Have you a problem with Irish?"

"No, sir. I've just never heard him talk before."

That was surprising, though not overly so. "Does he not talk at school?"

"No, sir."

The weight on Dermot's mind increased. He worried for Ronan. What kind of future did he have? If something were to happen to him, would Ronan be entirely alone?

The door opened before more questions could form in Dermot's overburdened mind. All the doubts he'd harbored seemed to melt away at the sight of Evangeline. He needed to sort all of this out, for his own piece of mind and tranquility of heart.

"Good afternoon." Her greeting encompassed all of them at once. Her gaze, however, focused on Hugo. "Have you been visiting with the McCormicks?"

"No, Miss Blake. Er . . . Yes." The lad shrugged and let both answers stand.

Evangeline met Dermot's eyes, her unspoken question crystal clear.

"We've come with a question for you, if you've a minute or two to spare," he said.

"Of course." She stepped back and motioned them inside. "It seems I am quite popular today."

As Dermot entered the room, he saw Mr. Farr at Evangeline's table, bent over a bowl of soup. Mr. Farr. Her grandfather. Would she admit to the connection now?

Ronan didn't hesitate or even seem to notice the exalted visitor, but crossed directly to his rocking chair and sat. Dermot would have to explain the rule about finishing up greetings and waiting to be invited before making oneself at home.

"What can I help you with?" Evangeline clearly didn't know to whom she ought to address the question.

"Might we talk a bit more privately, you and I?" Dermot asked.

Evangeline eyed him sidelong. She addressed Hugo next. "Are you hungry?"

An almost desperate plea entered the boy's expression. "Aye."

"I have soup in the pot at the fire. There is a clean bowl and spoon on the sideboard. Ladle yourself a helping, then sit at the table while Mr. McCormick and I talk."

"I thank thee, miss." The boy was off like an arrow.

Evangeline watched him with obvious concern. "He has been devouring our small teatime refreshments these past few days. I fear his family may be struggling to keep food on the table."

"I'm certain you're right."

She sighed, though the sound was quiet. "I worry for so many of them."

"I'm afraid I've not come with any news that'll settle your mind on that score." Dermot set his hand lightly on her elbow and led her to the far side of the room. "Tell me a little of Hugo. What kind of student is he?"

Evangeline glanced in the boy's direction then, lowering her voice, answered, "He is quite possibly the brightest student I have, along with Susannah Crossley. He is exceptionally smart."

That both argued in favor of hiring the boy and counted as a tragedy if he were pulled from school.

"Is he difficult?"

"He is stubborn, but he is also determined. When he puts his mind to accomplishing a task, he does it."

Reminders of Gaz Palmer tugged at Dermot's mind. "Is he lazy? 'Tis crucial that you be honest with me on this. Does he require a lot of pushing and reminding to do the work asked of him?"

She paused, her lips pressed together and her brow drawn in thought. "No, even early on, when he was unconvinced of the value of what we were doing, he didn't require hounding. He always wanted to know the why of everything. Why we had school. Why letters were called what they were. Why they made the sounds they made. Always 'why'? And, while that was a little frustrating for a teacher attempting to direct the efforts of dozens of children, I do not think it was indicative of him not wishing to work. To be truthful, I think he was afraid."

He'd not been expecting that. "Afraid of what?"

"Of not being good enough. School was new and different and challenging. If he could undermine its legitimacy, then failing at it would not be a bad reflection upon him."

"Do you think he'd approach any new task that way?" *Bricklaying, for example.*

Evangeline's focus shifted to Hugo. She motioned toward him. "He doesn't seem particularly intimidated just now."

Hugo Palmer, whose station in life was nearly as humble as it could possibly be, had struck up a conversation with King Midas himself.

"Why don't you want to work at the mill?" Mr. Farr asked him.

"The mill?" Evangeline whispered to Dermot.

"I'll explain in a bit." He wanted to hear if Hugo had the courage to be truthful with a man so much connected to the factory.

"I've heard too much about it," Hugo said. "I'd guess no one wants to work there—not really."

Mr. Farr pushed aside his bowl and gave the lad his full attention. "What have you heard?"

"Those what've been working there from t' first are starting to have troubles with their breathing. They say t' air inside is thick like it is in t' cotton mills in Manchester."

Mr. Farr's eyes narrowed. "The mill manager is supposed to employ scavengers to gather up stray bits of wool and fluff."

"T' scavengers are children." A fire entered Hugo's words and posture. This desperate, hungry, poor little boy suddenly had the bearing of a warrior. "They're charged with lying flat and crawling beneath great moving machines, picking up bits of fluff. Mark my words, one of them will pay with a finger or a hand, and t' air'll be no cleaner for it, not when t' overseer won't allow a single window to be opened to let in fresh air. Tha've set them to an impossible task, and they're punished for not managing it."

"You feel the overseer is unreasonable?"

"T' air is thick and hot as can be. T' workers are covered in sweat and struggle to keep moving. Mrs. Crossley grew overly hot yesterday and fainted. He didn't see it as proof that change was needed; he just took her job away from her."

Dermot hadn't heard that. The Crossleys would be in dire straits without her income. Evangeline pressed her hand to her heart, listening raptly but in obvious dismay.

"Us father worked there until a few days past," Hugo continued. "Came home every day smelling of oil from t' machines and of wool, a stench so strong no amount of washing rid him of it. T' smell inside t' mill must be unbearable for him to reek so strongly of it afterward."

To Mr. Farr's credit, he sat and silently listened, not interrupting or arguing.

"He'd sit by t' fire, rocking back and forth, muttering about noise—that he couldn't bide it. I've heard others talk about it. T' deafening noise of t' place."

Evangeline took hold of Dermot's hand. He felt the clutch

clear to his heart. How was it that this woman, who had been less than honest with him from the moment they'd met, still had such claim on his affections?

Hugo wasn't finished with his evaluation of the factory. "I've a friend there. He used to bahn to school but had to start working in thy mill. He's different now, tired and worn down. He looks"—Hugo mulled over the word before settling on—"broken. My family needs money, but I'll not earn it that way. Not if I've another choice."

"And so you want to work for Mr. McCormick instead of for me?" Mr. Farr asked, not unkindly.

Hugo nodded. "T' men what work for him say he works 'em hard, but he's fair."

Mr. Farr leaned closer, his elbows and forearms resting on the table. "And the mill workers don't say that?"

"No, sir."

Mr. Farr turned toward Dermot. "Have you heard the same thing?"

"I have."

Evangeline received the same question.

"So have I, though never before in this much detail," she answered. "Most in this town feel employment at the mill is an act of desperation. I've seen families actually grieve over the necessity of seeking a position there."

Mr. Farr clasped his hands together and rested his chin on them. His thick, white brows inched closer together. "Do you get the impression that this misery is the result of the mill manager more than the mill overseer?"

Evangeline crossed to the table and sat beside him. "You are asking if I think Mr. Barton is to blame?"

"A difficult question, I know."

"That I cannot tell you. The overseer is almost universally despised. But whether or not his behavior is the result of instructions he has been given by Mr. Barton, I do not know."

Mr. Farr nodded slowly, thoughtfully. "I think that is something I had best discover."

"The houses Mr. McCormick is building will bring you more workers, something the factory, as I understand it, needs." Evangeline spoke calmly but firmly. "But if your mill has a reputation for being a purgatory, you will always struggle for workers."

Mr. Farr rose. "I need to sort this out before I return to Leeds."

"Of course." Evangeline stood as well. She saw Mr. Farr out, but upon returning, immediately addressed Hugo. "Will you really no longer be in school?"

"Can't be. Us family need t' money."

She rubbed her temple. "But you have been doing so well, and there is so much more you could learn."

"Can't be helped, miss."

Evangeline paced away from the table. "First John and now Hugo." She spoke more to herself than to anyone else. "How many of my children will be forced to leave?"

She thought of them as her children. Evangeline Blake might have been kin to Mrs. Barton, but it didn't seem they were cut from the same cloth at all. Dermot's train of thought stopped short. Had learning about her family undermined his view of her so much that he had begun thinking of her in terms similar to how he thought of Mrs. Barton?

Evangeline stopped her circuit in front of him. "Ronan won't have to stop coming to school, will he?"

"He'll not." An idea, firm and formed, entered his mind with such force that he spoke it out loud. "I've been in need of workers to clean tools and run supplies. If Hugo and John Crossley will agree to it, one of them can come to work in the mornings while the other is here at school, then they can switch in the afternoon. They'd be paid, which should keep them out of the factory, but they can still have some learning."

Evangeline's gaze softened. "You'd do that?"

He nodded. "This world requires children to work more often than it ought. But I know John, and I know he'll work hard. And you've told me Hugo will as well."

"I will, Mr. McCormick." Hugo was on his feet, watching intently.

"They'll help me, which'll make their wages worthwhile. They'll still get to learn, which'll improve their lives going forward. That's worth a great deal."

Evangeline's eyes bored into his. "Could it work, do you think? Would their families agree to it?"

"Us family would," Hugo insisted. "I know it."

"Hie home, lad," he said. "Talk this over with your parents."

"Yes, sir. I thank thee, sir." Hugo rushed from the room, but popped back in an instant later. "I thank thee for t' scran, Miss Blake." He disappeared once more.

"I cannot tell you how many times I heard the children say 'scran' before I knew they meant 'food,'" Evangeline said with a small smile. "Oh, I hope the Palmers and Crossleys will accept your offer. My heart aches to think of those two dear boys losing their chance to learn, their chance for a few hours of peace and calm."

"I'll talk with the families," he said. "I feel certain Hugo and John'll be back in school come Monday."

She began clearing the bowls and spoons from her table, cleaning up after her visitors.

"Mr. Farr was here calling on you," he said.

She looked up at him briefly, confusion in her expression. "You saw him here yourself."

"I've never known him to pay personal calls while in Smeatley." He left the observation there, leaving the opportunity open for her to tell him the nature of her connection to Mr. Farr. But would she?

She set the bowls on the sideboard. "He wished to talk about the school."

"And only the school?" He hardly dared breathe while he waited for her answer. Did she intend to keep lying to him?

"We spoke of a few different things." Truthful, but not thorough. "Perhaps he means to be more personable when he comes to Smeatley now."

"Do you suppose that's what it was? A sudden urge to be friendly?"

She stood rooted to the spot, her hands clasped in front of her, her posture one of deep discomfort. "It would not be a terrible thing for him to be a little less formidable."

She clearly didn't mean to tell him the truth. Disappointment swelled in his chest. "Rouan was on the steps when Mr. Farr left here yesterday. He overheard your conversation."

She clearly didn't realize the significance of that. Though he'd have preferred she tell him her own self, he was too weary of half-truths.

"He heard Mr. Farr acknowledge you as his granddaughter."

Evangeline's eyes opened wide. Her face paled. "And he told you?"

"He did, though I shouldn't have had to hear it from him."

She took a single step closer. "I was required to keep it a secret. It was part of the terms of my employment. Mrs. Barton—"

"Your *aunt*," Dermot pointed out.

She nodded; her eyes pled for him to understand. "She was very clear that I would be fired if our kinship was made known. I would have lost my job."

"And you could find no reason to trust me with that bit of yourself?"

"I was not permitted to do so," she said again. "If my aunt had discovered—"

"You thought me so unreliable?" He shook his head. "Did you not trust me to keep a confidence?"

"It isn't that."

"Then what is it? I told you a closely kept bit of information about my life and Ronan's. I trusted you with that. But you didn't dare tell me something important to you."

"Dermot."

He held up a hand. He wasn't ready to hear her justification. Too much hurt weighed on his heart and mind. "I'd learned to trust you, Miss Blake. I thought we had a mutual trust, a mutual—" Disappointment cut his words short. "It seemed I was mistaken."

He collected Ronan, offered a quick farewell to Evangeline, then left. Through it all, she stood still and quiet. But she never looked away from him.

He didn't turn back, didn't even glance. He couldn't. His heart had given itself to her, and she'd not even told him the truth of who she was.

CHAPTER THIRTY

Mr. Trewe's sermon was, as always, focused on the godly quality of hard work. The lecture Evangeline heard in her heart, however, was one on honesty.

She hadn't been fully truthful with Dermot, but what choice had she had? When she'd first arrived, she hadn't known him well enough to trust him with such a sensitive bit of information. And Lucy's well-being depended upon Evangeline keeping her position, which meant keeping her secret. But she hadn't told him even after she knew she could depend upon him. Doing so hadn't even occurred to her.

Heavens, now I'm lying to myself in a church.

She had nearly told Dermot everything Friday evening when he'd held her and reassured her despite her nervousness to face her family. He hadn't even known they were her family. The words had hovered unspoken on her lips—but she hadn't told him.

Evangeline closed her eyes, shutting out the sights and sounds of Sunday services. She should have told him long before now.

But if he'd known her true origins, he would likely never have allowed her to be his friend.

Friend. He was so much more than that to her. She loved him. She'd known as much for weeks but hadn't admitted it to herself until that late, lonely moment outside his door. Had he been awake after all but simply hadn't wanted to see her? He had probably known about her family by then.

I have ruined everything.

Mass came to a close. She followed the townspeople out of the chapel, though her thoughts were far away. Dermot and Ronan did not attend services in Smeatley, and their absence was both relieving and disheartening. She missed them both and wished they were nearby. She wished she knew how to set things right between herself and Dermot.

She still struggled to find comfort in the churchyard—it was hard not to think of her lost family—yet she found a measure of peace as she made a slow circuit of the grounds. The townspeople stood about, chatting as they often did after services. Evangeline didn't join them immediately. She kept to the edge of the church-yard and breathed through her worry and loneliness. Somehow it would be made right again. Somehow.

She pasted a smile on her face and approached the spot where the Crossleys, Haighs, and Palmers had gathered. They all turned to look at her when she arrived.

"A good morning to you all," she said.

No one said anything.

Daniel Palmer, a cousin of Hugo's who worked at Hillside House, stood among them as well. Perhaps he would take up a conversation.

"How are you, Daniel?" she asked.

He dipped his head. "Well enough, Miss Blake." With a bow

not unlike those he offered to Aunt Barton, he slipped quickly away.

Odd. She turned to Mr. Palmer. "I hope I did not offend him somehow."

Mr. Palmer held his hat in his hands and didn't look her in the eye. "It's not for we to be offended, Miss Blake."

"I understand Mr. McCormick intended to visit you and discuss an opportunity for Hugo," she said.

Mr. Palmer nodded. "He were very generous. Hugo'll be back at school tomorrow, mark tha."

"I am so pleased to hear it."

Mrs. Palmer snatched up her husband's hand and they left as quickly as Daniel had. Evangeline often spoke at some length with the Palmers on Sundays. Yet they were clearly anxious to avoid her today.

She turned to the Haighs. "Is Cecilia here today? I did not see her."

"Aye." Mrs. Haigh spoke the single syllable in a clipped tone.

"Is something the matter?"

"Neya." Mrs. Haigh nudged her husband away, but paused to offer Evangeline a curtsey.

A curtsey? Why had she curtseyed? And why had Daniel bowed?

Only the Crossleys remained. Though she was confused and concerned, she was eager to speak with Mrs. Crossley. She had not been able to visit with her for far too long. Her friend had been at the factory; Evangeline had been drowning in her uncertainties.

"How have you been?" she asked.

Mrs. Crossley smiled fleetingly.

Evangeline looked to Mr. Crossley for some kind of explanation.

"Daniel tells we tha are kin to t' Bartons," he said.

Her breath froze in her lungs. Daniel had told them. They knew. They all knew. "And—and that is why they don't want to talk with me?"

"What are we to say?" Mrs. Crossley said.

"The same as always," Evangeline insisted.

But Mrs. Crossley shook her head. "It i'n't t' same, though. It can't be."

They stepped away. She received no final word of parting. They offered no indication of regret at the chasm spreading between them. Dermot had left in much the same way the day before. He'd not looked back even once. He hadn't hesitated even a moment.

Evangeline was alone. So very alone.

The next day, Evangeline pushed through her lessons with a heavy heart. The children behaved differently than they had before. Some of her students had grown quieter, others more defiant. They eyed her with suspicion and a degree of worry that broke her heart. Word of her origins had clearly spread.

The factory families came to claim their children at the usual hour. Evangeline stepped outside to offer her farewells, wishing she knew what to say to mend things between them. Seeing the distance growing between her and these families who had become her friends deepened her heartache.

Mrs. Haigh, who usually greeted her with a wave and a friendly "Ey up," offered only a quiet "Good evening, Miss Blake" with her head lowered as if she were a servant greeting her mistress.

The Shaws and Sutcliffes struck similarly humble miens. Mrs. Bennett didn't greet her at all, but hurried off as quickly as she came. No one stopped for a chat. No one offered the usual friendly farewells.

She set Ronan to the task of reading aloud the nursery rhymes she had written down for him. He seemed to like reading, though he did it so quietly she could hardly hear him. If that was what made him comfortable enough to undertake the work, she didn't mind.

"Rub a dub dub," Ronan read in a mumble. "Three men in a tub."

Evangeline stepped to the mantel as Ronan continued. She touched the pad of her finger to her family's image tucked behind its protective glass.

I am helping here. I think you would be proud of that She knew this was not the life they had envisioned for her, but she was pleased by all she had achieved. The struggle of facing uncertainty—and the sense of accomplishment she felt at having overcome it—had made her a better person. Stronger. If only her family were with her to share in that.

Into her moment of quiet reflection came a most unwelcome interruption: Aunt Barton's voice. "Is this how you undertake your teaching? By ignoring your student?"

Evangeline met her mother's photographic gaze and, for just a moment, could so easily see the expression she had often worn when speaking of her sister. Forbearance mingled with frustration mingled with a kind of sad affection. Evangeline offered a brief smile of condolence; she had come to understand that same blend of feelings quite well over the past months.

She turned away from the mantel and, as serenely as she could manage, said, "He prefers to practice his reading with a certain degree of privacy. Knowing that is how he learns best, I make certain he is afforded it."

A smirk turned the corners of her aunt's mouth. "Does his father also prefer a 'certain degree of privacy' at this house?"

That was too pointed a remark to be misunderstood. "There are times when I am surprised that you and my mother were at all related. *She* comported herself with utmost decorum and ladylike civility. *She* would never have lowered herself to utter such base and unfounded remarks."

"Yes. Your sainted mother." Aunt Barton's nose wrinkled. "She knew how to capture a man's attention."

"I beg your pardon."

"Be careful who you idolize, Evangeline." She moved to one of the narrow back windows and looked out, though not with any obvious purpose.

"If you have come here only to insult me and my family, I would ask you to leave. This is my home, and I will not allow your words to sully it."

"Is that so?" Aunt Barton actually laughed. "You seemed to have little objection to bandying about my husband's good name only two days ago."

"I did no such thing."

Aunt Barton brushed a finger along the windowsill, then eyed it with distaste, apparently finding more dust than she deemed acceptable. "Mr. Barton was subjected to an inquisition over the running of the mill, something he has not been called upon to endure even once thus far. That, no doubt, was your doing."

What could Evangeline say to that? To an extent, the inquiries *were* partially her fault—she had told Grandfather what she'd heard of the mill, after all. She was not obligated to respond as, in that moment, Dermot did, having apparently arrived in the doorway.

"Mr. Farr's questioning of your husband can be laid at the feet of a few people, though the necessity of it lies firmly with his own self."

Aunt Barton spun about. Her surprise quickly gave way to displeasure and a narrowing of her eyes. "You make yourself quite free here, walking in unannounced and unbidden."

"The door was open," Dermot said. "Your disparaging remarks would've brought any decent man in to defend an innocent lady such as your niece."

"*Your niece.*" Aunt Barton flung an accusatory glare at Evangeline. "You have been telling people of our kinship? That was a specific requirement of your living and working here. This is grounds for dismissal and eviction."

"She told no one." Dermot stepped further inside. "Mr. Farr did. He referred to her as his granddaughter within the hearing of one of her students, though I believe the knowledge has grown more general since the dinner Miss Blake took in your home— a more subtle revelation but, again, one brought about by Mr. Farr. If you mean to rake anyone over the coals for this, it'd best be him, though I'd pay a year's salary to watch you try."

"You would speak so flippantly to the wife of your master?"

"I have no master, and I work for no man." Dermot eyed her for a long, unhurried moment. "What's more, Miss Blake does not work for you, either, nor does she work for your husband. She's employed by the school board, of which you're not a member and of which your husband is only acting head. Mr. Farr's opinion is the only one that truly matters. I saw him here

Saturday. Her position seems quite safe. Yours and your hus-band's, however . . ." The thought dangled unfinished.

Aunt Barton's lips pursed into a tiny bud of anger. "Very brash words for one of your birth."

"And very uncouth words for one of yours." Dermot did not shrink in the least.

Evangeline didn't bother hiding her pleasure at being so fiercely defended. "I need to assist my student in gathering his supplies, so I am no longer in a position to receive visitors. Good day to you, Mrs. Barton."

Aunt Barton crossed in front of her, slowing long enough to whisper in menacing tones, "This day's work will cost you your sister's company. Mark my words."

"You do not frighten me," Evangeline answered in full voice. "I have every confidence that Grandfather took your measure long ago, and I believe he is fully capable of taking mine."

No more was said, though Evangeline felt the truth of her words. Her grandfather was not one to be swayed by petty resent-ment or vindictiveness. He might not side with Evangeline in the end, but she did not believe that would be the result of anything her aunt said or did.

Aunt Barton left in a huff.

"Come along, Ronan," Dermot said. "We're for home."

He faced Ronan, his back to her. His tone was colder than she was accustomed to.

"Are you still angry with me?" Evangeline asked.

"I was never angry with you, woman. Frustrated and disap-pointed, yes, but not angry."

Her heart sat heavy in her chest. "And now you mean to treat me differently as well. The whole town does."

"'Tis difficult to know how to act around you when none of us is entirely certain who you are anymore."

"I'm still the same person," she insisted.

"Aye, but none of us knew the whole of that person. You lied to us."

Long after he'd gone, his words hung heavy in her mind. *"You lied to us."* She hadn't wanted to, but what choice had she had? She would have lost her position. Aunt Barton had been quite clear that Grandfather had insisted—

The truth of things struck her quite suddenly. Grandfather had not hidden their connection. His invitation to supper had been one way the town had learned the truth. Yet Aunt Barton had insisted the secrecy was *his* requirement. Evangeline had been misled from the beginning. What else had been a half-truth at best?

She had lost Dermot's good opinion over a lie—two lies. The one her aunt had originally told, and the one she herself had maintained in the months since. She had come to Smeatley alone and now feared she would return to that isolation.

CHAPTER THIRTY-ONE

Mrs. Crossley." Evangeline hurried down the path from the schoolhouse, barely catching the woman before she stepped out onto the street. "Forgive me if this is an impertinence, but I had hoped you might have a moment or two to continue the stories we were writing down."

Her request was met with the same polite distance with which most of her students' parents had treated her the past few days. "I'd not deny thee, miss, but my days are right busy."

"Of course." Her heart dropped, but what could she say? She had been less than forthright with her neighbors, her students, their families. What right had she to expect them to still be on friendly terms with her? And, yet, how could she simply stop trying? "Perhaps you could tell me one bit of the story each time you are here. The process will take longer but will be worthwhile."

She thought for a minute before nodding slowly. "Next time I come, I'll tell thee a little more."

"Thank you." That was all she was able to say before the family slipped away. She'd not asked how they were, if Mrs. Crossley had found work. *I ought to have asked that first.* How selfish to have begun with her own concerns when theirs were so much weightier.

It was little wonder she now spent her evenings alone. Though she had hoped to have made a difference in the lives of her students, she was not truly a part of their lives. She was not really a part of anyone's.

She dragged herself back to the schoolhouse, watching the factory families' children play in the yard. The day would end just as it always did. Their voices would fill the air for a time, then the schoolyard would fall silent. Dermot would take Ronan home. She would remain behind with nothing but a framed photograph for company.

Cecilia Haigh and May Palmer were playing hopscotch. George Palmer and Jimmy Sutcliffe chased each other around the yard. Matthew Bennett circled a nearby tree, his hand rubbing its trunk as he spun. The children, at least, seemed happy. While at school, they were free to be children, playing and running and leaving behind the many, many cares of the world. She was grateful for that.

She didn't quite make it all the way inside before Jimmy called after her. "Miss Blake. Someone's come for thee."

Daniel Palmer, Hugo's cousin, came quickly up the walkway to where she stood and handed her a folded bit of paper. He dipped his head and left as swiftly and quietly as he had arrived. She hadn't even time to thank him.

She unfolded the paper and saw a coat of arms and the words "Post Office Telegraphers" emblazoned at the top. She had never before received a telegram.

It was from "H. Farr" in Leeds. *Grandfather.*

The message was not long. *I wish for you to come live with me in Leeds. Arrangements can be made as soon as you are ready.* That was all he'd written, a mere two sentences.

He wanted her to come to Leeds. That was precisely what she had hoped for months earlier. Being told she had to remain in Smeatley, working and living on her own, and attempting to prove her worth to her grandfather from a distance had dealt her such a blow. Yet, the offer now left her entirely upended.

She peeked inside her living quarters. Ronan was practicing his reading, something he preferred to do alone. The children outside were happy and content in their play. She remained in the entryway and sat on one of the lower steps of the staircase, the telegram still in her hands.

"I wish for you to come live with me in Leeds." She reread the sentence in a confused whisper. He wanted her to come. He hadn't commanded or insisted, something she appreciated after having been browbeaten so often since her family had passed on. Perhaps Grandfather had decided she was capable of choosing her own path in life.

Except his telegram hadn't truly *asked* her to come nor inquired as to her desires for her future. He might not have ordered her to move to Leeds, but he'd come worryingly close.

Still, she had held firm through the few disagreements they'd had during his recent visit. That must not have bothered him or he would not have offered his home to her. She likely need not worry that she would be living under his thumb.

And she would be near Lucy. Perhaps she could even convince her grandfather to allow Lucy to live in his home as well, away from the school where she was so unhappy. They would be together at last. She would not be living in her own home, but she would be with her sister.

And without her children. Without her independence. Her home. Ronan. Dermot. Her dear, darling, beloved Dermot.

She folded the telegram between her palms and rested her hands on her lap. What was she to do?

She needed someone to talk to—not to make the decision for her, but to listen and help her sort out her own thoughts. How often Dermot had done precisely that for her. He listened. He offered his viewpoint. But he never forced his ideas on her. Of all the people she had known since coming to Smeatley—even before then, if she were being entirely honest—he alone had never seemed to doubt her ability to make her own choices, and he had never insisted she was meant to simply do as she was told without question or argument. And when she had first come to his door and confessed that she could not cook or clean or do any of the things necessary for looking after herself, he'd never treated her like an imbecile or a child.

She had returned that confidence by not telling him the truth. That had been wrong of her. She ought to have trusted him enough for that.

When he arrived to fetch Ronan that evening, she couldn't bring herself to look him in the eye. Regret rendered her silent.

Dermot didn't make the swift exit he'd taken the past few days. "What has you as quiet as a mouse?"

"I am mulling over something." She busied herself pretending to straighten her small stack of papers.

"Are you needing a listening ear?"

She shook her head. Though she would have liked to talk over her many concerns with him, trusting his judgment as she did and knowing he would truly listen, she didn't feel she deserved his generosity. Hours trapped in her own spinning thoughts had left her spirits rather dismal.

Dermot moved closer to her. "What's happened, Evangeline?"

She met his gaze at last. The kindness and concern she saw there nearly undid her. "I've had a telegram from my grand-father."

"Have you?"

She nodded. "He wants me to come to Leeds."

"For a visit?"

She shook her head. "He wants me to live there with him."

Nothing of Dermot's thoughts were visible in his expression. "How do you feel about his offer?"

His gentle inquiry opened the floodgates. "I don't know how to feel or what to think. On the one hand, I would be near Lucy, perhaps could even arrange for her to live at my grandfather's house as well."

"That would remove her from the school where she is now," Dermot said.

"Precisely. And my grandfather's home, as I understand, is a pleasant place with many of the comforts my sister was once accustomed to."

Dermot nodded. "You were once accustomed to them as well."

"Part of me longs for that bit of my old life again, not having to cook every meal or clean every corner of my house, to live with some comfort and ease."

He indicated they should sit on the bench near the fire. She didn't object. She felt burdened enough to remain still for days on end. He sat beside her. He hadn't done that in days. She pushed down the surge of hope that rose up inside. She would not allow herself to contemplate that he intended anything but kindness.

She pressed on. "Coming to Smeatley and working as a teacher was not my choice. Living in this dim, cramped room with no warning and no prior experience of all the many things I needed to know to be successful was not a welcome challenge, I will admit."

Dermot sat, patiently listening, just as she'd known he would.

"But I have come to love this schoolhouse and the children I teach and this town and all of the challenges that come with it. I don't know that I could abandon any of that now."

"Are you speaking out of obligation to a commitment or out of a personal connection?" he asked. "I think you need to know which it is. You're deciding on your entire future."

There was a great deal of truth in that, though she wasn't certain of her answer. If she stayed, would she be doing so because she felt it was expected of her? If she chose to go to Leeds, would she be doing so for similar reasons?

"If I stay, I might never have Lucy with me again," she said.

"That is possible."

"But if I go, I would lose my sense of purpose. I am doing so much good here, Dermot, and I don't think it is arrogant to say so. I have seen the difference I have made in these children's lives. Who is to say the teacher hired to take my place would care for them personally? How many might fall by the wayside because they were seen as merely a name on a ledger rather than the dear, lovely children they are?"

Dermot nodded. "A sound argument, that."

"But Lucy is in Leeds," she countered.

"Another sound argument."

"What am I to do?" She stood and paced away. "How can I possibly pick between them?"

"Pick a third option."

She turned back to face him. "What third option? I was only given two."

His smile was gentle and kind. "What you were given and what is available to you are not always the same thing, my dear. You needn't resign yourself to only what you've been offered."

"A lady is meant to do as she's told and not to argue."

He folded his arms across his chest and eyed her with one arched brow. "You've grown fiery in the weeks you've been here, Evangeline Blake. Don't turn fainthearted now."

She *had* grown fierce. At first she'd been almost ashamed of her boldness, but the change had been necessary. "Being firm has proven far more effective," she admitted. "And I don't think it has made me a bad person."

"Far from it," he said. "And firmness is just what you're needing now. Think on it. I'm certain there's a third choice you've not stumbled upon yet."

She wanted to believe it. But what possible extra choice could there be? Lucy was in Leeds. Evangeline's work and her students and the life she loved were in Smeatley. How could she have her sister with her without leaving her entire life behind?

"What if—" She paused, wanting to make certain the thought taking shape had the substance she hoped it did. "What if Lucy came here?"

Dermot didn't respond or interrupt. Bless him, he meant to let her sort it out.

"That was what I had hoped for from the beginning," she reminded herself. "That was what my aunt said would happen— at least, she hinted at it enough to make me believe that was the outcome. Why should that change now?"

She pressed her palms together and set her fingertips against her chin. Lucy coming to Smeatley. That was not an outlandish idea. Dermot, however, had once been quite set against it.

"You do not think that life here would be a misery for her?" she asked.

"It'd not be easy," he answered, truthful as always. "But she'd have you, which'd help a great deal. And I believe the town would look out for her, being fond of you as they are."

She sighed. "They are not so warm as they once were."

"They're worried. The Bartons have not been kind to the people of Smeatley, although Mr. Barton is better than his wife."

Evangeline could acknowledge the truth of that.

"Knowing you're family to them, the Smeatley folks are worried you'll turn against them in the end."

How could they believe that of her? "I never would."

"I know it, and I think deep down they do as well, but there is the worry all the same."

"What can I do to convince them of my heart?"

"I believe time will tell. They'll see that you're still the kind and generous person they've seen you to be, and they'll learn to overlook your family relationships."

The hope he offered fell short of what she truly needed to hear.

"What of you, Dermot McCormick?" she asked quietly. "Could you ever learn to overlook it?"

He shrugged. "The connections don't bother me too much. We can't choose our family, after all."

"You chose yours." She indicated Ronan, sleeping in the rocking chair nearby.

"We choose who we keep," he said.

If only he would choose to keep her. "You've hardly spoken to me in days."

He rose and crossed to her. "I'm only human, you know.

I make a show of being hard and unfeeling, but I've vulnerable spots as well. You hit one, I'm afraid."

"I am sorry."

"I've had almost no one I could fully trust in all the time I've been in Smeatley. There's always been a barrier. But you seemed to have bridged that lonely gap. 'Twas a blow to know you'd lied, however indirectly."

"I've spent the past months making decisions based on fear." Her voice broke, but she pushed forward. "I have nearly forgotten how to be guided by hope and trust and—" She tried to take a deep breath, but couldn't entirely manage it. "I shouldn't have kept such a crucial part of my life a secret from you."

"'Twasn't your doing that made the secrecy necessary."

Some of the tension in her chest eased. "I still should have told you the truth."

"Aye. You should've. But I ought to have been more understanding about why you didn't." He took her hands in his. Her heart lodged in her throat, but for a different reason this time.

"Please tell me there is a chance you will forgive me," she pled. "I cannot bear this distance between us."

He pressed their entwined hands to his heart. "I've forgiven you, lass. I'm simply stubborn." He raised her hand to his lips and kissed it lightly.

She closed her eyes. A tear spilled, followed by another. Her breath shook.

"Oh, Evangeline." He pulled her into his arms. "I don't like seeing you cry."

She leaned against him, her emotions overwhelming her. "I have missed you."

His hand rubbed her back in soothing circles. "And I've missed you something fierce."

"You truly won't hold my family connections against me?" She was fully aware of the kind of people her aunt and uncle were.

"My family are poor Irish farmers who essentially sold me to a brick mason," he said. "You might very well hold a great many aspects of that against me."

"Though I do mourn the difficulties of your childhood, nothing about those origins gives me pause," she said. "Your past has made you who you are, and I"—she could not quite bring herself to speak the word *love*—"care a great deal for the person you are."

He laid his head atop hers, their embrace growing more comforting even as it grew more intimate. "And I care a great deal for the person you are, which makes our current arrangement far less awkward than it would be otherwise."

She leaned back enough to look up into his eyes. "When I first met you, I would not have guessed that you had a sense of humor."

He grinned down at her. "You made me nervous, woman, though I'd not have admitted that even to m'self."

"Why did I make you nervous?"

He ran a hand along her arm as he stepped back. "Because you were too good to be living in this run-down part of town. You were a reminder that I fit here because I hadn't accomplished any of the things I'd set out to do when I first stepped foot in this area of the world."

"And that made you nervous?"

He moved to the chair where Ronan slept. "I knew you'd discover, eventually, that I was a failure."

"You are no kind of a failure." She followed his path. "And why would my opinion matter so much?"

"I don't know." He tossed her an exasperated look. "But it did, almost from the beginning."

"Does it matter still?" She held her breath, waiting for the response.

"It matters a great deal."

Her heart pounded hard against her ribs. "I would miss you if I went to Leeds."

Dermot scooped Ronan into his arms. He paused as he passed her. "I'd miss you, too, Evangeline. I'd miss you something terrible."

She knew in that moment that she had regained the affection he held for her before her deceptions had pushed him away. But how far those "affections" went, she could not say.

"I hope my grandfather accepts my request to remain here, with Lucy."

"I intend to hope very hard." He gave her one more smile before slipping out the door with his precious armful.

He would miss her if she were gone. Her opinion mattered to him. He cared about her. In his embrace, she had found peace and contentment. She had found something that felt more like home than anything she had experienced since leaving Petersmarch.

She desperately hoped her grandfather would listen to her plea, because she could not bear the thought of leaving.

CHAPTER THIRTY-TWO

The week following the arrival of the telegram from Evangeline's grandfather, Dermot spent every evening at Evangeline's home, he and Ronan taking their meals with her and remaining for a time afterward. Evangeline had taken to sitting in his arms while they talked about their day, their memories, their thoughts for the future. Ronan even joined in the discussions now and then, expounding on the proper way to mix mortar or offering endless facts about sheep. 'Twas by far the most pleasant few days Dermot had known. Returning to her each day felt like coming home.

He stepped across the threshold of her living quarters, then paused, listening to Ronan reading.

"To fetch a p—p—" The boy struggled a moment.

Evangeline stood at the fire, stirring a pot. Though she didn't offer any assistance, she was clearly listening.

"Pail," Ronan finally said.

Evangeline nodded, but didn't interrupt.

"Of water." Ronan did not read loudly, but he was intent

on his paper. "Jack fell doe." Ronan shook his head. "Jack fell down and brock—*broke*—his crown, and Jill came—" His brow creased. He studied the words on the page. His little mouth moved, but no sound emerged.

Evangeline didn't turn to look at the boy, but she had stopped stirring. Indeed, she stood with all the tension of one fully expecting to be called upon to move swiftly at any moment.

Ronan looked over at her. "This one," he said.

She sprang into action, kneeling on the floor beside his chair. They put their heads near each other, and she spoke of vowels followed by consonants and what that meant for the sound they made. Dermot had listened during a few of their lessons and, though he'd not yet learned to read himself, he at least recognized the terms she was using.

Ronan listened intently. When she finished her explanation, he returned his attention to his reading. After a couple of unsuccessful attempts, he settled on the word "tumbling."

Evangeline nodded. "Very good." She patted his hand, something he permitted but did not seem to enjoy. Still, that was progress.

Ronan kept at his lessons. Evangeline returned to the fireplace. She did not take up her spoon again, though. She paused in front of the photograph of her family. Her gaze lingered on their faces. Fate had been unkind in the extreme, taking away all her family at once.

Dermot quietly crossed to her side. She must have heard him approach. "I miss them," she whispered.

"I know." He moved to stand directly beside her, then put an arm around her shoulders.

After a moment, her defeated posture gave way to

determination. "I hadn't meant to greet you with sadness. I have news to share, actually."

"Have you?"

She led him by the hand to their usual place on the long, spindle-backed bench near the fire, and sat, waiting for him to do the same. This time, she did not settle into his embrace, but sat facing him.

"I received another telegram today from my grandfather." A small smile appeared on her face, which gave him hope that the telegram had held good news. "My letter to him explained that he was being unfair by not sending Lucy to Smeatley when that had been our original agreement and I had kept up my part of it."

This woman had a backbone of steel, something he'd not have guessed in those early days and weeks when she'd been so dedicated to being prim and proper. "What did Mr. Farr say to that?"

"He admitted that I was correct."

Dermot whistled long and low. "'Tis no small feat to receive an admission of guilt from a man of his standing."

"I know." She fair glowed with pride, a sight he truly enjoyed. "Now, he has not agreed to let Lucy come live with me, but he has said she can come to visit."

"You'll be seeing her again, then."

She nodded, her eyes sparkling with excitement and, if he was not mistaken, unshed tears. "After all this time, I will have her with me."

"I'm happier for you than I can say. You've needed your family here—the family you're fond of, at any rate."

She hopped up. "Lucy will be arriving Saturday afternoon. Will you come with me to greet her at the train station?"

Dermot watched her with a contented joy. 'Twas a wonderful

thing to see her so happy. "Of course I will." He wanted to meet the sister who meant so much to her, and he wanted to be with Evangeline during a moment that she'd waited for all these weeks. He wanted to be part of all her precious and important moments.

Saturday morning dawned bitterly cold. Dermot dressed Ronan in his warmest clothes with an extra scarf wrapped around his head.

"Miss Blake's sister arrives this morning," he explained. "She loves her sister very much, so we will make certain Miss Lucy feels welcome here."

Ronan nodded, though Dermot couldn't imagine he would greet this new arrival with anything other than his usual wariness. He only hoped Lucy was as patient and understanding with the lad as Evangeline was.

They hadn't quite reached Evangeline's door when she stepped out of it, bundled against the cold and overflowing with anxious energy. She checked the door more than once to see if it was locked. She fiddled with her coat buttons and adjusted her scarf.

Dermot set his arm around her waist, walking beside her toward the street. "You're nervous."

"What if she isn't happy to see me? What if she blames me for leaving her at that school for so long? What if she hates me?"

He held her a touch closer. "Let's not open that door until we're certain fate's knocking at it."

"You're telling me not to go borrowing trouble?"

"I'm attempting to set your mind at ease."

She smiled up at him, and he, who had spent so long

guarding his heart, lost a little more of it to her. "You being here with me sets me more at ease than I can say."

"We're happy to be here." He adjusted Ronan's loose scarf. "I've heard so much of Lucy. I'm looking forward to making her acquaintance."

"She is a sweet girl," Evangeline said. "Rather quiet, really. I don't know what she'll make of this town or the people in it. Given that they've been more distant with me lately, I worry she'll be given something of a cold reception."

He wished he could offer her reassurance. The people of Smeatley were a headstrong lot, and they clung to what was familiar and what most closely resembled their own experiences.

The train platform was not overly busy. It seemed the factory was not sending or receiving any shipments that morning. Evangeline watched the tracks. She walked back and forth, rubbing her hands. Her eyes never lost their worried glint.

Mr. and Mrs. Barton arrived in the midst of Evangeline's pacing. Neither looked excited to be there.

"McCormick," Mr. Barton said in acknowledgment.

"You've come to greet your niece?" Dermot guessed.

Mr. Barton nodded. "It seems all the town knows of our relationship with the Blakes now."

"Mr. Farr revealed it." Dermot wanted to make certain Mr. Barton did not blame Evangeline the way his wife had. "One can't help wondering if forcing Miss Blake to be entirely without family these past months truly had been one of his requirements in the first place."

To his credit, Mr. Barton looked abashed. "My wife—" He didn't finish, but fell into an uncomfortable silence.

Dermot offered him no escape. Let the man wrestle with his conscience; it'd do him good.

Mrs. Barton took notice of Dermot and Ronan for the first time. "Why am I not surprised to see you here?"

He ignored the implied disapproval. He returned his attention to Evangeline, who was moving swiftly back to where he stood.

"The train is coming." She clutched his arm. "She'll be here in a moment."

If not for the Bartons standing nearby, he'd've wrapped an arm round her. As it was, he hoped his smile proved support enough.

The familiar rumbling began underfoot. Evangeline held more tightly to his arm.

"Only a moment more," he said.

In a cloud of steam, the train arrived. Its wheels squealed as it slowed painstakingly to a halt. Evangeline didn't look away, didn't even seem to blink.

A lone figure emerged a few cars down from the engine. She wore a dress of unrelieved black and a wide-brimmed bonnet. She struggled with the traveling bag clutched in her hands.

"Is that your Lucy?" he asked.

"I believe so." She took a single step forward. "Yes. Yes, that is Lucy."

She rushed headlong toward her sister and threw her arms around her, sending the bag to the ground with a thud. Her sister returned the embrace without a word.

Dermot moved quickly to where they stood, though making every effort not to disrupt the reunion. He picked up Lucy's bag, then took a step backward to give them a measure of privacy. Ronan joined him. The Bartons didn't move.

"My dear, sweet Lucy," Evangeline said, still holding fast to her sister.

"Do not make me go back, Evangeline. Please do not make me go back."

Those desperately whispered words reminded Dermot of the fear that he'd seen in Ronan's eyes the day he'd struck the bargain that had saved the boy from a life of misery. He'd not allowed himself to think much about that time—doing so still cut deeply—but seeing a similar scene play out now brought the memory fresh to his mind.

He tucked Ronan up close against him, grateful that the lad allowed it in that moment. He didn't always.

Evangeline held her sister at arm's length, looking her over with the same worry she'd worn all morning. "I will do everything in my power to make certain you don't have to return."

"What power do you have?" So much defeat lay in that question, so much despondency.

"Grandfather allowed you to come, something I insisted on. I believe I have more influence with him than I realized."

"You told him what to do?" Lucy sounded both doubtful and impressed.

"I did." Evangeline turned toward Dermot. She smiled, though tears hung on her lashes. "Lucy, this is Dermot McCormick and his boy, Ronan. They are neighbors of mine, and my dearest friends."

Though "friends" was not the word he'd have preferred, something in the tender way she looked at him added a note of something more to the declaration.

"We're right pleased to meet you, Miss Lucy," he said, doffing his hat. "Your sister speaks of you often."

"He is Irish," Lucy said in a surprised whisper.

Evangeline smiled. "He is *very* Irish. He is also very kind and clever and helpful and . . . rather wonderful."

If ever a woman had offered a more welcome bit of flattery than that, Dermot wasn't aware of it. Despite the bitter wind punishing them all, he felt warmed to his core.

"M' mother'd be right pleased to hear you say that, Evangeline."

Lucy, keeping close to her sister's side, eyed Dermot more closely. "Are you two sweethearts?"

Dermot grinned, while Evangeline blushed a deep shade of red.

Lucy appeared to bite back a smile of her own. "Never mind. I think I know."

Dermot thought he knew as well. 'Twas a fine thing to have an answer to that particular question.

"This is Ronan," he told Lucy. "He's a good lad, though a quiet one. He's not likely to greet you warmly, but you needn't take offense at that."

Evangeline leaned closer to her sister and said, "He is very much like our James."

Lucy made a sound of understanding and nodded. "I am happy to meet him, though I will not press him for conversation."

Their brother James must have been quite like Ronan for Lucy to have understood the situation so quickly and so entirely.

"We had best go greet your aunt and uncle," Evangeline said. "They have come as well."

"If we must," Lucy said.

Dermot walked alongside them, Ronan tucked against him. They moved slowly toward the Bartons, who made no effort to close the gap.

"Grandfather did not send you alone on the train, did he?" Evangeline asked.

"A servant came along," Lucy said, "but she was on her way further along the route and did not disembark here."

Evangeline breathed a sigh of obvious relief. "I felt certain he wouldn't have left you entirely unprotected, yet you were alone when you stepped from the train."

"Grandfather does not particularly care for me, but he is not entirely thoughtless." Lucy spoke so matter-of-factly, as if indifference from her mother's father was acceptable. How lonely she must have been these past months. 'Twas little wonder Evangeline had worried so much for her.

Lucy offered a brief curtsey to her aunt and uncle, though she neither spoke to them nor looked them in the eye.

"Now that you are here, we can be on our way," Mrs. Barton said. "Mr. McCormick, I am certain, will place your bag in our carriage."

"While I appreciate the offer of a ride in your vehicle," Evangeline said, "we are happy to walk. I should like Lucy to see the town, which she can easily do between here and our home."

"You misunderstand," Mrs. Barton said. "Lucy is staying with us. That was your grandfather's arrangement."

Lucy shrunk against Evangeline, who stood firm. "I haven't the slightest intention of agreeing to that arrangement. Lucy will be coming home with me."

Lucy turned wide eyes on her sister, apparently surprised by the stand she took.

"You are in no position—" Mrs. Barton began.

"She is my sister, and she will be coming home with me." Evangeline stepped beyond her aunt. "I made the mistake of leaving her in your care once, and you sent her away. I will not allow that to happen again."

"Robert," Mrs. Barton said. "Do something."

"I am doing something," he answered. "I am taking you home and leaving the girls in peace."

For a brief moment, Dermot held Mr. Barton's gaze. He hoped his hard expression communicated how little he approved of the way Evangeline had been treated by her family. Far from shrinking from the silent criticism, Mr. Barton nodded. "You'll look after the Blake sisters, I presume."

"I've every intention of doing so," he answered.

Mrs. Barton assumed her all-too-familiar tone and expression of distaste. "I imagine you do."

"Enough," Mr. Barton spoke sharply. "You have offered enough unwarranted insults to last most people a lifetime, and I, for one, will not endure it any longer."

He stepped away from his wife and moved toward their waiting carriage.

"Do you mean to leave me here?" she called after him.

"I mean to return home," he said, not slowing or looking back. "If you wish to come as well, I suggest you hurry."

No more was said. No peace was restored between them. Dermot did not know the history that had led to such animosity in their marriage, but he found himself feeling unexpectedly sorry for the Bartons. They were so obviously unhappy, and that misery infected most everyone they encountered. Somehow, Evangeline had managed to rise above it.

Her determination, her hope in the face of sorrow, her strength had thoroughly captured him. Which presented a question he was not yet ready to answer: what would he do if her grandfather insisted that Lucy return to Leeds and Evangeline chose to follow? How could he possibly live without her?

CHAPTER THIRTY-THREE

After some initial shock at the humbleness of Evangeline's living quarters, Lucy settled in nicely. She quickly spotted her treasures from home on the mantelshelf. "You still have them."

"Of course I do. They have been waiting there for you."

Lucy took George's shepherd from its perch and cradled it lovingly in her hands. A moment later, she did the same with Father's pipe.

"I can read to you from James's book tonight, if you'd like," Evangeline offered.

"Just as Father used to," Lucy said, her voice heavy and quiet.

"Yes. Just as Father used to."

Lucy's head slowly turned until she faced the photograph directly. She leaned closer. The tips of her fingers rested on the edge of the mantelshelf, but she did not touch the frame or glass.

"Mother," she whispered.

Evangeline blinked back tears as Lucy stood for minutes on end looking longingly at the frozen faces. She whispered each of their names, not in greeting or recognition, but in tones of utter heartbreak.

"May we go somewhere else for a while?" Lucy asked.

"Of course," Evangeline said. "The view from the top of the street is lovely. Shall we go see it?"

"I would like that."

Evangeline walked with her beyond the street's end, all the way out to the edge of the moor. The endless sea of grass-covered hills rolling out into the distance left Lucy speechless. Evangeline drank in the view as she always did. She didn't imagine there was a place in all of England as breathtaking in its starkness as this harsh but beautiful land.

"Would you like to meet one of my favorite families? They live here on the moor. Three of their children attend the school; one acts as my helper in class. She reminds me a great deal of you, actually, though perhaps a bit more outspoken."

Lucy nodded, so they made their way along the damp, dirt path. Lucy had so many questions. Why were there so few trees? What kind of grass grew in such a barren place? The tiny frogs that dotted the trail as it passed near a small spring captured her attention. She bent low, watching them, fascinated to discover the small dots below her feet were not rocks but tiny creatures.

"The moor is full of surprises," Evangeline told her sister. "It is an often unforgiving place, and it tests the mettle of all who live on it or around its edges, but it is wonderful all the same."

"I think you like living here," Lucy said.

"I could not imagine living anywhere else." The admission did not surprise Evangeline, though she had never spoken the words out loud before.

"Even Petersmarch?" Lucy pressed.

She thought a moment but knew her answer immediately.

"I should like to visit again someday, but I don't know that it would feel like home any longer. The house is not ours. The family living there belongs to us only distantly. This place, with all its challenges and struggles, has become home to me."

Lucy threaded her arm through Evangeline's. "I want to see all of it."

Evangeline pointed out the fields where the Crossleys' sheep had once roamed and spoke of the tragedy that had befallen them. She told her sister about the Palmers and their endless struggles. She talked of the factory, though not in tremendous detail; her sister did not need to know just yet how closely their family was tied to the suffering in this town. She shared a number of stories about her students and the progress they were making. She spoke of the inspector and his disapproval.

"Do you mean to continue teaching them from the stories you and Mrs. Crossley have written down?"

"I do." She knew the consequences but would not change her mind. "The method is working, whether or not Mr. Garvey is willing to admit as much. And though these people might well lose their language and their stories in time, I will not be part of the reason they do."

"You have become so fierce," Lucy said.

Evangeline laughed to hear her sister speak so incredulously. Had she truly been so fainthearted before? "Dermot says I have fire in my soul."

"I think he likes fire." Lucy's giggle gave away her meaning.

"You are playing matchmaker now?"

"This match was made long before I arrived."

Oh, it was a relief to see her sister smiling. She had done little of that since arriving in Smeatley, and none at all during their family's final days. Smeatley, with all its frustrations, was good for the heart.

"Do you like Dermot?" Evangeline found herself unexpectedly anxious about the answer.

Lucy did not hesitate. "I do. He is direct, which would have made me nervous if not for the way he kept looking at you."

"What way is that?"

"As if you were the very last piece of blackberry tart." Lucy sighed in that dramatic way all twelve-year-old girls seemed able to manage.

Evangeline chose to see the description as a compliment, though she had never before been compared to a pastry. "I think Father would have liked Dermot. How could he not?"

Lucy did not agree as readily as Evangeline expected. Indeed, her expression had grown guarded.

"Do you not think so?"

Lucy's brow drew downward. She didn't speak for a long moment as they continued their walk over the moor. "I remember the gentlemen Father introduced to you. They were not like Mr. McCormick. They were well-to-do and influential and came from fine families. I think Father and Mother always meant you to make a match of that sort."

There was a great deal of truth in Lucy's observation. Would Dermot have truly met with disapproval? Surely not. There was not a better man in all the world. He had cared about her when no one else had. He had stood as her friend during difficult moments and had not hesitated to tell her his thoughts when she asked for them. He saw her as capable and clever when even her own family had assumed she would fail at the tasks laid before her. He was good and kind and tenderhearted. How could her parents have wished for anything less for her?

Lucy spoke before Evangeline managed to find her voice. "Do you suppose Grandfather will object to him?"

"I happen to know Grandfather is impressed with him. He spoke highly of his work on the back-to-back houses and the way he manages his crew."

With a wisdom that belied her years, Lucy countered that observation. "Appreciating his work is a far cry from approving of him as a grandson-in-law."

Heat rose to Evangeline's face. "Things have not progressed so far as all that."

Lucy shrugged. "Not yet."

"There is one benefit to being a woman of independence living more or less on her own." Evangeline spoke with more surety than she felt. "I get to make decisions for myself." She only hoped *this* was one of those decisions.

When they reached the Crossleys' home, Lucy eyed it with curiosity but, thankfully, not dismissal. Having been raised in a fine home with all the advantages, Lucy would be unfamiliar with such poverty as was common in this small town.

Susannah answered their knock. "Ey up, Miss Blake."

"Good day to you, as well. I've come to introduce my sister. I should very much like for her to be acquainted with your family."

"I'd've guessed she were thy sister." Susannah seemed pleased. The Crossleys had been distant of late, but Evangeline hoped they were warming back up to her, however slowly.

"Let t' ladies come in," Mrs. Crossley called out. "It's right parky outside."

Lucy shot Evangeline a look of confusion.

"She was merely saying how cold the weather is."

Lucy nodded, though her expression didn't entirely clear.

They stepped inside. A blessed warmth immediately

enveloped them. The weather had, indeed, turned "parky" of late. Evangeline suspected winters in Yorkshire would be cold indeed.

To her surprise, she found Dermot sitting at the table between John Crossley and Ronan, two buckets on the tabletop in front of them. They, along with the rest of the Crossley family, watched Evangeline and Lucy. Having spent a good amount of the walk here speaking of Dermot and speculating upon his intentions, Evangeline couldn't prevent herself from coloring up. She only hoped the others would attribute the red in her cheeks to the cold air.

"Put t' wood in t' hole, Susannah," Mrs. Crossley instructed. "Tha'll let out all t' warm air."

Evangeline had finally sorted out that particular turn of phrase. When she'd first heard it, she'd though the word "hole" was "oil," owing to the unique Yorkshire pronunciation. "The wood" referred to the door. "The hole" referenced the open doorway. "Putting the wood in the hole" meant closing the door. It was a rather lovely way of saying such a commonplace thing.

With the door firmly closed, Susannah guided them to the crackling warmth of the fireplace. Evangeline looked to Mrs. Crossley as they passed, hoping to see a welcome there rather than an indication of intrusion. She received a genuinely pleased smile. Relief settled over her like a comforting blanket. Perhaps her deception, however unavoidable, would be forgiven.

"Tha're sister to us Miss Blake?" Mrs. Crossley asked Lucy.

Had Evangeline looked as confused those first few weeks as Lucy did now? She made a quick translation. "She is asking if you are my sister."

"I am," Lucy answered.

Mrs. Crossley made quick work of introducing her family, though Mr. Crossley and Thomas were away from home.

Susannah asked Lucy if she'd like to see the new kittens in the stone barn. Lucy looked to Evangeline for permission. She nodded, grateful for Susannah's easy nature and willingness to befriend the quiet and uncertain.

The girls, nearly of an age, stepped outside. Lucy would find the welcome Evangeline, herself, had wished for.

"She looks a great deal like thee," Mrs. Crossley said.

"I have heard that a few times since her arrival. I hadn't realized before that we resembled one another so closely."

Dermot rose. He nudged the two pails on the table closer to the boys. "Keep eyeing these, lads. I've a woman to greet, and I mean to do it well."

He crossed to where she stood. His earnest gaze brought Lucy's comparison to blackberry tarts firmly to mind. Quite suddenly, Evangeline could not stop herself from laughing.

"You're not supposed to find the prospect of me greeting you so entertaining, lass."

She set a hand on his arm and hoped her expression, though no doubt still filled with laughter, proved apologetic. "I was only thinking back on something Lucy said, and I could not help myself."

He took her hand in his and kissed it, as he'd taken to doing every time they saw each other. He'd also made a habit of lingering over his good night when he left her house each evening. She hoped he would do so again when they parted today.

"And now you're blushing." His gaze narrowed, though amusement sparkled beneath the surface. "I can hardly wait to see what you do next."

Evangeline glanced at Mrs. Crossley, uncertain what she thought of Dermot's unabashed flirting, but she simply waved them off.

"Kiss her fully if tha'd like," she said. "We'll not tease thee much."

Dermot chuckled low and deep. "I'll not put you to the blush more than I already have, my dear. I will say, though, it's a fine thing to have you here. I don't always get to see you twice in one day."

"You are always welcome for an extra visit. *I* don't impose a limit on knocks per day."

"I'll remember that." He released her hand, but didn't step away. "At the moment, though, Ronan and I are teaching John how to mix mortar and how many bricks are needed for a piling and such things."

"He is a very bright boy."

Dermot turned back toward the table. "They both are." He sat between the boys and turned toward John. "What have you decided about the mixtures?"

"This'n"—John tapped a bucket—"would be best in wet weather. This'n"—he tapped the other bucket—"would be best in dry weather."

Dermot nodded. "You've the right of that. Now tell me why."

Mrs. Crossley brought Evangeline a cup of hot tea while John gave Dermot his explanation.

"Thank you," she said, holding the cup between her hands and reveling in the warmth.

"Dermot has spent t' afternoon helping us John learn about bricklaying. He'll be saved from t' mill yet, I'm certain of it."

"I do hope so." Evangeline took a sip. Some of the chill she'd felt on the moor began to dissipate. "How is Johanna? I worry about her."

"She's been stronger these past weeks," Mrs. Crossley said. "We've some hope of her getting better."

"May I see her?"

Mrs. Crossley motioned her toward the small bedchamber where the little girl had been on Evangeline's previous visits. She stepped inside and found Johanna wrapped in a blanket, sitting more upright than she had been. Her face was still pale but her eyes were more alert.

"Good afternoon, sweetheart." Evangeline sat on the edge of the bed near Johanna's trundle. "Your mother tells me you are feeling better."

"A little bit." Even her voice sounded stronger.

"Has Susannah continued with your lessons?"

Johanna nodded. "I don't learn fast, but I'm working hard."

"I'm certain you are."

Mrs. Crossley pulled a rocking chair close. "I've given some thought to what tha said about us stories, Miss Blake. It'd be a shame not to finish 'em."

"I agree."

"If you've any paper with thee, we could work on it a bit now."

A surge of disappointment spread over her. "I don't have any."

"I've my slate," Johanna offered.

"Oh, Johanna." Evangeline set her cup of tea on the chest at the end of the bed. "Would you allow me to borrow it, just so I can write down your mother's stories? I will make certain Susannah brings you another tomorrow."

Johanna's gaze turned hopeful. "Can I bahn to school and get it for missen?"

"You'd like to come yourself?" Evangeline looked at Mrs. Crossley. "Could she?"

"Could I?" Johanna pleaded.

Mrs. Crossley held her arms out. "Climb on us lap, little one. Tha can listen while I tell Miss Blake a story."

Johanna slowly pulled herself onto her mother's lap. Mrs. Crossley wrapped her arms around her daughter. "If tha is well enough tomorrow, I'll fetch thee to school."

Johanna leaned against her mother. "I'll be well. I know it."

Mrs. Crossley stroked her daughter's hair. She looked at Evangeline. "T' slate is in t' trunk."

Evangeline pulled it out, along with the bit of chalk set carefully beside it. She resumed her place on the edge of the bed. Excitement bubbled up. This was more than merely a continuation of their earlier project. In that moment, she knew she had not lost Mrs. Crossley's friendship. She had been forgiven, and she still had a place in this town.

CHAPTER THIRTY-FOUR

ucy joined Evangeline in the school room Monday morning. She stood a bit apart, watching the students fill the benches. Her stiff posture spoke of deep discomfort. Lucy had ever been a quiet and uncertain girl. Susannah, however, hadn't a timid bone in her body, neither was she one to give up easily.

Evangeline watched in mingled awe and gratitude as Susannah patiently and kindly pulled Lucy into the circle of students, asking her help, insisting she was wanted and needed. By the time they took their afternoon tea, Lucy had tentatively taken up the tutoring of a small handful of students. She grew more comfortable as the day wore on, and, by the time the students began filing out for the evening, several paused to hug her as they left.

Amazement and happiness filled Lucy's expression. All Evangeline could do was smile her understanding.

She put an arm around her sister's shoulders. "You were wonderful today, darling. Simply wonderful."

Spots of embarrassed color touched Lucy's cheeks. "I didn't always know what to do."

Evangeline met Susannah's eyes. "A common feeling, is it not?"

Susannah laughed. "Aye. It's allas like 'at."

"But," Evangeline said, "that makes every moment of progress even sweeter."

A smile tugged at Susannah's lips. "If tha are expecting nowt, tha'll be happy with owt."

Lucy turned wide eyes on Evangeline.

Again, Susannah laughed. "Tha looked just as confused when tha first came to Smeatley. Us words sit odd on south-folk ears."

Evangeline squeezed Lucy's hand. "She said that if you are expecting nothing, you'll be happy with anything."

"Ah. You were purposely lowering my expectations of you as teachers?"

"Neya." Susannah shook her head. "We're just right terrible at it."

That set them all to laughing. How quickly Lucy and Susannah had taken to one another. They were good for each other. Susannah was often lonely amongst the other children, and had needed a friend. Lucy, under Susannah's influence, was lighter and happier. Both girls were a balm to Evangeline's soul.

"Us mother is coming to do t' stories with thee," Susannah said.

"Perfect." Evangeline fetched her inkwell and paper from the lectern. "Would you girls straighten up here so I can meet her downstairs?"

They agreed and set to work, chatting and smiling. Susannah was patient enough to help Lucy through the unfamiliar Yorkshire words. And Lucy, bless her, had grown so immediately fond of Susannah, something she'd mentioned again and again after their visit to the Crossley home, that she was simply delighted to be with her new friend.

Evangeline hurried down the steps. Ronan sat on the bottom-most one, a slate on his lap, writing on it with a nub of chalk. She sat down beside him. He had written a full dozen words, a few of which she had only introduced him to that day.

How very tempted she was to put an arm around his shoulders, but she knew him well enough to know that touch was not always welcome, not even always from Dermot.

"You are doing so well, Ronan," she said. "Your letters are beautifully formed. You learn words very quickly. I am inordinately proud of you."

He nodded and kept writing.

"Do you like school?" she asked, knowing his propensity for blunt honesty.

"School is for letters and reading and bread at tea."

He had assigned school a purpose and a place. That had always been a sure indication that James valued and enjoyed something.

"And school is with you," he added. "And you are at supper, and you sing when the thunder happens."

He had a place for her. She had a purpose in his life.

Tears sprang to her eyes. In recent weeks, a number of her students had thanked her for the things she'd taught them. They greeted her after church on Sundays. Little Cecilia had even told her that she loved her. Yet that moment, sitting beside Ronan as he wrote word after word and casually spoke of her as an accepted part of his life, moved her as nothing else had.

"If we have time before your father comes this evening," Evangeline said, "we can read more stories from my brother's book." They did that often.

"Papa likes the stories. He told me."

Her smile grew and grew. Ronan was opening to her more with each passing day. And to know Dermot enjoyed their story reading time was an added bit of encouragement.

Ronan looked up from his slate and toward the door. His gaze remained long enough to pull Evangeline's attention there as well. Dermot stood framed by the light spilling in from outside. His brows pulled down sharply. His eyes did not waver from Ronan. He, surprisingly, looked almost emotional.

"Dermot?"

In a voice no louder than a whisper, he said, "He called me 'papa.'" His apparent amazement told her a great deal of their history she'd not yet been made privy to.

She rose and crossed to him. "He hasn't called you that before."

He shook his head. "Not ever."

"I do not think that means he doesn't care for you."

"I know it. 'Tis simply . . ." His shoulders rose and fell. "I've thought of Ronan as my son all these years, but I've always wondered how he thinks of me."

The boy was bent over his slate once more, seemingly oblivious to the emotions his father was experiencing, to those *she* was experiencing.

"James was not overly expressive either," she told Dermot. "We came to treasure those moments when we had a glimpse into his thoughts and feelings. Those moments were precious."

"Yes, they are." His fond smile was soft, pleased. "I see them more and more often, though I don't know if it's because I've learned to better recognize them or because he offers more than he once did."

"Perhaps both," she suggested.

Dermot let a quick whistle. Ronan looked up on the instant.

"We're planting trees in a few minutes," Dermot said. "I know you wanted to see that."

Ronan hopped to his feet. He brought Evangeline his slate and chalk. "These are for school."

She took them and nodded gently. "They are for school."

Ronan slipped past, stepping out the door.

"You'll return for supper?" she asked Dermot.

"Of course." He kissed her cheek, then followed his son outside.

What a day she'd had. Lucy had found some enjoyment in teaching. Susannah had shined as she'd directed Lucy's efforts. The children were reading better than ever. Ronan had, in his own way, expressed his fondness for her. And she had been present as Dermot had experienced a precious moment with his son.

Her first days in Smeatley had been so very difficult. The contrast between then and now was drastic and reassuring.

Not even a moment passed before Mrs. Crossley stepped inside the small entryway. She glanced back once before her smiling gaze settled on Evangeline. "Dermot McCormick seems in fine spirits."

"I believe he is pleased to be spending extra time with his son today."

Something like a laugh entered Mrs. Crossley's eyes. "I suspect his spirits are often lifted when he visits here."

Though a bit of warmth touched Evangeline's cheeks, she didn't flinch from it. She not only had nothing to be ashamed of in the time she spent with Dermot, she was actually inordinately pleased that the town fully believed he enjoyed his time spent with her.

"Susannah tells me you have a few minutes to spend on our stories this afternoon," Evangeline said.

Mrs. Crossley nodded. "I've a right lot of time, truth be told."

Worry touched Evangeline's mind. "You still have not found work outside the mill?"

"Not yet, but I will." She spoke confidently, but with a hint of misgivings.

They moved into Evangeline's humble living quarters and settled in. Not a word of the story passed between them before Susannah and Lucy burst in.

"We've had t' best idea," Susannah declared. Lucy beamed silently beside her. "T' children are reading well now. What if us had t' parents come hear 'em read, see how much they've learned?"

A demonstration day. Evangeline hadn't thought of that, but it was not a bad idea. The parents who had sacrificed to send their children to school would be given the chance to see the dividends those sacrifices had paid. And those in town who were unconvinced of the value of educating their children might begin to see worth in it.

A nervous excitement began to grow inside.

"We would need to choose a day when most families would be available," Evangeline said.

"Sundays," Mrs. Crossley said firmly. "They won't be at t' factory."

Sunday, then. "And we would need to find a place large enough for everyone to gather."

"T' front garden is large enough," Susannah said.

"The weather might be too parky," Evangeline worried aloud.

"They'll keep their coats on," Susannah insisted.

They'd settled the when and where and a bit of the how.

That left but one unanswered question, the one that sprang into Evangeline's thoughts in that very moment. "But will they come? I know my position in this town was thrown into chaos when my grandfather revealed my connection to him and the Bartons. I've not been very welcome since then."

Mrs. Crossley and Susannah exchanged silent looks that didn't bode particularly well.

"They are upset with me," Evangeline said.

"More confused," Mrs. Crossley said. "Tha are kin to a powerful family. We've not t' first notion how to treat thee now."

"I'm no different than I was before," she said.

"Aye, but us didn't know truly who tha was before."

It was the same argument Dermot had made, one she didn't entirely know how to address. "Would the people in town put aside their difficulties with me long enough to come hear their children read?"

Mrs. Crossly nodded. "I believe they would."

Evangeline met Lucy and Susannah's eager eyes. "We should do it."

The weather proved remarkably cooperative Sunday afternoon. Many local families, even some who had no children in the school, had gathered in front of the schoolhouse. Some sat on blankets, others atop the large rocks scattered around. A few stood.

Evangeline's students were both eager and nervous. They shook and bounced and smiled as their eyes darted about. She did what she could to smooth their uncertainty, but she was nervous herself. The school inspector had already offered a preliminary assessment of her teaching ability. The town would soon be given the chance to do the same.

Dermot sat a bit removed with Ronan directly beside him. She had no expectation of him joining in the readings; she was simply pleased he had been willing to come. School, after all, was not usually held on Sundays. He did, however, spend a great many Sunday afternoons with her, something she hoped was proving helpful in calming whatever uncertainties he was feeling.

The appointed time arrived, and Evangeline moved to stand before them all. Her heartbeat thudded against her temples. The thickness in her throat threatened to end her planned speech before it even began. All their eyes were on her now. She swallowed.

Say something. Anything.

But no words came. She had misled these people, and their distrust lay plainly before her. What was she do? Say?

Hugo Palmer shouted into the silence. "Ey up, Miss Blake."

"Ey up, yussen," she answered without hardly thinking. She'd answered in the Yorkshire manner. Would they be offended or think she was mocking them?

But grins broke out all over the crowd, even a few chuckles.

"I realize my south-folk manner of speaking likely did a right terrible job of that," she said. "I am learning, though."

Again they laughed, but not *at* her. They were clearly pleased. Relief began trickling over her.

"Your children have been learning as well, which I know is the reason you have come. I will not take up any more of their time but will, instead, give them a chance to show you how much they have accomplished."

She motioned Susannah up. The girl didn't hesitate for even the length of a breath.

"I've been helping t' newest students. They've summat to

read for everyone." She motioned for her students to join her. A slow trickle quickly turned to a flow and, in a moment's time, Susannah's students were surrounding her.

They each took turns reading a short passage. Nothing they shared was overly complicated, yet it represented weeks of work. Evangeline watched her children as they shared their achievements. Some were hesitant, others confident. Some stumbled over their assignments, others offered a smooth, flawless performance. Throughout it all, Evangeline stood with a hand pressed to her heart, so deeply pleased. Their parents, she noticed, were equally proud.

Her more intermediate students joined Lucy at the front of the group next. Lucy's face turned a tell-tale shade of crimson, yet she pressed onward, explaining that she had spent the last week with her group of children and they, too, had prepared something for their parents. They offered their efforts and were met with equal enthusiasm.

Evangeline stepped in front once more. "We have but one group of students left," she said, "our most advanced group. These children have become remarkably accomplished readers in a very short amount of time, and they have prepared something particular for all of you." She waved the small group up.

Hugo, John Crossley, Susannah, and Lucy all took their places near her.

"They mean to read to you the story of 'The Town Beneath the Waves.'" She stepped aside, intending to allow the children full rein over their performance.

Susannah, however, held her there. "Miss Blake didn't say that she wrote down this story in Yorkshire speak, not south-folk speak. She's teaching us to read just t' way we speak, in us own words."

Apparently that bit of information was not widely known. Eyes around the crowd pulled wide and a few whispers erupted. Evangeline hoped her approach met with their approval, heaven knew it didn't meet with the approval of the school board or the school inspector.

Susannah gave Evangeline a quick nod, an indication, she guessed, that she was now free to step aside. She slipped away and took a place beside the school, next to Dermot.

"You look nervous, darlin'," he said.

"I am," she admitted. "I mean for this to be an afternoon for the children to impress their parents with all they've learned, but I can't help feeling a little under inspection myself."

"From where I've stood," he said, "you appear to be meeting with their approval."

She took a deep, lung-shaking breath. "I hope you are right."

Up in front of the gathering, Susannah continued her introductory speech. The girl certainly didn't want for confidence. "Hugo, John and missen are known to thee and all. This is Lucy, what is sister to us Miss Blake. She helps teach t' students. Now, she's south-folk, so her Yorkshire speech is middlin' at best, but she can read like she was born doin' it."

Lucy reddened, but laughed. Weeks earlier, Evangeline would have struggled to picture her quiet sister standing before a gathering of strangers. Smeatley had already done her good, just as it had changed and transformed Evangeline into a stronger version of herself.

All four children held up the slates on which they had copied out their portion of the story they meant to read. It was not long, owing to both the inexperience of three of the children and Evangeline's desire to keep the gathering short, but she hoped it would be enjoyed just the same.

Hugo began. "'One day, a weary bloke clothed in rags appeared in t' town and tried to beg for scran and shelter.'"

John read next. "However, he were turned away from every door, apart from t' right last one, which were home to a humble couple who welcomed him as a guest, and offered him t' best of what they had, though they had little."

Did the people listening realize that some of the words they read were spelled phonetically, exactly as the children spoke them? She'd argued with herself over that, wondering how far to adjust her representation of their words, how much to push them to recognize the "south-folk" versions of them. She felt she'd found a happy middle ground, but she doubted herself still.

Lucy was meant to read the next line, but she hesitated. Evangeline moved to help her, but Dermot took gentle hold of her hand.

"Let the children sort it," he whispered.

Fast as anything, Susannah slipped an arm around Lucy's shoulders. "Do thy best," she said. "We'll not begrudge thee a south-folk accent tripping across us words."

The gathering smiled and laughed a little.

"Go on, wee girl," Mr. Crossley tossed out encouragingly.

"Aye. Tha'll do grand," Mr. Palmer added.

The townspeople were showing her dear sister support, something she herself had been missing ever since her grandfather's visit. Her heart warmed at the sound and sight of it.

Lucy nodded a bit and raised her slate in shaking hands. "'As he gallock t' town, t' bloke turned around and, casting off his rags, revealed hissen as a dazzling angel.'" She released a breath so tense it was audible throughout the garden.

Susannah gave her shoulders one more squeeze, then took up her own slate. "'To punish t' townsolk for their unkindness, he uttered a terrible judgement upon them: "Semerwater rise, and Semerwater sink. Swallow t' town, all save this house where they gave us scran an' sup." As he spoke, water rose up from t' ground and swallowed every building in t' town, all except t' home of t' couple who offered him scran and shelter.'"

The town was clearly familiar with the tale. No one needed to tell them the story was over. They launched immediately into applause. The four children bowed and curtsied.

Evangeline released a breath just as strained as Lucy had. She could not be entirely certain she hadn't been holding her breath through the entire story.

She smiled at Dermot, relieved.

"They were brilliant," he said.

"Yes, they were."

She slipped back up to the front of the gathering. "That is what we prepared for you today. Thank you all so much for coming and for the honor and privilege of teaching your children. I have come to treasure and love them. Please remain as long as you'd like. Children, I will see you in the morning."

The crowd rose and began mingling about. Evangeline fully expected to simply return to her rooms and prepare for the next day, but it was not to be. People approached her, commenting on the presentation, on the children's reading and abilities. She was complimented, even thanked. On and on the interractions went, each as positive as the last. She was doing good and her efforts were appreciated.

The school board might not approve. Mr. Garvey might not. Her aunt, uncle, and grandfather might not. But she had made a difference in the lives of the people of Smeatley, and that was worth the world to her.

CHAPTER THIRTY-FIVE

The fortnight Lucy had been in town was the best Evangeline had known in some time. They often walked along the edge of the moor, singing songs they'd enjoyed at home, remembering happy times with their family. Dermot and Ronan spent the evenings with them, and Dermot was kind and gentle, treating her sister with such tenderness. Ronan was as quiet as expected but had shown no discomfort with Lucy. And Aunt Barton had not come by, which was joyous in and of itself.

Susannah continued working with the newest and youngest students. Lucy found a knack for helping those who were neither new nor quite among the fastest learners. She was encouraging and helpful and patient, a natural-born teacher. With most of her students looked after by the two girls, Evangeline was able to focus on those who were progressing quickly through their studies as well as have the time to give John and Hugo as much attention as possible during their brief half-days at school.

Johanna had not come to school, which broke Evangeline's heart. She and Lucy, however, walked out to the Crossley home a few times to see Johanna and bring a bit of school to her. While there, Evangeline wrote down more of Mrs. Crossley's stories. Given time, they would have enough for a book. The children of Smeatley would have story after story in their own language and their own words, and eventually Evangeline would lose her job over it. She hoped, of course, that the children's progress would prevent her dismissal.

Even if it didn't, she would not have changed course. She would not place her own employment above the well-being, happiness, and dignity of her students.

Mr. Garvey arrived at the schoolhouse door two weeks after Lucy's arrival, intent on making his next inspection.

"Have one of your students read from their primer." He stood at the front of the room, his expression stern and bleak. He had not, it seemed, forgotten their less-than-satisfactory previous encounter.

"The school board has not provided us with primers for all levels of academic ability," Evangeline told him. "The students have practiced with papers I have written out for them that reflect their current level of knowledge. The alphabet, words, sentences of varying difficulty."

"Are these papers written to the requirements of the various Standards?"

Evangeline turned the words about in her head but could not make sense of them. "I am not certain what you mean."

"Ours is not an educational system based on chaos. Learning is divided into six Standards, which students are required to pass. Your work as a teacher depends upon them progressing appropriately through the Standards."

Yet another thing the school board had not told her. "I was given no information about the Standards, Mr. Garvey."

"Hmm." He wrote something on the notepad he held in his hand. "Have one of your pupils read from one of your practice papers. I will do my best to sort out the rest of it."

Evangeline called on Billy Crossley. He was not her best student, but he was not shy nor easily intimidated. She gave him a sheet with several sentences at his level of learning. "T' cat sits on t' mat. It eats a rat. T' cat is fat."

"*The*," Mr. Garvey said. "*The* cat. *The* mat."

"He said 'the cat' and 'the mat,'" Evangeline assured him. "His accent simply makes it sound different to your ears." They'd had this conversation before.

Mr. Garvey eyed her with disapproval. "Have you not been working on their speech, Miss Blake?"

"They have learned to read and write, do basic arithmetic, and are learning geography. That is the purpose of a school."

"The Committee of Council on Education has determined the purpose of this school," Mr. Garvey said. "Teaching proper language is one of those purposes. How many times do I have to tell you this?"

"They can read," she repeated, "write, do arithmetic, and read a map. They are receiving an education."

Mr. Garvey eyed her with tense frustration. "Are they still reading Yorkshire stories?"

She would not lie, but neither would she allow him to make her ashamed of all she had accomplished. "They are. And because of those Yorkshire stories, their skills have improved tenfold."

"You were given specific instructions." He slapped his notepad down on the lectern. "Did I not make myself clear?"

Evangeline squared her shoulders. As Lucy had said, she had grown fierce, and she had every bit of the fire Dermot said she did. "My first loyalty is to my students and their families. I have chosen to teach them in the way that best suits them."

"Give me the stories." He held his hand out. "I will dispose of them."

The students watched, wide-eyed and uncertain. Lucy was clearly confused. Evangeline would not be strong-armed or ordered about. Not anymore. "The stories do not belong to you. Neither do these children. Neither do their words."

Mr. Garvey scoffed. "Your job, however, does."

Evangeline didn't flinch. "Before you decide that I am unworthy of my post, will you not allow the students to show you what they have learned?"

"I suppose." He did not sound at all willing to be convinced.

Still, she would try. "Who else will read for Mr. Garvey?"

Cecilia Haigh stood. Her little hands shook, the paper she held crinkling in her grasp. "I'll read, Miss Blake."

She knelt in front of the nervous girl. "Are you certain? You do not have to." She knew Cecilia's bashful disposition well enough to realize how terrified she must have been.

"He doesn't think tha are a good teacher," she said, her voice quiet and tremulous. "I want him to know tha are."

Cecilia's defense of her was touching. "I thank you for doing this, and I am fortunate to have you as one of my students."

She stood and took a position behind Cecilia. She set her hands on the girl's shoulders, hoping to give her an extra measure of courage.

The entire class fell quiet as their usually silent classmate bravely read from the sheet she had been studying. Even Lucy, who had known Cecilia for so short an amount of time, seemed to understand the enormity of what was happening. When Cecilia finished and dropped immediately back onto the bench,

Lucy sat beside her and put her arms around her. Cecilia turned in to the embrace, burying her head against Lucy.

Jimmy Sutcliffe volunteered to read next. Then George Palmer offered to answer a mathematical question, as did Emma Bennett.

Mr. Garvey, though he listened without interruption, showed no sign of being truly impressed. If anything, he grew more noticeably frustrated. He disapproved of her methods—he had made that clear—and he found her children's Yorkshire manner of speaking to be an indication of her failures. Could nothing convince him otherwise?

"We do not mean to keep you overly long." Evangeline wished to end their day of lessons in peace.

"You were told of your obligation to address their language," he said.

She nodded. "I understand. I did what was best for my students."

"That is not for you to decide." Mr. Garvey wrote down something else. "We cannot have chaos in our schools."

"Does this seem chaotic to you?" She motioned to the orderly, quiet classroom.

"They need to be taught to speak properly, to use proper words."

Evangeline squared her shoulders. "Then I am not the right person for this job."

The classroom erupted with objections. Mr. Garvey's gaze narrowed. Evangeline stood firm. She would not bend on this.

"We have goals and rules for a reason, Miss Blake." Mr. Garvey took up his notepad. "We cannot have teachers flouting them, not without consequences."

She stood as one at a mark, unable to avoid the blow he dealt. She knew he had the power to dismiss her. He knew she knew that. Though she was afraid, she would not allow that fear to intimidate her into doing something she knew was wrong.

"Fetch your school log," Mr. Garvey instructed.

She was prepared for the request, having kept a daily record of the school since his first visit more than a month ago. She pulled the ledger, which Uncle Barton had provided after she'd explained the requirement, from its place beside the lectern. She held it out to Mr. Garvey, but he shook his head.

"It is the duty of the teacher to record the results of an inspection," he said.

"Truly?"

He nodded sternly. "Every teacher records every inspection."

She laid the book on the lectern, open to the next blank page. Mr. Garvey set his notepad beside the ledger.

"Copy my report precisely," he instructed, then looked over the students. "Return to your studies," he told them.

Her children bent over their slates even as she bent over the lectern. *Copy my report precisely.* She breathed deeply, took up her pen, and did as she was required.

"Miss Blake has not worked toward the approved Standards for her students. She has no concept of approved teaching methods. Her attitude is off-puttingly self-assured. Though she was told to focus portions of her teaching on the improvement of her students' speech, she has refused to do so. Inspection has found her incapable, and it is recommended she be removed from her post."

Heat flooded Evangeline's face as she copied down the demeaning words. There could be no doubt of her situation now nor of Mr. Garvey's intention to see her fired.

"I have copied it." She spoke with as much calm as she could muster.

"Did you sign it?"

Sign it? "Is that required?"

"Yes."

She did not permit her disappointment or humiliation to show. She simply signed her name in full, set down her pen.

"If that is all you needed, Mr. Garvey, I would prefer to return to our lessons."

Mr. Garvey took up his notebook and left, his expression one of satisfaction. Perhaps she should have groveled. Perhaps she should have bent to his dictates. Months earlier, when she had first arrived in Smeatley, she likely would have. She could not countenance the idea now.

Dermot's declaration from days earlier returned to her mind with force: "I have no master." Though she worked as a teacher under the direction of the town school board and at the discretion of the education committee, she was not their servant nor were they granted such complete power over her. She would not bend to the will of those who refused to see the truth in front of them. She knew what was right, and she would do it no matter the cost.

Lucy was helping Ronan with his studies when Dermot arrived. Evangeline immediately pulled him into the entryway, closing the door to her living quarters so she could speak openly without her sister or his son overhearing.

"What's happened, my dear? You look overset."

"The school inspector returned today."

He nodded, clearly knowing there was more.

"He warned me on his last visit I was not to teach the children using Yorkshire texts, but doing so has helped them so much. I could not deny them the ability to learn simply because it did not meet with his approval."

Dermot's gaze didn't waver, neither did he interrupt.

"And he insisted that I work to change the children's speech so they sound more—" Weeks earlier, she would have used the word "proper," but that didn't feel right any longer. "More like children outside of Yorkshire. More like me, really."

"And have you?" he asked.

"Of course not. Their words are not mine to take away."

He nodded slowly. "I'd wager the inspector was none too happy about that."

"I am going to be let go," she said on a tense sigh.

"Is it for certain?"

"Yes." The reality of it was beginning to settle over her.

"He'd not offer you a second chance?"

"This was my second chance." She dropped onto the stairs, resting her elbows on her legs.

Dermot sat beside her. "Did using those Yorkshire stories help your wee ones?"

"They began reading so much faster," she said. "Having words they knew made understanding them so much easier. And they were excited to read something familiar, to be able to recognize on paper the stories their own mothers had told them. It made all the difference in the world."

Dermot's arm settled around her. She inched closer to him and leaned her head on his shoulder.

"Teaching them in their own language was the right thing," she said. "What if it wasn't worth it, though? Their new teacher might care more for rules and regulations than for the children. Perhaps I should have simply done as I was told."

"You could have." He rubbed her arm, keeping her close by. "But that is not who you are."

It used to be.

"You do what you know to be right," he continued, "even when it is difficult. Being less than yourself would not make you a better teacher, and you would be miserable."

"I am going to lose my job."

"I know, my dear."

"And I'll lose my home."

"I know."

"And my children."

He leaned his head on hers. "I know."

Someone knocked at the door. Evangeline's heart dropped. Had Mr. Garvey returned, her dismissal papers in hand?

"Bide here, dear," Dermot said, slipping away and standing. "I'll see who's come."

She straightened her posture and attempted to regain her composure. She would end her time here with dignity.

It was not Mr. Garvey who stood at the door, but Uncle Barton. He and Dermot exchanged uncomfortable greetings.

Uncle Barton spotted Evangeline sitting on the stairs. "May we talk a moment?"

She rose on shaky legs, but didn't shy away from his gaze. The hint of an apology she saw in his eyes did not set her mind at ease. While she was grateful he seemed to regret his business there, he clearly intended to go forward with it.

He stepped inside and took his hat in his hands.

"I suspect Mr. Garvey paid you a visit," she said.

"He did." Her uncle fiddled with the brim of his hat. "The town school board answers to Mr. Garvey because he speaks for the Committee of Council on Education. Their authority on this matter is far greater than ours."

"I understand." For the briefest of moments, she looked to Dermot. He stood by the door, watching her with precisely the mixture of support and concern that she needed. "I know what his report told you—he required that I copy it into my school log—but I feel you should know what he left off. The children have improved tremendously in their reading and writing since last he was here. They are enthusiastic about their studies. Even those children who are only able to be at school for a portion of the day are progressing. My dismissal is the result of him ignoring the actual success of this school simply because he does not approve of the Yorkshire manner of speaking and that, Uncle Barton, is a tragedy. He would sacrifice their education in the name of conformity."

"Heavens, you are just like your mother." The observation was clearly not meant as an insult. Quite the opposite, in fact.

"You seem to think better of her than my aunt does."

He took a step closer, his expression pleading. "I am sorry for the way she has treated you. The grudge she holds is not your doing, neither was it your mother's, yet your aunt cannot seem to let it go."

"What happened between them?"

Her uncle shook his head. "It was a long time ago."

"I am being made to suffer for it, as is Lucy. That makes it a difficulty *now*."

He watched her for a moment. His expression, however, did not change. "I can't," he said. "I am still suffering for it as well. Talking about it only adds to the misery."

How horribly appropriate. She was made to suffer, but not

told why. She was being unfairly dismissed. Life often dealt blows she was unprepared for.

"How soon am I expected to relinquish my home and position?" she asked.

"Not until we find a new teacher, which will take a couple of weeks at least."

She nodded. "I will begin making plans."

Dermot pulled the door open.

The silent instruction was not missed by Uncle Barton. He set his hat on his head. "I truly am sorry. About a great many things."

"So am I." She didn't wait to watch her uncle's departure but turned and took the stairs up to the schoolroom. She hadn't taken the time to straighten up after her students left. Her mind had been in too much turmoil.

She picked up the slates scattered about the room. The impact of Mr. Garvey's visit had been felt by all of her students. They knew her time as their teacher was being cut short. The next couple of weeks would be heartbreaking.

Dermot's steps sounded on the staircase before he arrived in the schoolroom.

"The children left a bit of a mess," she said without looking up. "It was a difficult afternoon. I'll have to make certain they are in the habit of tidying up before I . . . before—" The words wouldn't come.

"Before you go to Leeds." He spoke with certainty though she had not told him her intentions.

She clutched the pile of slates to her chest. "I tried forcing a third option, Dermot. It didn't work. I have no job. I will soon have no home. My sister will be taken away from me. I have to go. There is no other choice."

"But you don't want to."

She turned toward him. "Of course I don't want to. My entire life is here. Everything and everyone I care about most is here in Smeatley. I am being forced to leave that behind, and it is breaking my heart."

He stepped closer. "Lucy would be in Leeds. You'd not be leaving her behind."

"Grandfather might send her back to that school. I still would not have her with me. I would be all alone and so very far from home."

"Mr. Barton says you have a couple of weeks yet before you need to go," he said. "That's time enough for me to find a new position. Leeds is growing fast. There'd be ample work for a brick mason."

Every thought stopped. Her lungs froze in her chest. "I don't understand."

He stepped directly in front of her and slipped the slates from her arms, setting them on the bench beside them. Tenderly, he took her face in his hands. "If you are going to Leeds, so am I."

"But what of your back-to-backs?" She spoke with no more volume than he did.

His hands slid to her shoulders, then down her arms. "They'll be done before the two weeks are out. I'll be ready to go."

She set a hand tentatively on his chest, tempted to clutch his shirt to prevent him from slipping away. So many questions ran through her mind, so many worries. "What of Ronan?"

The tiniest hint of a smile tugged at his lips. "I thought I'd bring him with me."

Even she could allow a moment's amusement at his laughing tone. "You would truly give up everything you've built for yourself here?"

"They're only things, Evangeline. Things matter very little when all is said and done." He wrapped an arm around her waist, tugging her to him. "But you mean the world to me. I will go wherever you are going, whether it be Leeds or London or Botany Bay."

"But you've worked so hard for the opportunities you have here," she whispered. "I don't want you to regret it."

He leaned ever closer and lowered his voice to match hers. "I'll not regret a moment."

She could feel his heart pounding beneath her hand, matching the rhythm of hers. His free arm wrapped around her as well, enveloping her in his warm embrace.

"Do you think you can be happy in Leeds?" Dermot's breath tiptoed over her lips.

"You will be with me," she answered. "I will be joyous."

His lips, tentative and gentle, brushed over hers. A breath shuddered from her. He kissed the very corner of her mouth. She touched her fingertips to his stubbled jaw. His kiss, uncertain at first, changed on the instant. There was no longer a question in it, but a declaration.

I will go wherever you are going, he had vowed. Life was once again forcing her down a path not of her choosing. This time, however, she was not walking it alone.

CHAPTER THIRTY-SIX

Dermot's first set of back-to-back houses was nearly complete. He'd wager they'd be ready for tenants in a week or two. The floors were laid. The windows were in. The stairs were finished and the banisters placed. He was waiting on a few of the final details: fireplace grates and iron handrails for the front steps. In the meantime, his crews were finishing the garden beds so the families living there would have a small place for their kitchen herbs and such.

He was proud of how it had turned out, especially considering the unlikeliness of being given such an opportunity again. A brick mason could always find work, especially in a town growing as quickly as Leeds and neighboring Bradford. He wasn't worried about starving for want of wages, but he'd not be head of his own crew nor overseeing a project on the scope of the one he'd been entrusted with in Smeatley. Further, he'd be back to being a nameless Irishman "taking jobs away from the English." He'd not enjoy that. But he'd be near Evangeline, and for that, he'd endure the indignities all over again.

Hugo Palmer came running toward him. "Mr. Farr's ambling up t' ginnel!"

Mr. Farr was in the alleyway? His arrival was unexpected, but Dermot was more than prepared to meet him. He was proud of the work he'd done and knew Mr. Farr would be impressed.

The man himself stepped out of the alleyway in the next moment. His discerning eye studied everything. Dermot kept to his position and waited, letting the work speak for itself.

"I walked through the first house." Mr. Farr spoke as he loomed over the men laying the brick for the planters. "You completed it within budget?"

"Well within."

Mr. Farr nodded. "You're also well within the schedule you proposed."

"You're welcome."

For that cheeky remark he received something resembling a smile, though it quickly dissolved into a ponderous expression. "The mill needs more workers. Between your houses and the changes I'm requiring to be made at the factory, we'll have no trouble filling all the positions we have."

Dermot was glad to hear the complaints lodged against the mill had been heard and taken into consideration. Though most of the town had never warmed to him, he cared enough for those he'd grown attached to for their happiness to matter to him. "Have you heard that your granddaughter is losing her position as teacher?"

Mr. Farr nodded and, to his credit, seemed to genuinely regret the situation. "I did attempt to convince Mr. Garvey otherwise, but he's not a man who can be reasoned with once his pride is on the line."

"An interesting choice to oversee the education of children."

"He wouldn't have been my pick."

Dermot motioned him inside the house nearest them; he'd rather his men not hear the remainder of the conversation.

Mr. Farr eyed the narrow window in the entryway as they stepped past, no doubt checking the workmanship. "Has Evangeline happened to mention what she means to do next?"

"What choice does she have? Her entire life's being taken away." He waited for Mr. Farr to look at him again. "She's resigned herself to what little choice she has over her future."

He had Mr. Farr's full attention. "Resigning herself? Does she not *want* to come to Leeds?"

How could he possibly lack even a basic understanding of his own granddaughter's character? "She cares about this town's children. She's devoted herself to them. And she's made a home here for herself and her sister. It's all being taken away, just as it was all those months ago."

"When her parents and brothers died," Mr. Farr said.

"When, after enduring such loss, her remaining family turned their backs on her."

Mr. Farr folded his arms over his chest. His gaze narrowed.

Dermot had his toe in the icy water; he might as well jump all the way in. "She was brought to this unknown place and told she had no family, no connections, no one she could turn to with questions or concerns to alleviate her loneliness. Her wee sister was snatched away from her without so much as a word of farewell, the only connection between them for months being the letters she received from Miss Lucy begging and pleading to be spared the misery she was enduring at the school where she'd been sent. Miss Blake was told to be independent, to prove herself capable and able to see to her own concerns and future. She's done precisely that, with not a soul in her family giving her the least help. Her aunt, in fact, has been cruel, and her uncle has done little to alleviate that cruelty."

Mr. Farr acknowledged the truth with a sigh. "There is history between them that Evangeline does not understand."

"She deserves to know," Dermot insisted. "Whatever is causing the misery, she's the one being made to suffer for it."

"She has suffered a great deal," Mr. Farr acknowledged.

"And she continues to," Dermot said. "She's being told she must choose the future others have decided for her and give up the very independence she'd been instructed to develop. So, aye. I said 'resigned' and I meant it."

"You're quite her fierce defender." 'Twasn't an observation offered with even the slightest degree of ridicule. Rather, Mr. Farr seemed impressed.

"She hardly needs me to be," Dermot said. "But I'll speak in her defense anytime 'tis called for."

"Even to one with power over the work you do here?"

"Even to you, Mr. Farr."

His sharp gaze narrowed. "And why is that?"

"Because she holds my heart in her hands. She is all the world to me, and though you may hold sway over one future stretched out before me, any future that doesn't include her isn't one worth groveling for."

Mr. Farr watched him, amazement on his face.

"She's being forced to Leeds," Dermot said, "so I'm going there as well."

"What of your back-to-backs?" Mr. Farr asked.

"These'll be finished before I go. I'll not leave m' word unfulfilled."

Mr. Farr shook his head. "I had come here intending to ask how many more you could build and how quickly. I'm prepared to make you a very generous offer, to strike a bargain that would see you in fine fettle for years to come."

Dermot folded his arms across his chest. "I'll go where she is, no matter the cost."

"You love her," Mr. Farr said.

"More than anything else in all the world, certainly more than these houses."

The man looked around the entryway, his gaze lingering on the doorway to the parlor and the stairs leading upward. "You truly did good work here, McCormick. It'd be a shame to lose your guiding hand."

"I know what's most important to me."

Mr. Farr gave a single twitch of his head, no more than half a shake. "You've given me a mind full to think about."

"And I've a grand lot o' work to do," Dermot said. "I'll get back to it, if you've no objections."

"Will you join us for supper tonight at the Bartons' home?"

The invitation could not possibly have caught Dermot more unsuspecting. "Me?"

Mr. Farr chuckled. "I would have been just as shocked by such an invitation at your age. I had hardly two ha'pennies to rub together and no claims to importance in the eyes of those who felt themselves above me." He slapped a hand on Dermot's shoulder. "I know a man of worth when I see him."

"And that'd be me?"

Mr. Farr nodded firmly. "Will we see you tonight?"

"If I'm permitted to bring m' boy. He'll not give anyone trouble."

"Of course."

'Twas Dermot's turn to nod.

"Seven o'clock," Mr. Farr said.

His shock remained for long minutes after Mr. Farr left. Dermot was to take supper with a fine family in a house far grander than any he'd supped in before, and he was to do so while biting back his true opinion of the man and woman who lived there.

This'll be an odd sort of night, I'm full sure of it.

Dermot and Ronan stood at the edge of Hillside House's front wall, waiting for the Blake sisters to arrive. Though Mr. Farr hadn't said that his granddaughters would be in attendance, Dermot hadn't the least doubt they would be.

After only a few minutes, his guess proved correct. Bundled against the cold, Evangeline and Lucy turned the corner from Market Cross. Matching smiles spread over their faces as they approached.

"Dermot." Heavens, he loved the eager way Evangeline said his name. "What are you doing here? The two of you must be frozen solid."

"Ronan," he said, "walk on ahead with Miss Lucy. I'm wanting to offer our Evangeline a good evening."

Lucy giggled. "Come on, Ronan. We'll give these two sweethearts a bit of privacy."

Just like her sister, Lucy knew precisely the right way to befriend Ronan. She simply moved at his side, not forcing conversation or nearness.

"Did you wait here simply to see us?" Evangeline asked. "I would have come by your house to bid you a good evening. That would have saved you the misery of this bitterly cold night."

"Aye, but not the bitterness of our miserably cold hostess."

After a moment, her confusion gave way to realization. "You have been invited to eat with the family tonight."

"Your grandfather invited me." He slipped his arms around her waist. "I haven't offered you a proper good evening yet, my dear."

"No, you haven't."

"And I'm afraid I'm too cold to do so now."

"A shame." She slipped backward, out of his loose embrace, and began walking toward the house.

"Wait, lass. I'm warm enough."

But she only laughed, the sound utterly flirtatious. The smile remained on her face as the Bartons' high-starched butler ushered them inside. The house was as suffocatingly lavish as ever. During his time working on the place, Dermot had far preferred staying outside. Still, he was an invited guest, and this was Evangeline's family. He could endure nearly anything for her sake.

Mrs. Barton stood in the parlor, her face lit by a dozen points of light from the chandelier above her head. Her hand rested lightly on a gold-leafed table. She eyed them all down the length of her nose. Her expression turned to a sneer when her gaze reached Evangeline.

Dermot leaned a touch closer to Evangeline. "Courage, my dear," he whispered.

She actually laughed. "I am not afraid of her."

Lucy looped her arm through Evangeline's. "Neither am I."

"Onward, then, generals." Dermot motioned the sisters ahead.

They stepped fully inside the parlor with all the dignity of royalty but none of the pomp. The strength he'd seen in Evangeline had begun blossoming in her sister as well. The two of them moved directly past their aunt to where their grandfather stood. He greeted them with quick embraces and a warmth Dermot had not expected to see.

Mrs. Barton seemed more frustrated than surprised. She, however, did not comment, something for which Dermot was grateful. Though he'd never before been invited to a fine meal in a fine house, he knew enough of manners and civility to know that aggravating one's hostess was frowned upon.

Ronan kept close to Dermot's side. To his credit, the lad kept calm and quiet, though his eyes didn't stray far from Evangeline. She had become a source of comfort to the boy. Following her to Leeds would be best for the both of them. He only hoped it would be best for Evangeline.

"Before we step inside for our meal," Mr. Farr said, addressing the room at large, including Mr. Barton, who stood off to the side, "I wish to address something of importance. A few things, in fact."

Evangeline met Dermot's eye. The silent pleading in her eyes pulled at his heartstrings. He set his hand on Ronan's back and moved the two of them to where his sweetheart stood. She slipped her hand in his. Ronan tucked himself against Dermot's leg. Lucy leaned against her sister's arm. Together they faced Mr. Farr and whatever he meant to say.

"It was rightly pointed out to me earlier that some things have been left unspoken in this family that ought not to have been."

Mrs. Barton paled. "This hardly seems appropriate—"

"So long as you mean to punish Evangeline for the difficulties of the past, it is more than appropriate," Mr. Farr said.

Evangeline held more tightly to Dermot's hand.

"Do you not intend to put a stop to this, Robert?" Mrs. Barton demanded of her husband.

Mr. Barton turned away. Mr. Farr shot his daughter a look of warning, then addressed Evangeline directly. "I never made any secret of the fact that I was not overly fond of your father."

"No, you did not."

"I had always imagined Elizabeth marrying someone with a background and temperament similar to my own. I even had someone in mind."

Mrs. Barton's frown turned ferocious. "I wholeheartedly object to this."

"Hush, Bertha," Mr. Barton said quietly.

"Elizabeth made her choice, and I confess I was disappointed," Mr. Farr continued. "However, the man I had chosen for her remained connected to our family, continuing in the business I was building, and he did, eventually, become my son-in-law."

"Uncle Barton?" Evangeline whispered.

Mr. Farr nodded. "That ought to have been the end of things, but it proved only the beginning."

"Were you unhappy?" Evangeline's question might have been directed to any one of her family members.

'Twas Mr. Farr who answered first. "All seemed fine at first."

"What happened?" Evangeline asked.

Mrs. Barton's harsh gaze fell squarely on her niece. "My husband was still in love with my sister, that is 'what happened.'"

Mr. Barton faced his wife. "I would not have married you if I had still been in love with her."

"I saw it in your eyes whenever you looked at her. You smiled in ways you never smiled at me. You were happier in her company."

Mr. Barton shook his head, holding up his hands in frustration. "I was fond of Elizabeth; how could I not be? But you saw what you chose to see."

"What I saw was a woman who could charm anyone. What I saw was you falling into her trap. I have spent all the years of our marriage living in her shadow."

Mr. Barton attempted to interrupt, but Mrs. Barton pushed onward.

"Then her daughter comes to this town, fully ready to trade upon the family name to secure her own comforts, and you were more than prepared to fawn over her, just as you did her mother." Mrs. Barton's shoulders squared in defiance. "It is time someone in the Blake family understood her place in the world."

Dermot glanced at Lucy, worried for the girl. But both she and Evangeline stood tall and determined.

Evangeline shook her head. "You punished me, denied me my own family—my sister—even attempted to strip me of my dignity, because your husband once courted my mother? Months of suffering that had nothing to do with me."

"He loved her," Mrs. Barton said. "He loved her more deeply than he ever loved me."

Mr. Barton looked exhausted, in both mind and body. "We might have learned to love each other more deeply, Bertha, but you never permitted it. You have spent years punishing me for not having met you first, and we have both suffered for it."

"And now you have made Evangeline and Lucy suffer as well," Mr. Farr said. "While I wish I had raised a daughter who could change that fault in herself, I very much fear you will continue to wield your disapproval of their mother as a weapon."

Mrs. Barton's expression hardened. "Perhaps it is a good thing she is not remaining in Smeatley."

"That is a topic *I* wish to address." Evangeline squeezed Dermot's fingers then stepped forward, facing her grandfather with the bearing of a warrior. "The law gives you guardianship of

Lucy, but she is my sister, and I will not relinquish her without a fight, and fight you I will, if I must. The school where you sent her was a purgatory. Forcing her to live away from her only remaining family was a cruel and heartless thing to do."

Mr. Farr was clearly surprised by her fierce words.

"I may be losing my place as a teacher, but I am fully able and willing to find another position. Further, I have more than earned the right to have access to some part of my inheritance, the smallest bit of which would allow me to secure a new home for myself and Lucy and see to our needs while I secure a new source of income. I have learned to support myself, to run a household, and to live an independent life. I have earned the right to have Lucy with me."

Evangeline did not cower as she spoke to the man who held such power over so many lives.

"If you will not allow Lucy to remain with me, if I am forced to go to Leeds in order to have her with me, so be it. But know that I will stand her champion every moment of every day, and I will do the same for myself. A lady may do as she is told, but this woman will do what she must."

"Good heavens," Mrs. Barton gasped.

Dermot caught Lucy's eye. The girl beamed with pride. Dermot couldn't hold back a grin of absolute admiration.

"Before you begin storming the citadel," Mr. Farr said, "allow me to tell you what I have in mind. I've been giving thought to what I want my mill to be in Smeatley. We're building housing for our workers so they'll not live in squalor. We're making changes to the hours and the demands on those employed in the factory so the workers will not be so miserable. And I'm looking to offer schooling to the children working there so they'll not miss an education simply because their families are in need of money."

"Are you in earnest?" Evangeline watched her grandfather with wide, hopeful eyes.

He nodded. "I mean to open a school at the mill, so they can spend a little time each day learning."

"That is a wonderful idea," Evangeline said.

"I know." Mr. Farr was nothing if not confident. "And I'd like you to be the teacher. Despite Mr. Garvey's objections, I believe you're a fine teacher. Your students read for me, you'll remember, and did a bit of deciphering. I was impressed, just as Garvey ought to have been."

"You were impressed?"

"Not merely by your teaching." He lifted a stack of papers from a finely carved side table. "These were nearly impossible to overlook."

Evangeline glanced back at Dermot. He shrugged, not knowing what the papers were. She stepped closer to her grandfather, eyeing his mysterious pile.

"Bits of writing?" She was clearly confused.

"Pleas," Mr. Farr explained. "Written by your students."

She took a shaky breath. "May I read them?"

"I'd assumed you would." He gave the pile to her.

Evangeline returned to Dermot's side. Her gaze was glued to the papers in her hand. "They are forming their letters more precisely."

Dermot knew too little of such things to agree or disagree. "What have the children written?"

"I'm almost afraid to read them," she admitted on a whisper.

"You needn't be," Lucy insisted, a little too knowingly.

"You had a hand in this," he guessed aloud.

Lucy shrugged. "Susannah and I might have borrowed some paper."

Evangeline's brows turned sharply downward as she focused fully on the words scrawled out before her. Her lips moved silently as she looked over each page in turn. A brief smile. A soundless laugh. A sheen of tears.

"They love you," Mr. Farr said. "More to the point, they have faith in you. They credit you with all they have learned and are begging for you to remain."

Her eyes hadn't left her students' notes. "I have done some good here after all."

"A world of it," Dermot said.

Mr. Farr hooked his arms behind his back and rocked on his feet. "You are a fine teacher and a fierce defender of those in your care. This town could not do better for its children."

"But the committee will insist—"

"The committee only has power over schools run by the town," Mr. Farr said. "Private schools have far more freedom."

Evangeline pressed the stack of papers to her heart with one hand and took hold of Dermot's hand with the other. Her voice emerged a touch breathless. "Privately run schools like one sponsored by a mill?"

"Precisely."

Evangeline looked at Dermot, hope in her eyes. He tossed convention aside and slipped his arm around her waist.

Mr. Farr gave a slight smile. "It would be difficult, teaching students who can't spend much time with you each day, but I've every faith in you, my girl. Anyone who can deliver a scolding as precise and bold as the one you just did can certainly undertake a challenge such as this."

He'd offered her the opportunity to remain in Smeatley, to continue working. It seemed almost too good to be true. Having been the recipient of far too many of life's disappointments, Dermot held his breath.

"What of the children who do not work at the mill, whose families are not employed there?" Evangeline asked. "I cannot abandon them. Any new teacher the board selects will follow Mr. Garvey's dictates, stripping them of their language and ignoring what they need in favor of what he wants. I cannot resign them to that."

Mr. Farr had a ready answer. "I'll turn no student away, whether they work for me or not. They'll simply pay their fee to our school rather than to the school board."

"What of those whose fees are being paid by the board?" Evangeline pressed. "They would be the poorest and most vulnerable of families."

"We can convince the school board to pay that fee to our school instead."

"I believe that we could work out an agreement," Mr. Barton said.

"That is not surprising," Mrs. Barton muttered.

"I believe the factory school would be very busy," Evangeline said. "I do not know that I can single-handedly manage such a large undertaking."

"I will help," Lucy said. "Susannah Crossley and I—we'll both help. We already are."

"They are," Evangeline acknowledged. "A teacher could not ask for two better assistants, but two such able helpers could ask for far more than volunteering their time and efforts."

Mr. Farr arched an eyebrow. "You are a shrewd negotiator, granddaughter."

"A family trait."

A smile of appreciation touched his stern face. "I would pay the girls for their efforts as well, though Lucy would be required to continue her own education."

Lucy turned pale. "I won't go back to that school, Grandfather."

Evangeline pulled her sister firmly to her side. "I won't allow you to send her back."

"*We* won't," Dermot added, keeping them both near.

Mrs. Barton's eyes pulled wide with shock at the bold declaration. Mr. Barton seemed nearly as surprised. Evangeline, however, stood firm, apparently convinced that Dermot would defend her sister as fiercely as she did. Their future was not yet entirely decided, but they had vowed to build it together and that was reassurance enough for her.

Mr. Farr held his hands up in a gesture of calm surrender. "I don't mean to send Lucy back. I will arrange for a tutor or governess. Your mother would have wanted that."

Mrs. Barton scoffed and turned away, crossing the room to the window.

"Remaining will likely mean enduring continued unkindness." Mr. Farr didn't have to say from whom. "I wish I could promise you otherwise."

"Her bitterness will not poison me."

Mr. Farr turned to Dermot. "And I'd like to talk with you about expanding your back-to-back housing project as well as the possibility of another mill in a few years' time."

"Another mill?" 'Twas an enormous undertaking, one that would see him in fine fettle.

"I'm not fully decided, but I'm considering it."

"I'll think on it, as well," Dermot said. "Though I'll not make any decision until Evangeline has made hers."

"'Evangeline'?" Mr. Barton eyed him curiously. "Are the two of you on a Christian-name basis?"

Dermot silently dared him to condemn them for it. Mr. Barton smiled with approval. Mr. Farr did the same. Mrs. Barton blessed them all by not bothering to turn around, though she was likely glowering at the window.

Evangeline looked at him. "Rows and rows of houses *and* a mill, Dermot. That's years' worth of steady, reliable work that would see you quite comfortable. You would have everything you've ever worked for."

"We've discussed this already, my dear. If life's taking you to Leeds, it's taking me there as well. In Leeds, *you* would have all the comforts; I'm certain your grandfather would see to that. If that's what you're wanting, that's where we'll go."

"No regrets?" she pressed.

"Not a one," he vowed.

"And we would be together," she said softly.

"Always," he answered.

"I want to teach the children, whether at the town school or the factory school. I want to see you build your houses and realize your dreams. I want to stay in Smeatley."

He pressed the briefest of kisses to her forehead. "Smeatley, it is."

"That bargain ought to be sealed with more of a kiss than that," Mr. Farr said. He offered his arm to Lucy. "Shall we go in to dinner?"

Lucy accepted the invitation. She motioned for Ronan to follow them, which, to Dermot's surprise, he did.

Mr. Barton stepped past his wife. "Come along, Berta. We've a dinner to host."

She followed, though reluctantly. The misery that existed

between the couple was tragic. Dermot hoped Evangeline would not be subject to it very often.

A moment later, Dermot and Evangeline were alone.

"I am still amazed that you would have gone to Leeds if I'd been required to go there," she said.

"I'd have gone to the ends of the world, darling."

She brushed her fingers along his jaw. "For such a disagreeable man, you've proven surprisingly tenderhearted."

He turned his head enough to kiss her hand.

"You've changed us all, Evangeline Blake." He wrapped his hand around hers, holding it lovingly. "You've changed us for the better."

"And we get to stay," she said.

"*We.*" He smiled, something he didn't use to do so easily. "I like the way that sounds."

"So do I."

He caught her gaze with his. "We never did seal our bargain."

Her mouth turned up at the corners. "I suppose we didn't."

Dermot set his hands at her waist. Evangeline hooked a finger around one of his jacket buttons, her head tipped up toward him.

"Do you know you smell like flowers?"

She smiled. "Is that a good thing?"

"I like flowers." He slid his hands around to her back, relishing the warmth of her in his embrace. "But I *love* you."

Dermot brushed his lips over her cheek, not truly a kiss, but a personal, tender touch. Her eyelids fluttered and closed.

"And I love you, Dermot McCormick," she whispered. "So deeply. So much."

"And I am going to kiss you, so deeply, so much."

She smiled, her eyes still closed. 'Twas an invitation he didn't intend to ignore. He pressed his lips to hers. She wrapped her arms about his neck, her fingers threading into his hair. He feathered kisses along her jaw. She sighed, leaning into his embrace.

"I thank the heavens for bringing you here," he whispered in her ear.

She slipped her hand from his neck to the side of his face and lightly kissed him. "Be certain to thank the heavens for allowing us to stay. Together."

"Together," he repeated, his lips brushing hers as he spoke.

He kissed her once more, relishing and cherishing the moment. He had been alone for so long, convinced he always would be. But they'd found one another, and they'd found love.

He held her, amazed at his good fortune. They would be required to join the others soon enough, but for now, this moment was theirs. He wished it would never end.

"Dermot?"

"Yes, my dear?"

"Does this mean you are lifting your one knock per day limit?"

He laughed. "You may knock whenever you like and as often as you'd like. Until the day my door and your door are the same."

"I like the way that sounds."

He held her to him. "So do I, my dear. So do I."

CHAPTER THIRTY-SEVEN

Dermot held Evangeline's hand as they stepped out of the chapel and into the snow-dusted churchyard. Theirs was not the most highly attended wedding in the history of Smeatley, but looking out at the beloved faces of her students and their families, the bright and cheerful eyes of her sister, and Ronan walking beside his father, Evangeline could not imagine a more perfect gathering.

She, of course, would have wished for her parents and brothers to have been there. But Grandfather had come from Leeds. He had felt more like family these last weeks, kind and attentive. Either he had changed from the gruff and cold man he'd been during his visits to Petersmarch, or she had misunderstood him all those years ago. Whatever the reality of the situation, she was grateful for his presence.

"Miss Blake! Miss Blake!" a handful of voices called out.

Dermot squeezed her fingers. "You'd best greet your little ones, else they're liable to knock you down—and me with you."

She touched the tips of her gloved fingers to his cheek. He

understood well the deep affection she had for these children and they for her.

"On with you," he said. "I'm not going anywhere."

She turned to face her students, offering them a broad smile. "I'm so pleased you've come."

They thronged her, peppering her with questions and echoing her name in the way they always did when wishing for her undivided attention.

John Crossley managed to make himself heard. "Are we to have school tomorrow, Miss— Mrs. McCormick?"

"Miss Susannah and Miss Lucy will oversee school this week while I am away."

"We will miss thee," Cecilia Haigh said. She spoke more often than she once had, though she would never be an orator.

"I will miss you, as well." Knowing how close she had come to losing her students and the life she dearly loved, Evangeline did not wish to be apart from them long. But the joyous reason for her absence far outweighed the pain of temporary separation.

The reminder brought her gaze to Dermot. Dear, kind-hearted, loving Dermot. He had been at her side during some of her most difficult days. Knowing they need never be separated again brought her profound relief.

He held his hand out to her again. She took it, warmth spreading through her.

"Have I told you often enough that I love you?" she asked.

He raised her hands to his lips and kissed her gloved fingers. "You have, but I'll not object to hearing it a few more times."

She leaned into his one-armed embrace. "I do love you. Coming here and meeting you is one of the best things that has happened in my life."

"And in mine." He pulled her closer. "We make a fine team, you and I. And together we will make a beautiful life."

He bent and kissed her. As he did, the church bells rang.

Tradition in Smeatley held that the bells rang to mark a wedding, tolling out a jubilant celebration. No longer would their peals reverberate against Evangeline's heart with loss and sorrow. From that day forward, they would soar with hues of love and sing of new beginnings.

ACKNOWLEDGMENTS

I had the invaluable opportunity to walk through the Bradford Industrial Museum's Moorside Mill in West Yorkshire. The incredibly knowledgeable volunteers were second-to-none, answering my endless stream of questions and encouraging my deep fascination of this bygone era, allowing me to watch the massive machinery run and experience the sounds, smells, and sights of a working nineteenth-century textile mill. The museum's fully restored 1870s back-to-back houses were a researcher's dream come true. Walking through them, studying the style and layout, made such a difference in my understanding of these mill-town houses.

The Cliffe Castle Museum in Keighley, West Yorkshire, offered tremendously detailed insights into the opulence, fashions, furnishings, and lifestyle of industrial Yorkshire's Victorian-era nouveau riche. The opportunity to walk the corridors and grounds of this beautiful historic home deepened my understanding of the people of this time and place.

I am deeply grateful for Normanby Hall's exhibition on

Victorian-era fashions and the tremendous help it was in solidifying in my mind the particulars of dress and clothing during this era.

An enormous thank you to Richard, who gladly and patiently answered my endless list of questions about Marsden Moor and even dug around for an out-of-print pamphlet filled with wonderful information. Learning of the history, the flora and fauna, and the unique ecology of the moorlands increased my love of this starkly beautiful area of England.

My sincere gratitude goes to my parents, Steve and Ginny, for walking the moor with me and shuttling me around Yorkshire, Lancashire, and Derbyshire in search of information, insights, and history-nerd adventures.

I am profoundly grateful to those dedicated souls, at the end of the nineteenth century, who loved the language of Yorkshire enough to write it down in all its beauty so future generations could fall in love with it even as it has faded over time.

DISCUSSION QUESTIONS

1. Throughout the story, Evangeline struggles to be both "lady-like" and independent. Was it possible at this time to be both? Discuss Evangeline's successes and failures as she struggles to reconcile these two requirements and to discover who she wants to be.

2. Today, we might diagnose Ronan as being on the autism spectrum, but in the Victorian era, such terminology was unknown. What role did Ronan's condition play in the story and in the relationship that developed between Evangeline and Dermot?

3. Dermot tells Evangeline, "We can't choose our family, after all." Do you agree? Are there people in your life or social circles whom you have "chosen" to be part of your family? What qualities do you look for in a person you choose to be friends with?

4. Family relationships are an important element in the story. Compare Evangeline's relationship with her sister Lucy to Aunt Barton's relationship with her sister. What made one relationship stronger than the other? Do you think the relationship between Aunt Barton and Evangeline will improve with time?

5. Dermot is an Irishman living in an English town, which makes him feel like an outcast. Have you ever moved to a new place and felt unwelcome? How did you overcome those feelings?

6. Evangeline is hired to teach school despite her lack of training in the profession. Have you ever been asked to perform a task that felt impossible to achieve? How did you approach the task? Where you able to be successful in the task? How was Evangeline able to turn an impossible situation to her advantage?

7. The language of Yorkshire plays an important role in the story. Have you learned a second language? How hard was it to learn? Why was it so important to Evangeline to preserve the Yorkshire dialect for her students?

ABOUT THE AUTHOR

SARAH M. EDEN is the author of several well-received historical romances. Her previous Proper Romance novel *Longing for Home* won the Foreword Reviews 2013 IndieFab Book of the Year award for romance. *Hope Springs* won the 2014 Whitney Award for "Best Novel of the Year" and *The Sheriffs of Savage Wells* was a Foreword Reviews 2016 Book of the Year finalist for romance.

Combining her obsession with history and an affinity for tender love stories, Sarah loves crafting witty characters and heartfelt romances. She happily spends hours perusing the reference shelves of her local library and dreams of one day traveling to all the places she reads about. Sarah is represented by Pam Victorio at D4EO Literary Agency.

Visit Sarah at www.sarahmeden.com.

FALL IN LOVE WITH A

PROPER ROMANCE

BY

SARAH M. EDEN

  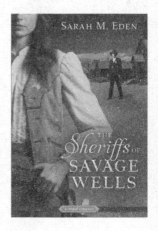

Available wherever books are sold

SHADOW
MOUNTAIN